# THE CAT IN THE WINDOW MURDERS

## FRANK L. GERTCHER

Wind Grass Hill Books

Terre Haute, IN

*The Cat in the Window Murders* is the third book in the Caroline Case mystery series. The murders are set in war-weary France just prior to the Great Depression. After arriving in Le Havre on the SS *Isle de France*, Caroline and Hannibal travel and stay in the finest hotels and resorts. They meet fascinating historical characters and experience newsworthy events and scenes in Le Havre, Rouen, Giverny, Paris, Mâcon and other ancient French towns. However, any similarity of the key storyline characters in this novel to persons living or dead is purely coincidental and not intended by the author.

Cover design by Phil Velikan

Cover art: 1920 flapper silhouette ©Incomible/Shutterstock.com; window image © mossolainen nikolai/Shutterstock.com

Packaged by Wish Publishing

Printed in the United States of America
10 9 8 7 6 5 4 3 2 1

*This book is dedicated to my wife Linda. She shares in my many adventures.*

# ALSO FROM FRANK L. GERTCHER

"…*An imaginative morality tale about free will, crime, punishment, and the possibility of redemption.*" — **Kirkus Reviews.**

"*Readers of murder mysteries will relish the many facets of* The Dark Cabin Murders, *which is anything but singular, involving readers in probes of inner being as well as mysteries and events that ultimately examine wider issues of the impact of life choices.*" — **Midwest Book Review.**

*Published 2018 • $29.95 • ISBN: 978-0-9835754-2-9*

## THE CAROLINE CASE MYSTERIES

Meet Caroline Case, a plucky madam in the 1920s who transforms herself into a budding detective when she starts investigating the death of her friend Alec. Full of historical detail and great storytelling, this book is sure to delight mystery lovers.

"*Surprisingly and pleasantly lighthearted for a tale involving prostitution, bootlegging and murder. The author skillfully alternates action scenes…with his focus on the gently evolving relationship between Caroline and Hannibal. Detailed descriptions of developments in forensic techniques and equipment add a historical bonus.*" — **Kirkus Reviews.**

*Published 2019 • $29.95 • ISBN: 978-0-9835754-4-3*

The year is 1928 and prohibition is the law of the land. Caroline Case now owns her own detective agency, and she finds herself caught up in the world of intrigue in Al Capone's Chicago. Mystery lovers will enjoy this romantic and exciting glimpse into the roaring 20s.

"*There is plenty of fuel for a high action drama, and Gertcher does not disappoint. Like the series opener, the novel is enjoyably lightened by humor and a strong protagonist. Caroline is smart, confident, and spirited, and in between the shootings, knifings, and a kidnapping is some solid sleuthing. A fun murder-and-mayhem detective story enhanced by historical details and a sturdy female lead.*" — **Kirkus Reviews.**

*Published 2020 • $29.95 • ISBN: 978-0-9835754-6-7*

# ACKNOWLEDGEMENTS

My thanks to all who contributed cultural and historical information about Europe. Contributors include my wife Linda, who shared my adventures with regard to European country roads, storied waterways, vast cathedrals and museums, dark and sinister city alleys and out-of-the-way eateries with indescribable menus. Also, Linda and the very talented Katherine Garretson provided valuable edits and review comments for the entire text of this book and the texts of my other books in this series. Stanislav Fele (1926-2016), my cousin from Ljubljana, Slovenia, shared many details of European life prior to and during the Great Depression. Details on the great French ocean liner SS *Isle de France* were provided by Natacha Potéreau from the archives of the Compagnie Générale Transatlantique, Le Havre, France. The contributions provided by the above kind-hearted people were, I'm sure, factually accurate. Any errors in this book concerning details on European culture, locations, organizations and history are strictly my own.

# THE CAT IN THE WINDOW
# MURDERS

# PROLOGUE

*I am Caroline Case Jones, and you are reading the third volume of my diary.*

If you read the first two volumes, you know that by hook or by crook, I have become quite wealthy.

During the early roaring 1920s, I managed several houses of 'sinful pleasure' in the Wabash Valley. In those days, I was simply known as 'Madame Caroline.' Prohibition was in full swing, and my establishments provided girls, booze and the opportunity to ignore social mores with gay abandon.

However, in 1921, my bootlegger friend Alec was murdered. I met Hannibal Jones, and together, we solved Alec's murder and several others. I fell in love with Hannibal, forensics and sleuthing.

In 1928, I sold my business interests, and Hannibal and I moved from the Valley to Chicago. We became full-time private detectives in 'the murder capital of the world.'

We solved several intriguing murders in Chicago. The murderers were brought to justice, legal or otherwise. Unfortunately, we also made enemies among the North Side gangsters who were at war with Al Capone. I was kidnapped, but I escaped and had many wild adventures. With the help of the Chicago police, my old friends in the Valley and even Al Capone, Hannibal discovered my whereabouts. Hannibal and his 'army' rescued me just as my enemies were closing in.

The year is 1929, and we are on our way to Europe. We arranged passage from New York to Le Havre on the new luxury ship, the SS *Isle de France*. Europe remains war-scarred and embroiled in social turmoil. Murders are frequent. Police forces are overburdened, underpaid and often corrupt. We have work to do, and solving murders is the name of the game.

# 1

## MURDER WAS SERVED

*Monday morning, June 17, 1929*

The events of Sunday evening are seared in my memory. Less than twelve hours ago, Hannibal and I arrived at the scene of the murder of an American heiress on the SS *Isle de France*. Two hours later, Captain Blancart asked for our help. We agreed to investigate.

It began in a marvelous setting. Hannibal and I had finished a stroll around the moonlit promenade deck on the newest ocean liner in the world. After our romantic stroll, we settled in our exquisite reserved private dining room, one of two occupied that evening. Our waiter came in, poured two glasses of 1921 Dom Pérignon, placed the bottle in an ice bucket, took our order for dinner and left discretely.

I looked around at the wonderful art deco stylings. "Oh, Hannibal," I said. "It's beautiful."

"And so are you, Mrs. Caroline Case Jones," replied Hannibal with a smile.

We raised our champagne glasses in a toast and then sipped in comforting silence.

"I hope the people in the private dining room next door are having a nice time," I mused as I sipped.

"Hummm," replied Hannibal with a slight frown. "We saw eight diners enter the room, all dressed to the nines, led by an older couple. The man was condescending to the staff. The lady glittered with diamonds. Her facial expression was sad, somehow."

His frown changed to a pleasant grin. "We are definitely having a better time." He raised his champagne glass and touched mine again with a musical tap.

Suddenly the lights went out. We had candles on the table, so we could still see. "What on earth?" I said.

Hannibal and I both looked toward the door. We expected our waiter to enter with an explanation. After several minutes, the lights came back on.

Suddenly, 'Aheeeh! Eeeh!' These screams were followed by several thumps and the sound of scraping furniture.

Hannibal and I both stood and looked for the source of the sounds. "Next room!" I exclaimed. Hannibal quickly moved to and through our door. I was right behind him. My heart raced as Hannibal and I entered the room next to ours. Several wide-eyed waiters joined us.

I saw a table in the center. Directly across, the older lady that we had seen earlier that evening was sitting in a chair, staring at us. I sensed that she was quite dead. The remainder of Sunday evening at the crime scene passed in a bewildering whirl.

Later, in our cabin, Chief Purser Henri Villar, at the request of Captain Blancart, asked for our help in solving 'this most perplexing murder.' According to Villar, our reputation had preceded us.

This morning, as usual, Hannibal had showered, shaved, combed his hair and was fully dressed before I slipped out of troubled dreams and got out of bed.

I observed his tall, trim form as I rubbed sleep from my eyes and toddled off to the bathroom. He was pacing back and forth at the far end of our luxurious main cabin area. I sensed that he was deep in thought. He wore tailored white slacks, a blue sport shirt, a white cardigan sweater and brown and white saddle shoes over dark blue socks.

"What a guy!" I thought to myself as I shed my Chanel black silk pajamas and headed toward the shower. I smiled as my mind turned to pleasant memories.

My body swayed as I toddled; I had to compensate for the motion of the ship. Fortunately, Hannibal had experience with trans-Atlantic crossings during the war. When we boarded, he gave me good advice on how to adapt to the pitch, roll and vibration. "Don't close your eyes, and keep your vision toward the horizon, not the floor," he said. "Let your body sway as you walk, and you'll be fine."

Hannibal was right of course, and after some initial queasiness, I adapted. Hannibal also said later after we were at sea that the vibration of the ship, which was sometimes moderate, was a design problem that eventually would have to be fixed. "It affects the operation and maintenance of the ship's machinery as well as the humans on board," he said.

After I had showered, combed my hair and put on my usual make-up, I changed into my Chanel white silk lounging outfit. I added a matching, white fox trimmed robe and soft fur-lined slippers.

I looked long into our bathroom mirror. "I am a very elegant private detective, if I do say so myself," I thought. I giggled a little, turned and emerged from the bathroom.

Almost instinctively, I headed for the steaming coffee pot. It rested on our coffee table near the large window side of our beautiful Grand Classe cabin, which was, by passenger ship standards, really a spacious apartment. Apparently, a steward had brought a silver coffee pot, sweet rolls, condiments, cups, exquisite small dishes and napkins on a silver tray while I was in the shower.

Hannibal gave me an appreciative look as I sauntered and swayed toward him and the coffee pot. I giggled again; I couldn't help it.

"OK, Caroline, concentrate on the task at hand," I thought to myself as I arrived at the coffee table next to Hannibal.

I conjured up an image of the previous evening, the private dining room next to ours and that thin older lady, dead, staring at me from her chair at the table across the room. The screams of the other females in the room echoed in my mind. With that sobering image, fleeting thoughts of romance disappeared.

"I need some coffee," I muttered.

Hannibal understood. "Me too," he responded with a smile.

I poured coffee, and Hannibal and I made ourselves comfortable on two very soft chairs.

After we settled in, Hannibal said: "The murder of the lady in the dining room occurred a few minutes before seven o'clock." He sipped his coffee and added: "At nine o'clock, Henri Villar, the ship's Chief Purser, relayed Captain Blancart's request that we help solve the murder."

"I know the Captain requested our help, but what legal authority does he have to investigate murders?" I asked.

"Good question," replied Hannibal. "We are in international waters, and maritime law applies. The Captain has absolute authority to investigate, arrest and hold persons suspected of committing a crime."

He paused a moment and then added: "When we reach Le Havre, control of the investigation and potential prosecution will transfer to the French judicial police, under the Gendarmerie Nationale."

"Does the ship have a jail?" I asked.

Hannibal smiled and replied: "Oh, yes. Every passenger ship, no matter how luxurious, has a jail, as you call it. On board ship, the jail is called a brig." He paused and added: "Ship security is low key most of the time, but rest assured that certain officers and crew have been trained to apprehend and detain anyone on board who is suspected of committing a crime."

"Good to know," I responded. "If we identify the killer, we can turn to the Captain and his officers to follow up with arrest and detention."

"Yes," replied Hannibal. "And they have the legal authority to use force if necessary."

Satisfied with regard to back-up, I said: "We accepted Captain Blancart's request for help for a fee, of course." I gave Hannibal a big smile.

Hannibal laughed and said: "You are always the entrepreneur."

I then looked at our passenger schedule on our coffee table. "Given a normal sailing time, we should dock in Le Havre on June 22." I frowned and continued: "Once passengers disembark, the murderer will undoubtedly try to disappear into France. We have four and a half days to solve the murder."

"Agreed," responded Hannibal. "Not much time, and the *Isle de France* is a big ship." He scanned his notes. "It has about 530 first class, 600 cabin class and 640 third class passengers. It also has over 800 officers and crew."

I nodded and replied: "We need to narrow down our list of suspects." I thought a moment as I looked through my notes on the table next to the coffee pot.

"We cannot rule out anyone yet, but we will know more if we interview the persons who were present near the crime scene."

"Yes," said Hannibal. "Sunday evening, I asked Chief Purser Villar to provide names and information. The steward delivered Villar's list this morning with the coffee service."

He chuckled and added: "You were in the bathroom making yourself beautiful." He held up a gold-embossed envelope with the Compagnie Generale Transatlantique logo as evidence. It was addressed to Major and Mrs. Jones.

I gave Hannibal a snooty look and said: "OK smarty, the time in the bathroom was well-spent. Let's see the list."

Hannibal laughed. I watched as he opened the envelope and took out a thick, folded set of notes. He smoothed out the creases and spread the notes on the coffee table next to the sweets tray and dishes.

We both scanned through the pages. After a moment, I said: "Villar confirms what we know; there were eight passengers at the table in the private dining room at the time one of the passengers, our elderly lady, was murdered."

"Yes," replied Hannibal. "The notes also identify the three ship staff members who were present, including the head waiter, his assistant and the butler, who came in from the adjoining pantry."

"Good," I responded. I looked closely and added: "Villar's list shows passenger names, ages, titles, addresses and cabin numbers."

"It also shows the names, ages, titles, brief job descriptions and crew cabin numbers for the butler and the two waiters," said Hannibal.

"Let's review our own observations," I said. I paused, thought a few moments and then said: "We were in the private dining room next door. The lights went out at about seven o'clock. After a couple of minutes, the lights came on, and we heard screams. We hurried toward the sound of the screams."

Hannibal leaned back in his chair and quietly sipped his coffee for a few minutes. Finally, he said: "When we arrived, we saw a large square table in the center of the room. Two place settings were on each of the four sides. Most of the chairs were in disarray; three were turned over. Directly across on the far side of the table, the elderly lady that we had seen earlier that evening was sitting in a chair, staring at us. Her body was tilted to her left, but it was held upright by the left arm and back of the chair. I checked her pulse and confirmed that she was dead."

"Yes," I replied. "Seven members of the dinner party were standing, all with expressions of disbelief on their faces. Except for the dead woman and overturned chairs, nothing seemed out of place."

Hannibal looked at his notes and said: "When we arrived, both dedicated waiters were standing near the back of the room. The butler entered the room from the walk-in pantry. I sent one waiter to find a ship's officer and the other to notify the Captain."

"Did you notice anything about the dead woman that would indicate the cause of death?" I asked.

"Yes," said Hannibal. "She had bruises on her neck; her head rested at an odd angle, and her jaw was twisted to her right. "From the evidence, I think her neck had been broken." He was quiet for a moment and then added: "If her neck was broken, that requires strength and some expertise."

"Did you see any blood?" I asked.

"No," replied Hannibal. "No blood and no visible wounds other than the bruises on the neck and the twisted jaw."

"We can get the ship's surgeon to verify the cause of death," I suggested. "Where would the body be kept?"

"The body is probably in the infirmary, and I'm sure the ship's surgeon will have already performed a preliminary autopsy," replied Hannibal.

"We need to work with the doctor," I responded. "Do we know his name?"

Hannibal flipped through Villar's notes. "Yes, here it is," he said. "The body is indeed in the infirmary, and it is in the care of Doctor Joseph Borec, Senior Surgeon." Hannibal read a few additional moments. "Villar also mentions Borec's assistant, Doctor Jean Dupuy."

"We need to talk with both men," I responded. "Let's also set up interviews with the two waiters and the butler, and then the seven passengers who were in the dining room. We may have others to interview after this first round."

Hannibal looked at me and grinned. "Are you planning to obtain fingerprints in addition to statements?"

"Of course," I replied. "We can set up the interviews, offer coffee and tea to the interviewees and get prints from the cups and saucers that they use." I thought a moment and then added: "I know you had a conversation with the young ship's officer who came to the dining room just after the murder." I paused and added: "Did you have the dining room and the adjacent areas sealed after the occupants left?"

"Yes," said Hannibal. "The young lieutenant, whose name is Arnaud Chatelain, understood the reasons." He smiled and added: "Only the body and the unused food in the pantry would be removed."

Hannibal then added: "I emphasized to Lieutenant Chatelain that great care had to be taken to not contaminate the crime scene and the nearby passageways and rooms. I also had the murder victim's cabin sealed. We can search it later."

I nodded and replied: "So, we will have a pristine crime scene to lift prints, and we can compare these to the prints taken from the people that we interview." I thought a moment and then added: "The ship's surgeon will have a microscope, tape, surgical gloves and other equipment. We can improvise a dusting powder."

"I think so," said Hannibal. He was then quiet for a few moments. Finally, he added: "We also need to check the light switches."

"Hummm," I responded. "Someone turned off the lights. It was likely either the murderer or his or her accomplice."

Hannibal was quiet again; I could tell he was thinking. Finally, he said: "The lights went off in our private dining room as well as the dining room with the murder."

I caught his drift. "Yes," I responded. "We need to identify the switch or switches that cause the lights to go out in both rooms." I thought a moment, then asked: "Were other private dining rooms in use at the time of the murder?"

"No," Hannibal said; "I asked our waiter about that the night of the murder. There are four private dining rooms next to the main first-class dining room, and only two were in use that evening, ours and the one next door."

I thought a moment and then asked. "Did the lights go out in the main dining room?"

"No," replied Hannibal. "I asked the waiter about that as well. Only the lights in the private dining rooms went out, as well as the lights in the butler's pantries and the passageway just outside the four rooms."

"Good," I said. "We should be able to narrow our search of light switches to a relatively small number." I paused and then added: "Fingerprints on these switches will be of interest."

"Yes," responded Hannibal "The ship's Chief Engineer should be able to provide details on the electrical system that controls the lights." He looked at his notes again and extracted a pamphlet. "Fortunately, our cabin passenger pamphlet identifies the ship's senior officers. The Chief Engineer is Yves Miossec. His assistant is Pierre Allain."

"Let's look at each person on Villar's list," I said. We read Villar's notes together, slowly.

Hannibal spoke first. "The victim was Mrs. Rosemary Davin Pierpont. Apparently, Villar obtained information from her passport. Mrs. Pierpont was 70 years of age, widowed, and she was booked in one of the four Grande Classe cabins on Deck B. I know both the Pierpont and Davin families. Rosemary was wealthy as a Davin heiress before she married John Edwin Pierpont."

"Hummm," I muttered. "We are in a Grande classe cabin on Deck A. There are only four such cabins on this deck as well." I paused, looked up and smiled: "Rosemary has good taste, like you."

Hannibal smiled in response. We returned our attention to the list.

After a moment, Hannibal said: "Rosemary had two adult children who were in the dining room when she was murdered: John Edwin Pierpont Junior, age 50, and Viscountess Abigail Pierpont Cornwall, age 38."

"I've never met a Viscountess before," I responded. I peered at the narrative after Abigail's name. "Abigail's husband, Viscount Arthur Blakely Cornwall, age 35, was with his wife in the dining room."

Hannibal responded with: "John Edwin Junior's wife is Julia, age 48. She was also in the dining room."

I continued reading. After a moment, I said: "Both couples are in outside first-class cabins for two on Deck A, one on the starboard side and the other on the port side." I smiled smugly. "I can tell starboard and port cabins by their numbers."

"Very observant," Hannibal replied with a smile. "The next pair on the list are Lucian Ambrose Morgan, age 45, and his wife Elizabeth, age 35." Hannibal continued reading. He then said: "Villar notes show that Lucian is a senior partner with the law firm Pierpont, Morgan and Stanley." He paused and then added: "I know the firm. They specialize in wills, trusts and wealth management for society patrons."

I looked up and said: "I see the name Pierpont as one of the senior partners. I wonder if that Pierpont is related to Rosemary's late husband."

"Yes," said Hannibal. "If I recall correctly, the attorney is Ambrose Pierpont, and he is the brother of John Edwin Pierpont Senior, Rosemary's deceased husband."

I smiled and responded: "You have moved in interesting circles, Mr. High Society."

Hannibal blushed and laughed a little. "I suppose so," he said.

I had gotten even for his remark about my time in the bathroom, so I smiled smugly.

Hannibal looked down at the list again. After a moment, he said: "Our last passenger is Harrison Beau Hadley, age 60." Hannibal paused again and added: "He resides in the first-class cabin right next to Rosemary's Grande Classe cabin; I can tell from the cabin numbers."

"Ah, Rosemary has a paramour," I stated.

"Quite likely," replied Hannibal. "Hadley is ten years younger." Hannibal looked up and smiled. "Interesting," he added.

I continued to read. After a few moments, I said: "The three crew members at the crime scene were Yves Lefevre, butler, Richard Girard, head waiter and Anton Guerin, waiter." They all reside in the crew quarters on Deck D."

"Yes," replied Hannibal. "Villar was very thorough. He also listed our head waiter and waiter. Both followed us into the room where the murder took place. Our butler, however, stayed in our own dining room."

Hannibal paused and added: "Our waiters were Maurice Dumont, age 28, and Henri Fontaine, age 21. Maurice, our head waiter, was the gossipy one." Hannibal grinned and continued: "We need to encourage him to nose around a bit."

"Now you are the devious one," I said with a grin. "I agree, and I think I can make it happen."

"Of course, you can," responded Hannibal with a laugh. "Let's figure out how to set up and conduct our interviews, collect fingerprints and process the crime scene."

# 2

## SOUNDS IN THE DARK

*Early Monday Evening, June 17, 1929*

Hannibal had a busy afternoon. As he told me later, he first contacted Chief Purser Henri Villar, who in turn, arranged with Lieutenant Arnaud Chatelain and Chief Steward Camille Millien to set up one of the four first-class private dining rooms for interviews. He also visited the Chief Engineer and asked about the location of light switches.

At Hannibal's request, Millien assigned Maurice Dumont and Henri Fontaine, our waiters, to set up coffee and tea for use during the interviews.

Both of our young waiters were excited about their introduction to sleuthing. In the presence of Lieutenant Chatelain, Hannibal explained to the pair how to set up and collect used cups and saucers and preserve residual fingerprints after each interviewee left the room. The butler's pantry next to the room would be used to store the clean and used cups and saucers.

Hannibal spoke softly but clearly, as if he were giving a practiced lecture. "During the interview process, we won't have time to lift fingerprints, we will do that together later. However, when you collect the cups and saucers between interviews, you need to wear surgical gloves to avoid contaminating prints on the cups and saucers. Lift each item by its edges and place it in a rack in the butler's pantry."

Hannibal demonstrated by putting on a pair of gloves and lifting a cup and saucer from a tray by their edges with the palms of his hands. Chatelain and the two waiters watched carefully.

Hannibal continued: "After you have placed the items in the rack, use a sheet of note paper to label each set of cups and saucers with the name of the interviewee."

I then added: "Please make sure that the interviewees are not in the room when you are wearing the gloves; we don't want them to suspect what we are doing and share information with the next interviewee."

Hannibal nodded and asked: "Are there any questions?" There were none.

Hannibal left Chatelain and the two waiters to set up the interview room.

Hannibal then visited the infirmary, obtained an English summary of a preliminary autopsy report and returned it to me in our cabin. We both planned to read it before the interviews. Doctors Borec and Dupuy very courteously helped Hannibal create a tool kit for dusting and lifting fingerprints.

While Hannibal was doing his work, I consulted the autopsy report and wrote out an interview schedule and a set of questions. We would begin with the three crew members and then continue with the seven passengers whose dinner was interrupted by murder.

Each person would be interviewed separately, and each interview would last fifteen to twenty minutes. I allowed ten minutes between interviews to collect and label appropriate cups and saucers. We would lift the fingerprints later, after the interviews were completed. In all, the interview and fingerprint collection process would take between three and four hours. We would start this evening; we had no time to lose.

We also had to process the sealed crime scene and Rosemary's cabin. Lieutenant Chatelain had the dining room, the adjacent pantry, the back passageway and the cabin sealed on Sunday evening.

After the murder, we had not observed any perishable blood or bodily fluids to process. We could therefore safely leave the crime scene and cabin processing until Tuesday.

Late in the afternoon, I decided to visit Lieutenant Chatelain. I needed his help to set up the interviews. Villar had thoughtfully provided the location of Chatelain's office on the Boat Deck.

Before leaving our cabin, I dressed in my new, Chanel form-fitting white dress that featured a round, conservative neckline. The bodice had an elegant navy-blue bow and matching dark blue buttons for detail. The dress also had puffed short sleeves with navy-blue trim. The hem was conservative at just below my knees, but there was a short slit in the back. My accessories included white silk hose, a navy-blue handbag and matching low-heeled shoes. My short dark hair was coiffed in the latest fashion. I was conservative, but slightly daring. "Nice, Caroline," I said to myself. I preened a little and giggled.

Satisfied with my appearance, I made my way to the Boat Deck and knocked on Chatelain's door. "Entre!" I heard from inside. I opened the door. I saw young Chatelain sitting at a fold-down desk on the left side of a tiny office. Shelves all around the room were stacked with books, manuals and papers.

Chatelain saw me standing in the doorway. He immediately stood up, banging his head on a nearby shelf in the process. After a grimace and a moment of recovery, he said: "Ah, Madame Jones; Entrez, s'il vous plait!" His eyes gave me a quick up-and-down look. I smiled sweetly.

"Merci, Monsieur le lieutenant," I replied, with the appropriate reserved tone. "Shall we speak English? My command of the French language is limited, I'm afraid."

"Of course, Madame," responded Chatelain, as he rubbed the newly acquired sore spot on the back of his head. "What can I do for you?"

He then stepped away from his desk and removed a pile of papers from a second chair in the right corner of the room. "Please!" he said, as he motioned me to the chair.

I smiled, entered the office and sat down. I observed Chatelain carefully for a moment, as he returned to his chair.

After he settled, I said: "I need your help in setting up interviews." I then gave him my list of names. "Can you have these people, listed in order, come to our interview room, one at a time, this evening?" I paused a moment and then added: "We have Chief Purser Villar's permission to conduct interviews as required."

Chatelain studied the list for a moment, then replied: "Yes, of course. The Chief Purser instructed me to help you in any way I can with regard to your investigation." He paused and then added: "Ship security is one of my many additional duties." His face had a wry smile.

We spent the next half hour laying out the details of the interview process. Chatelain was quick to catch on, and he understood both the interview objectives and the idea of collecting fingerprints.

Finally, I concluded with: "Shall we start with Monsieur Lefevre, the butler, at six o'clock? We should be able to finish by ten this evening with all ten interviews."

"Yes," replied Chatelain, with a thoughtful expression. "I will hold each subsequent interviewee, alone, in the private dining room next door and wait for your signal to send him or her in." We will use the two dining rooms other than yours and the crime scene."

"Parfait!" I responded. "Merci beaucoup, Monsieur lieutenant," I stood and offered my hand.

Chatelain smiled; he seemed pleased with my attempts to use French as best as I could. He took my hand gently, bowed formally and replied: "Monsieur Lefevre will be at your interview room door at six o'clock. The others will be summoned in order; the next in line will be waiting alone, in the room next door."

I thanked Chatelain courteously and took my leave.

## Monday at Mid-night, June 17

And so, it happened. Hannibal and I sat down at the interview table just before six, with note pads and pencils ready.

Hannibal wore a conservative navy-blue blazer, a light blue shirt, a blue and white tie, light-grey slacks and matching grey and white loafers over navy-blue socks. His attire was not too business-like, but not totally casual, either.

I wore my new, Lanvin-blue Railene dress with ivory trim, straight from Paris to New York, designed by Jeanne herself. It had a curve-hugging fit and lovely cream lace detailing. It also had a deep scoop neckline and very feminine cap sleeves, accented with cream-colored mother of pearl buttons. The sweeping cut of the back balanced the scoop neck design on the front for a flirty, elegant style The skirt had a slight fishtail design that ended in a hem just below my knees. I also wore creamy silk hose, cream-colored medium heel shoes and a double strand of choker pearls. I carried a matching small handbag. I was perfectly dressed for life aboard the SS *Isle de France*.

A single chair rested on the other side of the square table. Coffee, tea, condiments and of course, cups and saucers, rested on a side table. Our two waiters were ready. Maurice Dumont stood near the side table, and Henri Fontaine waited in the butler's pantry, ready to collect and replace used cups and saucers.

Hannibal and I sat in our chairs, sipped coffee and waited. At precisely six o'clock, we heard a knock at the door. "Come in!" said Hannibal.

I recognized Yves Lefevre, the butler, as he opened the door with his right hand. Lefevre was a medium height, powerful-looking man. He had a shock of greying hair and steely blue eyes. He was impeccably dressed in his butler uniform. He walked carefully, as if his feet hurt. "Odd," I thought to myself.

"Please, have a seat," I said courteously, as I motioned toward the empty chair on the other side of the table. "As you probably know, we have been authorized by the Captain to investigate the murder of Rosemary Davin Pierpont in the room next door last evening." I paused a moment and then added: "We need your help."

"I will do what I can," responded Lefevre cautiously, as he took his seat.

I turned to Maurice, my new sleuth recruit, and said: "Maurice, perhaps Monsieur Lefevre would like some coffee or tea." I then turned to Lefevre and said: "We want you to be comfortable; please join us in a cup of coffee." I raised my cup a little.

"Yes, merci," Lefevre responded. He relaxed a little and turned to Maurice.

Maurice smiled and said: "Shall I pour?" Do you take anything in your coffee?"

"Noir, uni s'il vous plait," responded Lefevre.

Maurice nodded, poured a cup of black coffee, placed it on a silver tray, and walked over to Lefevre.

Lefevre reached out for the cup with his right hand and lifted it from the tray. As he reached, I saw a nasty scrape and bruise on the back of his hand. After a few moments of relaxation, the questions began.

"As Mrs. Jones said, we need your help," said Hannibal softly. He paused, smiled and added: "We saw you emerge from the butler's pantry into the dining room when we entered, just after the lights came on. Can you describe what you observed from the time just before the lights went out until we entered the room?"

Lefevre took a deep breath. He began in a confident manner. I could tell he had rehearsed his answer.

"I was in the pantry, preparing the trays with the aperitifs for the two waiters," he responded. "The mix was French 75, made from gin, lemon, syrup and champagne." He paused, recalling his obviously practiced lines. He then continued: "The soup, which was potato-leek, had also just been delivered from the kitchen." He paused again and then added: "The lights went out, I heard scuffling noises in the dining room, and then the lights came on. As you saw, I entered just as you arrived."

Were you alone in the pantry?" I asked.

"Yes," responded Lefevre. "The kitchen server had just left, and I was alone."

"The lights were out for several minutes," said Hannibal. "What did you do during that time?"

Lefevre eyes flickered a little. He then replied: "It was pitch black in the pantry, and I did not want to knock over anything." He paused and then added: "I waited until the lights came back on and then entered the dining room, as I said."

"Why didn't you respond to the scuffling noises in the dining room?" I asked.

"What could I do?" Lefevre replied. I couldn't see anything." His tone was defensive.

"Where is the switch for the lights in the pantry and dining room?" Hannibal asked.

"I'm not sure," replied Lefevre. His eyes flicked down.

"Actually, the switch is in the passageway between the butler's pantry and the kitchen," said Hannibal. "It isn't far from the pantry, and the lights in the kitchen down the passageway did not go off; I checked."

Lefevre squirmed a little, but didn't say anything.

I decided to change the subject. "I understand that you have been with Compagnie Generale Transatlantique for over ten years,"

I stated. "Chief Purser Villar provided a summary of your employment record."

Lefevre nodded and said: "I have a good record with the company." He sniffed a little.

"I'm sure you do," I responded with a sweet smile. I paused and looked directly into Lefevre's eyes. "What did you do before you joined this steamship company?"

Lefevre squirmed again, puffed himself up a little and then replied: "I was employed by various aristocratic houses in Paris." He sniffed and added: "You can check."

"We will," I responded. "As soon as we dock in Le Havre." I watched carefully as Lefevre's eyes shifted around again. "Scared," I thought to myself.

I shifted the line of questioning again, by asking: "What did you do after Lieutenant Chatelain released you from the scene of the murder?"

Lefevre opened and then closed his mouth and stuttered a little before answering. Finally, he said: "With Lieutenant Chatelain's permission, I returned to the kitchen and instructed the kitchen servers to remove the food from the pantry." He paused a moment and said: "I then returned to my cabin."

I observed Lefevre's expression carefully for a few moments and then asked: "Do you recall the time that you left the dining room and kitchen area?"

Lefevre thought a few moments and then answered: "I saw the clock on the wall in the passageway just after Lieutenant Chatelain said we could leave." He added: "I think it was about eight o 'clock."

Hannibal shifted the line of questioning again and asked: "Did you serve during the war?"

"Yes, of course," responded Lefevre. "I was a volunteer." His eyes changed from shifting around to a steady look.

"Ah, the truth," I concluded. I then looked at Hannibal, who nodded. Our unspoken agreement was that the interview was over; we had enough information from Lefevre for the time being.

I then turned to Lefevre and said: "Thank you so much for your help. We will contact you if we have additional questions." I paused and then added: "Please close the door when you leave."

Lefevre let out a sigh, put down his coffee cup, rose from his seat, bowed stiffly, turned and left the room. I noticed again that his walk seemed pained. I looked at his shoes. They were new and obviously tight.

I could tell that Hannibal also noticed. He then turned to Maurice and nodded.

Maurice opened the pantry door and said a few words to Henri. Per our arrangement, Henri and Maurice carefully collected and labelled Lefevre's coffee cup, placed it in a rack in the pantry and added a clean cup to the side table. After this was done, Henri slipped out the back door to the pantry. He had been instructed to walk down the passageway to the pantry door that serviced the next private dining room, enter, and notify Lieutenant Chatelain to send in the next interviewee.

The process went smoothly; I was proud of our new recruits.

The next interviewee was Richard Girard, the head waiter in the room during the murder. After the usual preliminaries, he accepted a cup of tea, with three lumps of sugar. Maurice served the tea, and Girard took a deep breath and relaxed.

"Thank you so much for coming," I said after Girard had a couple of sips.

Girard took another sip. He eyed me carefully over the rim of his cup. "Oui, Madame," he replied. I noted that he held the cup in his right hand.

"What did you experience from the time just before the lights went out until Major Jones and I entered the dining room?" I asked.

Girard was silent for several moments. Finally, he said: "I was standing near the door to the pantry when the lights went out." He paused and then added: "I heard several exclamations from our guests, all along the lines of: What happened? and Why did the lights go out?"

He then said, carefully and slowly: "Just after the lights went out, I heard choking and scuffling sounds from the direction of the dining table." He paused, frowned a little and added: "Less than a minute later, I felt the air move as if someone moved past me. I heard squeaks along with steps on the floor." He continued: "After a few moments, I felt someone move by me again, along with squeaking shoes."

"Anything else?" I asked.

"No, just silence," responded Girard. "I did hear comments from a couple of the ladies present along the lines of: 'I hope the lights come on soon,' and 'What's that noise?' but nothing else."

"Interesting," I said. "What happened when the lights came on?"

"At first there was silence and then pandemonium," replied Girard. "Guests jumped up from their seats and chairs toppled over. There were screams. Everyone was looking at Madame Pierpont." He paused moment and then added: "I then saw you and Major Jones enter the door."

"Were any of the guests standing when the lights came on?" I asked.

Girard thought carefully for a moment. "Not that I recall," he responded. As best as I could tell, guests rose from their seats after the lights came on and they saw Madame Pierpont."

"Did you leave the room at any time after the lights went out?" Hannibal asked.

"No," replied Girard. He reflected a moment. "I don't recall moving much from the time the lights went out until the moment you and Major Jones walked in the door."

"Major Jones sent you to notify the Captain about the murder," I stated. "I recall that you returned at about half past seven."

Girard nodded.

I then asked: "After Major Jones and I left, do you recall the time that Lieutenant Chatelain released you from the crime scene?"

"Yes," responded Girard. "I looked at my watch, and the time was eight o'clock." He grinned a little and added: "I thought the time would be important."

I smiled and said: "You were correct."

Hannibal asked: "Did you or any of the other staff on duty in the dining room Sunday evening have any contact with any of the guests before Sunday evening?"

Girard thought a full minute. "Anton and I were newly assigned to the private dining room, and I did not speak to any of the guests before Sunday evening."

He paused a few moments and then added: "We knew who they were of course, Monsieur Lefevre pointed them out to us in the main dining room the day before, when he gave us our Sunday evening assignments."

"Did Monsieur Lefevre indicate whether or not he had contact with any of the guests earlier?" Hannibal asked.

"Why yes," replied Girard. "He said he talked with Mr. Pierpont two days earlier just after we sailed, when Mr. Pierpont made the room reservation."

We had a few more questions, but we did not discover anything else of significance.

Finally, I looked over at Hannibal, and he nodded.

"Thank you for your insight, Monsieur Girard," said Hannibal. "You can go, but we may have more questions later."

Girard drained his teacup, set it down, stood and said: "Oui, Monsieur." He then turned and quietly walked to the door.

Before the next interviewee arrived, I looked over at Hannibal and said: "Girard heard squeaky shoes." I paused and then added: "Interesting."

Hannibal nodded. Soon Maurice and Henri had everything ready. Lieutenant Chatelain sent in Anton Guerin, Girard's assistant.

Guerin entered the room and stood at attention. He was a thin young man and looked as if would blow away in even a slight breeze. His face had the look of a scared rabbit. "Not our murderer," I instantly concluded.

"Please be seated Monsieur Guerin," I said softly. "I'm so glad you are here. We need your help." I paused and then added: "Would you like some coffee or tea?"

Guerin took his seat and let out a big sigh. He looked first at me, then Hannibal and back to me. "Oui madame, merci beaucoup." Guerin had a cup of coffee, which he held in his right hand.

Hannibal then stated: "Thank you for finding a ship's officer last night. Lieutenant Chatelain was just the right person to contact."

Guerin visibly relaxed and sipped his coffee.

Hannibal and I then asked the usual questions about Guerin's activities before, during and immediately after the murder. He confirmed Girard's statement about the scuffling sound and added that he heard a cry of 'Oh!' and then the sound of squeaky shoes, but nothing else. He too had remained nearly stationary while the lights were out.

However, Guerin did reveal an important detail about activities after Lieutenant Chatelain released everyone at the crime scene. His revelation was in response to the following question from Hannibal.

"What did you do after Lieutenant Chatelain released you from the dining room area?"

Guerin thought a moment, then stated: "I returned to my cabin on Deck D." He paused, looked directly at Hannibal and said: "As I approached my cabin, I saw something unusual."

"Oh?" replied Hannibal. We both waited for Guerin to continue.

After a moment, Guerin said: "Monsieur Lefevre left a few minutes before me. As I approached my cabin from the mid-ship companionway, I saw him in the passageway. He headed aft in a hurry and exited the passageway to the service companionway that leads to the upper decks." Guerin paused and then continued: "He had shoes tucked under his arm." He paused again and added: "I followed."

"Interesting," I responded. "What else happened?"

"Well, Monsieur Lefevre exited the hatch from the companionway on Deck C, right on the Cabin-Class Promenade. I watched from the porthole in the hatch as he hurried to the stern and tossed the shoes overboard."

"Did Lefevre see you?" I asked.

"No, I don't think so," replied Guerin. "I hurried back down to Deck D and my cabin. I closed my door. A half-minute or so later, I heard footsteps in the passageway, and then the opening and closing of a door." He paused and then said: "I'm sure it was Lefevre, his cabin is two doors forward on the passageway."

"Please keep your story to yourself for now," I instructed. "Tell no one other than Lieutenant Chatelain, but only if he should ask."

"Yes, Madame Jones," replied Guerin. He smiled wanly and gave a deep sigh. I could tell that he was relieved and scared at the same time.

"Very good, Monsieur Guerin," said Hannibal. "You did the right thing." Hannibal looked from Guerin to me.

I nodded; I had no further questions. "Squeaky shoes again," I thought to myself.

# 3

## TIMING AND OPPORTUNITY

*Seven O'Clock, Tuesday morning, June 18, 1929*

Breakfast for both Hannibal and me consisted of coffee, juice, oatmeal and toast, which was brought to our cabin at six this morning.

Hannibal left right after breakfast; he wanted to consult with Doctors Borec and Dupuy. Hannibal, Maurice, Henri and I will meet to process the crime scene at about eight. I have about an hour of free time to write about the events of Sunday and Monday.

When Hannibal and I arrived at the crime scene on Sunday, Harrison Beau Hadley was standing next to a chair on Rosemary's right, looking over at Rosemary. Rosemary's sagging body leaned away from him.

On Monday evening, our passenger interviews began with Hadley. Anton Guerin, the waiter, had just left the interview room.

As Anton departed, Hannibal looked at his watch. "Seven ten," he said. "Slightly ahead of schedule." He then looked to Maurice, who nodded, opened the pantry door and spoke to Henri.

Hadley entered the room. He stopped just short of the chair, tipped his head back a little, sniffed and waited.

Hadley was handsome for an older man. He was thin and medium height. He had startling blue eyes and sand-colored hair, but the hair color didn't look quite natural. He was very well dressed. He wore a double-breasted navy-blue blazer with gold buttons, a white shirt open at the neck, and a gold cravat. He also wore white trousers and white shoes. His outfit was topped off with a cherry wood walking cane that had gold trim.

"What a dandy!" I thought to myself. To Hadley, I smiled sweetly and said: "Please, Mr. Hadley, have a seat. We need your help in solving this terrible murder."

Hadley's demeanor softened a little, but I couldn't tell yet whether his sad expression was feigned or real. "Take your time, Caroline," I thought. Hadley sniffed again and took his seat.

"Would you please join us in coffee or tea?" I asked. I smiled and raised my cup a little.

"Why, yes, thank you," replied Hadley. He turned to Maurice and said: "Earl Grey tea, two teaspoons of sugar and a spot of cream, please." His voice had a high-pitched tenor sound with a slight air of privilege.

Maurice played the perfect waiter and complied. Tea was served with both a cup and saucer. I observed Hadley as he sipped his tea. He held his cup in his right hand.

"Hadley sounds and looks for all the world like the salesman of ladies' shoes that I met once at Saks," I thought to myself. I smiled again. "OK, Caroline," my thoughts continued: "Don't stereotype and jump to conclusions."

I glanced at Hannibal. He kept a straight face, but his eyes twinkled a little. He began with a blunt statement and a question: "Mr. Hadley, you have a first-class cabin next to the cabin formerly occupied by Mrs. Rosemary Davin Pierpont. Are you a member of the Pierpont or Davin family?"

The question had the desired effect; Hadley was caught off-guard. His eyes cast down for a moment. He then tilted his head back, looked at Hannibal with an air of defiance and responded. "No, Rosemary and I are, I mean were, good friends." He then lowered his head a little, took a silk handkerchief from his trouser pocket and dabbed his eyes.

I read Hadley's body language: "Fake grief," I concluded. I glanced at Hannibal, and I could see that he agreed.

"I see," responded Hannibal to Hadley. Hannibal pretended to study his notes for a full minute. Hadley squirmed. Finally, Hannibal looked up and said: "As you would expect, we will interview the Pierpont family members this evening. Are you good friends with Rosemary's son and daughter?"

Hadley's eyes flickered again. He drew himself up a little and replied: "Yes, well, no, we had our disagreements."

"Over money?" Hannibal asked bluntly.

Hadley realized that Hannibal had his number. "Well, Rosemary and I traveled together, and sometimes the others objected."

Hadley' glance shifted from Hannibal to me and then back to Hannibal. Hannibal looked at me. I picked up his cue; it was time to change approach and keep Hadley off balance.

"Now Mr. Hadley, I'm sure you are deeply grieved over Rosemary's untimely death." I paused, gave Hadley my most sympathetic smile and said: "Please tell us about what you experienced from the time the lights went out in the dining room until Major Jones and I walked into the room."

Hadley took a deep breath, recovered a little and looked at me with sad eyes. He began his obviously rehearsed account.

"I was sitting in a chair to Rosemary's right. My chair was about two feet away, and we were holding hands over the chair arms. When the lights went out, Rosemary took her hand away and exclaimed: 'What happened?' Hadley paused and then added, with an even more sorrowful expression on his face: "Those were her last words to me."

I looked closely at Hadley. So far, his account seemed genuine.

Hadley continued: "I heard a scuffle and then Rosemary's voice saying: 'Oh!' After about a minute, I sensed that someone had stepped between Rosemary's chair and mine. I reached toward

Rosemary, but my hand touched someone else." Hadley looked at me with steady eyes.

"When your hand touched, what did you sense?" I asked.

"A man's clothing," replied Hadley. "The fabric was smooth but not silky, like a woman's clothing would feel. The fabric felt like worsted wool, like a man's jacket, I think."

"What happened next?" I asked.

Hadley paused, collecting his thoughts. "I grabbed at the person who stood between Rosemary and me. Then something hit me, like a fist." He turned his face. I could see a series of four bruises on the left side, in front of his ear, extending down to his jaw. Hadley continued: "I was stunned. The next thing I recall was the lights coming on."

"What did you see?" I asked.

"I was blinded by the light at first," replied Hadley. "As I focused, I turned toward Rosemary. She was leaning to the left, away from me. The person who hit me was gone."

Hannibal then asked: "Are you sure about the sequence of events?"

Hadley thought a moment, then said: "Yes." He turned from me and looked at Hannibal with a steady gaze. "First, I heard a scuffling sound, then Rosemary's voice saying 'Oh!' Less than a minute later, I sensed someone between Rosemary and me." He paused, reached up with his right hand, and touched his left cheek tenderly. "I grabbed, and then someone hit me." He put his hand down and added: "The next thing I remember was the lights coming on."

Hannibal and I looked at each other. I nodded. Hannibal turned to Hadley and asked: "Do you know if Rosemary had a will?"

Hadley was caught off guard again. He had obviously planned for more questions on events of Sunday evening. He stuttered for a moment and then replied: "I don't know; well, I suppose she does."

Hannibal gave Hadley a steely look and said: "I will check, but do you know if you are you mentioned in her will?"

Hadley stuttered again and his eyes blinked several times. He finally replied: "Yes, I think so. She may have mentioned it." He realized that he had a motive for murder.

Hannibal looked at me. I smiled and nodded. It was our signal that I had no more questions.

Hannibal turned to Hadley and said: "You can go now. However, we may have more questions later."

Sweat beaded on Hadley's forehead. He rose unsteadily from his chair, using his cane. He turned and walked toward the door.

"Close the door please, after you exit," said Hannibal. Hadley complied.

"I looked at Hannibal and said: "Not the killer, but he still may be involved."

"Agree," replied Hannibal.

Maurice quickly took care of the cup and saucer, and we were soon ready for Lucian Ambrose Morgan.

Before Morgan entered, Hannibal and I reviewed our file. "Morgan is probably Rosemary's attorney," Hannibal began. "We can follow up with regard to his knowledge of events Sunday night, but we have to be careful about attorney-client privilege."

"Yes, but this is a murder investigation, and we are operating under the authority of the Captain," I replied. "Within reasonable limits, I think he'll cooperate."

"Villar's notes provide some information obtained from Morgan's passport," Hannibal responded. "He is 45 years old, and he and his wife Elizabeth are in an outside first-class cabin for two on Deck A. He listed his employment as a senior partner in the New York law firm of Pierpont, Morgan and Stanley."

"I'm very interested in his knowledge about Rosemary's will," I said.

As I finished my statement, we heard a knock at the door. "Come in," said Hannibal. The door opened.

Lucian Morgan stood in the doorway. I recognized him from Sunday night. He was medium height, rotund, and had a bald head. He also had a cherubic expression on his face. Unlike most of the other passengers, he was dressed in a conservative business suit.

"He looks the part of an attorney," I thought to myself.

"Please come in and have a seat," I said. "We are so glad you could come and help us with this most distressing case."

Morgan nodded, smiled briefly, crossed the room and sat down. He looked at me with a steady gaze; his eyes expressed mild curiosity. He leaned back in his chair and waited, seemingly completely relaxed.

"He understands how to use body language to project a desired impression," I thought to myself. I returned his gaze and smiled in return. I then said: "Would you like some coffee or tea?" I raised my cup and pointed with it toward Maurice, who was standing by the serving table at the back of the room.

"Why yes, thank you," responded Morgan. "Tea please."

Maurice quickly provided the service, including a teacup and saucer.

I watched carefully as Morgan held the saucer in his left hand and the teacup in his right. He sipped slowly. "Right-handed," I concluded.

After a minute or so, Hannibal looked steadily at Morgan and said: "I believe we met some years ago, before the war, at a social function in New York." Hannibal smiled and added: "As I recall, you and I attended a ball, just before I shipped off to France."

I gave Hannibal a quick glance, as I tried to suppress my look of surprise. My look said: "You didn't tell me!"

Hannibal's eyes twinkled for my benefit as well as for Morgan.

"Why yes," responded Morgan. "You were in uniform, and quite a hit with the ladies, I believe." He gave me a quick glance and smiled like a sly cherub.

Hannibal gave a brief chuckle, and I gave him a dirty look.

"And you were already a successful attorney," replied Hannibal. "I remember that you escorted a lovely lady that evening."

"Yes," said Morgan. "That lady was Elizabeth." He smiled broadly and added: "Elizabeth is now my wife. We were married in 1921."

"Wonderful," I said sweetly. "I'm sure you have a happy marriage." I looked at Morgan steadily for a moment. Morgan returned my gaze with a knowing smile. He then said: "Yes, we do, thank you."

I gave Hannibal another quick glance. I had calmed down a little. Objectively, I could see that he was trying to establish a personal link with Morgan. "OK, Caroline," I thought to myself. "Follow Hannibal's lead."

Hannibal then said: "Harvard, class of 1907?"

"Why yes," replied Morgan. "I completed my undergraduate law degree that year." He added: "My graduate work continued until 1910."

"Ah, Juris Doctorate?" Hannibal asked.

"Yes," responded Morgan. "I went to work for Ambrose Pierpont in 1911."

"And now you are a senior partner," stated Hannibal. "Very well done, sir."

"Thank you," replied Morgan. His eyes twinkled, and he said: "As you probably know, Ambrose was John Edwin Senior's brother." His smile said: "I know what you are doing."

"I would guess that you are Rosemary Pierpont's attorney," I said. I wanted to get back in the game.

Morgan turned to me and answered: "Yes, I am." His eyes continued to twinkle.

"I understand attorney-client privilege," said Hannibal, but I'm sure you understand this is a murder investigation under the authority of Captain Blancart."

"And maritime law applies," responded Morgan with a slight frown. "Yes, I understand, and I will help you as much as I can." His eyes had a steady look, first at Hannibal and then at me.

"He will help, and he is not the murderer," I concluded to myself. I hadn't fully formulated the 'why' yet, but my intuition was seldom wrong.

Hannibal continued: "Did Rosemary have a will?"

"Yes," replied Morgan in a careful manner. "I helped with her will several years ago." He then said: "It's contents will be revealed in due course, consistent with proper procedure."

"Could Rosemary have made other wills that supersede the will that was made several years ago?" I asked.

"That is certainly possible," replied Morgan, as he turned his gaze toward me. "But as far as I know, Rosemary does not have another attorney." He added: "However, hand-written wills, made by individuals without an attorney, are relatively common and are often perfectly legal."

Hannibal looked over at me and smiled. His look said: "Good question."

I returned his smile. My confidence was back.

I then asked: "Are you also the attorney for Rosemary's children, John Edwin Junior and Abigail?"

"No," replied Morgan. His expression clouded a little. "John Edwin Junior and Abigail had legal issues that conflicted with those of Rosemary." He paused and then said: "I could not legally and ethically represent both Rosemary and her grown children."

"Did their conflicts involve money?" Hannibal asked.

"Yes," replied Morgan. "It is a matter of public court record that both John Edwin Junior and Abigail sued their mother with regard to their father's estate when he died in 1920." He continued: "The record shows that except for some personal items and real estate, the bulk of John Edwin Senior's estate, both the part that he held jointly with his wife and the part that he held separately, went exclusively to Rosemary."

"Does Rosemary provide allowances to her two adult children?" I asked bluntly.

"That is a matter of attorney-client privilege," stated Morgan blandly. However, his eyes flickered a little.

I read the unspoken message. "Yes," I concluded to myself. I smiled at Morgan, and he returned my smile.

Hannibal then shifted the line of questioning. "Can you tell us what you experienced from the time the lights went out in the dining room Sunday evening until the moment Mrs. Jones and I walked in the door?"

"Of course," replied Morgan. He then gave a very precise narrative about the events that occurred in the dark that evening. Most importantly, he confirmed Girard's and Hadley's stories about the sequence of sounds:  a muffled cry of 'Oh!' from Rosemary, silence for a few moments, then squeaky footsteps coming into the room. He also confirmed that the next sound was an impact like flesh hitting flesh, and that it came from the direction of Hadley. Finally, a moment later, he heard squeaky footsteps leaving.

After Morgan finished his narrative, Hannibal and I looked at each other. I nodded.

Hannibal turned to Morgan and said: "Thank you for a very clear presentation." His thanks were genuine, and I certainly agreed. Hannibal then added: "We are finished for now, I believe." He looked at me for a formal, courtesy agreement.

"Yes," I responded. "Thank you, Mr. Morgan."

"I will take my leave," said Morgan. He then looked first at Hannibal and then me. "I will help you in any way I can," he said, and then he continued. "Rosemary was my friend." This last statement was accompanied by a slight choking sound.

Without further comment, he rose from his chair, turned and walked to the door. He opened the door, stepped out and closed it quietly.

"Definitely not our murderer," I thought to myself. I looked at Hannibal. He smiled; I could tell that he agreed.

Maurice and Henri took care of the teacup and saucer, and soon we were ready for John Edwin Pierpont Junior.

Before Junior arrived, Hannibal and I reviewed our file. I began with: "Junior is 50 years old. He and his wife Julia are in an outside first-class cabin for two on Deck A."

"Yes," replied Hannibal. "Based upon Morgan's statements, he didn't get along with his mother in the time just after his father died."

"Hopefully, we can gain insight into his more recent relationship with his mother," I responded. Hannibal nodded in agreement.

A couple of minutes passed. The door opened without a knock. John Edwin Junior stood there.

Junior was a thin man with a sallow complexion. He was dressed haphazardly in white slacks and shoes. He also wore a rumpled white and blue striped shirt with an open collar, a light blue blazer and a 'boater' straw hat. His shirt was not quite tucked in on one side.

"Come in," said Hannibal. Please have a seat."

Junior walked in with an unsteady gait, tossed his hat on the table and sat down. He looked first at Hannibal and then at me in a leering way. I could smell his breath across the table.

"Bourbon," I thought to myself. "Drunk as a skunk."

"I am so sorry for your loss," I said with the sweetest smile I could muster. "I hope you can help us solve your mother's murder."

"I would like some coffee," responded Junior in a slurred voice.

Hannibal turned to Maurice and nodded. Without the slightest indication of distaste, Maurice brought a silver tray with a cup of steaming coffee, a little pitcher of cream, a small bowl of sugar, a teaspoon and a couple of napkins. He set the tray on the table next to Junior.

Junior then said, in a slightly slurred voice: "Cream and teaspoon of sugar, my good man."

"Of course, sir," responded Maurice with perfect politeness. Soon it was done.

Junior picked up his cup with his right hand and held it with both hands. He took several long sips. He then sat back in his chair and eyed first Hannibal and then me.

"Right-handed," I thought to myself.

To Junior, I said: "Do you know Yves Lefevre, the butler who served in the private dining room last evening?"

Junior's face expressed surprise; he had clearly expected questions about the events of Sunday evening. His eyes flickered up and down for a moment. He replied: "No, well, yes, he was introduced as one of the serving staff." He frowned and sipped his coffee again.

"When were you introduced?" I asked.

"Last night, of course," Junior replied. His eyes flickered again.

I changed the subject. "Traveling abroad is expensive," I stated. "Do you have a substantial income?"

"Yes, of course," Junior responded haughtily. "I give financial advice to the trust set up by my father, for which I am well-paid."

"Who manages the trust?" Hannibal asked with a bland expression.

"My mother and her lawyer," blurted Junior, with obvious distaste.

I looked intently into Junior's eyes and asked: "What did you do Sunday afternoon before coming to dinner?"

Junior sniffed, raised his eyebrows a little and replied: "I took a stroll on the Boat Deck promenade and then entered the smoking room for brandy and cigars with some acquaintances." He paused and looked at me, again in a haughty way. "You can check with the bartender!" He added triumphantly.

"I'm sure you did," I thought to myself. I smiled wryly and then looked over at Hannibal.

Hannibal changed the subject again: "Please tell us what you observed from the time the lights went out and the moment Mrs. Jones and I entered the dining room on Sunday evening."

Junior began a rather disjointed recital. He didn't add anything that we didn't already know, except that he didn't remember much.

After a while, Hannibal and I looked at each other. I nodded.

Hannibal turned to Junior and said: "Thank you, Mr. Pierpont. We appreciate your help. Please feel free to go. However, I hope you will make yourself available if we have further questions."

I looked into Junior's eyes, smiled sympathetically and said: "Again, we are very sorry for your loss."

"Thank you," replied Junior, without much sincerity. After an unsteady rise from his seat, he made his way to the door, which he left open after he exited. Maurice walked over and closed the door.

"That drunk couldn't kill a fly," I stated matter-of-factly. "Still, he was involved."

"Agree," replied Hannibal, with a wry smile.

We were soon ready for Arthur Blakley Cornwall, Viscount of Abbington.

"According to Villar's notes, Cornwall and his wife Abigail resided with Rosemary at her New York home during a visit just before boarding this ship," Hannibal said.

"Interesting," I replied.

Soon we heard a knock at the door. "Come in," said Hannibal. He stood up from his chair.

The door opened. A very handsome man in his mid-thirties stood in the doorway. He was well dressed in a light blue business suit with a single-breasted jacket, cuffed trousers and a British-style regimental tie. He had sandy hair and a light, trimmed moustache. He was tall, muscular and tanned.

"Please have a seat, Lord Cornwall," stated Hannibal, and he bowed slightly, in a formal yet reserved manner.

Lord Cornwall, Viscount of Abbington, nodded in an aristocratic way, entered the room and sat down. Hannibal also took his seat.

"Well done, Hannibal," I thought to myself. "I have no idea how to properly address members of the nobility."

"I remember reading the official accounts of the 1917 Battle of Passchendaele when I was in France," said Hannibal. "You were prominently mentioned in the dispatches."

"Thank you for remembering," replied Lord Cornwall courteously. "I was a Captain then, and I tried to do my part." He then said in a smooth voice: "Please call me Arthur." He looked first at Hannibal and then me. "He said: "Is this lovely lady Mrs. Caroline Case Jones?"

"Yes, I am," I replied with a slight smile. I eyed 'Arthur' cautiously. There was something too perfect in his demeanor. "So nice to meet you, Lord Cornwall. You may call me Caroline when we are in a more informal setting." I added: "Would you like some tea or coffee?"

"Of course, Mrs. Jones," replied Cornwall. "Tea, please." His smile didn't change.

Soon Cornwall had tea. I noticed that he was left-handed.

I began the questioning. "I understand that Lady Cornwall, your wife, is the former Abigail Pierpont, daughter of John Edwin and Rosemary Pierpont."

"Yes," replied Cornwall. "She is devastated over the loss of her mother."

"I'm sure," I stated. "I understand that Rosemary Pierpont was quite wealthy. Will Lady Cornwall inherit a substantial estate?"

Cornwall's eyes blinked, but he recovered quickly. "Yes, I suppose," he responded. "I'm sure Rosemary had a will, and it will be read eventually."

He paused and then added: "My attorney will contact Mr. Morgan, Rosemary's attorney, at the appropriate time." He paused again, acquired a sad expression and then said: "Now is not the time, of course."

"Your passport lists your residence as Abbington Estate, near Newbury, England," said Hannibal. "Do you and your wife live there most of the time?"

"When we are not traveling about," replied Cornwall. "It's a big house, and we are having it re-modeled. Quite expensive and time-consuming, you know."

"Other than the will held by Mr. Morgan, do you know of another later will that Rosemary may have had?"

Cornwall's eyes blinked again. He hesitated a brief moment before replying: "Just after Easter, during a family discussion, Rosemary did mention that she was considering changes to accommodate Mr. Harrison Hadley." He added: "I'm sure you will check; several non-family members heard the discussion."

I could see that Cornwall had made an effort to maintain his composure. "Did the discussion take place at Rosemary's home in New York City?" I asked.

"Yes, Abigail and I were there on an extended six-month visit," replied Cornwall. "In fact, we just left her home in New York to board this ship." He paused a moment and then added: "We planned to cross the Channel from Le Havre to Dover after we dock." He smiled and continued: "I must check on the remodeling work at home."

"Was John Edwin Junior and his wife Julia also present during this discussion at Rosemary's residence?" I asked.

"Yes," replied Cornwall. "So was Mr. Morgan, and I know you have already spoken to him."

"Your first mistake, Lord Cornwall, I thought to myself. "Morgan didn't say a word about such a discussion." To Cornwall, I just smiled and asked: "Did you ever see a new will?"

Cornwall blinked again. "No," he replied. "I don't think Rosemary ever got around to making one."

"Time to change the subject, Caroline," I thought. I looked over at Hannibal, who understood.

"Would you please tell us what you remember from the time just before the lights went out in the dining room Sunday evening until Mrs. Jones and I arrived?"

"Yes, of course, responded Cornwall. "Just before the lights went out, everyone in the dinner party was seated at the table. Two waiters were at the serving tables in the back. I didn't see the butler; I suppose he was in the pantry or back in the kitchen."

Cornwall paused, collecting his thoughts. "We were all engaged in light dinner conversation when the lights went out."

He leaned back as if recalling events and said: "Several people, including my wife, made exclamations like 'What happened?' and so on. After a minute or so, I heard footsteps enter from the pantry door, then an exclamation from Rosemary, then more footsteps."

He paused for effect and added: "When the lights came on, we saw Rosemary."

Cornwall leaned forward, folded his hands on the table, acquired a sad expression and gave a big sigh. He then added: "After that, everyone at the table jumped up from their seats. Abigail and Julia screamed."

He looked intently at Hannibal. "At that moment, you and Mrs. Jones walked in the room."

"Are you sure everyone in the dinner party was seated when the lights came on?" I asked.

"Yes, positive," replied Cornwall quickly. His eyes blinked again.

Hannibal and I looked at each other. I nodded.

Hannibal stood, turned to Cornwall, bowed slightly and said: "Thank you so much for your help, Lord Cornwall. I hope you will make yourself available if we have more questions."

I remained seated; I didn't know the protocol, and even if I did, I probably would have remained seated. "Bad attitude, Caroline," I told myself. "You are going to Europe, and you better learn how to operate in aristocratic society."

Cornwall looked at me, smiled and stood up. "Of course," he replied. He then turned, walked to the door and exited. He closed the door softly behind him.

After he left, Hannibal and I had a brief discussion before we asked Maurice to signal for Elizabeth Morgan. Maurice notified Henri about the next interviewee and then busied himself with Lord Cornwall's teacup and saucer.

# 4

## METHOD AND MOTIVE

*Seven Thirty, Tuesday morning, June 18, 1929*

I only have about thirty minutes before meeting Hannibal, Maurice and Henri at the crime scene. My entries will be hurried; I can refine them later. I still need to record our interviews with Elizabeth Morgan, Abigail Cornwall and Julia Pierpont on Monday evening.

After Lord Cornwall left, Maurice made a new pot of tea and brought out some sweets on a silver tray. I gave Maurice my coffee cup; Hannibal kept his.

Hannibal and I each reviewed our notes. Questions for the ladies would be different than the men. After a minute or so, we heard a knock at the door.

"Please come in," I said in a clear but soft voice. The door opened. I recognized Elizabeth Morgan from Sunday night. Hannibal stood as Elizabeth entered. He walked around the table and assisted Elizabeth as she took her seat. After a few moments, everyone settled.

Maurice, the perfect waiter, brought a tray with a pot of tea and sweets over to the table. Elizabeth smiled graciously as she chose plain tea and a small plate of sugar cookies. I noted that she was right-handed. Maurice offered the same to me, and I accepted a cup of tea.

I looked carefully at Elizabeth. She was a few years older than me, and she was beautiful. She had light brown hair, coiffed in the latest conservative fashion. Her skin was smooth and creamy. Her hands, which she folded demurely in her lap after she was seated, had lovely pink, manicured nails. I also saw a simple, platinum wedding band. She didn't wear lipstick; she didn't need it.

She wore a fashionable, conservative dress, as befitting the wife of a wealthy attorney. "Form-fitting, Lanvin blue with white trim, silver buttons for accent and two lovely strands of pearls," I noted to myself. "Excellent taste."

I liked Elizabeth instantly. "Careful, Caroline," I admonished myself. "This is a murder investigation." I took a deep breath and said softly: "I know this is a distressing time for everyone." I paused for effect, watched Elizabeth's face carefully and continued: "We hope you can help us solve this terrible murder of Mrs. Pierpont."

Elizabeth smiled, looked directly in my eyes and replied: "Rosemary was my friend. I will help in any way I can." She sipped her tea slowly. She held her cup in her right hand, and her saucer remained on the table.

I could not detect any attempt at deception. I then said: "Would you please describe what you experienced from just before the lights went out in the dining room Sunday night until the moment Major Jones and I entered the room?"

Elizabeth put down her cup, took a deep breath and replied: "Lucian and I were sitting across the table from Rosemary and Harrison before the lights went out. We were engaged in light dinner table conversation. Others at the table were also talking, but I didn't pay much attention to what they were saying."

She continued: "I did catch snippets of whispered conversation between Arthur and Abigail; they seemed very concerned about paying bills."

"What exactly did you hear?" asked Hannibal.

Elizabeth looked at Hannibal with a steady gaze. She replied: "Well, Arthur said: 'The contractor wants payment.' Abigail replied: 'We have to do something.' She seemed very upset."

"Do you recall any other comments?" I asked.

Elizabeth thought a moment. She then turned to me and said: "Not from Arthur and Abigail."

"Did you hear any comments made by others?" Hannibal asked.

"A little, but not much," responded Elizabeth. "I did notice that John Edwin and Julia were having a heated discussion over something." She smiled wryly. "John Edwin had been drinking; his voice carried quite well."

"Do you recall what John Edwin said?" I asked.

Elizabeth frowned and said: "Well, I recall one comment John Edwin made: 'Things have been taken care of.' I don't remember any other words." Elizabeth added: "I also remember that Julia put her finger to her lips and said: 'Shhh.' John Edwin was quiet after that. Shortly afterwards, the lights went out."

"What did you experience after the lights went out?" Hannibal asked.

Elizabeth recounted her observations. She didn't add anything to what we already knew, except that her recollections matched the stories of her husband, Girard and Guerin.

Hannibal and I looked at each other. We had finished our questions. Hannibal stood and said: "Thank you, Mrs. Morgan. You have been most helpful."

Elizabeth took the cue, rose from her seat, looked first at Hannibal and then me and said: "I hope you can solve this. Lucian and I will be available if you need us." With that comment, she turned, walked to the door and exited quietly. She closed the door.

I thought for a couple of minutes as Maurice and Henri performed their duties. Finally, I said: "I think Lucian should be present when we process Rosemary's cabin. He is her attorney."

"Good idea," replied Hannibal. "Who knows what might turn up?" He added: "We can do the cabin after we process the crime scene."

Our next interview was with Abigail Pierpont Cornwall. Hannibal stood when we heard the knock at the door. Maurice walked over and opened it. Lady Cornwall made a grand entrance.

"Attractive woman," I thought to myself. "She's ageing well."

Hannibal bowed slightly, in the appropriate formal manner. "Please have a seat, Lady Cornwall," he said.

Maurice helped her with her chair and offered her tea and sweets. She took tea with sugar and cream and sipped it daintily. She used her right hand.

"Puts on unnecessary airs," I concluded. Still, Lady Cornwall was dressed in the latest casual fashion, entirely appropriate for a holiday at sea. She wore a loose-fitting white dress with navy-blue buttons and wide belt. She also wore a matching broad sun hat with a slight vail. Pearls gleamed from her neck, ears and left wrist. I didn't like her. I remained seated.

I smiled sweetly and said: "I am so sorry for your loss, Lady Cornwall." I paused as she nodded in an aristocratic way. Her blue eyes glittered. I continued: "I hope you can help us with this most distressing event." I then looked over at Hannibal.

Hannibal said: "Unfortunately, this is a murder investigation under the authority of Captain Blancart." He paused and his steely eyes stared directly at Lady Cornwall. "We hope you will cooperate." Hannibal's voice was soft, but it held an implied threat.

Lady Cornwall's eyes narrowed a bit. "Yes," she responded. She sniffed slightly and sipped her tea.

Hannibal asked: "Do you know if your mother had a will?"

Lady Cornwall sniffed again as if the question was impertinent. After a moment, she answered: "Yes, I suppose she did."

Hannibal then stated: "Rosemary Pierpont was quite wealthy." He paused and asked: "Do you expect to inherit a substantial amount of money?"

Lady Cornwall's eyes blinked. She sniffed again and replied: "I don't know; I don't concern myself with those things." She added: "You'll have to ask my attorney or my husband."

Hannibal looked over at me and smiled. I made a point of writing a note. "Liar," I wrote. I also wrote: "Cool customer." Lady Cornwall raised her eyebrows and fidgeted a little.

"Time to change the subject," I concluded. Precisely as I had done with Elizabeth, I asked: "Would you please describe what you experienced from just before the lights went out in the dining room Sunday night until the moment Major Jones and I entered the room?"

Lady Cornwall gave a recitation that matched perfectly with her husband's.

After she finished, I made a point of again making notes. Lady Cornwall watched me carefully and sipped her tea.

After a couple of minutes, I looked up at Hannibal. He nodded and his eyes twinkled. He then stood, turned to Lady Cornwall and said: "Thank you so much for your help, Lady Cornwall." He didn't bow. "We hope you will be available if we have more questions."

Right on cue, Maurice walked over to the door and opened it. Lady Cornwall raised her eyebrows, put down her teacup, sniffed, stood, turned, and without another word, walked out the door. Maurice closed the door. All three of us chuckled. "Doesn't like being dismissed," I said.

Our final interview was with Julia Pierpont. I reviewed my notes while Maurice and Henri performed their tasks.

"Julia Pierpont, age 48, married John Edwin Junior in 1905, I mused. "I can imagine what nearly twenty-five years with that drunk must be like," Hannibal laughed.

Soon we heard a soft knock at the door. Hannibal stood, and Maurice walked over and opened the door. Julia stood in the doorway quietly.

"Please come in and have a seat," said Hannibal. Julia entered. Her walk was unsteady. Maurice helped her with her chair and offered her tea and sweets. Julia took a cup of tea and a sugar cookie.

"She is right-handed," I observed. Julia was dressed in appropriate fashion, but her clothes seemed to hang loosely. "She's lost weight since she bought that dress," I surmised. "I wonder why?"

Julia answered my question with a hiccup. I looked closely. "She has been drinking," I concluded. Julia hiccupped again. I looked at her face. Lines radiated from her eyes, and her cheeks had a slight florid tint. Veins showed in places near her nose.

"Alcoholic," I decided. I had no doubts; I had seen plenty of examples during my earlier life on the Wabash. "I can't detect an odor of liquor, so she's probably addicted to good quality gin, which has no easily discernible odor." Somehow, Julia's situation elicited my sympathy.

I smiled and looked Julia in the eyes. "I'm sure you and your husband are grief-stricken by your mother-in-law's murder, I stated. "Can you think of anyone who would want to do her harm?"

Julia took a deep breath and replied: "No, Rosemary and I got along fine." Julia paused and then added: "If she had enemies, I don't know them."

I noted that Julia addressed her relationship with Rosemary first. "A defensive answer," I concluded. To Julia, I said: "Your husband said that he receives payments from his mother's trust." I paused and watched Julia's eyes. "Do either of you have other sources of income?"

"No, well yes," answered Julia with a little hesitation. "John Edwin has investments." Her eyes blinked.

"Do you know if Rosemary had a will?" Hannibal asked.

"Yes," responded Julia. "She discussed her will with us several times." Julia's expression hardened a little.

"Not a pleasant discussion," I concluded. To Julia, I asked: "Have you seen Rosemary's will?"

"No," replied Julia a little too quickly. "Rosemary discussed it with us, but I have never seen it." Her eyes blinked.

Time to change the subject, so I asked: "Would you please describe what you experienced from just before the lights went out in the dining room Sunday night until the moment Major Jones and I entered the room?"

Julia thought a few moments, then gave an answer that matched, more or less, what we heard from Lucian Morgan and his wife Elizabeth. She did add that she heard a chair scrape on the other side of the table just after Rosemary's outcry and before she heard squeaky shoes. Her narrative was interrupted by a few hiccups, but it was coherent, unlike her husband's recitation.

When she finished, I looked at Hannibal and nodded. Hannibal stood and said: "Thank you for your help, Mrs. Pierpont." He paused for effect and said: "I hope you will be available if we have further questions."

Julia gave Hannibal an uncertain look. She then looked at me and then back to Hannibal. After a moment, she said: "Yes, of course." She put down her teacup and got up from her chair. Maurice walked her to the door.

After she was gone, I sighed, leaned back in my chair, and said: "We have a lot to discuss."

"Yes," responded Hannibal. "However, we need to process the crime scene first."

Lieutenant Chatelain entered the room and said: "I sent each of the interviewees away, in turn. He paused took out his watch and added: "It's only nine forty-five." He smiled.

Maurice piped up and said: "Henri and I can process the fingerprints from the cups and saucers, if you show us how." Henri, who had just entered room, added: "Yes, we want to help."

I looked at Maurice, then Henri and then Lieutenant Chatelain. Chatelain grinned. Finally, I looked at Hannibal. Hannibal nodded and said: "I have the dusting powder, adhesive tape and blank paper."

I looked at our three co-workers and said: "We would love your help. It would save us valuable time."

Hannibal and I spent the next hour working with Lieutenant Chatelain, Maurice and Henri. After a couple of examples, all three had the process down correctly.

After the interviews on Monday, Hannibal and I returned to our cabin, prepared for bed, wrote profusely, got in bed at about one o'clock and slept soundly. We were both exhausted.

I have finished my entries about Monday night. Whew! I hear Hannibal in our main cabin area; he's back from his visit with Doctors Borec and Dupuy. I wonder how that turned out. I'm sure Hannibal will tell me as we go to the crime scene and meet Lieutenant Chatelain, Maurice and Henri.

Hannibal looked in at me as I wrote in my notebook. "In addition to meeting with Borec and Dupuy, I visited Lucian Morgan this morning. He will meet us at Rosemary Pierpont's cabin at eight-thirty."

"Excellent," I said. "I think Morgan's help will be very useful if and when this murder goes to court."

# 5

## EVALUATE THE EVIDENCE

*Noon, Tuesday, June 18, 1929*

Lieutenant Chatelain, Maurice and Henri met us at the crime scene just after eight this morning. Chatelain still had our fingerprint lifting kit from last night.

"Good morning gentlemen," I said, as Hannibal and I walked up to the private dining room door. "Shall we go inside?"

"Yes, Madame," replied Chatelain. He then removed the seal across the door latch, and the five of us entered the room.

We were quiet for a few moments. The place was dimly lit with light from the open doorway to the butler's pantry. The table was still set for eight people, and three of the eight chairs lay on their sides. One of the chairs directly across the table from the door had been moved back slightly, and Rosemary's body had been removed.

"Spooky," I thought to myself.

Hannibal broke the silence. "Do you gentlemen remember how we lifted fingerprints from the cups and saucers last night?"

Chatelain, Maurice and Henri all murmured assent. Chatelain added: "We finished with the cups." He paused and smiled. "You will have my report that identifies the names and the associated fingerprints later today."

"Thank you, Lieutenant," replied Hannibal. He looked at the three men in turn and added: "Thank you all."

Silence followed Hannibal's thanks. The air in the room seemed cool and somehow heavy.

Hannibal broke the spell, temporarily at least. "We need to use the same technique as with the cups and saucers, except that this time, we will lift prints from a variety of surfaces. Inspect for prints first, use the black powder, and then lift each print with a strip of cellophane tape. After you have a print on the tape adhesive, carefully stick the tape on a blank sheet of paper so that the print clearly shows from the paper through the tape."

He paused, looked around at each man and then continued: "Write underneath the tape the date, time and location where the print was lifted. A quick sketch would also be helpful. Add any brief remarks that will help Doctor Dupuy determine the exact location where you found the print." He paused again and asked: "Any questions?"

There were none. Chatelain and Hannibal laid out the items from the kit on the floor to avoid contaminating prints on furniture surfaces. Hannibal also dumped a pile of extra surgical gloves from a sack that he had brought from Doctor Dupuy's office.

Hannibal looked at me, and I nodded. I then continued the instructions. "Dust for prints on the chairs, the edges of the table, all door handles and all light switches. We are especially interested in the switch on the wall in the passageway near the door to the butler's pantry."

Hannibal smiled and said: "Each room has its own switch. However, I checked with the Chief Engineer, and the switch in the passageway is the only one that controls all the lights in the private dining rooms, the butler's pantries and the passageway."

Henri looked at me and asked: "Are you and Major Jones going to stay here with us?" He had a slightly apprehensive look, as if the spooky room had scared him a little.

"No," I said with a re-assuring smile. "The three of you, working together, can handle the crime scene. Major Jones and I will do some work in Rosemary Pierpont's cabin."

Chatelain said: "I will break the seal on Mrs. Pierpont's cabin door and let you in. Afterwards, I will return to this room and assist these two men." He looked at Henri and smiled. "Will you two be OK until I return?"

Henri drew himself up and sniffed a little. "Oui, Monsieur Lieutenant," he responded. Maurice just grinned.

Hannibal and I watched for a few minutes as Maurice and Henri put on gloves. Each took a container of powder, a roll of cellophane tape and sheets of paper. The pair then started looking for prints. Chatelain picked up the same items and then walked through the butler's pantry toward the passageway. Hannibal and I watched.

After about five minutes, the lights came on in the dining room. Chatelain returned and said: "I took care of the light switch in the passageway." He held up a sheet of paper. I could see a piece of tape with a clear print and some writing.

"Good," I replied. The brighter light in the room helped, and Maurice and Henri moved about with more confidence. "Shall we head to Mrs. Pierpont's cabin?"

Hannibal looked at his watch and said: "Eight-fifteen." He looked at me and smiled: "Perfect."

Lieutenant Chatelain, Hannibal and I walked down the passageway, past the First-Class Dining Room and continued aft on the starboard side. The B Deck Grande Classe cabins were up one deck. We used the grand staircase to make our way to Rosemary's cabin, which was the first of four Grande Classe cabins on our left. Chatelain removed the seal on the door latch. Chatelain, Hannibal and I entered the cabin.

At precisely eight-thirty, Lucian Morgan arrived. After a few moments of greetings, Chatelain left and headed back to the crime scene. Morgan, Hannibal and I were alone. Morgan looked first at me and then Hannibal. His face had a look of curiosity, and he waited.

"I think we should look for personal papers," said Hannibal. "Anything that would shed light on a motive for murder."

"Yes," replied Morgan. "In my presence as Rosemary's attorney and given the authority delegated to you by the Captain, such a search is entirely proper."

The search began. I felt a bit eerie looking through Rosemary's personal effects. However, I suppressed my feelings and thoroughly searched bureau drawers, suitcases and even bathroom toiletries. Hannibal did the same on the other side of the cabin.

After about ten minutes, I found a large envelope in a steamer trunk that rested next to a closet by the entryway. I opened the envelope and emptied the contents on a small writing desk nearby. The first thing I saw was a business-sized envelope labeled: 'Last Will and Testament, by Rosemary Davin Pierpont.' It had a notarized, unbroken wax seal over the envelope flap. The envelope also had a date: June 15, 1929, just two days before the SS *Isle de France* sailed from New York harbor.

"Hannibal, Mr. Morgan, look at this," I said. Both walked over. I handed the will to Hannibal, who, after a moment, handed it to Morgan. Hannibal and I waited.

After reading the envelope and looking carefully at the seal, Morgan said: "I have not seen this document." He paused a moment and then added: "Given the circumstances and since I am Mrs. Pierpont's attorney, I think it is entirely appropriate that I open this envelope. You two are witnesses to my actions."

He broke the seal and opened the envelope. The three of us read the hand-written will. After a while, Morgan said: "This is a perfectly legal document, and it supersedes Rosemary's will of 1925, which I have in my office in New York."

"Hannibal said: "1925? He looked first at Morgan and then me. "Did you notice the reference to a will dated November 1, 1928 in the second paragraph?"

After a moment of study, Morgan said: "There must have been a second will, dated November 1, 1928. This is the third, most recent will."

All three of us read the will again. Finally, I said: "Wow!"

Morgan then said: "I will take this will to Chief Purser Villar, along with my written statement that explains what we have done. I will also list you two as witnesses. Later, you can endorse my statement, if you choose, in the presence of Chief Purser Villar. I know Villar will keep both documents, the will and my statement, in his safe."

"Very good," responded Hannibal. "Thank you, Mr. Morgan." I nodded in agreement.

After a moment, I said: "Let's tidy up a bit. If you both agree, I will go down to the crime scene, return with Lieutenant Chatelain, and we can re-seal this cabin."

"Good idea," responded Hannibal.

"I will take my leave and do what I promised," said Morgan. He paused and then added: "I am glad we are working together." His voice was sincere.

Hannibal remained in the cabin while Morgan and I went about our tasks.

## Five in the Afternoon, Tuesday, June 18

What a busy day! Lieutenant Chatelain, Maurice and Henri completed their work at the crime scene. Chatelain delivered his report about an hour ago. It included all the crime scene fingerprints and location descriptions. In turn, Hannibal took it to Doctor Dupuy. Villar has Rosemary's will and Morgan's statement, along with our endorsements.

Hannibal and I read Lieutenant Chatelain's report and Doctor Borec's official autopsy report.

Our 'team' still had to analyze and compare the fingerprints taken from suspects to the fingerprints lifted from the crime scene. Doctor Dupuy promised to complete this task by tomorrow at noon. We should be able to present our results the day after tomorrow, in an appropriate forum, one day before we dock in Le Havre on June 22.

Hannibal and I are ravenously hungry; we've had nothing to eat since breakfast except for a hurried snack at noon. Hannibal made a dinner reservation for six this evening, and we will discuss our findings after we return to our cabin.

### Nine in the Evening, Tuesday, June 18

Just before six, we strolled from our cabin to the grand staircase on Deck A. We descended to the main First-Class Dining Room entrance on Deck C.

I wore my elegant, form-fitting Chanel crêpe de Chine little black evening dress. It had a V-neckline and long narrow sleeves. The hem ended just above my ankles, but the dress had a slit in the back to make walking easy. My outfit was accessorized with short, triple strings of white pearls, dark silk hose, black high-heeled shoes and a matching small handbag. I had a black silk evening wrap for the cool breeze on deck. The diamonds on my engagement and wedding rings sparkled in the light. I was able to arrange my hair in a reasonable fashion, but I must get to the salon soon!

Hannibal wore his informal white jacket tuxedo, black trousers, black tie and cummerbund. His highly polished black shoes gleamed. What a handsome escort!

The dining room was full, but the maître de courteously found us a quiet table for two. We each started with a glass of champagne. The head waiter for our table took our order. Hannibal coached me on reading the menu, all in French, of course.

We both laughed merrily at my awkward attempts to understand French. Finally, after much trial and error on my part, Hannibal and I both had soupe à L'oignon and a light salade du jardin. For an unusual, tasty main course, I had J'avais une blanquette de Veau avec des brins de céleri et des tranches de poivron rouge et de petites pommes de terre nouvelles. Hannibal had Magret de Canard.

"Let's see," I said with a grin; For us American girls, we have veal and duck with all the trimmings."

Hannibal laughed and replied: "Close enough."

Our main course was accompanied with a single glass each of Grand vin rouge de la Côte de Bordeaux. For dessert, we each had crème brûlée and a glass of classic late harvest Chenin Blanc. We had a wonderful time, and our murder case was temporarily forgotten.

We strolled back to our cabin at about eight-thirty. When Hannibal unlocked and opened the door, I saw a folded paper on the floor. "Hannibal," I said: "Look!" I pointed.

Hannibal picked up and unfolded the paper. It was a note. We both read: "J'espère que vous avez passé une merveilleuse soirée. Suggérez que vous portiez votre attention sur les activités de croisière et oubliez votre préoccupation pour les choses qui ne vous concernent pas."

I stumbled through the words. After a moment, I said: "I can't do a direct translation, but I think that it essentially means: "Mind your own business."   I looked up at Hannibal. He saw the question in my eyes.

"You understand the note perfectly," Hannibal replied.

We both studied the note closely. "It's written in flowing script," said Hannibal. "The writer knows French punctuation, and has good hand-writing."

"The paper is from a standard ship notepad, and they are everywhere, even in our room," I said. "The writer used a pencil and wrote with his or her right hand."

"Hummm," Hannibal mused. "Time for a little unauthorized snooping. I'll visit Maurice and Henri."

He looked at me and smiled. "Please wait here, and keep the door locked until I return." Without another word, Hannibal stepped out of the door. I bolted it from the inside and waited impatiently.

After half an hour, I heard a soft knock. I went to the door. I asked softly: "Hannibal?"

"Yes," came the reply. It was Hannibal's voice.

I unlocked the door, and Hannibal entered. He looked at me, smiled and said: "Mission underway."

# 6

## MURDERER REVEALED

*Wednesday Morning, June 19, 1929*

The investigation reports from our teammates are done. We have the autopsy, the comparison of fingerprints and Rosemary's latest will. Hannibal and I also have voluminous notes taken during the interviews and the first draft of our report that documents our findings to date.

Hannibal and I know the answers. We will spend the day working on our report, except for the final chapter. The report will be addressed to Chief Purser Villar. We will also do a summary for Captain Blancart.

We have yet to use our information and our wits to spring a trap for the guilty. With Villar's permission, we have scheduled a meeting with all of the potential suspects in one room. Lieutenant Chatelain will be present, along with his Sergeant at Arms.

The meeting will be held tomorrow, June 20, at nine in the morning. Chatelain set aside one of the private dining rooms for the meeting, and he agreed to add extra tables and chairs. Maurice and Henri will do the set-up. They will also be present during the meeting to serve coffee, tea and sweets, and for other reasons.

Depending on the outcome of our meeting tomorrow, we may have a second meeting on June 21. A lot will depend on the reaction of our potential suspects. We have already consulted with Chatelain, and he understands our plan. The final chapter of our report and the Captain's summary will be written after our meetings. Tomorrow will be exciting!

## Thursday Afternoon, June 20

My expectations about the meeting were correct. What a meeting! We prepared by reviewing our notes and reports. We dressed conservatively, very different from our interview sessions. The idea was to impress the innocent, partially guilty and guilty with our business-like appearance.

I wore my Schiaparelli summer suit with blouse, vest, jacket and skirt. The blouse was white satin, and it had a small collar and long sleeves. The light blue satin vest had a low, round neckline and a double-row of dark blue buttons in front. The dark blue twilled crepe jacket was fitted and cut to give a yoke-like appearance. It had a wide notched collar, and it was flared all around at the waist. The matching skirt was full and finished with a thin belt. I wore a narrow tie that matched the color of the skirt and jacket. My accessories included creamy white silk hose and medium-heeled dark blue shoes. I also carried my black leather notebook. I felt professional, yet stylish.

Hannibal wore a classic grey worsted wool single-breasted business suit, a light blue shirt a dark blue tie and black shoes. He looked like a thoroughly modern attorney, ready to try his case, or perhaps a banker, ready to meet wealthy clients. He also carried a black leather notebook.

Hannibal and I arrived at the meeting room early, about eight-thirty. Maurice and Henri were already there, with coffee, tea, sweet rolls and miniature cannoli set on serving tables at the back of the room. I couldn't help myself: I ate a cannoli and washed it down with coffee. Mmmmn! Maurice and Henri both grinned at me.

I looked around the room. It was set up exactly as Hannibal and I had instructed. It had five square tables, all with white linen tablecloths and place settings, as if for a morning tea. One table was smaller and set near the back of the room. It had two chairs. Hannibal and I set our notebooks on this table. Three larger tables were arranged in the middle of the room, and each had four chairs. Two of these tables were for the seven passengers and one was for the three staff members who were all present at the murder. Another small table was set by the main door, and it was reserved for Lieutenant Chatelain and his Sergeant at Arms.

Chatelain and his Sergeant arrived at about eight forty-five. The Sergeant was a large man, and he had a no-nonsense expression on his face. Hannibal briefed the pair as I finished my second cannoli.

Our 'guests' began arriving at about nine. Chatelain had instructed all of them to attend the day before. He also told them that Hannibal and I had important facts to present about the events of Sunday night, but nothing more.

As they entered, Maurice escorted them to a table. By nine-fifteen, everyone was seated and enjoying coffee or tea, sweet rolls and cannoli. Maurice and Henri moved about the room, providing polite and efficient service. Hannibal and I sat at our table and watched the actions and body language of our 'guests.'

As planned, everyone relaxed a little, even Lefevre, Girard and Guerin. Lefevre occasionally looked intently at John Edwin Junior. The Cornwalls remained somewhat aloof, yet their eyes had cold, calculating looks. John Edwin Junior and Julia whispered together furtively. Hadley had moved his chair slightly to provide distance between himself and the Cornwalls. He sipped tea quietly. The Morgans both sat back in their chairs with expressions of mild curiosity. And yet, among all, there was an air of expectation.

At precisely nine-thirty, Hannibal rose from his seat, looked around the room at each person, in turn. Whispers and conversations stopped.

"In cooperation with Lieutenant Chatelain and others, Mrs. Jones and I have completed our fact-finding work. We will present results during this briefing." He paused for effect and then continued: "However, we still have a few questions, and we will ask these at appropriate moments during our presentation." Hannibal looked over at me and smiled.

I remained seated, sipped my coffee, and then put my cup down. I said: "We have a timeline. First, the lights went out in your dining room. They also went out in our room next door and in the passageway behind the two dining rooms."

I looked around the room at several faces and then continued: "This happened at about five minutes before seven o'clock. Just after the lights went out, several persons in your dining room made comments like 'What happened?' and so on. This was followed by an exclamation of 'Oh!' from Mrs. Pierpont." I paused and then said: "A few moments later, several persons in this room told us that they heard squeaky shoes as someone walked across the room." I looked directly at Lefevre, and so did Hannibal.

"Mr. Hadley, who was sitting to the right of Mrs. Pierpont, told us that after he heard the shoes, someone moved between his chair and the chair of Mrs. Pierpont. Also, Mr. Hadley stated that the person who was between the two chairs hit him."

Lefevre eyes widened and he shifted nervously in his chair.

I pressed home my indictment. "Several persons in this room also testified that they heard an impact sound from the direction of Mr. Hadley. After that sound, they heard squeaky shoes again, crossing the floor."

I paused and stared intently at Lefevre's eyes. "You, Monsieur Lefevre, are the person who walked across the room. You were the person between the chairs occupied by Mrs. Pierpont and Mr. Hadley. You were also the person who struck Mr. Hadley. A few moments afterwards, you walked back across the room."

I paused for moment, then continued: "Our evidence includes the bruised and skinned knuckles on your right hand and Mr. Hadley's nasty bruise on his left cheek. Most importantly, we found your left-hand fingerprints on the right arm of Mrs. Pierpont's chair.

Finally, we know you tossed your shoes overboard later that night from the Cabin-Class Promenade on Deck C."

Lefevre's mouth opened as if he were about to say something, and he gripped the arms of his chair. After a moment, he closed his mouth and clamped his jaws tight. His eyes stared back at me intently.

I stared right back and stated: "In addition, we know that you were the one who turned out the lights. Your right thumb and index fingerprints were on the light switch in the passageway just behind the butler's pantry." I paused and then continued: "That switch is the only one that controls all of the lights in the private dining rooms, butler's pantries and passageway."

Lefevre started to rise from his chair. The Sergeant of Arms walked swiftly over and placed a firm hand on Lefevre's shoulder. Lefevre sat back down. However, his eyes had a murderous look, and he continued to stare at me.

I looked up at Hannibal, who said firmly: "Remain seated, Monsieur Lefevre." He stared intently at Lefevre and continued: "There is still the issue of motive. Why did you turn out the lights and approach Mrs. Pierpont in the dark?"

Lefevre took several deep breaths and looked around wildly. I was reminded of a cornered animal. Finally, he said: "I, I didn't do it!" He turned around and stared at Junior. If looks could kill, Junior would have been dead instantly.

Junior recoiled, opened his mouth and stared wide-eyed at Lefevre.

I returned my attention to Lefevre. "Did Mr. Pierpont pay you to kill his mother?" I asked in a soft but clear voice.

Lefevre pointed to Junior and shouted: "He, he promised me ten thousand American dollars!" He started to rise from his chair again, but the Sergeant shoved him down, this time with both hands.

Junior rose to a half-standing position. Lieutenant Chatelain got up and swiftly moved over behind Junior's chair. Junior looked up, saw Chatelain and sat back down. "No!" he said in a shrill voice. Julia stared at her husband with wide eyes.

I glanced over at Lord and Lady Cornwall. The expressions on their faces changed from total surprise to smug satisfaction. "Interesting," I thought to myself. "They didn't know."

I looked at Junior. So did the Sergeant. His attention was distracted from his restraint of Lefevre. I sensed movement. It was Lefevre. I got up swiftly. As I did so, I slipped off my shoes.

Lefevre made the most of the Sergeant's distraction. He rose from his chair. In a swift fluid motion, he swung up his right fist. He hit the Sergeant under the jaw, almost lifting him off his feet. The Sergeant went down.

As the Sergeant hit the floor, I took several fast steps and came up behind Lefevre as he started toward the door. I slammed my bare left foot just behind his right knee. Lefevre's knee buckled, and he spun counter-clockwise. His body faced me, and his arms swung wildly as he lost his balance.

The forward motion of my body still produced momentum. I slammed my left fist into Lefevre's middle, up under his ribs. The full weight of my body was behind the blow. Lefevre went down on his back, right next to the Sergeant.

I stood over Lefevre, put my hands on my hips and said in a clear voice: "Don't move!"

Hannibal arrived by my side. He glanced over at me with a grin. "Need any help?" He asked.

I looked up. I'm sure there was fire in my eyes; my blood was up. After a moment, I took a deep breath, let it out, and replied: "No, I don't think so." I smiled.

Hannibal turned his attention to Lefevre, who was trying to catch his breath. He reached down and with both hands, grasped Lefevre's collar and hauled him to his feet.

Chatelain, who had been startled by all the swift action, recovered and stepped over to Lefevre's side. He and Hannibal slammed Lefevre back down in his chair.

I turned my attention to the Sergeant, who slowly got up. I watched as he looked first at me, then Lefevre and then back to me. "Merci beaucoup, Madame," he said with a sheepish expression. I smiled and nodded.

I glanced around the room. Everyone except Junior sat with their mouths open. Junior had risen from his chair and had started toward the door. "I wouldn't do that," I said firmly as I looked in Junior's direction.

Junior heard, turn towards me, and stared for a moment. He thought better of his actions and returned meekly to his chair.

The Sergeant returned to his post next to Lefevre. Chatelain stood behind Junior. Hannibal and I glanced at each other, and I nodded.

We then returned to our table. Hannibal remained standing, and I sat down. I took several deep breaths, calmed down and waited. I looked at each person around the room. The air of expectation returned.

In a soft but clear voice, Hannibal said: "I'm sure the proper authorities will have questions about the relationship between Mr. Pierpont and Monsieur Lefevre."

Lord Cornwell then said: "Well done, Major and Mrs. Jones." He smiled and then added: "You have motive, opportunity and your killer."

"It would seem so," replied Hannibal with a bland smile.

Hannibal then looked at Chatelain. "I suggest that Monsieur Lefevre be held in the brig. I also suggest that Mr. Pierpont be restricted to his cabin." Chatelain nodded in agreement.

I understood Hannibal's approach. Lefevre was clearly a dangerous, violent person. Junior, on the other hand, had not demonstrated violence, and as long as we were at sea, he was not a flight risk.

"I think everyone has had enough for today. Mrs. Jones and I have reports to write." Hannibal paused and then continued: "However, I would like to re-convene in this room tomorrow morning at nine o'clock. I would like everyone to be here, except Monsieurs Lefevre, Girard and Guerin." He added: "We have Pierpont family matters to discuss."

He then looked at Chatelain and said: "Would you please see to it that all designated persons come tomorrow, including Mr. and Mrs. Pierpont?"

"Of course," replied Chatelain.

Everyone left except Maurice and Henri, who busied themselves with clean-up.

Hannibal interrupted their activities. "Let's sit and talk for a moment," he said. "I am most interested in the results of your work yesterday in the cabins of our recent guests." Soon the four of us were in quiet but intense conversation.

Later that afternoon, Hannibal and I visited Doctor Dupuy in his office. We had new evidence to analyze.

## Friday afternoon, June 21

As planned, Hannibal and I re-convened our meeting in the same dining room at nine o'clock this Friday morning.

The Cornwall, Pierpont and Morgan couples arrived promptly at nine o'clock. The Pierponts had Lieutenant Chatelain as an escort. As before, Junior looked scared. Julia looked bewildered. Hadley entered the room shortly after nine. His face expressed apprehension and curiosity.

Maurice and Henri served coffee and tea but not sweet rolls and cannoli. I was disappointed.

Hannibal stood and said: "Night before last, Mrs. Jones and I found a note on the floor inside our cabin door." He paused, looked around and continued: "The note was written in French, in pencil and on notepaper commonly found everywhere on the ship." Hannibal then looked at me.

I picked up the narrative. "The handwriting was in well-practiced flowing script. The person who wrote it knew French and wrote with a right hand." I paused and then said: "We had each of your cabins searched by the room maids while you were at our meeting yesterday morning." I looked over at Maurice.

Maurice walked over and stood by Hannibal. He looked at me, grinned and said: "Ahem! Yes." He then began his well-practiced speech. I couldn't help but smile.

"Henri and I know several of the maids who service the rooms. We asked them to retrieve every room notepad, like this one, and identify which room it came from." He held up a notepad as evidence. "Afterwards, the maids replaced the notepad taken from each room with a new notepad." He paused, looked at Hannibal and added: We gave the four notepads from the rooms to Major Jones yesterday."

Hannibal said: "Thank you, Maurice." He looked around at faces in the room and continued: "Mrs. Jones and I took the notepads to Doctor Dupuy, the ship's Assistant Surgeon. The three of us used a magnifying glass to look carefully at the top sheet of each pad. We found one that had imprints that matched the note that Mrs. Jones and I found under the door."

As Hannibal was talking, I looked around the room at faces. As expected, only two expressions were of interest.

"Lady Cornwall, the exact imprint of the note was on the top sheet of the notepad from your room." He paused and then continued: "Would you explain why you would write such a note?"

For a moment, Lady Cornwall lost her poise. Finally, she stuttered and said: "I, I don't know what you are talking about!"

Lord Cornwall looked at his wife with astonishment. He said: "Why on earth?"

Lady Cornwall stuttered again and said: "You told me!" Then she stopped and tried to regain her usual icy pose. She looked at Hannibal and said: "So?"

Hannibal smiled and said: "Another interesting fact is that you are right-handed and your husband is left-handed."

Again, Lady Cornwall said: "So?"

Lord Cornwall's reaction was a look of dawning consternation.

Silence reigned in the room for several moments.

Hannibal changed the subject. "We also have the problem of the missing will, dated November 1, 1928." He then looked at me.

I sipped my coffee again, set down the cup and said: "On Tuesday morning, Mr. Morgan, Major Jones and I searched Mrs. Pierpont's cabin. We found Mrs. Pierpont's will, dated   June 15, 1929. In the second paragraph, it mentions that this will supersedes a will dated November 1, 1928." I paused, looked at Lucian Morgan and said: "Mr. Morgan, would you please tell us about Mrs. Pierpont's wills?

Morgan smiled and said: "Yes. Rosemary filed a will with me dated March 1, 1925. I have no record of a will dated November 1, 1928."

I then looked at Hadley and said: "Do you recall a will dated November 1, 1928?"

Hadley gulped a little and then replied: "I don't recall a date, but in early December, Rosemary told Arthur, Abigail, John Edwin, Julia and me that she had written a new will. He puffed up slightly and added: "She also said that I would receive a substantial bequest."

"Did she say how much?" I asked.

"Yes, replied Hadley. "Ten million dollars in stocks and bonds." He then looked at the Cornwalls and the Pierponts and said: "The others, especially Abigail and John Edwin, were very angry because Rosemary said that the remainder of her fortune would go to a trust for charitable purposes." He paused and then added: "At the time,

Rosemary was upset about the spendthrift ways of Abigail and John Edwin."

Hannibal smiled and then asked: "Mr. Morgan, does Mrs. Pierpont's will, dated March 1, 1925, say anything about a charitable trust?"

Morgan smiled ruefully and replied: "No. The 1925 will divides Rosemary's estate equally between her son and daughter."

Hannibal looked at the Cornwalls and Pierponts, in turn. He said: "I believe we have motive for murder. The question is: "Who actually killed Mrs. Pierpont?

Lord Cornwall spoke up in a confident voice. "You have Lefevre, and he was promised payment by John Edwin to murder his mother!"

"How awful!" Lady Cornwall added. She gave the Pierponts a scornful look.

"Yes, he was promised payment," I responded. "However, Lefevre did not kill Mrs. Pierpont."

Stunned silence reigned in the room.

Hannibal picked up a report from our table and said: "I have the autopsy report signed by both Doctor Joseph Borec, Ship's Surgeon, and his assistant, Doctor Jean Dupuy."

Hannibal looked around the room. "Rosemary Pierpont died of a broken neck. Further, the neck was broken by a person standing on the left of Rosemary's chair. We know this because her jaw was dislocated from her left to right, and the neck vertebrae was crushed on her left side."

Hannibal paused and then continued. "The killer reached around Rosemary's back, then under her chin with his right hand. He grasped her left cheek and pulled to Rosemary's right. At the same time, he grasped Rosemary's right ear and surrounding hair in his left hand and pulled to Rosemary's left."

Morgan stirred slightly. Like a good defense attorney, he asked: "You have proof that this technique was used?"

Hannibal smiled and replied: "Yes." He looked over at Cornwall and said: "Lord Cornwall, Doctors Borec and Dupuy found your left thumbprint on Rosemary's diamond-encrusted silver haircomb that was in her hair just above her right ear. They also found your right index fingerprint on her art-deco pendant earring in her left ear."

Hannibal took a deep breath, exhaled slightly and stated in a clear voice: "Arthur Blakely Cornwall, you murdered Rosemary Pierpont. When the lights went out, you took the opportunity of the moment, moved to Rosemary's left side, broke her neck and swiftly returned to your chair."

Hannibal paused and then continued: "Shortly afterwards, Monsieur Lefevre entered from the butler's pantry, arrived on Rosemary's right side, discovered that she was already dead, struck Mr. Hadley, and then returned to the pantry."

Lieutenant Chatelain stepped forward and stood in front of Lord Cornwall. The Sergeant at Arms moved behind Cornwall and folded his arms.

Lord Cornwall glanced up at Chatelain and then turned slightly and glanced at the Sergeant. He gave a brief sigh, smiled and looked at Hannibal and then me. "Very well done, Major Jones and Mrs. Jones."

After his comment, Cornwall stood and waited.

Lieutenant Chatelain said: "Follow me please." He turned and walked toward the door.

Cornwall and the Sergeant followed. After a moment, the door closed with a soft click.

# 7

## LOOSE ENDS

*Friday evening,* June 21, 1929

It's Friday evening, and Hannibal and I are back in our Grande Classe cabin. We just returned from dinner in the main First-Class dining room. We had a pleasant time with Lucian and Elizabeth Morgan.

I like Elizabeth. She is beautiful, well but conservatively dressed, well-spoken and modest. Yet during our dining experience, I sensed that she had a past that did not originate in high society. I like that, given my own background. I may learn more, over time.

Lucian, of course, is the perfect, smart and well-spoken attorney. Based on experience with our recent 'American heiress' case, I'm convinced that he is meticulously honest. Hannibal and I agree that he will handle Rosemary Pierpont's estate in an ethical manner.

This brings me to the loose ends of the case, which was the main topic of conversation during dinner. We have the matter of the wills written by Rosemary, the likely punishment of the guilty and not so guilty, and the fate of the innocent.

After we were seated in the dining room and exchanged the usual pleasantries, we ordered champagne and sipped quietly.

Our waiter returned and took our orders for dinner. My companions all laughed at my concentrated efforts with French, and I laughed with them. Our poor waiter was so confused.

The soup course arrived, and Elizabeth began the discussion. We continued through salad and the main course.

"As I understand it," Elizabeth began; "Rosemary wrote three wills: one in 1925, a second on November 1 last year, and the last one on June 15, just before we sailed."

"Yes," responded Lucian. "The one dated June 15 supersedes the other two." He paused and added: "I saw the one she filed with me in 1925 and the one dated June 15. I have no idea what happened to the one dated November 1, 1928."

"Still, the November will was referenced in the June 15 will," I said. Maybe the will dated in November will eventually turn up." I smiled wryly and added: "Unless it was destroyed."

"Maybe," responded Lucian. "It doesn't really matter from the point of view of probate. The last will takes precedence."

"Did you read the last will?" Elizabeth asked. She looked around the table at Lucian, Hannibal and me.

"Yes," I replied. "I think John Edwin Junior, the Cornwalls and even Harrison Hadley will be in for surprises and probably dismay." I smiled wryly. "Rosemary was clearly at odds with her children, and even her infatuation with Hadley was beginning to fade."

Elizabeth responded: "How sad. I felt sorry for Rosemary; she was never the same after John Edwin Senior died." Elizabeth looked at her husband and asked: "Would it be impertinent for me to ask what Rosemary wrote in her last will?"

Lucian looked at his wife and smiled. "No, since both Hannibal and Caroline saw the will, I see no reason to keep it secret from you." He paused and then added: "The probate court will review the will dated June 15$^{th}$, and I'm sure that it will be upheld."

Hannibal looked at Lucian, who nodded.

Hannibal then turned to Elizabeth and said: "Rosemary reduced the bequest to Hadley from the ten million that he thought he was going to get to one-hundred thousand." He paused a moment and then added: "She also left the remainder of her estate, all of it, to a charitable trust that she had already set up with Pierpont, Morgan and Stanley."

"Yes," said Lucian with a wry smile. "I believe that I will take over management of the trust."

"Oh, my goodness," replied Elizabeth. She began to smile as the implications formed in her mind. "John Edwin Junior and Abigail will be furious."

"Based on recent events," they already were," I stated matter-of-factly. "The result was conspiracy to murder and actual murder."

"I see," said Elizabeth. She looked at her husband. "Do you think that Arthur Cornwall will be convicted?"

Lucian thought for a moment then replied: "Probably. Lieutenant Chatelain, at the direction of Captain Blancart, will turn Cornwall over to the Gendarmerie Nationale judicial police when we dock in Le Havre."

Lucian grinned and added: "He will also turn over the evidence, including the autopsy report, fingerprint files and the reports generated by these two." He nodded first to me and then to Hannibal. "The Gendarmerie Nationale will refer the case to the French judiciary for prosecution."

"What about Abigail?" I asked.

"Unless her husband turns over evidence to the contrary, she will not even be prosecuted," replied Lucian. He smiled and added: "Her only 'crime' was composing a cryptic note to you and Hannibal, which, I think, is not much of an offense."

Hannibal said: "In almost all cases, even murder, testimony against a spouse cannot be forced in court." He thought a moment and then added: "I doubt that Arthur Cornwall would even try to testify against his wife; it's not in his character."

"I agree," said Lucian. "Still, Abigail lost her family fortune, and I believe, based upon their statements over the past years, she and Arthur have many debts."

"Hummm," I replied. "She may have to get a job." I smiled and added: "I wonder what skill set she would list on a job application?"

My companions all chuckled.

After a moment of silence, Elizabeth asked: "What about John Edwin Junior?"

"As best we can tell, no money was passed from John Edwin to Yves Lefevre," replied Hannibal. "It would be John Edwin's word against that of Lefevre about a promise of ten thousand, and I doubt that a court would convict on that basis."

"So, Junior's punishment is the same as that of Abigail," I stated with a smile. "He was disinherited, and he may have to get a job."

Smiles touched the faces of my companions.

"What about Lefevre?" Elizabeth asked.

"Interesting," replied Lucian. "He did not commit murder, and his only real crime was assault with regard to Harrison Hadley." Lucian thought a moment and added: "Unless Hadley testifies, which I doubt that he will, Lefevre will get off scot-free."

"He will probably lose his job with Compagnie Generale Transatlantique," said Hannibal. "I'm sure Lieutenant Chatelain will see to that."

"Finding another job may be a problem, without a recommendation from his previous employer," I responded. "His future does not look bright."

"What about Hadley?" Elizabeth asked.

"Well," I responded, He gets one-hundred thousand, so the smart move would be a genteel retirement."

"Yes," said Lucian. "We'll see." He paused and smiled. "In any case, he has the opportunity, and his gigolo past with ladies like Rosemary may not be sustainable in the future."

"Getting old," I said. The others smiled in agreement.

Silence reigned for a while.

After a while, dessert was delivered. It was scrumptious, and our table talk turned to the nature of our beautiful ship, what we planned to do in France and so on. We had a merry time.

Over dessert, I asked one more question about the case. "What about Julia?"

"Her situation is sad," replied Elizabeth. "Still, her options include divorce from her drunken but now less wealthy husband."

"Yes," added Lucian. "Her family is quite wealthy, and she may return to them." He thought a moment and added: "I hope she seeks treatment for her alcohol problem."

Elizabeth, Hannibal and I all nodded.

"I wish her the best," I thought to myself. I then changed the subject: "We dock tomorrow," I said. "I understand that docking is a fascinating procedure. Shall we meet on deck to watch?"

"Great idea," said Lucian. He looked at Hannibal and grinned. "Escorting two lovely ladies to the Sun Deck tomorrow as we dock would be our pleasure, don't you think?"

"Of course," replied Hannibal. He raised his glass of champagne and said: "To the ladies!" Hannibal and Lucian tapped champagne glasses in a toast.

Elizabeth and I smiled coyly.

# 8

## SHADOWS OF LEHAVRE

*Saturday afternoon, June 22, 1929*

The SS *Isle de France* entered the d'Avant du Port de Le Havre about noon today. We passed through the channel with the Quai des Remorqueurs on the starboard side and a little further, the Quai de New York on the port side. The ship then turned slightly to port and with the help of several tugboats, docked at the Quai des Transatlantique in the Bassin de l'Eure.

After about an hour of preparation by the crew, we passengers were allowed to disembark with our hand luggage. Our remaining complement of luggage would be waiting for us at customs just across the quai. Hannibal had already arranged for our main luggage to be taken from customs to the newly re-modeled Grande Hôtel Frascati at Place'1, Rue de Perrey.

As we walked down the gangway, Hannibal described our hotel accommodations. "The Frascati was originally built in 1839," said Hannibal. "It had major expansions in 1871 and 1891. It was remodeled in 1911, after a fire. Last year, the Compagnie Industrielle Maritime, the new owners, began the latest re-model." He looked at me, and with a smile, added: "It's now ready for us."

"Sounds wonderful," I replied with a warm smile. I slipped my right arm in his left. "How do you find out these things?" I looked at his face and watched his expression.

"My secret," responded Hannibal with a twinkle in his eyes. "Anyway, the official inauguration banquet at the Frascati will be in

August, but the Compagnie Industrielle Maritime has already opened the hotel for business," said Hannibal. "We have a grand suite."

"OK, smarty," I said with a giggle. "Since we have a grand suite, you are forgiven for your little secrets."

After the expected routine at customs and the departure of our luggage, Hannibal and I took a cab from the quai across the bridge between the Bassin de la Barre on the left and the Bassin Vauben on the right. At my request, the cab driver agreed to give us a little tour of the town on our way to the hotel. I was so excited!

The driver continued north on Rue Lorriune to the Boulevard de Strasbourg. We turned left and continued past the Hôtel de Ville on the right and the Jardin Public on the left. The Hôtel de Ville was really the town hall.

"It's relatively modern," said Hannibal. "It was built in the nineteenth century."

The manicured gardens were full of beautiful flowers, trees and fountains. Like a typical tourist, I gawked out the window of the cab at the lovely buildings, the flowers and the comings and goings of hundreds of people. Hannibal smiled; I think he was pleased that I was so enjoying myself.

We continued on Boulevard de Strasbourg for about three kilometers past the gardens, then turned left for a short distance on Rue Augustin Normand. We then turned right on Rue de Perrey.

The Grande Hôtel Frascati was south on Rue de Perrey about three more kilometers, near the Batterie Royale. We checked in, our luggage arrived and we were escorted to our grande suite on the top floor.

Our large bay window looked out to sea. The sun was low in the late afternoon sky, and we could see ships arriving and leaving Port de Le Havre. What a wonderful view!

Hannibal called down to the concierge and made dinner reservations in the grand dining room. Since sunset would be at about ten o'clock, he made a reservation for eight o'clock. He asked for a table on the window side so we could watch the sunset and the lights of passing ships. How romantic! What should I wear?

I decided on my Chanel little black dress, diamonds and a gorgeous black evening wrap. I preened in the bathroom mirror for a while and added final touches to my hair.

After several minutes, I grinned and said out loud: "Not bad for a small-town girl from the American Midwest." I puffed my hair a little more, put my hands on my hips and did a little twirl. As I did so, I saw Hannibal standing in the doorway.

"Caroline, tu es la plus belle femme que j'aie jamais vue," Hannibal said softly. He walked over and caressed my shoulders.

I turned, touched his cheek and put my arms around his waist. I then reached up, kissed him warmly and stepped back. "That sounded like a complement," I replied with a grin. "Let's finish dinner early." I kissed him again.

"You must have a plan," Hannibal responded with a chuckle. "I'm looking forward to finding out."

I giggled again. "You have to be patient, dinner first."

Hannibal just laughed.

We still had over an hour before dinner. When I finished preening, I walked into our spacious parlor and turned on the lamps. I then walked over to the bay window, and the lamps behind me gave golden light. In retrospect, I know that I was silhouetted in the window.

From my point of view, the window framed a lovely scene of the outer harbor. Gold and purple tinted clouds accented the sea view to the west. The sun, already past zenith, produced a golden haze. After admiring the view of the sun, sea and clouds, I turned my attention to the promenade along the beach. Lamp posts lined the walkway and couples strolled by. "Exquisite," I thought to myself.

I noticed a man standing next to one of the nearby lampposts. He was short and rotund but very well dressed. His attire included a dark suit, vest and matching homburg hat. He was looking up at me.

I stared back, and he noticed. He then touched his hat, bowed slightly and walked on down the promenade. After a short walk, he turned on the walkway that led to the hotel. I continued to watch as he entered the door and disappeared inside. "Interesting, I thought to myself. "I wonder what that was all about?"

## Saturday evening, eleven o'clock June 22

Hannibal is in the bathroom getting ready for bed. I have already put on my lovely black silk nightgown and matching robe, and I have time for a few notes in my diary.

Before we went downstairs to dinner, we found out more about the man I saw from the window. About ten minutes after the man entered the hotel at the door to the promenade, we heard a knock.

Hannibal walked over to our entry hall and answered the door. I remained in the seat just under the bay window. Rays of sunlight gleamed all around me, and I was comfortably warm.

I heard our door open and a brief conversation. After a few moments, Hannibal walked into the parlor, followed by the well-dressed man who I had seen earlier by the promenade lamp post. The man carried his homburg in both hands, and he smiled as he and Hannibal stopped in the middle of the room.

I rose from my seat, held my hands demurely together in front and waited.

"Caroline, please meet Capitaine Inspecteur Pierre Soucet from the Sections de recherche de la Gendarmerie Nationale," said Hannibal.

"Ah, Madame Caroline Case Jones," said the man smoothly. He smiled in a sincere way. "Je vous ai vu à la fenêtre. Vous me rapellez du joli chat noir de la maison de mon enfance." He bowed formally, hat still in hand.

I followed his French; I had never been called a lovely black cat before.

I thought a moment. "It's my outfit," I realized. "I'm wearing a black, form-fitting dress, and I have dark hair." My thoughts continued: "While I stood silhouetted in the window earlier, I also had on my black evening wrap." I paused in my thinking, and concluded: "OK, I look like a black cat."

I decided to accept the intended complement. After all, this was France. "Je vous remercie, Monsieur le Capitaine," I answered correctly, with a slight smile.

Hannibal grinned.

"Hannibal always knows what I am thinking," my thoughts continued. I gave him a snooty look.

I turned back to our guest, smiled and asked: "What can we do for you, Monsieur le Capitaine?"

Captain Inspector Soucet responded to my question in accented but excellent English. I was relieved, I had almost exhausted my vocabulary of appropriate responses in French.

"Lieutenant Chatelain from the SS *Isle de France* told me all about you and Major Jones. He described your work with regard to the murder on the SS *Isle de France*, including the collection of fingerprints and other evidence, your skills with interviews, your comprehensive documentation and of course, the resulting identification of the murderer."

Soucet paused, looked at me with a steady gaze and added: "You come highly recommended as excellent private investigators."

"Thank you," I responded. Hannibal and I both waited.

Soucet turned, looked first at Hannibal and then back to me. I could tell that he was evaluating our reactions. After a long moment, he seemed to come to a conclusion. He said: "I need help on a different case."

"Good heavens!" I thought to myself. "We just arrived, and we haven't even had dinner yet!" I'm sure my face had a moment of surprise, but I think I quickly recovered. To Soucet, I said: "Oh? How can we help?"

Hannibal, who stood back from Soucet's view, grinned, raised his eyebrows and then folded his arms. I'm sure he understood my reaction and attempt at recovery.

I gave Hannibal a quick glance that said: "Wipe that smile off your face." He didn't.

Soucet also smiled. I couldn't tell yet what his smile meant.

Soucet then took a breath, let it out slowly, and responded: "Unfortunately, Le Havre has always had its share of pickpockets, street robbers and occasional crimes of passion among its inhabitants. After all, it is a rough and tumble port city, second only to Marseille."

He paused and then continued: "Recently, I am afraid that Le Havre's criminals have begun to prey upon our unsuspecting visitors in a systematic fashion, and their crimes have expanded to burglaries and even murder."

"This is different," I thought. Soucet had piqued my interest. To Soucet, I simply replied: "I understand." I then waited for him to continue.

Soucet gave a deep sigh and said: "Like Paris and Marseille, which are very large cities, Le Havre's criminals have become organized. They operate with almost military precision. Hotel rooms are robbed when guests are out during the day; stolen goods are carefully selected, and fingerprints are not found."

He added: "Over the past year, all of the victims arrived by ship, they were invariably wealthy, and they stayed in our finest hotels."

"What about murder?" I asked.

Soucet nodded and said: "Last week, Sir Albert Brunswick from England was murdered in his hotel room. Apparently, he surprised a robbery in process." Soucet grimaced and added: "The murder was quite brutal."

Hannibal walked over to my side and asked: "Have there been other murders?"

"Yes," replied Soucet. "Seven over the past year. Four have occurred since January, all with striking similarities." Soucet paused and added: "City officials, including the Maire, have become deeply concerned."

He paused and then said: "I have been sent to Le Havre from Paris, and I have many responsibilities." He looked first at Hannibal and then me and added: "I have no one on the local force who is qualified to investigate this most complex problem."

"I can imagine the pressure on the police," I thought to myself. To Soucet, I asked: "How can we help?"

"I believe we have an organized gang operating in Le Havre," stated Soucet. "Determine the structure of the gang, identify its members and its contacts and especially, find the mastermind, if one exists." Soucet looked over at Hannibal and then to me. His eyes had a pleading look. "Will you take the case?"

Hannibal and I looked at each other. After a few moments, Hannibal looked at Soucet and asked: "May Mrs. Jones and I discuss the case over dinner? We can give you an answer first thing in the morning."

"Of course," replied Soucet. He looked into my eyes and then smiled. I think he already knew the answer. He turned to Hannibal and said: "My card, Monsieur. Please call me when you decide." He gave Hannibal a gold-embossed calling card and shook Hannibal's hand.

He then turned to me and said: "Bonsoir, Madame Jones. J'ai hâte de travailler avec vous." He smiled, bowed slightly, turned and walked toward the door. Hannibal followed. The pair exchanged goodbyes, and Soucet departed.

"Soucet is anxious to work with us," I translated to myself. "How interesting!"

## Sunday morning, June 23

Dinner was both merry and sobering. The merry part involved champagne, wonderful food and my diligent yet comical attempts to learn French. The sobering part involved the discussion of our possible case, which we chose to call: "The Shadows of Le Havre.'

I will document the merry part first. Hannibal wore his summer tuxedo and I wore my Chanel little black dress and matching wrap. We certainly looked the part of wealthy tourists. I took Hannibal's arm, and we followed the Maître d'hôtel to a table for two by the window. The setting was lovely. I sniffed and tried to look sophisticated.

Hannibal looked at me with a twinkle in his eyes and said: "Vous avez l'air ravissante ce soir Mme Jones, et je suis honorée d'être votre escorte."

I drew a blank. My lips moved as I tried to silently translate the words from French to English. Hannibal smiled, raised his eyebrows and acted the perfect gentleman. Of course, that was the perfect way to infuriate me. I knew that he knew that I was lost in translation.

"Humph," I finally uttered. "Merci beaucoup, Monsieur Jones." I tossed back my head and sniffed again.

Hannibal grinned, chuckled for a brief moment and then did his best to keep a straight face. I watched for another moment, then burst out laughing at both Hannibal and myself. Our tit for tat continued during our ordering from the menu and the meal. We had a wonderful time.

After dessert, we watched the lights along the promenade and the harbor. It was lovely. We then began the sobering discussion of the evening. The question was: Did we want to take on Soucet's case?

"This will be different than anything we have worked on before," Hannibal began. "According to Soucet, the burglars know enough to avoid leaving fingerprints and other traceable evidence." Hannibal looked at me carefully. "Our ability to use forensic techniques may be limited."

"Yes," I replied. "We can still use other techniques of detailed observation and deductive reasoning."

"OK," Hannibal responded, as he sipped his champagne. "However, we may be dealing with a gang rather than one or two people." He paused a moment and added: "It reminds me of Chicago and the North Side Gang."

"Europe is very different than Chicago," I replied.

"We have limited knowledge of the customs, the cities, the countryside and the laws," responded Hannibal.

"Very sobering," I replied. I leaned back in my chair, looked Hannibal in the eyes, and summed up my thoughts in a phrase: "Limited tools, dangerous criminals and unknown territory." I grinned and added: "What are we waiting for?"

Hannibal laughed and raised his champagne glass in a toast. I raised mine, and our glasses touched with a musical clink.

Hannibal sipped his champagne and looked at me over the rim of his glass for a moment. His eyes twinkled. As he set the glass on the table, he said: "Do you know what fee you want from our friend Capitaine Inspecteur Soucet?"

"Lots," I responded. Hannibal laughed and we toasted again.

# 9

## MURDER FILES

*Monday morning, June 24, 1929*

Hannibal left about an hour ago. He had to pick up our Duesenberg at the Quai des Transatlantique. I don't expect him back until this afternoon.

In the meantime, I called Inspector Soucet at the number on his card. The call took a while to complete. Fortunately, the hotel concierge spoke English, and he worked with the operator to complete my call. Completing the connection was a laborious process.

I waited patiently. After about fifteen minutes, Soucet came on the line. After our exchange of formal greetings, I said: "Major Jones and I decided to accept your kind offer. We will take the case."

"Je suis tellement reconnaissante, Madame Jones," Soucet replied. "I have several case files. Shall I send them by courier to your hotel?'

"Oui, s'il vous plaît," I responded. "Les fichiers arriveront-ils aujourd'hui?" Secretly, I was proud of my growing ability with the French language. I'm sure my fractured grammar was a source of amusement, but I'm trying.

Soucet responded in perfect English. "Yes, Madame. My courier will arrive this afternoon."

We briefly discussed our fee. Soucet was most generous, and it was soon settled.

## Monday evening, June 24

Hannibal found me at a table next to our bay window late this afternoon. I was engrossed in my homework when he arrived.

Earlier, I had the hotel service staff deliver the table, a couple of chairs, a pot of coffee and two cups, a small side table and lots of notepads and pencils. I had set up a serviceable office for work next to our window. Soucet's files were stacked on the floor all around the table, the coffee table and the second chair.

I was dressed in my new Chanel pants and blouse combination. "I look very modern," I thought to myself. The black pants fitted me closely at the top but widened from my lower legs to my ankles. The blouse was a conservative burgundy in color, and showed my figure to full advantage.

Hannibal came in through our entryway and stopped in the middle of the room. His eyes swept the scene. He then returned his gaze to me and gave a low whistle. "Already at work, I see," he said with a smile. "You look beautiful."

I grinned, raised my coffee cup in mock toast, and replied: "Of course I do. I will fill you in when you are ready. Did everything go well with our car?"

"Yes," replied Hannibal. "The hotel valet will keep it in the garage and bring it out whenever we need it. All we have to do is call the front desk." He carefully moved the stack of files on the second chair to the floor, and sat down.

He looked at me and grinned. "You've been busy," he said. "Any results?"

"Well, yes," I replied. I shuffled my pages of notes, put them in order and said: "We have seven murder victims: four British, one British citizen who resided in Canada and two U.S. citizens. Four were male, and three were female."

I read my notes for a moment. "For each victim, we have a passport, an autopsy report with photos of the victim, a police statement, a statement by the surviving spouse and a statement by either the British or the American Consul's office in Le Havre." I frowned and said: "The passports and the Consul's statements are in English, but autopsies and police reports are in French; you'll have to read them."

Hannibal smiled and asked: "Are the surviving spouses still in town?"

"Not according to the statements by the British and American Consuls," I replied.

I flipped pages of my notes, read and added: "The respective consulates made arrangements for the surviving spouses to return home, along with the bodies of the victims."

"New passports?" Hannibal asked.

"Yes," I replied. "The consulates issued a new passport to each of the surviving spouses." I frowned a little and continued: "When they arrived, each couple only had one passport. The wife was listed on the husband's passport as a dependent." I sniffed and added: "Just like ours."

I paused, and Hannibal smiled. "He knows what I'm thinking," I thought to myself. His next comment confirmed it.

"Following standard procedure, the four surviving men and ladies, now single, would have been issued new passports in their own names," said Hannibal. "Perhaps, someday, each person, male or female, married or not, will be issued an individual passport."

"Let's hope so," I responded, and I sniffed again. "Anyway, we have the original passports, and they provide a wealth of information."

"Did you look at the autopsy reports?" Hannibal asked.

"Yes," I replied. "I was able to read a little. One statement was of particular interest; it was the same in each report." I picked up one of the autopsy reports and leafed through it. "Here it is," I stated slowly: "La victime a été étranglée par une garrote à double boucle."

"Very interesting," replied Hannibal. "The victims, male and female, were all strangled with a double loop garrote."

"What's that?" I asked.

"It's a method of strangulation used by the French military, particularly the Foreign Legion," replied Hannibal. "A double coil of cord, usually silk, is dropped around a victim's neck and pulled tight. The cord has handles on each end. Even if the victim pulls on one of the coils around his neck, he only succeeds in tightening the other."

Hannibal grimaced and added: "Very efficient. I encountered several cases during the war, when French soldiers garroted German sentries during intelligence gathering raids."

"Wow!" I exclaimed. "You never told me."

Hannibal sighed. His eyes had a far-away look. After a moment, he looked at me and said: "It's not something I care to think about." He looked at me with a sad but steady gaze. "I suppose I will have to, with this case." Hannibal paused again.

I waited; I'm sure my face expressed concern.

After a full minute, Hannibal said: "The method is not well known. We probably have one murderer, with seven victims." He paused and then added: "Our murderer most likely had experience in the French military."

I decided to change the subject. "I looked at each passport," I said. "Fortunately, like the consular statements, they are written in English." I smiled; I was trying to give Hannibal something different to think about.

Hannibal took a deep breath, looked at me, and his eyes twinkled. It was the old Hannibal. "Did you find anything in the passports that connect our victims, anything in common?" He asked.

"Nothing with regard to travel or experiences," I replied. I picked up my summary notes on the victims and read out loud.

"Anne, Lady Wallace, British, was murdered on June 2nd last year, in her hotel room here at the Frascati. She and her husband, Sir Walter Wallace, arrived on the SS *Carmania* on May 31st. Sir Walter returned to London on June 15."

I looked up at Hannibal and asked: "Shall I continue?"

"Please," replied Hannibal. He leaned back in his chair and observed me with his usual steady gaze.

"Sir William McKenzie, British resident of Canada, was murdered on June 22, in his hotel room at the Continental. He and Mary, Lady McKenzie, his wife, arrived on the RMS *Albertic* on June 24. Lady McKenzie returned to Canada on July 15.

I saw Hannibal nod again, and I continued.

"Baron Harrison Newberry, British, was murdered on July 4 last year, in his hotel room at the Normandie. He and his wife Lady Margaret Newberry arrived on the RMS *Tuscania* on July 2. Lady Newberry returned to London on July 12."

I looked down the page at the next case and read aloud.

"Lady Olivia Bolton was murdered on August 30, last year, in her hotel room at the Moderne. Lady Bolton and her husband Lord John Bolton, a Viscount, also arrived on the RMS *Tuscania,* on August 27. Lord Bolton returned to Southampton and then Edinburgh on September 4."

I paused and then continued.

"The next victim was American," I said. "Mr. Walter Smith was murdered on September 24 in his hotel room at the Bordeaux. Smith and his wife Florence arrived on September 22 on the SS *Isle de France* from New York. Mrs. Smith returned to New York on the *Isle de France* the following week."

I looked down the list and said: "The next victim was also American, followed by another British."

Hannibal nodded.

"Hazel Brown was murdered on March 28 of this year, in her hotel room at the Moderne. She and her husband Ralph arrived on the SS *Isle de France* on March 25 from New York. Ralph returned to New York on the *Isle de France* the following week."

"The last victim was British. Sir Albert Brunswick was murdered just last week on June 14. Sir Albert and Jane, Lady Brunswick, his wife, arrived on the SS *De Grasse* on June 12. The murder took place in his hotel room at the Continental. Lady Brunswick returned to Southampton and then London on June 22, the day we arrived in Le Havre."

I looked up at Hannibal. He had closed his eyes. I could tell he was thinking.

Finally, he opened his eyes and said: "Seven murders, four males and three females. I do not see a pattern on ship arrivals or hotels."

"Yet they were all killed by garrote in their respective hotel rooms," I responded. "The surviving spouse statements all say that their hotel rooms were robbed of jewelry and cash. I think the police reports will provide more details."

"Yes," replied Hannibal. "The victims may have interrupted burglaries, but I will check." He paused a moment and added: "I will also check the whereabouts of the respective spouses during the murders. Since the authorities did not hold them, they must have been cleared by witnesses."

"Hummm," I responded. "We can't interview the spouses; they are all gone. However, we can check the police reports and the hotels and follow up on witnesses. There may be relevant events, not in the reports, that shed light on the murders."

"I will work on the reports written in French and give you a translation," replied Hannibal with a grin.

"Merci beaucoup, Monsieur," I replied with a wry smile. "I'm trying, but my French vocabulary, and especially my ability to pick up on the nuances, need some work."

"In the meantime, perhaps you can pick up a pattern from the passports, spousal statements and consular reports," responded Hannibal. "Occupation, wealth and income, or nuances from the passports themselves may give us clues."

"Right," I responded. "Shall we do room service for dinner, with lots of coffee?"

## Tuesday noon, June 25

Hannibal and I retired to bed after two o'clock last night. Unfortunately, I was full of coffee from our marathon work session, so I was up a half-dozen times. Since we had a night light in the hallway leading to our bedroom, I saw the time on the clock on the nightstand. I finally fell into deep slumber about five this morning.

Later this morning, I heard Hannibal in the parlor. He was trying to be quiet, but I could still hear him padding about in his slippers; the floorboards squeaked. He also talked on the phone.

Finally, I opened one eye and saw daylight shining through the window. I quickly closed my eye. "It's too early!" I mumbled. I covered my head with my pillow. That didn't work either. I had to go to the bathroom again.

I gave up, removed the pillow, opened both eyes and tried to focus. The sunlight through the window was blinding. "OK, Caroline, get up!" I muttered.

After a bathroom visit, including a shower and brushing my teeth, I began to function, more or less. I combed my hair, fixed my face and put on my new Lanvin casual pants outfit. This time I wore a red blouse with my stylish navy-blue pants. However, I remained barefoot.

I padded softly into the parlor. Hannibal was at the table, writing. He was dressed in a casual light blue shirt, navy-blue sweater vest and summer weight grey trousers. He still had on his slippers. He looked wide awake and fully functional. "How does he do it?" I muttered to myself.

Hannibal looked up, smiled and said: "I ordered breakfast earlier." He raised a coffee cup in a mock toast and added: "It's on the portable table in the entryway. It came a few minutes ago, so it should be hot." He motioned with his cup.

"Thanks," I muttered. My tongue still felt thick. I padded on bare feet to the entryway and found a portable table covered with white linen. It had a silver coffee pot, cups, condiments, two glasses of orange juice, silverware, napkins and two covered dishes.

I lifted the lid on one dish and saw eggs Benedict, little sausages, hash browns and toast. I suddenly realized that I was ravenously hungry. I returned the cover and wheeled the little table into the parlor toward Hannibal. "Breakfast is served," I announced.

Hannibal chuckled, rose from his chair and moved both chairs to each side of the arriving portable table. Soon we were seated and enjoying a delicious breakfast.

After about ten minutes of diligent attention to food, I sat back, picked up my coffee cup and sipped slowly. My mind was in gear again.

Hannibal watched me for a few moments. Finally, he said: "Last night, I recall that you said there was something unusual about the passports. What did you find?"

I took another sip of coffee, set down the cup and reached around to our work table. I found my notes and made myself comfortable again.

After a few moments of reading, I replied: "Well, there were no similarities in occupation. Sir Walter was a shipping magnate from London, Sir William was a mining engineer in Canada, Baron Newberry had income from his estates in England and Ireland, Sir John owned a newspaper in Edinburgh, Walter Smith owned textile factories in New England, Ralph Brown was an executive with a steel company in Pittsburg and Sir Albert was an importer of tea from Ceylon." I paused and then added: "However, all were obviously wealthy."

Hannibal nodded and asked: "Anything else?"

I frowned a moment, then replied: "Yes." I got up from the portable table and spread out seven passports on the work table. I opened each to the page with the Le Havre arrival stamp. I then opened our passport to the same page.

After propping each passport open to the desired page with other files, I said: "The arrival stamps were made with a red ink hand stamp. Do you see anything unusual?"

Hannibal got up, walked around to the work table and peered closely at each passport, in turn. Finally, he raised up and said: "There is a small, unusual imperfection at the top of each stamp mark on the seven, but not on the stamp on our passport."

He thought a moment, and his eyes widened a little. "The seven were all made with the same hand stamp!" He turned to me, smiled and said: "Good eye; you are very observant."

"All of the ships docked at the Quai des Transatlantique in the Bassin de l'Eure. As I recall, there are about a dozen lines at customs, each with a clerk, to process well over a thousand passengers from each ship."

I paused and then continued: "Perhaps the same customs clerk checked in each of our murder victims." I grinned and added: "That is not a coincidence. We need to check with the supervisor at the Customs House."

# 10

## L'OBSERVATERU SUR LE QUAI

*Wednesday evening, June 26, 1929*

After breakfast this morning, Hannibal and I navigated the streets of Le Havre in our Duesenberg. An hour later, we made it to the Quai des Transatlantique.

Le Havre traffic is worse than Chicago. Right of way goes to the fastest car and the most daring driver. Unless forced to the side, drivers go down the center of the road. In places, the cobblestones rattled everything in the car, including me. Then there are roundabouts. I had never experienced these before. I was scared to death.

Actually, after a while, the drive was exhilarating, like a fast carnival ride. Hannibal drove with confidence and skill. I was impressed. I observed carefully as he worked the pedals, shifted gears and steered the car without taking his eyes off the road.

"I will ask him to teach me to drive when we get ready to tour the countryside on our way to Paris or on a sight-seeing tour; maybe I can get a French driver's license," I mused.

Before we left the hotel, Hannibal had contacted Soucet by phone. He explained that we wanted to obtain more information about the case from the customs office at the Quai des Transatlantique. Soucet promised to make a phone call to the Chief Customs Inspector's office at the Quai.

Thanks to Soucet, we were expected. When we arrived at the customs house, we entered a side door away from the dozen customs stations on the main floor. We found the Chief Customs Inspector's suite, and Hannibal introduced us to the secretary in the Inspector's outer office.

The secretary was a nice young lady. Her name was Suzette, and she spoke perfect English. We were promptly escorted to the inner office, which was spacious and well-appointed.

Inspecteur en chef des douanes Quentin Colbert was a small, dapper man, with a moustache and pointed goatee. He stood, smiled and bowed slightly as Hannibal and I entered his office. "Bienvenue, monsieur et madame, que puis-je faire pour vous?

I thought to myself: "Inspecteur Colbert has a prestigious job and apparently lives well." I smiled sweetly.

Hannibal introduced us in proper French. He explained our association with Capitaine Inspecteur Soucet of the Gendarmerie and outlined our findings with regard to the customs stamp on the passports of the murder victims.

Colbert was most helpful. Unfortunately for me, he didn't speak English. He declared: "Chaque employé a personnalisé le bureau qui lui a été assignés, avec des feuilles de règles, des tiroirs remplis de crayons, des tampons à main, des photos et même des vivres cachés dans les tiroirs." He grinned and then added more details.

I did my best to follow Colbert's very fast French. Roughly speaking, he said that each desk on the main floor of the customs house was the assigned clerk's little kingdom, and the desk assignments never varied. He promised to find the flawed hand stamp and identify the associated clerk.

Colbert also promised to give Hannibal a phone call with the name of the clerk and as much information as he could from the clerk's employment file.

Hannibal explained that we didn't want to alert the clerks as to our suspicions. Colbert understood. He said he would personally check the hand stamps that evening, after the clerks had left.

Through Hannibal, I asked for a list of names of all travelers who passed through that clerk's station over the past year.

"I want to verify that our murder victims were serviced by the clerk in question," I stated to Hannibal. "Also, we can compare the clerk's list to police reports of burglaries of ship passenger hotel rooms."

"Good idea," replied Hannibal. "There may have been burglaries that did not end in murder."

Hannibal explained the idea to Colbert in French, who replied in very fast French.

For my benefit, Hannibal translated his reply: "Colbert said that each clerk keeps a logbook. It would require a few days to take photos of logbook names, dates and arriving ship names for the past year, but it could be done at night, and the clerk would never know."

Colbert added: J'ai un appareil photo adapté."

I understood that he had a camera. I smiled.

Colbert grinned again. I think he was enjoying his opportunity to participate in a police-sponsored investigation.

After an exchange of phone numbers, Colbert personally escorted us to the side door, away from the customs stations.

"Colbert gets the idea," I thought to myself as we exited. "The clerk in question will not know who we are and what we are up to."

After another exhilarating ride through the streets of Le Havre, we arrived back at the Frascati. We had a late lunch in the café in the long gallery facing the sea.

I ordered from the menu for both Hannibal and me. The waiter was very kind and patient. Hannibal and I both burst out laughing at my efforts, and the waiter joined in. We three had a merry time.

After much ado, Hannibal and I both had soupe à l'oignon et une salade. Nous avons partagé une baguette avec du beurre frais crémeux et de la confiture de fraises. Nous avons également partagé une bouteille de Perrier. The Perrier sparkling water was my one concession to British and American rather than French preferences. I was so proud of myself!

After we returned to our room, Hannibal called Soucet, who promised a list of hotel room burglaries. We were done for the day. I looked at the clock. It was already three in the afternoon.

I collapsed on the bed. "Time for a nap," I mumbled. "Wake me in time for dinner." I heard Hannibal chuckle as I closed my eyes.

I woke up when I heard Hannibal at the door. He had ordered room service. I opened one eye and looked at the clock; the time was eight in the evening. I rolled to a sitting position on the edge of the bed and rubbed sleep from both eyes. My hair was a mess.

The room service waiter, a perfect gentleman, pretended not to notice my disheveled appearance. He and Hannibal pushed our work table and papers out of the way and set up dinner next to the bay window. I watched for a moment, then headed for the bathroom.

When I emerged, my hair was combed and I had washed my face. The waiter was gone. Hannibal stood by the table, smiling, waiting for me. We had a wonderful evening, and we watched the sunset.

## Thursday evening, June 27

This morning, a courier delivered Soucet's list of Le Havre hotel room burglaries. There were twenty-seven, including the seven that ended in murder, over the past year.

Soucet's list was very thorough. Thankfully, it was written in English.

"Soucet is such a thoughtful man," I concluded.

The list included details for every burglary, including descriptions of missing items. Most of the items were expensive jewelry pieces set with diamonds, rubies, sapphires, pearls and other gemstones.

The exceptions included a set of monogramed gold cufflinks, a couple of silver cigarette cases and a gold tie clip. The cufflinks, cases and clip had the engraved initials of their respective owners.

This morning, Colbert called with a name. The clerk with the flawed hand stamp was Jacques Barre. Colbert also said that he was making progress on photographing logbook pages, and he would be finished by Saturday morning.

In the meantime, he would send Suzette over with details on Barre, including a photograph and his employment record. How efficient! Hannibal thanked him profusely.

As promised, Suzette delivered the file on Barre at about noon. "I prepared an English translation," she said with a smile.

"Thank heaven!" I thought to myself. To Suzette, I said: "You are very kind. Thank you so much." I smiled warmly. She nodded politely and took her leave.

"I like Suzette; we could be friends," my thoughts continued. Oh, well.

Hannibal and I discussed next steps over lunch. I brought our file on Barre, a summer ship arrival schedule, a city map and a streetcar schedule. The two schedules were written in English and designed for tourists. We sat next to the window in the Frascati long gallery café again. This time, Hannibal ordered lunch; I was busy reading.

As we sipped Perrier and waited for soup, salad and a baguette, I began the conversation on Barre. "According to Colbert's file, Barre is not married." I continued to read. After a moment I added: "He lives at 10 Rue du Chéllou."

Hannibal nodded, and I continued reading.

After a few minutes, I said: "Barre's works Monday through Friday, from eight in the morning until five in the evening. He has an hour for lunch at noon."

Hannibal responded: "I doubt that Barre is our burglar, He would have been at work when the murders took place."

"He probably identifies likely targets and others do the dirty work." I responded. "We need to identify his accomplices."

Hannibal then said: "Let's look at our map." He unfolded our Le Havre city map and laid it out on the table.

After a moment of reading the index and then the map, he said: "His apartment is here, near the Jardin Public." He pointed and then looked at the kilometer scale in the corner. "It's about nine kilometers from the Quai des Transatlantique."

"That's a fairly long commute to work," I replied. "I doubt that he has a car. Such a luxury would be too ostentatious for a customs clerk."

"Yes," responded Hannibal. "He would avoid a flashy lifestyle, especially if he has money from nefarious sources."

"Agree," I replied. I watched Hannibal's face; he was obviously thinking.

After a couple of sips of Perrier, he said: "Office workers in this town usually ride the streetcar to and from work."

I pulled out my streetcar schedule and studied it for a moment. "If so, for his commute, he probably rides the streetcar from the corner of Rue du Chéllou along Boulevard de Strasbourg to Rue de Lorraine, changes near the Caserne Klébler, and continues to the Quai."

Hannibal looked over and studied the schedule. "Yes," he responded. "Still, with stops, the trip takes an hour each way." He pointed to the times on the schedule.

I did some quick calculations in my head. "He would have to leave home at six thirty and catch the early morning streetcar a block from his apartment. He would arrive at work by eight. On the return, he would probably catch the five-thirty or six o'clock streetcar and get home by six thirty or seven."

Hannibal nodded and then looked at our schedule of ship arrivals by month. "Ships unload passengers either at nine in the morning or two in the afternoon, Monday through Friday," he said. "Barre has a long day."

"Yes," I responded. "I wonder what he does on weekends?"

"Well, the Jardin Public is only a block away from his apartment," I said. "Perhaps he visits the park."

Hannibal leaned back in his chair, sipped his Perrier, and said: "We have a good working hypothesis for his schedule." He paused, thought a moment and then added: "We need to confirm or correct it by observation."

"Yes," I replied; "Who Barre meets may lead us to accomplices."

We were silent for a few minutes. I then said: "Shall we set up surveillance near his home to see how he commutes, where he goes and who he contacts?" I smiled mischievously and added: "Who knows what will turn up?"

Hannibal watched me carefully for a few moments, grinned and then said: "Want the job?"

"Of course!" I replied with a big smile. "What fun!"

Hannibal laughed and responded: "You can watch Barre's apartment this Friday. Begin in the morning and see if he leaves his apartment."

Hannibal paused and added: "Our friend Colbert can watch Barre while he's at work, including his lunch hour. I will call him this afternoon."

"Good," I replied. "This weekend, we can continue our surveillance, depending on what turns up."

"How exciting!" I thought to myself.

To Hannibal, I said: "Today, perhaps we can do a drive-by reconnaissance of Barre's residence, the nearby Jardin Public and the streetcar route."

Hannibal nodded and said: "Good idea. We can drive north on Rue du Perrey, turn on Rue Normand and then turn on Boulevard de Strasbourg and be at the Jardin Public within half an hour. From there, we can turn on Rue du Chéllou and scout out Barre's residence."

My thoughts continued: "For tomorrow, I need to blend into the scene so Barre will not notice me."

I looked at Hannibal, grinned and said: "I should dress in typical clothes that secretaries and shopkeepers wear in Le Havre." I then asked: "Can we go shopping this afternoon?"

Hannibal laughed and replied: "Of course. We can't have you looking like a lovely socialite on holiday. We can shop on Boulevard de Strasbourg after we do our reconnaissance."

I thought a moment and then asked: "While I'm checking out Barre tomorrow, what will you be doing?"

"I will follow up with the witnesses identified by the police," Hannibal responded. From the looks of the reports, not much was done after the police verified the whereabouts of the spouses at the time of the murders."

"OK," I replied. "As soon as we get Colbert's logbook photos, we can compare the entries to the police list of twenty-seven burglaries, including the ones associated with our seven murders," I responded. "We can do that this weekend, after we return to our hotel room."

Lunch ended at one-thirty. Hannibal and I had a plan. We headed for the lobby, found the valet, and requested our Duesenberg.

Just before two o'clock, we were on the road, driving on Rue de Perrey. We turned on the Boulevard de Strasbourg. Thirty minutes later, we passed the Jardin Public.

I looked for street signs. At the next corner, I saw the sign for the Rue du Chéllou. A quaint brasserie with street-side tables and umbrellas rested on the corner. "Perfect!" I thought to myself. "I have my observation post."

Hannibal turned right on Rue du Chéllou. Well-kept brownstone apartment buildings lined a shaded street. "Nice neighborhood," I said to Hannibal. He nodded and pointed. "Number 10 is on the left."

I looked. The building was a typical three-story apartment house, much like the others on the street. Hannibal continued driving to the corner and turned right. After a block, he turned right again. After a minute or so, we were back on the Boulevard de Strasbourg. We turned right. I looked back, and I could see the trees of the Jardin Public some distance behind.

Nice shops lined the street. We passed a streetcar heading in the opposite direction. I turned and watched it stop at the corner of Rue de Chéllou.

After a short distance, I spotted dresses displayed in the window of a shop. I could also see several other dress shops just a few doors down. "Perfect!" I exclaimed. "Let's go shopping!"

Hannibal laughed, turned on to a small side street and parked. The next two hours were pure delight.

# 11

## THE PROBLEMS OF BEING SNEAKY

*Friday Evening, June 28, 1929*

Being sneaky is more difficult than I had thought. First, I had to be at my surveillance post before Jacques Barre caught the streetcar. Unfortunately, I had to get out of bed at four in the morning to get to my post in time. Second, I had never seen Barre before; all I had was a photo taken by his employer. And finally, the weather was windy, rainy and cold. Burrr!

At six o'clock this morning, Hannibal dropped me off a block away from the corner of Boulevard de Strasbourg and Rue du Chéllou. I kissed Hannibal goodbye and said: "I'll take a cab back to the hotel when I'm finished."

"OK," Hannibal replied. "Be careful."

"I will," I responded. "You know me."

"Yes," said Hannibal. He smiled and added: "I do know you."

"Hummf!" I replied. Then I smiled and said: "I will."

I came prepared. I wore a tan, water-resistant trench coat over my off-the-rack dress that I bought on Thursday. I also wore a dowdy-looking matching hat and sensible shoes, and I carried an umbrella.

I thought I looked just like a working girl from one of the local offices or shops. However, I carried a very large purse. Inside, I had Hannibal's camera, a notebook, pencils, Barre's photo and my Smith and Wesson revolver. Like Hannibal said, a girl has to be careful.

Hannibal's camera was a German Ermanox, the latest in camera technology. It had a kind of low power telescope, which meant that distant objects could be made to look close up. It also worked well in low light situations. I had used it before, back on the Wabash.

Fortunately, the brasserie that I had spotted during our reconnaissance yesterday was open for breakfast. I bought a newspaper from a newsstand just outside, walked in and found a table in the corner by the window.

I could see the streetcar stop sign at the corner of Strasbourg and Rue du Chéllou. "OK, Caroline, you're ready for action," I said to myself. The clock on the wall behind the service counter read six-fifteen.

I looked around. The place was empty, except for me. A few people hurried by outside in the rain.

A grey-haired lady wearing an apron stepped out of the kitchen in back and walked over to my table. She had a big wooden spoon in her hand. She smiled and asked: "Bonjour Madame, voulez-vous le petit déjeuner?"

"Oui, madame," I replied in reasonably good French. "Du café, des fruits et peut-être un petit pain sucré, s'il vous plaît."

The lady raised her eyebrows and looked at me long and carefully. Finally, she said, in perfect English: "You are American, Yes?"

I was totally abashed. I had tried so hard to be a local French girl. Well, there was no point in lying; I could tell from her expression that the old gal was pretty sharp. I decided to take a huge risk.

"Yes, I am," I replied. I looked directly in the older lady's eyes. "I am working with the police on a criminal investigation." I smiled wryly. "I am doing my best to be unnoticed by the person we suspect of a crime."

"Humm," responded the older lady. Her eyes twinkled. "Why would an American girl be helping the police in Le Havre?"

"I am Caroline Case Jones," I replied. "Major Hannibal Jones, my husband, and I are private investigators. Capitaine Inspecteur Pierre Soucet from the Sections de recherche de la Gendarmerie Nationale hired us to help solve seven murders of tourists in Le Havre."

Everything was out on the table. I looked in the old lady's eyes. I'm sure my gaze had a pleading look.

"Who are you investigating?" asked the lady.

"Jacques Barre," I replied. "We think he is involved."

To my utter surprise, she grimaced and replied: "I know him. How can I help?"

At first, I didn't know what to say. The lady's eyes regained their twinkle and she smiled. She then looked up and out the window. "The streetcar has arrived," she said. "Jacques Barre is walking toward it."

I turned and looked outside. Sure enough, I spotted a small, thin man in a trench coat and homburg hat as he hurried toward the streetcar. He carried a lunch pail. I recognized Barre from the photo in my purse.

The streetcar took off, Barre on board. It headed down Boulevard de Strasbourg, toward the docks. The subject of my surveillance was gone.

I turned back to the older lady. My mouth was open. I closed it and waited.

She pulled up a chair, sat down and laid her spoon on the table. She looked at me for a long moment. I squirmed a little.

Finally, she said: "My name is Annabelle Fouquet. I lived in America for many years. This is my restaurant. Like I said earlier: How can I help?"

I stuttered and then said: "What can you tell me about Jacques Barre?"

Annabelle leaned back in her chair, watched me for a moment and then said: "Barre is not a nice man. He comes in my restaurant several times each week. He is rude and demanding. He tried to make time with my young niece, who waits tables in the evening." Annabelle's eyes squinted a little. Carrie is only sixteen."

"I'm so sorry," I replied. Visions of my past came up from buried memories. I'm sure my sincerity was expressed in my demeanor.

Annabelle nodded. Her expression softened.

I then asked: "Does Barre meet anyone in your restaurant? Do you know any of his associates?"

Annabelle leaned forward and folded her hands on the table. She then said: "He does meet with someone nearly every Saturday, here in my restaurant." She paused, as if she were recalling past events. She then said: "They have lunch, and then they do a strange thing."

I'm sure my face expressed the obvious question.

Annabelle responded after a few moments. "They exchange envelopes." She paused, then added: "It's the same every Saturday."

"Anything else?" I asked.

"Yes," replied Annabelle. Barre addressed the other man by the name 'Grégorie." I also saw a name on Barre's envelope. It said 'Durant.' They each pay for lunch, and they both leave. Barre walks down the street, and Durant takes a streetcar toward the Hôtel de Ville."

"What time does this Saturday meeting take place?" I asked.

"Eleven o'clock," replied Annabelle. "It never varies."

"Would you allow me to hide in your kitchen tomorrow and take photographs of Barre and his companion?"

Annabelle's eyes twinkled again. "Of course," she responded. She then added: "Like I said earlier, I don't like Barre. I have long thought that he may be involved in something; he has that look about him."

I smiled and said: "I understand intuition; it works for me, and I'm not often wrong."

Annabelle replied: "Yes, I see. You took a chance with me." She chuckled and added: "You were right."

I laughed openly, and Annabelle joined in. She then said: "Would you like that coffee, fruit and sweet roll now?"

What a morning! I had the name of Barre's contact and an opportunity for surveillance on Saturday at eleven o'clock. I also made a new friend.

After breakfast, Annabelle gave me a tour of the kitchen. It was neat, clean and had wonderful smells. I noticed a glass transom above the door.

Annabelle saw my glance and said: "It's a perfect spot for taking photos; you can see the entire dining area from up there." She smiled and added: "I have a step ladder in back."

"Very resourceful!" I replied. "May I see?"

Annabelle led the way to a storage closet at the back of the kitchen. A tall, sturdy step ladder rested against the wall.

"We can set the step ladder next to the door and move it under the transom when you need to take photos," Annabelle said. "I'll have it out for you on Saturday morning."

"Wonderful! "I replied. I'll be here around ten-thirty tomorrow."

I lingered in the dining room for another half-hour, enjoying another sweet roll and making notes. Annabelle brought more coffee. Finally, the rain stopped. I paid my check, thanked Annabelle profusely and left. By that time, the restaurant had a dozen or so customers.

Outside, I hailed a passing cab. After another thirty minutes, I arrived back at the Frascati. It was raining again as I got out of the cab.

Hannibal was on his own expedition, so I removed my damp clothes, took a warm bath and dressed in my two-piece black rayon

Schiaparelli lounging pajamas. I combed and fixed my hair; I wanted to look nice for Hannibal when he came back from his work.

My outfit had a daring top that accented my figure, a smooth form-fitting midriff and billowy legs. A short, long-sleeved matching jacket provided a modest cover. I also wore black slippers. I felt warm and looked very alluring, if I do say so myself.

Hannibal arrived at about four o'clock in the afternoon. I was standing by the bay window, looking out, when he stepped through the door. Several lamps were on that gave the room a golden glow. I knew that from Hannibal's point of view, I was silhouetted against the gray, rainy sky outside the window. I turned and faced Hannibal.

Hannibal stopped, smiled, looked me up and down and said softly: "Ah, exquis, tu ressembles à un joli chat noir à la fenêtre."

I recognized the words; I had heard 'the black cat in the window' phrase from Soucet a few days earlier. I liked it. I walked slowly over to Hannibal and gave him a long kiss.

Later, after a room service dinner, Hannibal and I settled in to compare notes.

I described my visit to the brasserie, my brief glimpse of Barre and my very interesting conversation with Annabelle. "We now have two names: Jacques Barre, our nefarious customs clerk, and Grégorie Durant, his contact. We also know that they exchange envelopes every Saturday."

"Hummm," replied Hannibal. "Barre is most likely selling a target list of wealthy passengers who arrive by ship. Burglaries and murders are the results."

"I will take photos tomorrow for evidence," I responded. "What did you find out at the hotels?"

Hannibal flipped through his notes. After a moment, he said: "I visited each Maître d'hôtel at five hotels: Frascati, Continental, Normandie, Modern and Bordeaux. All five Maître d's remembered the respective murders."

I sat back in my chair and waited.

Hannibal slipped into his military briefing mode and continued. "Pierre Clément at the Frascati confirmed that on June 2, 1928, Sir Walter and Anne, Lady Wallace left the dining room at about eleven in the morning. Sir Walter went to the smoking room to meet a business partner. Lady Wallace returned to the couple's room on the top floor of the hotel."

Hannibal flipped a page in his notes and continued. "Lady Wallace's body was discovered by Ouellette Paquet, a maid, just after two." Hannibal paused, flipped through his notes and added: "Apparently, no one saw any suspicious persons in or near the room."

He then looked at the police report. "The police dusted for fingerprints. They found prints of Sir Walter, Lady Wallace and the maid, that's all."

Hannibal looked up from the report. After a moment, he stated: "The story was much the same at the other four hotels for each of the remaining six murders, with one exception."

"Oh?" I responded.

Hannibal studied his notes again. "When Sir Albert Brunswick was murdered at the Continental on June 12, a little over two weeks ago, Byron Caron, the Maître d', told me that Francis Delacroix, a waiter, was on his way to a room near the murder scene with a tray."

Hannibal paused and then added: "This was new information, and it was not in the police report."

I nodded and waited for Hannibal to continue.

"Caron said that he did not know about Delacroix's errand until after the police completed their brief investigation," said Hannibal. "Of course, I interviewed Delacroix."

"And?" I asked. Hannibal smiled; he could see that he had my complete attention.

"Delacroix saw a man in the hallway near the murder scene at about three o'clock. He said that the man looked at him, turned, and walked quickly down the hall, away from him. The man was dressed in a delivery uniform of a local laundry service. He had a laundry bag in his hand. He also wore gloves."

"Description?" I queried.

"Medium height, dark complexion, muscular build, dark hair peppered with gray and a moustache. He also said that the man had light blue eyes, which stood out from his dark complexion."

"Wow!" I responded. Delacroix may have seen the murderer." I thought a moment and asked: "Why didn't Delacroix tell his boss or the police?"

"I asked that question of Delacroix," replied Hannibal. "He said that he assumed that the man in the hallway was a laundry delivery man. Also, after his shift, Delacroix went on holiday. He didn't return until today."

Hannibal paused and then added: "He didn't know about the murder until this morning. When he heard the gossip among his fellow waiters, he told his story to Caron immediately, which was just before I arrived."

"Did Caron confirm Delacroix's absence and return?" I asked.

"Yes," said Hannibal. "I think we have a pretty good description of the murderer."

I thought for several minutes, then said: "We need to tie Barre to Durant and Durant to the murderer."

"Yes," replied Hannibal. Your surveillance tomorrow will be most interesting."

"We will be getting the photos of logbook pages from our friend Colbert soon," I responded. "He promised have them ready tomorrow."

With that, Hannibal and I ended our discussion of the case for this evening. I made these diary entries, and Hannibal made more notes.

We had a glass of wine, watched the sunset at just after ten o'clock, and then went to bed. What a day!

# 12

## CONNECTIONS

*Saturday Evening, June 29, 1929*

Our first connection had been established: Barre to Durant. With Annabelle's help, I followed up by being a snoop in her brasserie this morning. In preparation, Hannibal drove me to the corner of Boulevard de Strasbourg and Rue du Thiérs, a block from the brasserie.

Hannibal spent the day comparing police reports to Soucet's list of burglaries and Colbert's logbook photos. The logbook photos had been delivered just after eight o'clock this morning. Except for Soucet's list and Colbert's file on Barre, everything was in French. Hannibal had to perform the analysis. We would review his analysis and the results of my snooping when I got back to the hotel.

I arrived at my drop-off point at about ten o'clock. Fortunately, the weather had changed, and the sun was out. It was still cool, so I wore my second off-the-rack dress, a trench coat and sensible walking shoes. I looked frumpy again. "The things I must do to be a sleuth," I grumbled to myself.

I also had my big purse. It contained my notebook and Hannibal's camera. I left my revolver, umbrella and hat in our hotel room. The hat, which I didn't like, made me look even more frumpy. "My hypocrisy only goes so far," I concluded. I tossed my head back and sniffed as I walked.

I finished setting up in Annabelle's kitchen just before eleven o'clock. The brasserie had a double door between the kitchen and the dining area, and the glass transom above the doors went all the way across. Annabelle and I set up the ladder on the left, and the right door was free for passage. Barre and Durant arrived at eleven o'clock, as expected. I was on my ladder, well-hidden and ready.

Durant was neatly dressed, middle-aged, medium height and clean-shaven. He had a dark complexion and dark hair. "Probably of Mediterranean descent, maybe Italian," I surmised as I watched.

The Barre and Durant meeting lasted over an hour, with much animated conversation. I couldn't follow the French, but I caught enough to conclude that they were discussing money. I also heard the phrase 'une bijouterie à Paris' mentioned several times. I made notes and took photos of the envelope exchange.

As the pair neared the completion of their lunch, I climbed down from my ladder, put away my stuff, whispered 'bonjour' and 'merci beaucoup' to Annabelle and quietly slipped out the back door. I was on a mission.

Based on Annabelle's information, I expected Durant to catch the streetcar in front of the brasserie and head toward the Hôtel de Ville. I hurried around the building to Strasbourg, turned right and walked to the streetcar stop a block away, at Rue de Ténelle.

I could see the brasserie and the streetcar stop in front. I bought a newspaper from a nearby newsstand. I watched as Barre and Durant exited the brasserie. Barre walked around the side and disappeared on Rue du Chéllou. Durant waited for the streetcar, which would be coming from my direction on Strasbourg.

The wait wasn't long. I got on the streetcar, purchased my ticket and found an unobtrusive seat in back. As expected, Durant got on at the next stop. I pretended to read. Durant sat a few seats in front of me.

Within fifteen minutes, we stopped. Durant got up, paid his fare and stepped off the streetcar. I followed discretely and paid my fare. As I stepped off, I looked at the street sign. "Rue de Metz," I observed.

I let Durant get about two dozen meters ahead. Fortunately, the sidewalk was crowded near Strasbourg, and Durant gave no indication that he noticed me. He passed the intersection of Rue de Orangerie, continued for half a block and turned left onto a walkway that led to a gated courtyard and apartment building.

The Rue de Metz past Orangerie was quiet and tree-lined. There was no traffic and few pedestrians. I crossed the street and continued past Durant's apartment building. "Nice place," I thought to myself. "Durant lives well."

As I passed Durant's building on the other side of the street, I noted its number: '25 Rue de Metz,' which I committed to memory.

I looked around at the buildings on my side of the street. Directly across from Number 25, I saw a sign in a window. It read: 'Chambre à louer.'

I searched my memory for the right translation. Finally, I had it, and I said: "Room for rent!"  I then shushed myself. "Careful, Caroline," I muttered, "not out loud." Anyway, I had found an observation post. "I need Hannibal," my thoughts continued.

I was finished for the day. I turned around and walked back to Boulevard de Strasbourg. Within a few minutes, I caught a cab and headed back to the Frascati. Success!

I saw Hannibal as I entered our room. He was sitting in a chair by our work table. He had a pot of coffee on the side table and cup in his hand. Open reports were scattered across the work table and all around on the floor.

Hannibal looked up at me, smiled and said: "You look all bubbly; did you have a good day?"

"He always knows," I thought to myself, "how does he do it?"

To Hannibal, I replied: "Yes, of course," as if there was never a doubt. "I followed Durant, and he lives at 25 Rue de Metz, just off Strasbourg on the west side of the Hôtel de Ville." I paused and then added: "I also found a good place where we might be able to observe his apartment building."

"Excellent," replied Hannibal. "What did you find for an observation post?"

"I saw a sign in a window in an apartment house across the street from Durant's place," I replied. "It read: chambre à louer."

"Ah, room for rent," replied Hannibal. "Good idea."

I dropped my big purse on the floor, took off my trench coat, slipped off my uncomfortable shoes, fluffed my hair, and sauntered over to Hannibal.

I sat on the table right in the middle of his files. I swung my legs back and forth over the edge of the table. Hannibal laughed, set his coffee cup on the side table, stood, leaned over and gave me a warm kiss.

I kissed him back and asked: "And what did you find out today?"

"Well," replied Hannibal after a couple more kisses; Barre processed every one of the twenty-seven ship passengers or couples whose hotel rooms had been robbed." He paused and then added: "We have uncovered a large operation."

"I agree," I responded. "From my hiding place in the brasserie, I took photos for evidence, including several that showed Barre and Durant exchanging envelopes. I also listened to their conversation."

"Perfect," replied Hannibal. "Did you hear anything of interest?"

I thought a moment then said: "I couldn't follow the French very well; they talked too fast for me. However, it was clear they were talking about money. I also picked up the phrase: 'une bijouterie à Paris' several times."

"Ah," responded Hannibal, "a jewelry shop in Paris."

I swiftly made the connection. "An outlet for their stolen jewelry!" I exclaimed.

"I think so," replied Hannibal. "I think we should tell Soucet what we have discovered and advise him about our plans for continued surveillance."

"Can we do that in the morning?" I said. I then giggled and gave Hannibal another kiss.

Hannibal chuckled. "You have lots of good ideas," he replied.

And so, the evening passed.

## Sunday Evening, June 30

Hannibal and I were very busy this morning. Before we left the hotel, Hannibal phoned Soucet and told him about our findings and planned activities. Hannibal and I then took a cab to our planned surveillance post about nine o'clock; we couldn't risk being obvious with our Duesenberg.

We surreptitiously rented the room across the street from 25 Rue de Metz and set up shop. The room had a perfect viewing window to Durant's building. The landlady was very cordial, especially after Hannibal gave her double her asking price, with a week's rent in advance. Ah, the advantages of an expense account.

In his negotiations with our new landlady, Hannibal outlined what we were doing, including our association with the Gendarmerie Nationale. She was all a-twitter; I could tell she was so excited to participate in our little investigation. She readily agreed to supply us with sandwiches, snacks and a constant supply of coffee. Hannibal also got her to pledge complete secrecy; she was to tell no one.

We brought Hannibal's camera and binoculars from the Frascati. We were both armed; Hannibal had his forty-five and I had my revolver. We set aside our tools of the trade and began our vigil. All we had to do was watch out the window.

We started Sunday at noon. Nothing happened. Durant never left his apartment. We finally went back to the Frascati at about eight in the evening. Surveillance can be so boring.

## Monday Evening, July 1

Hannibal and I arrived at the rented room early this morning. We had another long, boring day. However, at about six o'clock in the evening, Durant left his apartment building and walked along

Rue de Metz toward Boulevard de Strasbourg. He was dressed neatly, as if for an evening out.

Hannibal and I slipped out the back door of our building and followed at a discrete distance. Durant turned right on Strasbourg, passed the Squaré Sainte Roché and entered a cabaret at the corner of Rue Louis Philippe. We waited for several minutes, and then entered the cabaret.

The interior was smokey and dimly lit. American-style jazz music played from a small stage at the back. Several of the musicians were black men. I was reminded of the working-class speakeasies in Chicago and the Wabash Valley.

The music was very good. I had heard gossip at the Frascati about expatriate American jazz musicians in Paris. Apparently, some had settled in Le Havre.

Hannibal and I found a small table in the corner across from the bar, near the front door. A waiter came over, and Hannibal ordered wine and snacks. We made ourselves comfortable. The wine and snacks soon arrived.

My eyes adjusted to the dim light. I spotted Durant on the other side of the room at a table. He had four companions. They had several bottles of wine on the table, and each man had a glass.

Hannibal patted me on the hand and said: "I'll be back shortly; enjoy your wine." He quietly slipped over to the bar and talked briefly to the bartender. The bartender nodded. Hannibal slipped into a hallway behind the bar and disappeared.

I continued to observe Durant and his companions. Durant was doing most of the talking. The others listened intently and occasionally made comments. I couldn't hear their voices over the sound of the music.

I looked closely at each man, committing each detail to memory. One man was of particular interest. As best as I could tell from his sitting position, he was of medium height. He had a dark complexion and a muscular build. He had dark hair and a moustache. When he turned to the light, I could see that he had startingly blue eyes, which stood out from his dark complexion. "He fits Delacroix's description!" I concluded.

The other three men seemed less sinister than the first; but still, they appeared hardened and not to be trifled with. After about ten minutes, Hannibal returned to our table. We continued to sip wine, nibble at our snacks and observe.

About thirty minutes later, two newcomers entered the cabaret. Both were burly men, and they made half-concealed glances at Hannibal and me. I squirmed a little. Hannibal watched carefully for a moment, then returned his attention to Durant and his companions.

As the evening progressed, the conversation at Durant's table became more jovial. Apparently, business talk had ended, and the group began to enjoy the music and the surroundings. Several of the men looked around the room, including Durant.

Durant was smiling. Apparently, he made some jovial comments, because his companions laughed. After a moment, Durant's gaze fell upon me. His eyes widened, and he no longer smiled.

Clearly, he recognized me. "Oh, my," I thought to myself: "Not good." My thoughts raced. "He must have noticed me when I followed him on Saturday."

Durant turned to his companions and the group huddled together. Occasionally one would look in our direction. I could see they were discussing Hannibal and me.

After a minute or two, Durant's four companions got up from the table and walked slowly over toward us. Durant remained at the table, watching.

I looked over at Hannibal. His eyes had a steady gaze as he watched the approach of the four men. "Get ready," he said softly. I slipped my revolver out of my purse.

Hannibal waited until the four arrived at our table. One tried to slip behind Hannibal. That was a mistake. Hannibal rose from his chair, and with a sweeping backhand, hit the man behind him full in the face before he could raise his guard. The man staggered backwards.

Hannibal's intense, blazing stare never left the remaining three men in front. The nearest swung his right fist at Hannibal's face. Hannibal ducked, braced his feet and brought his right up into the man's midriff with a crashing blow. Air escaped from the man's lungs in a whoosh, and he doubled over.

The remaining two men started forward. Suddenly, the two burly men from the bar were there, and a general melee ensued.

One of the men from the bar shouted: "Gendarme!"

My mind raced. "Of course!" I concluded. "Hannibal called the police from the bar!"

I returned my attention to Durant. As the fight started, he had risen from the table, turned and was headed for the back door behind the stage.

I slipped off my shoes, held my revolver loosely in my right hand, rose from my chair and ran lightly across the room. I came up behind Durant. As on the ship with Lefevre, I landed my practiced blow with my left foot behind Durant's right knee.

He spun half-way around and went down on his back, hitting the back of his head on the floor with a sharp 'whack' in the process.

My momentum carried me forward. My silk hose on my feet let me slide to a halt. I turned and took three steps back toward Durant. I dropped with my full weight, knees first, on his middle. Air and a shriek escaped from Durant's lips at the same time.

I was ready with my revolver. I shoved the snub-nosed barrel into Durant's open mouth. I pulled the hammer back.

It made a very loud click-click sound. I noticed the sound because the music had stopped. Even the melee behind me had ended. The cabaret was as quiet as an empty church.

I glared down at Durant and stated in a clear and matter-of-fact manner: "One move, Monsieur Durant, and your brains will be all over this floor." I'm sure my eyes had the same look that I saw in Hannibal's eyes as he dealt with his opponents.

Whether Durant understood English or not, he got the point. He didn't move.

After half a minute of silence, I heard a familiar soft voice. "Ah, Madame and Monsieur Jones, you have the situation under control, I see." It was Soucet.

# 13

## RINGS WITHIN SHADOWS

*Thursday Evening, July 4, 1929*

Hannibal and I took Tuesday off. The bad guys are the in the custody of Inspecteur Soucet and the Gendarmerie, and Soucet will follow up. We have had enough excitement for a while.

After sleeping late on Tuesday morning, we had a late breakfast in the café, located in the Frascati gallery, facing the sea. The view was wonderful.

The day was warm and sunny, so we decided to explore. I wore a light, Lanvin-blue full skirt with petticoats, a white blouse and a matching blue cardigan sweater. I tied a yellow silk scarf around my neck for accent. I had silk hose and sensible white walking shoes. Hannibal wore tan trousers, a light blue open-collar shirt, a navy-blue sweater vest, and matching brown shoes. We were perfect, classic tourists.

About ten o'clock, the valet brought our Duesenberg around front, and we drove across the Seine toward Honfleur, a nearby picturesque little port town on the Côte de Grâce.

Once we crossed the bridge, Hannibal let me drive the Duesenberg. Fortunately, very few cars were on the road. I narrowly missed a donkey cart and one poor cow. Watching the road, working the pedals, shifting gears and steering the car all at the same time was more complicated than I thought. "I can do this," I told myself. I'm sure my expression was one of grim determination.

From Hannibal's point of view, the episode was hilarious, I think. He did laugh a lot, in a cautious, nervous way.

No thanks to my erratic driving, we arrived safely in Honfleur at about noon. I parked near the Quai Sainte Catherine on the Vieux Bassin, and Hannibal gave a big sigh of relief. We looked in the many shops along the quai, bought a few trinkets, and walked around the bassin.

There were several little Mom and Pop restaurants along the quai. We had a late lunch, and Hannibal drove back to the Frascati. Darn! I realize, however, that my driving needs a little work.

Wednesday was different. Soucet called at about ten o'clock, just after we returned to our room from breakfast.

Hannibal answered the phone. I remained in the parlor, standing by our big bay window, sipping coffee. Outside, the weather had turned cool and windy again. "English Channel weather," I mused. I watched as grey clouds scudded across the sky. The warm coffee cup in my hands felt good.

I had dressed in my second Chanel pants and top combination. I had bought two sets, of course. I had enough of working girl clothes, at least until my next snooping assignment.

To account for the weather, my pants were light-weight black worsted wool. The high-waisted top accented my slim figure. The legs were wide, with a billowy look.

The top was really a form-fitting, light-weight cashmere sweater. It was also black, but with burgundy trim at the high, close-fitting neck and at the wrists of the long sleeves. For accent, I wore a silk scarf around my neck. It was burgundy-colored to match the trim on my sweater. I finished with black, medium heeled shoes and diamond stud earrings to accent my engagement and wedding rings.

Hannibal walked back into the parlor after his conversation on the phone. I turned and smiled. I knew that I was silhouetted against the window.

As I expected, Hannibal gave me a long, appreciative look. "The cat in the window again," he said. He smiled and walked over toward me.

"Was that Soucet on the phone?" I asked.

"Yes," replied Hannibal. He gave me a warm kiss and I responded. After a moment, Hannibal continued: "Soucet wants us to visit him at the Palais de Justice this afternoon." Hannibal grinned and added: "He seemed very pleased with our work."

"Where?" I asked.

"The Palais de Justice is on the Boulevard de Strasbourg, a kilometer or so past the Hôtel de Ville," replied Hannibal. "It's about a thirty-minute drive."

We left the Frascati at about one o'clock. Hannibal and I both wore light jackets. Mine was short and made from black Persian lambskin. It complimented my Chanel outfit. I felt very chic and modern.

As we approached the car in front of the Frascati, I asked: "May I drive?"

Hannibal raised his eyebrows and gave a big sigh. "I suppose so," he said. "You need to practice in-town driving, and there are probably no donkey carts or cows on our route." He gave a chuckle.

"OK," smarty," I replied with a toss of my head and a sniff. "You just wait; I'll do better this time."

And so, I did. I navigated the roundabout at the intersection of Rue de Perrey and Boulevard de Strasbourg, dodged the streetcar as we passed the Hôtel de Ville, turned left on Rue Jean-Babtiste Benot Eyriés and parked in the lot at the back of the Palais de Justice. My gear-shifting skills had also improved; I didn't grind them even once.

"OK, Caroline," I thought to myself, as I shut down the engine. "You didn't hit anything. Don't press your luck; let Hannibal drive back."

To Hannibal, I smiled sweetly, with a touch of triumph. "How was that?" I asked.

"Outstanding," replied Hannibal with a smile and a twinkle in his eyes. "You'll be giving driving lessons to Frenchmen any day now."

"Hummf," I responded. Hannibal took the hint, got out of the car, walked around and opened my door for me. He still had a grin on his face as we walked into the Palais de Justice.

We found Capitaine Inspecteur Soucet's office down the hallway on the first floor. The door from the hallway opened into a little anteroom. A uniformed sergeant sat at a desk halfway across the room. As he stood to greet us, I recognized him from Monday at the cabaret. He was one of the burly men who assisted Hannibal in the fight.

The Sergeant smiled and said: "Bonjour, Monsieur et Madame Jones. Bienvenue; l'Inspecteur vous attend." He bowed slightly and motioned us toward the inner office. He then walked ahead a little and opened the door.

As we entered, Soucet saw us, rose from behind his desk and said: "Ah, so good to see you, Major and Madame Jones." He smiled warmly and motioned us to two ornate chairs in front of his desk. "Please make yourselves comfortable."

Hannibal assisted me with my jacket and then removed his own. He laid them on a spare chair that rested in the corner near the door. We both sat down in the two chairs in front of Soucet's desk.

I glanced around the office. It was paneled in oak and had many filled bookshelves at the back. Three large windows let in light along the left wall. A large oak work table and a half-dozen chairs rested near the windows. Files were neatly stacked on the table. Small side tables held lamps and decorative pieces. A fireplace took up the middle of the right wall, and a beautiful clock rested on the mantelpiece. A merry fire danced in the fireplace to ward off the coolness of the room.

Everything in the room was neat and in place; it reflected the personality of its occupant. "Very nice," I thought to myself. To Soucet, I smiled and said: "So good to see you, Inspecteur. I hope you are satisfied with our work."

"Oh, my yes," responded Soucet. "We have six men behind bars, including a murderer, and lots of evidence, including your well-written report. Convictions in court are almost certain."

"Thank you," I replied. Hannibal and I waited, Soucet had asked us to visit him for a reason.

Soucet smiled, leaned over and took an envelope out of his drawer. He walked around his desk with the envelope in hand. He glanced at Hannibal with a mischievous grin, turned to me and handed me the envelope. "Your fee, Madame Jones," he said. "I hope the amount is satisfactory."

I've never been shy about taking money for services rendered. I opened the envelope and peeked at the check. It was in U.S. dollars and drawn on an American branch bank in Paris. The amount was twenty thousand dollars. I gasped a little; the check was written for twice our agreed upon amount.

Soucet observed my expression and chuckled. Hannibal just grinned; I don't think the amount mattered to him, as long as I was pleased.

I finally said: "Thank you, Monsieur Inspecteur; you are very generous." I looked at Soucet carefully. He had an inscrutable expression, with a hint of a smile. His eyes twinkled.

"OK," I thought to myself. "What's the catch?" There had to be something else. I was right.

Soucet returned to his chair behind his desk, sat down and put his hands together in a little pyramid. He glanced at Hannibal and then looked at me with a steady gaze. His smile was gone.

"You have uncovered something much larger than you know," he began. "Durant headed a local operation for a vast criminal network." He paused for effect and then continued: "When we searched the apartments of Durant, Barre and the others, we found not only evidence to convict, but evidence of connections to Le Milieu, the French underworld."

Both Hannibal and I had expressions of astonishment.

Soucet smiled again and said: "I hope you will agree to help us by continuing your investigation." His eyes twinkled as he looked carefully at me. "The path leads to Paris, and you will be well-paid for your efforts."

Hannibal and I looked at each other. I nodded. How exciting!

Hannibal turned to Soucet and replied: "We would be happy to help." Hannibal's eyes twinkled, and he added: "Madame Jones wants to go shopping in Paris anyway."

Hannibal and Soucet laughed merrily. I gave both of them a snooty look and responded with: "Hummf!" I couldn't help it; I then joined in the laughter. After a few moments, Soucet got down to business. "Let's go to my work table," he said.

After we were seated, Soucet opened a file from one of the stacks on the table. "First, I will tell you what we found that relates to our murderer."

He then read from the file. We found out many things about "Léo Martel, our murderer, when we searched his rather disreputable apartment near the Bassin du Commerce. In addition to a double loop garrote, we found military records."

Soucet paused, looked first at Hannibal, then me and said: "Martel spent five years in the French Foreign Legion. He was wounded in battle during the Rif War in Morocco in late 1926. He became a French citizen in 1927, Français par le sang renversé."

Hannibal looked at me and translated: "French citizen by spilled blood," he said.

"Yes," responded Soucet. "We do not know his background before his service in the Legion, except that he was born somewhere in North Africa, probably of mixed European and Berber ancestry."

Soucet paused, read a little more and said: "Martel was poorly educated, and he apparently fell on hard times when he moved to Le Havre. However, he had combat skills learned in the Legion. He must have been recruited by Durant in 1928; since we found lists of tourist names, written by Durant, in Martel's apartment, dating back to early 1928."

Soucet continued: "We also found several pieces of jewelry that matched descriptions of pieces that were taken from Sir Albert and Lady Brunswick's room on June 14." Apparently, these had not yet been turned over to Durant for disposal."

Soucet smiled and concluded: "We have motive, method and opportunity. Our murder victims, certainly Sir Albert, were killed by Martel when they interrupted a burglary." Soucet looked at me with a steady gaze. "Thanks to you and Major Jones, Martel, a very brutal man, will be tried for murder."

"I see," I responded. "What about the other three burglars?"

"Ah, yes," replied Soucet. "Hervé Lachance, Renée Savage and Louis Renaud. All three are petty criminals, and they are well-known to the gendarme in Le Havre." They did not kill anyone, but they will serve long prison sentences for burglary and for assault in the cabaret." Soucet's eyes twinkled, and he added: "You two did very well in the cabaret. I was impressed." He chuckled a little.

Soucet then smiled grimly and said: "After intense questioning, the three burglars talked. They implicated Durant in setting up the other burglaries."

I did not want to know about gendarme methods of questioning, so I changed the subject. "What about Barre?"

Soucet nodded and said: "As you know, Jacques Barre was a customs clerk at the Quai des Transatlantique. The evidence against him is overwhelming. He sold information on likely targets for burglary to Durant. He will be tried for conspiracy to commit burglary and for selling confidential government information." Soucet smiled and added: "Barre will go to prison for many years."

The room was silent for a few moments. Finally, Hannibal asked: "What about Durant?"

"Now, we come to the key," replied Soucet. "We have established that Durant was a beau voyous, a member of the Unione Corse, a Le Milieu crime family. Evidence found in his rather expensive apartment connects him to a parrain in Paris."

I'm sure my face had a blank look. "Parrain?" I asked.

"In English, parrain means godfather," Hannibal responded. "I think, in the context of Le Milieu, parrain means the head, or leader, of a criminal organization."

"Oh," I said, "Like the criminal gangs in Chicago."

"Yes," responded Soucet. "Very much like your Al Capone."

That comparison brought back memories. How exciting! To Soucet, I asked: "How did you connect Durant to a parrain in Paris?"

"Durant had a pre-paid pass on the train that runs between Le Havre and Paris," replied Soucet. "He also had an envelope full of cash in his apartment. The envelope had a name on it. It said: 'Emporium Or, Argent et Joaillerie, Simon Goldhirsch, propriétaire.'

Again, I looked at Hannibal, who said: "In English, it means 'Gold, Silver and Fine Jewelry Emporium, Simon Goldhirsch, Proprietor.' Simon Goldhirsch must be a contact."

"Yes," said Soucet. "And that is the lead you must follow."

Soucet gave a sigh and continued: "My sources in Paris tell me that Goldhirsch has connections to Paul Carbone, a known Le Milieu parrain. We have been trying to put Carbone behind bars for years, but we don't have the evidence."

Soucet paused, and his face acquired a sad, far-away look. He then added: "Also, we in the Gendarmerie Nationale do not get the cooperation of the Sûreté Nationale; in particular, Jean Babtiste Pascal Eugéne Chiappe, the Paris Préfet de Police."

"Oh!" I thought to myself. "Do we have a case with police corruption?" To Soucet, I smiled and said: "Interesting. We will do our best." I grinned mischievously and added: "After shopping in Paris, of course."

Hannibal and Soucet laughed.

# 14

## DEATH ON THE ROAD

*Saturday morning, July 6, 1929*

Today, I will start packing for our trip from Le Havre to Paris. Since we plan to drive, we will have to send most of our belongings by rail to Hôtel Ritz, 15 Place Vendôme, Paris. We leave next Wednesday. I have to select a few outfits to take with us in the Duesenberg. Decisions, decisions!

Last night, Hannibal and I laid out a route on a tourist map. The drive will be a little over 200 kilometers, and we will make a leisurely trip. We will pass through the towns of Caudebec-en-Caux, Jumiéges, Rouen, Pont-de-l'Arche, Vernon, Giverny, Mantes and finally, the suburbs of Paris. With a couple of stops along the way, we will check in at the Ritz on Thursday, July 18.

Our investigation in Paris awaits. Hannibal phoned Inspecteur Soucet and told him about our itinerary. Soucet said he would advise his contacts in Paris, and a representative of the Gendarmerie would contact us at the Ritz.

We plan to spend six nights and five days in Rouen and another two nights and one day in Giverny, visiting the sites. According to Hannibal, Rouen rests on the Seine, and it is the capital of Normandie. He also said that it has a beautiful medieval cathedral. I read somewhere that Giverny was the home of Claude Monet, the impressionist painter. He died just three years ago. Hannibal said we could drive by Monet's house and gardens. Of course, I want to see everything. Maybe we can buy some Monet paintings.

On Monday, I have a special errand; I want to get a French driver's license. Hannibal got one during the war. He renewed it when he picked up our Duesenberg at the quai. A license can be issued by the French Ministére de L'Intérieur, Département de la Sécurité Publique. Hannibal said they have an office in the Hôtel de Ville on Boulevard de Strasbourg. All that is required to qualify for a new license is an affidavit by two persons who already have a French driver's license.

I guess I should be nice to Hannibal and the Inspecteur, since I want them to lie and say I know how to drive. Hannibal said he would get me a booklet that explains French signs and rules of the road. He also promised to help me decipher the French. Driving to Paris will be such fun!

## Monday evening, July 8

Success! I have a French driver's license. I promised Hannibal that I would work very hard to become a safe driver. With Hannibal's help, I will read the 'Driving in France' booklet tonight, after dinner. Hannibal raised his eyebrows when I prattled on about driving through the French countryside. Oh, well; I'm determined to prove myself, mostly for my own satisfaction.

We leave Le Havre day after tomorrow. I am still in a tizzy over which outfits to take in the car. Hannibal plans to have our trunks picked up first thing tomorrow for shipment to Paris. Final decisions on what to wear will have to be made tonight.

## Wednesday evening, July 10

Hannibal and I arrived at the Grande Hôtel D'Angleterre in Rouen this evening. We drove across the Pont Jeanne d'Arc. The hotel was at 21 Quai de Havre, on the Seine. We have a suite with a view. What a picturesque setting! We had a light dinner with room service, and we are both dead tired. I will write a few pages, and then I'm off to bed.

We had a very unusual drive from Le Havre. On our first day on the road, Hannibal and I solved a killing.

I was driving. We had passed through Caudebec-en-Caux, where we stopped for gas and a quick look at the cathedral. The road was gravel and bumpy, but the day was warm and beautiful.

We made good progress. By late morning, we were just outside of Jumiéges, a small village about twenty kilometers from Rouen. Only one car was on the road ahead of us, and I kept my distance. The one-lane road rose and passed over a small hill. The car ahead disappeared for few moments as it passed the crest.

We reached the top of the hill. Twenty meters ahead, the other car was stopped dead in the road. I pushed down on the clutch and slammed on the brakes. Our Duesenberg stopped about two meters from the other car's rear bumper. "Oh my! That was close!" I said aloud. I glanced over at Hannibal, who had braced with both hands on the dash.

Hannibal looked at me and said: "Are you OK?"

"Yes," I replied. "What on earth is going on with that car?"

After my response, Hannibal took a deep breath and looked at the scene in front of us. He then said: "Let's check." He got out of our car and walked toward the car ahead. I shut down the engine, let out on the clutch, got out on my side and followed.

As I approached, I could see a nameplate on the back of the car. It read 'Austin.' A sweeping glance told me that it was a coupe, green and new. An elderly gentleman in tweeds opened the door on the right side. "Steering wheel on the right, old man in tweeds, definitely British," I concluded.

A woman in a bonnet and very conservative dark dress stepped out on the left. She peered around the front of the car and screamed: "Aheeeh!" several times, followed by: "Oh, my heavens!"

Other than being panic-stricken, the woman seemed OK. I passed by her and looked in front of the Austin. A very large black and white cow lay on its side. Its feet were crushed up against the bumper of the Austin. As I watched, the poor critter breathed its last. Foam formed at its mouth.

Hannibal was talking to the driver on the other side of the car. The elderly man was very upset, and Hannibal was doing his best to calm him down.

I turned back to the lady, who, fortunately, had stopped screaming. "Are you OK?" I asked. "I'm Caroline Case Jones. Major Jones, my husband, and I will help you if we can."

After a moment of stutters, the lady took out a handkerchief, dabbed her eyes and looked at me. Finally, she replied: "Yes, I think so. Please help."

She looked over at Hannibal and her companion on the other side of the car. After a moment, she seemed satisfied. She turned back to me and tried to smile. "I'm Susan Warmly, and John, my husband, and I are on our way to Rouen on holiday."

She then turned and looked at the cow. "That poor creature!" She took a deep breath, turned back to me and said: "It was just lying in the road, and John couldn't stop."

I looked at the cow. The car bumper had hit the cow's feet, that was all. There were no other injuries that I could see and no damage to the car. However, the cow's mid-section was greatly distended. "The critter looks like a big black and white balloon," I thought to myself.

I heard a voice in the distance. I looked up. A man in work clothes was striding up the road toward us. He was saying over and over: 'Vous avez tué ma vache! Vous avez tué ma vache!'

I looked over at Hannibal. My glance asked the obvious question.

Hannibal saw my look and responded: "The farmer said: You killed my cow!"

The Frenchman approached Hannibal and John. Hannibal tried to interpret and mediate, with only moderate success. John had a bewildered look; he obviously didn't understand French. After a few minutes of this, the Frenchman turned and stormed off back toward a house in the near distance.

Hannibal turned his attention to John. I could hear him say: "The farmer is going to call the local gendarme. Why don't you sit in your car and wait?"

After a moment, John said: "Yes, yes." He then tottered over to the open door of the Austin and sat down. After a couple of deep breaths, he turned to Susan and said: "Please, my dear let's both sit and wait."

I turned to Susan, smiled and said: "John is going to sit and try to relax until the policeman arrives; perhaps you should do the same."

After a brief uncertain look, Susan said: "Yes, of course." Soon it was done.

I looked over at Hannibal and said: "Shall we investigate?"

Hannibal grinned and responded: "Yes. After all, we have a killing. Not quite a murder, but close enough." He paused and added: "It will take time for the gendarme to arrive; there is a ferry crossing between Jumiéges and our location."

I walked over to Hannibal, turned so the Warmly's couldn't see, chuckled a little and said: "I'll check out the crime scene, you check out the victim."

I looked around. "Details, Caroline," I told myself. I saw erratic hoofprints in the dirt along the side of the road. I followed them.

I could see a pasture on the left side of the road. It was enclosed by dense hedgerows and trees. I followed the tracks along the road for about twenty meters.

The tracks led toward a gate that provided access to and from the pasture. The gate was about three meters wide, made of crisscrossed split saplings and had vertical struts on each end. The strut on the left was attached to a wooden gatepost with two iron post and ring hinges. The strut on the right had a sliding wooden latch that slipped into a notch in the gatepost on the right. The gate was firmly closed.

I looked to the sides of the gate. I could see smashed hedges and broken split saplings just to the left of the hinged gatepost. Cow tracks led from the opening. "The cow got out of the pasture and on the road here," I muttered. I looked back toward the two cars. Tracks led from the hole in the hedgerow toward the dead cow. "Confirmed," my thoughts continued.

I walked over to the gate and peered into the pasture. The grass was still wet with heavy dew. I could see clipped plants and grasses all along the hedgerow to the left of the gate. I looked closely at the plants; some were clipped, others were not. "The cow grazed here," I concluded.

Some of the unclipped plants were about three feet tall and had tassels, but most were about a foot tall. I searched my memory. "Sorghum," I remembered from my days on the Wabash. "Farmers grow sorghum for silage."

I looked into the distance. I could see a field on the other side of the pasture. Rows of sorghum gleamed in the late morning sunlight. I turned back to the sorghum by the gate and hedgerow. "This sorghum is wild; it was probably seeded from last year's crop in the next field over," I concluded.

"Wet sorghum, hole in the fence and bloated cow," I summarized. I knew the answer. "Time to return to Hannibal," I said to myself.

Hannibal was waiting. As I approached, I asked: "How is your investigation going?"

"All done," Hannibal responded: "Bloated cow, masticated, foamy greenery in the cow's mouth and an odor of bitter almonds." He paused and then added: "No damage to the car."

Hannibal continued: "The bitter almond odor is typical of hydrogen cyanide gas. I remember reading reports during the war. The French used it in 1916 on the western front." He grimaced a little and continued. "Although highly poisonous, hydrogen cyanide wasn't a practical weapon; it was lighter than air and dispersed quickly. The French changed to phosgene and later mustard gas."

Hannibal then looked at me and asked: "What did you find?"

I quickly explained my observations.

Hannibal nodded. "Sorghum, especially new growth and wet, is an excellent source of hydrogen cyanide." He smiled grimly and added: "Our lab in Chicago investigated a number of cattle poisonings in the Midwest. We wrote a report for the Illinois Department of Agriculture, advising farmers on proper techniques for growing and processing sorghum for silage."

"Umm," I mused. "Our findings are consistent. Further, the impact of the car's bumper with the cow produced only non-fatal injuries to the feet and legs."

Hannibal nodded and took out his pocket watch. He looked and then said: "I checked the time when we got out of the car." He smiled and added: "Our investigation took twenty minutes."

"A new record," I replied. "Our farmer and the gendarme should arrive any time now."

Hannibal walked over to John and I comforted Susan. We didn't have a long wait. An ancient black sedan appeared in the distance on the road, coming from the direction of Jumiéges. The farmer came out of his house and met the sedan. Soon the farmer and a uniformed gendarme arrived in the clattering car. Both got out and walked up to the dead cow.

The farmer chattered on and on in French, presumably about his dead cow. The gendarme nodded occasionally, glanced at Hannibal, then me and then at poor John Warmly. The gendarme had a worn, tired expression.

"Overworked and underpaid," I concluded as I watched. After about five minutes of long-winded, one-sided conversation between the farmer and the cop, the pair walked over to Hannibal and John. I walked around the car and stood next to Hannibal.

The gendarme glanced at John, then looked carefully at Hannibal. He touched his cap and said: "Pardon, Monsieur. Pourriez-vous vous identifier et me dire ce qui s'est passé?"

I caught the nature of the question: "Essentially, the man asked: "Who are you and what happened?"

Hannibal introduced the Warmly couple, me and himself. He then said: "Monsieur and Madame Warmly ne parlent pas français. Parlez vous anglais?"

"Yes, of course," replied the gendarme. "I am Gendarme Officier Pierre Macon. I fought side by side with the Americans during the war."

He looked closely at Hannibal, smiled and said: "You are American." There was no doubt in his statement.

The conversation continued in English. Only the farmer was left out; which seemed to satisfy everyone else, including Gendarme Officier Pierre Macon.

Hannibal turned to me and said: "Caroline, please tell Monsieur Macon what you observed."

I quickly explained my findings. Hannibal, Pierre and I then walked to the pasture gate. I explained and pointed as we walked. The farmer remained with the Warmlys, glaring at them and then looking at his dead cow.

The three of us returned to the cow. Hannibal slipped into his military briefing mode.

"Cows have chambered stomachs," he began. "They digest by fermenting grass and other plants. Unfortunately, the chambered stomach is also an excellent medium for the liberation of hydrocyanic acid."

He walked around the cow, observing carefully. He continued his lecture. "The acid was rapidly absorbed into the cow's blood. This prevented the blood from carrying oxygen."

He looked up at Pierre and then me and added: "The cow got plenty of hydrocyanic acid from the young, wet sorghum."

Hannibal pointed to the side of the cow and said: "The cow is also bloated. This was caused by an increase in the gas pressure within the cow's chambered stomach as the wet sorghum and other grasses fermented."

He then pointed to the cow's mouth. "Note the frothy foam. Gas was trapped in the stomach in the form of a foam. The swollen stomach put pressure on the cow's lungs, causing them to slowly collapse."

Hannibal waived his hand toward the erratic trail of cow's footprints, and said: The cyanide-poisoned and bloated cow staggered into and through the hedge and collapsed on the road. The cow died as a result of hydrocyanic acid poisoning and asphyxiation."

Hannibal looked over at John Warmly and continued. "The cow was in its final death throes when you came over the hill and bumped into the cow's legs and feet." He smiled and added: "You did not kill the farmer's cow."

Pierre bent over and looked closely at the cow's mouth. He sniffed. "Mon dieu!" He exclaimed. You are right. I smell the poison gas. I was there in 1916 when it was used."

Pierre then turned to the farmer and explained the situation in French. After a while, the farmer's face expressed sorrowful acknowledgement. "He understands," I concluded, with a smile of satisfaction.

The farmer looked at his dead cow for several moments. Tears formed in his eyes. He turned to the Warmlys and said: "Je comprends la situation. Je suis vraiment désolé pour mes actions. Vous n'avez pas tué ma vache."

The Warmlys looked at Hannibal and then Pierre. Their faces expressed the obvious question. Hannibal translated: "The farmer understands. He apologizes. You did not kill his cow."

"Oh, I am so sorry for his loss," replied John Warmly. "Please tell him." He nodded toward the farmer. Hannibal made the appropriate translation.

Pierre and the farmer had a long discussion in French. I followed enough of the conversation to know that Pierre wanted the farmer to help him clear the road of the dead cow. The farmer nodded. Pierre walked over to his police car and returned with a long rope.

Hannibal, Pierre and the farmer used the police car and rope to drag the deceased off the road.

Afterwards, goodbyes and thanks were said, and the Warmlys continued their journey. Hannibal and Pierre talked a while about common experiences during the war. Pierre then climbed in his ancient car and clattered back toward Jumiéges.

Hannibal turned to me, grinned and said: "Pierre said the cow's death will be ruled a suicide. Shall we continue our journey?"

"Good idea," I replied. "Case closed. Would you like to drive?"

# 15

## PRELUDE IN ROUEN

*Thursday evening, July 11, 1929*

We arrived last evening at the Grand Hôtel on the quai in Rouen. We had a nice dinner and a sound sleep. Our first day started well. As usual, Hannibal got up early. I heard him order coffee from room service on the phone in the parlor. I lounged in bed, listening to the sounds of Hannibal's activities and songbirds out our bedroom window. Finally, just after eight o'clock, I stretched, yawned and got up.

I was wearing my shear black Schiaparelli lounging pajamas. My hair was all tousled and down in my eyes. I was barefoot. I toddled over to our large window and looked out over the Seine. The view was spectacular. Sunlight bathed me in a warm golden glow. I stretched and yawned again.

I sensed Hannibal's presence. I turned. Hannibal was standing in the doorway between the parlor and the bedroom. He had two cups of steaming coffee. He smiled and said: "Ah, the cat in the window again." He paused, sipped from one of the cups and added: "You look lovely. Want some coffee?"

I padded over to Hannibal, kissed him lightly on the cheek and replied: "Yes, please." I stepped back, smiled and added: "You are a very nice man." I stepped forward and kissed him again, this time on the lips.

Hannibal chuckled a little and said: "Careful, you'll spill our coffee."

"Hummf," I responded. I then giggled a little. "Let's sit in the parlor and plan our day." I brushed the hair from my eyes, took Hannibal's arm, and we walked into the parlor. Soon we were comfortable on the sofa with coffee cups in our hands and a tourist map of Rouen laid out on the coffee table.

I studied the map between sips of coffee. After a few minutes, I said: "We can walk along the quai to the Rue Jeanne d'Arc, turn left and walk a block to the Rue aux Ours. If we take a right, we will be headed toward the Rue de la Champmeslé. After another left, we will come to the Rue du Petit Salut. We turn right, walk another block, cross the Rue Grand Pont, and we will be at the Place de la Cathédrale." I smiled triumphantly. "An easy walk, with lots of shops along the way."

Hannibal laughed. "Shopping in mind, I see," he responded. "How about breakfast first?"

I suddenly realized that I was ravenously hungry. I looked at the clock on a table over by our entryway. It read eight-thirty. I thought a moment and said: "OK, I'll be ready by nine-thirty. Let's order a couple of sweet rolls and orange juice from downstairs to take the edge off, then have a nice lunch at a brasserie near the cathedral." I then added: "I'm sure we can find one."

"Sounds good," replied Hannibal. "Are you sure you can be ready in an hour?"

"Yes, smarty," I responded. "You just take care of ordering our sweet rolls and orange juice." With that, I set my coffee cup down and scurried off to the bathroom. I heard Hannibal chuckle as I passed through the doorway.

I was primped and ready at precisely nine-thirty. I had a smug look on my face as I sauntered into the parlor and said: "Is breakfast ready?" Hannibal laughed and replied: "Of course." Sweet rolls, orange juice and coffee rested on a silver tray on the coffee table.

I wore a Chanel navy-blue full skirt with petticoats, a white silk blouse and matching navy-blue cardigan sweater. I tied a beautifully patterned white and blue silk scarf around my neck for accent. I had silk hose and sensible white walking shoes. Since we were in a strange town, I had left my jewelry tucked away in the hotel concierge safe. Hannibal wore grey trousers, a light blue open-collar shirt, a navy-blue cardigan and black shoes. Like our day in Honfleur, we were a perfect tourist couple.

Shortly after ten o'clock, we strolled out of the hotel on the quai. The day was gorgeous. We stopped and shopped in nearly every store between the hotel and the Place de la Cathédrale. In deference to our limited space in the Duesenberg, I only bought a few trinkets. Hannibal was very patient.

As we walked across the Rue Grand Pont, I could see the Cathédrale primatiale Notre-Dame-de-l'Assomption de Rouen in all its glory. "I can see why Monet created a series of paintings of this beautiful place," I said to Hannibal.

"Yes," Hannibal responded. "Quite a view."

We stood and stared for a good five minutes. Finally, I said: "Let's find a place for lunch." We both looked around.

After a minute or so, Hannibal pointed and said: "I see a small hotel and brasserie near the corner on the Place de la Cathédrale." He looked at me and asked: "Shall we give it a try?"

I looked where Hannibal had pointed. "Looks good," I replied. We walked the short distance to the hotel door and looked inside. The small lobby was decorated in a Renaissance theme, with paintings, displays of armor and weapons and even a few tapestries. I had never seen such a place. "Amazing," I said. "I would love to have lunch here and look at the displays."

"OK," replied Hannibal. "I would like it as well." He opened the door and we stepped inside.

A neatly dressed, middle-aged gentleman walked in from the brasserie door to the right of the lobby and said in perfect English: "Ah, welcome, Monsieur, Madame." His eyes twinkled and he added: "You are American, yes?"

I laughed and replied: "Yes we are, Monsieur. Is it that obvious?"

"We have many American visitors," replied the gentleman with a smile. "I am Bernard Paquet, and this is my hotel and brasserie." He paused and then added: "I overheard your conversation in English outside my door. Voulez-vous déjeuner?" He smiled broadly.

I understood that Monsieur Paquet was having a little fun with me. I liked him immediately.

I sniffed, tossed my head back and replied in my best French: "Oui, Monsieur Paquet. Nous aimerions déjeuner, s'il vous plaît." I grinned broadly and added: "I have just about exhausted my vocabulary in French, Monsieur Paquet." I laughed. Paquet and Hannibal both joined in.

"Well done, my lady," replied Paquet. "Please call me Bernard."

"And I am Caroline, and my escort is Hannibal, my husband," I responded. Hannibal smiled and offered his hand to Bernard. He then said: "You have made friends, Bernard. We would love lunch." He added: "Surprise us!"

Bernard laughed. "I will. My wife is an excellent cook."

With that, the three of us walked through the lobby and over toward the interior brasserie door. As we passed a small concierge alcove, I noticed a very attractive young lady sitting at a desk. She had been crying, and she had a very sad expression.

I hesitated a moment as Bernard and Hannibal walked ahead toward the door. I then told myself: "It's none of your business, Caroline." I turned and hurried to catch up.

Still, I couldn't help myself. As Bernard, Hannibal and I arrived at the interior door to the brasserie, I looked at Bernard and said: "The young lady at the concierge desk seemed to be in tears. Is something wrong?"

"Funny that you should ask," replied Bernard. "Her name is Michelle Potéreau. She is new to Rouen. She said she came from Paris. I gave her a job a couple of months ago."

He paused a moment and then continued: "She is a good worker, but she has been very sad lately." He paused again and then added: "I think she has problems with her male friend." Bernard didn't seem to want to elaborate.

"Oh," I replied. "Well, I hope things work out for her." With that, we three entered the brasserie.

I saw a dozen patrons sitting at various tables. Some appeared to be tourists, but most were local folks. Several smiled as we entered. Bernard found us a table next to the window, where we had a full view of the cathedral. "How very nice!" I thought to myself. I put the image of the crying girl out of my thoughts.

Lunch was soon served. Bernard said it was called 'garbure,' which was a lightly seasoned stew made of ham, cabbage and other vegetables. He served it steaming hot, with baguettes and sweet cream butter on the side. He brought us two glasses of a classic Bordeaux red table wine to drink.

For dessert, we had a golden-brown pastis landais. Bernard explained that it was made with a combination of eggs, butter, flour, yeast and powdered sugar. I could tell it was flavored with vanilla and rum. Bernard brought us a hot green tea to sip with the pastry.

What a delicious lunch! As we finished our last cup of tea, Hannibal paid our bill, and I asked Bernard if we could view his displays of antiques.

"Of course!" said Bernard. "I am very proud of them. Renaissance, you know."

Hannibal and I followed Bernard into the lobby. He explained the details of the suit of armor in the main lobby and the many weapons hanging on the walls. I recognized various swords, halberds, spears, crossbows and so on. Bernard had names and histories for all of them.

We even got a tour of one of the side hallways. I moved a little ahead, while Bernard and Hannibal discussed a particular display.

On the left wall near the end of the hallway, I could see a display of a dozen or so daggers and short swords arranged in a pattern. I noticed that one of the spaces had little hooks in the wall, but no weapon. I looked closely. Bernard saw me staring at the empty spot on the wall and walked over. I pointed to the empty space.

Bernard looked, and his face expressed consternation. "One of my stilettos is missing!" He looked all around on the floor, behind a nearby bureau and so on. He found nothing. "It was Fifteenth Century Italian, with a blade about twenty-five centimeters long, and it had a brass hilt," Bernard continued. "I can't imagine what happened. I will check with my cleaning staff!"

Hannibal and I could tell the tour was over. We expressed our concern, thanked him profusely for the excellent lunch and the most interesting tour.

"Yes, yes," replied Bernard. He smiled wanly. "Please come again, you are always welcome." Hannibal and I discretely took our leave. Bernard bustled off toward the kitchen.

As Hannibal and I stepped outside, I looked at the cathedral. What a magnificent place! "Can we go inside?" I asked.

"I believe so," replied Hannibal. "Let's check." We walked across the street and onto the path toward the main entrance.

As I looked up at the three soaring spires, Hannibal said: "The iron and bronze-plated Lanterne tower is over one-hundred fifty meters tall." He paused and smiled as I stared. "Look at the sculptures above the main door. They symbolize the family tree of Jesus." He pointed to the left and continued: "The sculptures above the Portaile Saint Jean portray the martyrdom of Saint John." He then pointed to the right and said: "On the right above the Portaile Saint Etienne, you can see sculptures of the stoning of Saint Stephen, the first Christian martyr."

"Oh, my," I replied softly. I was overwhelmed by the intricate beauty of the entire façade. My eyes scanned the whole scene and then stopped at the huge stained-glass window above the main portal. I pointed.

Hannibal smiled and said: "Wait until you get inside. You can look back and up at the window from the main nave." He paused. I could tell he was reviewing old memories. He then said: "You will see the window in all its glory."

Hannibal lifted the latch and opened the massive main door. It swung open easily and silently. We stepped inside. The first thing I noticed was the cool, dimly lit immensity of the place.

The main nave seemed to stretch on forever. Light filtered through many stained-glass windows all around. I could see the alter and choir stalls in the distance. I looked behind and up. Hannibal was right, the huge round window above the main portal was magnificent. I felt very small.

We were about to walk into the main nave when we saw a young man, dressed in a black cassock with a white clerical collar, standing at the end of the aisle to the left. "A priest," I concluded. "I hope we haven't done anything wrong."

The priest approached silently; his hands were folded in front. He had a worried, somber expression. Hannibal and I waited respectfully.

"Good morning, Father," said Hannibal as the priest approached. I looked at Hannibal. I was slightly surprised that Hannibal used English.

"Ah, you are American," replied the priest. Hannibal and I both nodded. "So am I," added the priest. He smiled slightly. I am Father Cyril."

"How did Hannibal know?" I thought to myself. "He has a knack for reading people." My thoughts continued: "It must be the bearing and the way Americans walk." I didn't have time to follow up on my speculations; the priest was speaking softly and earnestly.

"The cathedral is closed, unfortunately." He turned and nodded toward three people seated in chairs some distance away in the main nave. "There was a serious incident yesterday, and the Gendarmerie have temporarily closed down the cathedral until they complete their investigation."

I looked carefully at the three seated persons. One was a uniformed gendarme. Another was a middle-aged woman. She was dressed in black and wore a veil. She was crying softly. The third was an older man, well-dressed in business attire. His face had an aloof expression.

"Of course, Father," I heard Hannibal say. "We will leave immediately."

"Thank you," replied Father Cyril. "I'm sure we will re-open in a day or so. You are welcome to call me and check." He reached in his cassock pocket, took out a card and added: "The phone number of my diocese office is on the card." He smiled warmly and said: "It's nice to meet fellow Americans."

Hannibal smiled in return and said: "I am Hannibal Jones." He turned to me and added: "My wife Caroline."

"Pleased to meet you, Father," I responded. I offered my hand.

Father Cyril turned to me, took my hand gently and said: "My pleasure, Mrs. Jones."

I returned his steady gaze. "Seems like a nice man; however, he was reticent about the closure of the cathedral," I thought to myself.

Father Cyril turned back to Hannibal, shook hands, and nodded toward the door. We took the hint and left quietly. As we departed, I looked back at the three people sitting in the main nave. The gendarme was staring in our direction. "Curious," I muttered.

I glanced at Hannibal. I could tell that he had also noticed the trio in the nave.

After leaving the cathedral, Hannibal said: "Shall we take a leisurely stroll back toward the hotel?" He grinned and added: "I'm sure you can find more shops of interest."

"OK, smarty," I responded.

We had an impromptu dinner in another brasserie on the quai near the hotel at about six o'clock. By seven-thirty, we were back in our room. "What an interesting day," I mused as I prepared to change into my lounging clothes. Hannibal sat in the parlor, reading a French newspaper.

Before I could go into the bathroom and change, I heard a knock. Hannibal got up and walked to the entryway. I peered around the corner from the bedroom. Hannibal opened the door. The uniformed gendarme that we saw in the cathedral stood in the doorway. Behind him stood another man, dressed in business attire.

"Puis-je vous aider, Monsieur?" I heard Hannibal say.

The uniformed man responded: "Bonsoir, Monsieur. Êtes-vous le Major Hannibal Jones?" He peered past Hannibal and saw me. He then asked: "Et Madame Caroline Jones?"

"Oui," replied Hannibal.

The man in the business suit stepped forward and said, in perfect English: "Ah, Monsieur and Madame Jones. I am Inspecteur Émilien Duchamps." He nodded toward the uniformed gendarme. This is Gendarme Rémi Moreau. Yes, we would very much appreciate your help."

He paused and then added: "Capitaine Inspecteur Soucet called and told me you would be in Rouen, and Father Cyril said you visited the cathedral today." He paused again, gazed steadily at me and continued: "We have a most unfortunate murder on our hands."

# 16

## THE PROBLEM WITH CONFESSIONS

*Friday Morning, July 12, 1929*

Last evening, Inspecteur Duchamps and Gendarme Officier Moreau visited Hannibal and me at our hotel room for over an hour. They told us about the murder in the Rouen Cathedral. It happened on Wednesday, July 10, the day we arrived in town.

According to Duchamps, Father Cyril found the body. He discovered Mathis Sartré, a wealthy businessman, face down, lying in a pool of blood, on the floor in the north transept of the cathedral, near the Portaile des Libraires.

"Sartré had been stabbed from the front, through the lungs and probably through the heart," said Duchamps. He paused and added: "The autopsy will tell us more."

"The victim saw his attacker," I surmised to myself. "Any defensive wounds?" I asked.

"None," replied Duchamps. "He had just one stab wound, in front, under his breastbone. There was bloody froth at the wound site and in the victim's mouth."

My thoughts raced. "The victim was surprised, so he most likely knew the person who killed him," I concluded. I returned my attention to Duchamps.

"Father Cyril found the body at about ten o'clock in the morning, just after attending confession for a parishioner," Duchamp was saying. I focused on Duchamps comments as he continued: "Father

Cyril immediately reported his findings to the Gendarmerie and to Archbishop André du Bois de la Villerable."

After a moment, Duchamps said: "I am the chief investigator on this case." He smiled and then added: "Capitaine Inspecteur Soucet told me about your exploits on the *Isle de France* and in Le Havre."

He then explained: "In addition to a phone call to me with your itinerary between Le Havre and Paris, Inspecteur Soucet sent a letter to Sections de recherche de la Gendarmerie Nationale. You are well-known to the Gendarmerie throughout France."

"Good heavens!" I exclaimed. I wasn't quite sure what to think concerning our apparent notoriety. I got up from my seat and walked over to our window. I looked out at the golden sun low in the sky. I turned around and faced Duchamps and Moreau. Both were sitting in chairs across from Hannibal, who remained on the sofa.

My mind returned to the murder. "Hannibal and I met Father Cyril yesterday at the cathedral," I said. He told us there was an incident." I turned to Moreau. "I also saw you just before we left the cathedral."

Moreau replied: "Oui madame; Je me rappelle." He nodded affirmatively.

"Understands some English, but he's not fluent," I surmised to myself. "Like me with French." I smiled at Moreau.

Hannibal looked at Moreau and asked: "Monsieur Moreau, qui étaient les deux personnes avec vous à la cathédrale hier?"

I understood Hannibal's question; I was thinking the same. Who were the two people with Moreau in the nave of the cathedral?

Moreau turned to Duchamps with a questioning look.

Duchamps nodded and said: "The lady was Madame Abrialé Sartré, the wife of Monsieur Mathis Sartré, our victim. The gentleman was Monsieur Antoine Bonfils, his business partner." Duchamps paused and then added: "Neither could name witnesses to confirm their whereabouts on the morning of July 10."

"Motive?" Hannibal asked.

Duchamps nodded and replied: "Monsieur Sartré had a large life insurance policy, and his wife is the sole beneficiary. Also, Monsieur Bonfils will acquire Sartré's share of their very lucrative textile manufacturing business."

"Have you taken fingerprints?" I asked.

"Yes," responded Duchamps. "Since they had no witnesses to confirm their whereabouts on Wednesday morning, we took photos and fingerprints." He paused a moment and then added: "However, we have nothing from the crime scene for comparison."

"Witnesses to the murder?" I asked.

"None that we know about," responded Duchamps. Duchamps paused for quite a while. Finally, he said: "Something is going on with Father Cyril, but I cannot get him to explain. Since he was at the crime scene, we also took his photo and fingerprints."

"Very thorough," I responded with a smile.

Duchamps smiled in return and replied: "We try."

"Murder weapon?" Hannibal asked.

"None has been found," replied Duchamps. "From the appearance of the wound, we know it was a knife or similar weapon."

"Has the crime scene been cleaned up?" I asked.

"Yes," responded Duchamps. "The body was removed and the blood cleaned off the floor." He looked at me carefully and continued: "I know what you are thinking. However, the Archbishop insisted that the cathedral be re-opened as soon as possible." He shook his head sadly and added: "We had no choice."

Hannibal and I looked at each other. Hannibal turned to Duchamps and asked: "How can we help?"

Duchamps replied: "Investigate. Your reputations for detailed work and unique insights are well known."

Duchamps' eyes twinkled. He looked intently at me and said: "Madame Jones, you are known as 'the cat in the window.' After seeing you framed in the light from the window behind you, I agree with that assessment. You also have a reputation as a lovely and very intelligent lady."

He turned to Hannibal and said: "You, Monsieur Major Jones, are well-known in France for you exploits during the war, as an accomplished scholar and also as a very successful businessman."

"Well!" I thought to myself. "Flattery works. How can we refuse?" I looked at Hannibal again. He grinned.

Duchamps looked first at me and then Hannibal. He said: "Of course, you will be well paid."

"Precisely the right comment," I thought to myself. "You have closed the deal." I looked at Duchamps and smiled sweetly.

Hannibal looked at me and suppressed a chuckle. He then turned to Duchamps and said: "We will take the case."

Duchamps gave a big sigh. "Thank you, Monsieur and Madame," he said. "I will send you the appropriate files, including the autopsy report, photos and fingerprints, first thing tomorrow." He looked at Hannibal and added: "I will leave the sealed files at the front desk."

Duchamps reached into his jacket pocket and took out a pink card. I recognized the form; it was a French driver's license. He handed the card to me and said: "You may find the photo on Monsieur Sartré's driver's license of interest."

I looked at Sartré's license. Like mine, it read: 'République Française, Permis De Conduire Les Automobiles.' The number in the top left corner was 54022. Also, like mine, the license had a black and white photo of the driver in the lower left corner. Various signatures, including Sartré's, filled the lower right, next to the photo.

Monsieur Sartré's image stared at me from the license. I saw a handsome, clean-shaven, middle-aged gentleman with regular features. His hair was parted in the middle. I looked up at Duchamps and asked: "Good photo: may we keep the license for use during our investigation?"

"Yes, of course," replied Duchamps. "I brought it for that purpose."

"Thank you, Inspecteur," replied Hannibal. He rose from his seat. Duchamps and Moreau did the same.

After the usual pleasantries, Duchamps and Moreau departed. Hannibal returned from the entryway, and we both sat on the couch. For a few minutes, we remained immersed in our own thoughts.

Finally, Hannibal said: "We have two people with motive, a dead body and a suspicious priest. We need an autopsy report that accurately describes the wound. We also need a murder weapon."

"I think we should spread our net a little wider," I mused. "Remember the missing Renaissance stiletto in the brasserie across the street from the cathedral? That might not be a coincidence."

"Agree," replied Hannibal. "In addition to Father Cyril, Madame Sartré and Monsieur Bonfils, we should visit our friend Bernard at the brasserie."

I nodded, thought a moment and said: "We should also visit the sanitized crime scene. Who knows what might turn up?"

"Yes," replied Hannibal. "Let's go to the cathedral first, talk to Father Cyril and visit the crime scene." He thought a moment and added: "Afterwards, we can talk to Bernard."

"Duchamps said we will have the police files tomorrow," I responded. "I'm sure the reports are in French; you will have to interpret for me."

Hannibal nodded and replied. "We can read tomorrow night. The day will be busy." He thought a moment and then added: "I still have Father Cyril's phone number; I will give him a call tonight."

Soon the call was made, and we had an appointment at nine in the morning. I looked at the clock on the table in the entryway. "Ten o'clock," I said. "Let's get some sleep and get up early. We'll have to hurry if we want breakfast before our meeting at the cathedral."

## Saturday Evening, July 13

The hotel front desk clerk called just after seven o'clock this morning. Duchamps' files had been delivered. Hannibal went downstairs and picked them up while I finished getting ready. When Hannibal returned, we sorted out the photos of Madame Sartré and Monsieur Bonfils. I put them in my purse, along with Monsieur Sartré's driver's license and some tools of the detective trade. We left the rest of the files in our room for reading tonight.

Hannibal and I dressed appropriately for a visit to the cathedral. I wore a conservative black dress and black shoes. I also wore a matching hat with a veil. I carried my large, very full black purse. Hannibal wore a conservative charcoal-grey business suit.

After a quick breakfast at our hotel, we made it to the cathedral just before nine o'clock. Father Cyril met us inside the main door. After the usual pleasantries, Hannibal explained that we were working with Inspecteur Duchamps with regard to the murder of Monsieur Sartré. I watched his expression carefully.

Father Cyril gave a sigh and said: "I understand. I suppose you would like to visit the crime scene." He paused and then added: "The cathedral will re-open today at noon."

"Yes," I said. "But before we do, can you tell us how you came to discover the body?"

Father Cyril looked at me closely for a moment, then responded: "I was in the confessional near the choir stalls with a parishioner." He motioned with his hand toward the choir stalls in the distance. I could see a confessional along the wall near the stalls.

Father Cyril continued: "When we finished, I left the confessional and walked past the ambulatory toward the north side aisle. As I passed through the north transept, I saw the body lying on the floor near the Portaile des Libraires." He gave a sigh and continued: "I hurried over and saw that it was Monsieur Sartré, a prominent parishioner."

"What time was this?" Hannibal asked.

Father Cyril replied: "I checked my watch; I thought the time would be important. It was ten o'clock."

"What happened next?" Hannibal asked.

"Well," replied Father Cyril, "I left the cathedral through the Portaile des Libraires and went immediately to my office in the diocese building next door. I called the gendarme. I then sent a secretary to the palace next to the diocese to notify the Archbishop."

I looked intently at Father Cyril and asked: "Did you see anyone else as you discovered the body?"

Father Cyril blinked a couple of times before he replied. "I did not see anyone as I walked from the confessional through the north transept toward the Portaile des Libraires."

"Who was with you in the confessional?" I asked pointedly.

Father Cyril blinked again. He then replied: "I cannot tell you." He paused, glanced at Hannibal and returned his gaze to me. "The seal of the confessional is inviolable; it is absolutely forbidden for a priest to betray in any way a penitent in words or in any manner and for any reason."

I was not ready to back off. I then asked: "Do you know if the person with you in the confessional was at or near the crime scene before confession?"

Father Cyril blinked again. "Again, the seal of the confessional is sacrosanct," he replied.

I looked at Hannibal. No words were spoken, but he understood what I wanted to do.

"Do you recall if Monsieur and Madame Sartré visited the cathedral on July 10?" Hannibal asked.

Father Cyril reached into his cassock pocket and took out a small appointment book. He read for a moment.

Finally, he looked up and said: "There was a ten o'clock meeting scheduled on July 10 for a charity working group in the conference room in the diocese building. Monsieur and Madame Sartré are members of the steering committee." He looked down at the book again. "However, according to the secretary, neither showed up for the meeting."

"Did you attend the working group meeting?" I asked.

"No," responded Father Cyril. "I was in the confessional. A parishioner came in that morning."

"Do you recall the time?" I asked.

"I left my office just before nine o'clock," replied Father Cyril. "I went straight to the confessional and entered my side shortly thereafter."

"Did you see anyone in the main cathedral when you entered?" I asked.

"Just the cleaning staff," responded Father Cyril. "They were leaving through the Portaile des Libraires. They clean on Wednesday, and they always finish about nine."

"Do you know if they cleaned the confessional?" Hannibal asked.

"I think so," replied Father Cyril. "They always sanitize it completely every Wednesday."

"Father," said Hannibal softly, "I have many questions about what you saw concerning Monsieur Sartré's body. Such questions would best be addressed in your office rather than in this holy place."

"I understand," replied Father Cyril. He looked at Hannibal's face and then returned his gaze to me. His eyes squinted a little. "After we visit the crime scene, we can leave through the Portaile des Libraires. It's a short walk to my office." He motioned with his hand toward the end of the north aisle.

I returned Father Cyril's gaze with a steady look of my own. I then said: "With your permission, I will remain in the cathedral and view the crime scene in detail."

"As you wish," replied Father Cyril. "Monsieur Jones and I can leave you there and continue to my office through the nearby portaile." He then turned and led the way from the main entryway along the north aisle.

Soon we passed into the north transept. I glanced around. I could see the ornate stairs on either side of the portaile.

Father Cyril said: "I found Monsieur Sartré's body here." He pointed to the stone floor just ahead, near the stairs on the left of the portaile. He gave a brief description of the position of the body. There was really not much to see except a clean stone floor.

Hannibal and Father Cyril soon departed through the portaile. The atmosphere of the crime scene was cool and very quiet. Light came through stained glass windows on both sides of the transept. I was completely alone. "I've never been in a place like this before," I thought to myself.

I stood on the spot where Father Cyril said he found the body. I made a complete turn all around. I could see another portaile on the other side of the main nave. As I turned back and faced the Portaile des Libraires, I saw a small chapel to my right. An alter rested under the stained-glass window at the far end of the chapel.

I turned a little more. A wall divided the chapel from the continuance of the north side aisle. I could see the choir stalls in the center of the main nave. An ornate wooden confessional rested against the wall near the choir stalls.

I walked slowly toward the confessional. I looked carefully at every nook and cranny along the way. "Nothing," I muttered.

I reached the confessional and looked around. "No one here," I concluded. I opened the penitent's door and looked inside. A velvet-covered kneeling rail with brass fittings was fixed slightly above the floor on the right. A little shelf rested above the rail for the penitent to rest his or her hands in a prayerful fashion. A lattice mesh separated the penitent side from the side for the priest. I looked all around inside.

The light streaming from the stained-glass window across the main nave brightened a little. "The sun must have passed from behind a cloud," I thought to myself.

After a few moments, I saw a tiny gleam from something under the kneeling rail. I stepped back, kneeled on the floor just outside the booth and looked under the rail. I saw a brass handle.

I opened my purse. Inside, I had surgical gloves, a pocket knife, a small can of black dusting powder, a roll of cellophane tape and a few sheets of white paper. I also had a neatly folded linen table napkin that I had swiped from the hotel dining room at breakfast.

I finished within a few minutes and gathered my tools of the trade. My 'evidence' was wrapped carefully in the linen napkin. I then stood up and looked around. "Alone: time to join Hannibal and Father Cyril," I said softly to myself.

# 17

## SUSPECTS ALL IN A ROW

*Saturday Evening, July 13 1929, Continuation*

After I finished at the confessional, I located Father Cyril's diocese office without much trouble.

Both he and Hannibal looked up when I quietly walked into the room. Father Cyril stood up from his seat behind his desk and motioned me to a chair next to Hannibal. I walked over to the chair, and Hannibal assisted me as I sat down. After a moment, the social pleasantries ended.

I looked around. The office was quite plush. It had oak paneling, a matching desk, many filled bookcases, tall windows and a large oak table with a dozen chairs. Many Christian symbols decorated the room. "Father Cyril hosts meetings here," I thought to myself.

I returned my attention to Father Cyril, who had been speaking. "Monsieur and Madame Sartré were prominent parishioners," he was saying. "They contributed to many local charities."

"And Monsieur Bonfils?" Hannibal asked.

"The same," replied Father Cyril.

"Can you think of anyone who had a grievance with Monsieur Sartré?" I asked. I watched Father Cyril's expression intently.

Father Cyril blinked a couple of times. "You will have to ask others about Monsieur Sartré's non-church activities." He smiled wanly. "His church work, as well as the church work of his wife and business partner, are matters of public record."

"I understand," I responded with a smile. I thought to myself: "It's that sanctity of the confessional thing again." However, my thoughts followed the logic of Father Cyril's body language. "Never mind, the body language has given enough hints." My eyes retained their steady gaze as I watched Father Cyril's face. He blinked again, twice.

Hannibal looked at me and I nodded. Hannibal turned to Father Cyril and said: "I believe we are finished for now. Caroline and I will be busy today, but we hope you will host a meeting on Monday, here in your office." May we invite others who will shed light on this murder in the cathedral?"

Father Cyril raised his eyebrows a little and replied: "Of course. I believe I can speak for the Archbishop. He wants this terrible event closed as soon as possible." He paused a moment and then asked: "Will Inspecteur Duchamps attend?"

"Yes," responded Hannibal. "Others who are directly involved with the case will also attend. I will call you with a list of names. We can also set a time."

Father Cyril nodded and then rose from his seat. After the usual pleasantries, he escorted us to the diocese building door. Hannibal and I continued on our own around the side of the cathedral towards Bernard's brasserie and hotel. As we walked, I filled him in on my findings in the confessional.

"Very good," said Hannibal when I finished. "We have only one missing piece."

"Yes," I replied. "I think our friend Bernard will help." I thought a moment and then added: "He might also clarify motives; our priest could only give unintended hints."

Hannibal smiled and nodded.

Bernard Paquet greeted us as soon as we stepped into the lobby of his hotel.

"Welcome," said Bernard. "Lunch will be available at eleven, and you are early." His face had a puzzled look.

"Perhaps we will have lunch another day," said Hannibal. "In addition to being tourists, we are private detectives. We are helping the Gendarmerie investigate the murder of Monsieur Mathis Sartré."

Bernard digested this revelation. Hannibal continued: "The murder happened in the cathedral on Wednesday, July 10th. Your missing stiletto may have been the murder weapon."

I then took the photos of Madame Sartré and Monsieur Bonfils and Monsieur Sartré's driver's license out of my purse. I identified the names and showed the photos to Bernard.

"Oh, my heaven," responded Bernard. "Madame Sartré was in my hotel last Tuesday, two days before you came in for lunch." He paused as he searched his memory. "There was a confrontation between Madame Sartré and Michelle, my concierge."

He looked again at Sartré's driver's license and said: "I have seen Monsieur Sartré on several occasions. He always spoke with Michelle, not me." He paused and added: "He never ate in my brasserie."

He looked over at the photo of Bonfils and said: "I have never met the other gentleman. You said his name was Bonfils?"

"Yes," replied Hannibal. "Are you sure?"

"Yes, yes," replied Bernard. He then looked at me and asked: "Are you sure my missing stiletto was the murder weapon?"

"Possibly," I responded. "Do you have a private place where we can discuss it?"

"Yes, of course," replied Bernard. "Come into my office." He stepped back and motioned us inside. He then led the way to a small office near the concierge alcove. I looked for Michelle Potéreau as we passed her desk; she was not there.

Bernard's office had a small desk and several chairs. Soon we were all comfortably seated.

I opened my purse and took out the stiletto, still wrapped in the linen napkin, and laid it on the desk.

Bernard's concentration was intense as I unfolded the napkin. His eyes widened. "Oh, my heaven!" He exclaimed again. "It's my missing stiletto!"

Bernard had many questions. Soon we were deep in discussion about where the weapon was found and so on.

Finally, I said: "We would like to lift fingerprints from several locations in your hotel." I paused while Bernard shifted his stare from the stiletto to my face. "Would you mind?"

"Please do what you think is necessary," replied Bernard. "Oh, my heaven!" He exclaimed again.

Hannibal and I divided up the work. I dusted and took fingerprints from the concierge desk, including drawer handles, items in the drawers, the desk surface, etc. Hannibal dusted and lifted fingerprints from the walls and hooks that held the stiletto. Bernard followed us and watched our efforts with intense interest.

We also took Bernard's fingerprints, just to be thorough. As expected, Bernard was very cooperative.

We finished our work in less than half an hour. We planned to do comparisons when we returned to our hotel room. The three of us returned to Bernard's office.

After we were all seated, Hannibal and I asked many questions about Madame Sartré's visit on July 9th, the day before the murder. Bernard answered them all without hesitation.

In response to our questions, Bernard said: "I caught a few words between Madame Sartré and Michelle as I sat in this office." He nodded toward the concierge desk just outside. "Both were standing near Michelle's desk."

Hannibal and I waited for Bernard to continue.

After a few moments, he said: "Apparently, something had been going on between Michelle and Monsieur Sartré." Bernard's voice dropped to a whisper as he said: "Madame Sartré said: 'Stay away from my husband!' several times."

Bernard leaned forward in his chair and continued: "After a few minutes of heated accusations, Madame Sartré stormed out of the concierge alcove. I stepped out of my office. Michelle was in tears."

He paused and then added: "As I recall, Madame Sartré went down the hallway. I turned to Michelle and asked her what was wrong. She wouldn't say, she just cried. About a minute later, I heard my front door slam. I think it was Madame Sartré."

Our discussion lasted for another half hour or so, but there were no other revelations. Hannibal and I thanked Bernard for his forthright help. "We will let you know how our investigation turns out," Hannibal said, as he and I rose from our chairs.

"Please do," replied Bernard. "Oh, my heaven," he said softly as leaned back in his chair and closed his eyes. Hannibal and I quietly took our leave.

Hannibal and I walked from Bernard's place back toward the hotel. "Let's order room service when we get back to our room," I said. "We have a lot of work to do."

"Good idea," replied Hannibal. "I will call Father Cyril and Inspecteur Duchamps and set up a meeting for nine on Monday morning." He looked closely at me and asked: "Do you think we can be ready?"

I thought a few moments. "Police reports, autopsy fingerprint comparisons, timelines and our report," I mused. I looked up at Hannibal and said: "Yes, I think so."

We were quiet most of the way back to the hotel. The sun disappeared behind gray clouds, and rain started pattering on the sidewalk as we reached the hotel entrance. "A fitting ending to our day," I thought to myself as we entered the lobby.

## Sunday afternoon, July 14

Dawn seemed to arrive just after I went to bed last night. I rolled out at just before eight o'clock this morning. I sat on the side of the bed and rubbed the sleep from my eyes.

Last night, Hannibal and I read and analyzed the police and autopsy reports until the wee hours of the morning. "Getting awake is going to take a while," I mumbled.

I peered around the corner into the parlor and focused my eyes. Hannibal was already at our table, hard at work. My thoughts continued: "How does he do it?" I rubbed my eyes again, got up and toddled into the bathroom.

After a shower and attention to my hair, I dressed in my navy-blue slacks that accented my slim figure. The lower legs of the slacks billowed out in the latest style. I also wore a white silk blouse and my yellow silk scarf around my neck. Since we planned to work in the room most of the day, I decided to remain barefoot.

"I need my trunks with my full wardrobe," I muttered to myself. "It's getting harder to mix and match while we are on the road." I thought a little more and decided that I would treat myself to a shopping excursion as soon as we reached Paris.

The thought of shopping made me feel better. I padded barefoot out of the bathroom and into the parlor. I looked at Hannibal. He was wearing his tan trousers, a light blue open-collar shirt, a navy-blue sweater vest, and matching brown shoes.

"He needs to go shopping too," I thought to myself. "Oh well, work first," I concluded. I smiled at Hannibal and said: "Bonjour, Monsieur. How are you this fine morning?"

Hannibal looked up, grinned and responded: "Are you ready for coffee and breakfast?" My tummy growled in response. So, our day began.

After a room service breakfast and my third cup of coffee, I looked at the files neatly arranged on our work table. Hannibal had laid out materials for our three suspects, all in a row.

"All three had opportunity, and two have a motive," I said. "We have a murder weapon and fingerprints. Can we lay out a timeline?"

"I think so," replied Hannibal. "The autopsy report places the time of death between nine and nine-thirty. Father Cyril discovered the body at ten o'clock. Father Cyril saw one, but we know that two parishioners visited the confessional after nine and prior to ten o'clock."

"We also know that the cleaning staff left at about nine, and according to Father Cyril, they always clean the confessional," I responded.

"One of the two parishioners who visited the confessional is the murderer," Hannibal concluded.

"Let's look at fingerprints again," I said. "I think we will have our answer."

Hannibal and I spent the rest of the afternoon writing our report for Inspecteur Duchamps. We finished at about four. Hannibal called the concierge and we made early dinner reservations. Tomorrow will be a most interesting day!

## Monday evening, July 15, 1929

Hannibal and I arrived at Father Cyril's office this morning at about eight-forty-five. As we had arranged with Inspecteur Duchamps and Father Cyril, all of our participants arrived around nine. Duchamps told us later that he and Moreau had found Michelle Potéreau at her apartment and escorted her to the meeting. Father Cyril had made sure Madame Sartré and Monsieur Bonfils attended. Hannibal and I had no problem convincing our friend Bernard Paquet to show up.

As the last of the participants filed into the office and seated themselves around the table, Hannibal looked at his watch. "Nine-fifteen," he said. "Time to start." He looked over at me and nodded.

He then rose from his seat and said: "Madame Jones will present our findings, and I will interpret for those who do not speak English."

I rose from my seat and began. "At the request of Inspecteur Duchamps, Major Jones and I have investigated the murder of Monsieur Mathis Sartré in the cathedral between nine and nine-thirty on Wednesday, July 10th. We have motive, method, opportunity and convincing evidence." I paused for effect and then added: "We believe we have identified the murderer."

Hannibal interpreted my statement into French. I looked around the room at every face. Our two suspects squirmed a little. Father Cyril took a deep breath, let out a sigh and leaned back in his chair. The others all paid rapt attention.

I continued: "Mademoiselle Potéreau arrived at the cathedral shortly after nine o'clock on Wednesday morning. She went to the confessional. Father Cyril was already inside. She made her confession." I paused and then added: "I found Mademoiselle Potéreau's fingerprints on the shelf."

I looked intently at Michelle Potéreau as Hannibal spoke in French. She put her hands to her face and looked over at Father Cyril, who remained impassive.

I then glanced at Madame Sartré. She gave out a sigh and looked at Michelle with a withering stare and a grim smile.

"Monsieur and Madame Sartré also arrived after nine and before ten. They were scheduled to attend a meeting in the diocese conference room at ten o'clock." I paused as Hannibal interpreted and then continued: "For some reason, they passed through the cathedral on their way to the diocese building just behind the cathedral. However, they never arrived at the meeting."

I watched Madame Sartré as Hannibal interpreted. She took a sharp breath and her expression changed to an uncertain look. "Time to shift to another topic," I thought to myself.

I then continued: "On July 9, Monsieur Bernard Paquet witnessed a confrontation between Madame Sartré and Mademoiselle Potéreau in his hotel across the street from the cathedral." I glanced at Bernard, who nodded.

Hannibal interpreted. Madame Sartré's eyes widened. Michelle Potéreau glanced first at me, then Sartré and then back to me. She swallowed convulsively.

"On her way out of the hotel," I continued, "Madame Sartré took a stiletto off the wall in the hallway. Although there were no witnesses to this event, Major Jones found her fingerprints on the wall and on the hooks that held the stiletto."

Madame Sartré's expression changed to apprehension as Hannibal spoke. I then shifted my presentation again. I wanted Sartré to stew a little.

"On July 10, Father Cyril witnessed the cleaning staff leave the cathedral shortly after nine in the morning. He also stated that they always cleaned and sanitized the confessional." I paused as I watched Father Cyril nod affirmatively.

"I know Madame Sartré was in the cathedral after nine and before ten on July 10 because I found her fingerprints on the brass fittings of the kneeling rail in the confessional. I also found a stiletto under the kneeling rail. It had dried blood on the blade. The grip of the hilt of the stiletto had no fingerprints. However, I found a thumb print on the underside of the hilt guard." I paused, stared at Madame Sartré and then added: "The thumbprint was yours, Madame Sartré."

I watched Madame Sartré's expression change to fear as Hannibal interpreted. I then continued: "Madame Sartré, you found out that your husband was having an affair with Mademoiselle Potéreau sometime before July 9. You confronted her in Monsieur Paquet's hotel on the 9th and stole a stiletto from the hotel on your way out."

Hannibal interpreted. I glanced at Michelle Potéreau. She was staring at Madame Sartré.

I continued: "On the tenth, you must have seen Mademoiselle Potéreau enter the cathedral as you and your husband were on your way to the meeting in the diocese building. You convinced your husband to walk through the cathedral on your way to the meeting, probably with the intent of confronting both your husband and Mademoiselle Potéreau."

I paused and then added: "Once inside, you must have seen Mademoiselle Potéreau enter the confessional." I watched Madame Sartré's face as Hannibal interpreted. She looked wildly around at the others at the table. All were staring at her.

I then continued: "You saw your opportunity. You murdered your husband in the north transept. You then hid nearby as first Mademoiselle Potéreau and then Father Cyril left the confessional. Mademoiselle Potéreau must have left the cathedral through the main nave to the front door or through the portaile on the other side of the main nave. Father Cyril turned toward the Portaile des Libraires and discovered the body. After Father Cyril left, you planted the murder weapon."

Hannibal interpreted. As he finished, Madame Sartré rose from her seat, pointed her finger at Michelle Potéreau, and screamed: "Vous en êtes la cause!" She then started toward Potéreau. Fortunately, Moreau intervened, restrained Sartré and forced her back in her seat.

I looked around the table. Emotions expressed on faces ranged from extreme sadness to utter bewilderment.

Michelle was crying softly. My heart went out to her. "A young girl seduced by an older married man, probably with promises that he never intended to keep." My thoughts continued: "She will need help."

I looked over at Father Cyril. He first had an expression that indicated relief. He looked at Madame Sartré and Michelle Potéreau. His expression changed to sorrow and then pity. He then looked at me. He smiled wanly and nodded affirmatively. He leaned back in his chair, folded his hands in an attitude of prayer and closed his eyes.

I looked at Bernard. He was staring at me. His expression was one of frank admiration. "Oh, my heaven," he muttered several times.

Bonfils looked utterly bewildered. I smiled grimly and thought: "Monsieur Bonfils has a lot to think about," I concluded. "He lost his partner and his partner's wife. He now is the sole owner of a textile business."

I looked at Inspecteur Duchamps. He smiled and nodded.

"I think we have earned our fee," I thought with satisfaction.

I turned to Hannibal. He smiled and whispered softly. "Well done."

# 18

## ASSASSINS

*Tuesday morning, July 16*

It's eight o'clock in the morning and I am out of bed. How unusual! I am also fashionably dressed in navy-blue pants, a white silk blouse, matching navy-blue cardigan sweater, my white and blue silk scarf and sensible white walking shoes. I am fully primped and ready to leave Rouen.

Hannibal is downstairs paying the bill, arranging for a bellman and ordering up our car. We will eat breakfast downstairs after the car is packed.

Rouen proved to be busy, exciting and productive in terms of a nice fee from Inspecteur Duchamps for solving his murder case. We also got an insider's view of the cathedral, bought a few trinkets and made some new friends. However, I want to see Giverny and then Paris. I desperately need to do some real shopping!

Hannibal made reservations for two nights at the Hôtel Baudy in Giverny. He said it was a quaint, rustic little place and a hangout for artists of the impressionist school. It also has a restaurant with courtyard dining. Sounds like fun!

When I was a girl, I remember reading Indiana newspaper articles about impressionist artists. The local Clinton Carnegie Library had a picture book of their creations. I was captivated by the vivid colors, the depth of the images and the splashy brushstrokes.

I still remember some of the artist's names. In addition to Claude Monet, I remember Frederick Carl Frieseke, Richard Miller, Lawton

S. Parker, Guy Rose, Edmund Greacen and Karl Anderson. They were called 'The Giverny Group,' and they were a sensation at the time. Now I get to visit Giverny. What a treat!

According to Hannibal, many artists from around the world come to Giverny to observe Monet's gardens and to paint the wonderful flowers, waterways and other Monet-designed features. I hope we can talk our way in.

Hannibal also said that since Claude Monet died in 1926, his house has been occupied by Blanche-Hoschedé Monet, Claude Monet's daughter-in-law and stepdaughter. How does he know such things? The relationship sounds complicated. Anyway, she is an artist in her own right, and perhaps she will let us see the gardens.

Hannibal said I could drive, as long as I didn't get into any more situations with dead cows on the road. Humph! I smiled sweetly and said: "I promise." Hannibal just laughed.

## Tuesday night, July 16

We made it. I drove all the way and didn't hit anything. The distance was only about seventy kilometers. The countryside between Rouen and Giverny was beautiful, and we made a leisurely trip. We drove into town a little after noon.

I was surprised at the size of Giverny; it's just a little village on the right bank of the Seine. Except for the Eglise Sainte-Radegonde church, the Hôtel Baudy, a few local shops and a village marketplace, the only attraction is Monet's house and gardens, which is really a private residence.

We parked our car next to the hotel, took out overnight bags, locked the car and entered the lobby. We were greeted by a nice young man at the front desk. Hannibal took care of our check-in, and I glanced around, just people-watching.

Hannibal soon finished. Our small suite wasn't quite ready yet, so we sat on comfortable chairs in the lobby. As we discussed plans for dinner, two attractive women entered through the front door.

One looked middle-aged and the other appeared young, perhaps still a teenager. They were well-dressed in conservative clothing that somehow didn't seem French. Both carried small bags and purses.

They had expressions of fear, especially the older woman. She kept looking over shoulder toward the door. Hannibal and I stopped our conversation and watched discretely.

The pair whispered to each other in a language I did not understand. I did catch the name 'Lesya' as the older woman addressed the teenager. After a few minutes, the older lady stepped up to the desk clerk and spoke in heavily accented French.

I followed enough of the conversation in French to understand that the woman wanted a room. The clerk asked to see passports. The woman presented two. The clerk looked at the passports carefully and handed them back. The woman stuffed the passports in her purse.

The clerk eyed her for a moment, handed her a key and pointed to the register. The woman picked up a pen and quickly wrote. As she did so, she said: "Excusez-moi, pouvons-nous garer notre automobile hors de la vue de la rue?"

Hannibal and I both heard the woman's question. I turned to Hannibal. He whispered in my ear: "The lady obtained a room, and now she wants to hide her car."

"That's odd," I whispered back. "They both look scared." Hannibal nodded.

We watched as the clerk raised his eyebrows a little. The lady took folded money from her purse and gave the money and her car keys to the clerk.

"Oui, madame," the clerk replied. Without another word, he walked out the front door. After a few minutes, we heard a car start and drive away.

The two women smiled wanly at us as they crossed the lobby and walked up the stairs, presumably toward their room. Hannibal and I looked at each other.

After a moment, I got up, slipped quietly across the lobby and looked at the register. I returned to my seat just as the desk clerk entered the lobby from the back.

Hannibal looked at me, grinned and whispered: "OK nosy, what did you find out?"

"The woman's first name was Olha, but I couldn't make out the last; the writing was scrawled on the page. The scrawl looks intentional. They are in room 12, just down the hall from us." I replied. "I overheard the name 'Lesya' earlier; it's the name of the younger woman."

"Hummm, responded Hannibal; "Olha and Lesya, both scared. They had their car hidden. Based on the passports they presented and the language they used between themselves, they are foreigners."

"On the run," I stated matter-of-factly. "I've seen it before."

Hannibal nodded and said rhetorically: "But why?" He paused and thought a moment. "Aren't you hungry? Let's continue our discussion about dinner."

"OK," I responded reluctantly. I was hungry. "Let's go down for dinner about six this evening."

A very attractive French woman was in the Hôtel Baudy courtyard when Hannibal and I arrived for a romantic outdoor dinner. She was at a large table with two men and another woman.

Hannibal and I were the only other couple in the courtyard; apparently Olha and Lesya either stayed in their room or made other arrangements.

Before we could find a seat, the lady waved us over to her table. We walked over. In perfect English, she introduced herself.

"I am Blanche Monet; would you care to join us rather than dine alone?" She smiled and added: "My friends here are also Americans." The others at the table smiled and nodded. One of the men said: "We're from New York: how about you?"

"How does everyone seem to recognize us as Americans?" I mused to myself. "It happens all the time." I smiled and said: "Indiana."

Of course, we said yes to Blanche's invitation. Hannibal handled the introductions. From Hannibal's description, the lady was Claude Monet's heir!

Blanche and her friends were all fluent in both English and French. I did my best with the French, and everyone understood.

Blanche and the others were artists. During our conversations, she said she lived in her father-in-law's house, worked in the old studio and kept the gardens.

Hannibal ordered several bottles of wine. Later, dinner was served, family style. We had a merry evening. Toward dusk, I asked Blanche if we could visit the gardens on Wednesday.

 Blanche said: "Of course. Many artists visit, and you are more than welcome."

"Oh, thank you," I replied. "I have heard so many wonderful things about them."

Blanche nodded graciously. The evening passed in pleasant conversation, mostly about art, artists and various views and colors in Monet's gardens. We all finished dinner at about nine o'clock.

After dinner, Hannibal and I strolled back through the lobby toward the stairs that led up to our room. Two very sinister-looking men in business suits and slouch hats were having a conversation with the desk clerk, who we had met earlier. The men were speaking in heavily accented French. The clerk appeared apprehensive.

Hannibal and I walked past the two men and headed toward the stairs. As we started up, I heard a soft "Oh!" I looked. Lesya stood at the top of the stairs. Her hands were up to the sides of her face and her eyes were wide open in an expression of horror. She turned and ran silently down the hallway.

At the top, I stopped and peeked back over the rail. Hannibal stopped in the hallway and watched me.

After a few moments of conversation with the clerk, the men in the lobby below presented passports and signed the register. The pair had a brief conversation between themselves in a foreign language. One went outside and returned shortly with two suitcases.

I slipped past Hannibal and we both moved quickly and quietly down the hall to our room. Hannibal was ready with the key, and we got inside as footsteps sounded on the stairs. Whew!

After our door was closed, I looked at Hannibal and said: "Olha and Lesya are on the run and hiding in their room. Lesya clearly recognized the two men who just checked in. All of them speak in a language that is neither French or English. What is going on?"

"Interesting," replied Hannibal. That was all he said. He then kissed me.

I responded briefly and said: "Later dear, we have a mystery on our hands."

Hannibal stepped back, grinned and shook his head in a resigned fashion.

I turned back to our door and listened. The two men were opening the door to the room next to ours. Curiosity was getting the better of me. I waited until the hallway was silent, opened our door and looked out. I glanced back at Hannibal.

He shook his head and said: "Be careful!" How does he always know?

I stepped out, closed our door and tip-toed down the hall toward room 12. After a knock on the door, I said softly: "I'm Caroline Case Jones. Perhaps I can help."

A full minute passed. Finally, footsteps sounded from inside. The knob turned slowly, and the door opened. A very frightened face appeared. It was Olha. She looked at me, and her fright subsided a little. After a moment, she said, in heavily accented English: "You are American?"

"Yes," I replied. "Your companion was frightened by the two men who just checked into the hotel."

Olha opened the door and said: "Yes, they are hunting us. We saw them drive up from our window. One of their friends killed my husband. Please help us!"

"May I come in?" I asked softly.

Olha opened the door wider. I slipped by her, and she closed the door silently. Lesya was sitting on the edge of the bed. Her eyes had a pleading look.

For the next hour, Olha and Lesya told me their story. I resolved to help, but I needed Hannibal. After re-assuring Olha and Lesya, I slipped silently out the door and down the hall to our room.

After a soft knock, Hannibal opened the door. Together, we refined the plan that began in my mind while Olha and Lesya were telling me their story.

Hannibal added details about Olha's history. He explained that the story of Symon Petiura, Olha's husband, was in the newspapers, both in France and the United States, in 1926 and 27. Olha had said that she and her daughter Lesya had been on the run for over two years!

Our plan would begin at breakfast. I slept fitfully during the night.

At about seven in the morning, I heard stirrings in the hallway. Hannibal and I were already dressed and waiting. I stepped to the door and listened. As expected, the two men from next door were just outside, speaking in a language that I didn't understand. They walked down the hallway toward the stairs.

"OK, Caroline," I muttered. "Time for action." I looked over at Hannibal, and he nodded.

I opened our door and walked down the hallway toward the stairs. As planned, Hannibal remained in the room.

The two men from the room next door were at a table in the courtyard drinking coffee. The waiter was just leaving toward the kitchen door; the men had ordered breakfast. I smiled and sat at a nearby table. One of the men smiled in return; the other just stared in a cold manner. I shivered a little.

The waiter returned and I ordered sweet rolls, fruit and sandwiches in my best French. I explained that Hannibal and I would eat in our room. "Trop de vin hier soir," I added. The waiter laughed; he remembered that Hannibal had ordered several bottles of wine last evening.

Breakfast arrived for the men at the next table. The waiter brought my order in a paper sack, as requested. I waited to make sure that the men were occupied and then walked into the lobby.

Hannibal had just finished his conversation with the desk clerk, who was the same young man who had checked us in. Both Hannibal and the clerk nodded. I walked up the stairs. Hannibal went outside with the desk clerk.

Upstairs, I knocked on the door to room 12. Olha and Lesya were ready. I gave them our breakfast and walked over to the window.

An old Citroën appeared near the front of the building. The desk clerk stepped out. Hannibal joined him; he had finished his errand around the corner in the parking lot. I turned to Olha and said: "Go now, your car is waiting." I smiled and added: "You will not be followed."

Olha and Lesya had all of their belongings and the sack with breakfast. In a trembling voice, Olha said: "Thank you, thank you." Tears were streaming down her face.

I smiled and just said: "Go!" The pair slipped out the door and hurried down the hallway. I watched from the window.

As Olha and Lesya drove off in their Citroën, another car arrived in front of the hotel. Three men in gendarme uniforms stepped out. I watched from the window as Hannibal, the desk clerk and the three gendarmes had a brief conversation. The men all walked toward the front door. I left Olha's and Lesya's room, hurried down the hallway and down the stairs.

Hannibal was waiting in the lobby. He grinned and held up two passports. "Found these in the room next door," he said. According to our plan, the desk clerk called the gendarmes. They will ask our two sinister neighbors for their passports, and they won't be able to produce them." His smile broadened. "They will be arrested. Let's get out of sight in our room."

We had just closed our room door when we heard heavy footsteps in the hallway. I put my ear to the door and listened. I could tell from the accented French that the one of the men from next door was irritated about being asked to show his passport.

The door to the room next to ours opened. I could hear rummaging around, exclamations and then what were probably curses.

After a few moments, a loud voice, in perfect French, said: "Comme vous n'avez pas de passeport, vous êtes en état d'arrestation. Viens avec nous!"

"Mission accomplished," I said with a smile. "Of course, you disabled their car, right?" I looked at Hannibal.

"Certainly," he replied. "I doubt that Giverny has a repair shop that has replacement sparkplug wires." He grinned and said: "These passports will magically appear at the front desk when we leave. By the time all of this is sorted out, Olha and Lesya will have several days head start."

I looked at the passports. I saw hammer and sickle emblems. "Union of Soviet Socialist Republics, I believe," I said.

"Yes," replied Hannibal. "Soviet assassins on a mission."

I walked over to one of our comfy chairs, sat down and breathed a big sigh. Hannibal sat in the adjoining chair and watched me for a few minutes.

Finally, I said: "I understand that Olha's husband was Symon Petiura, and he was murdered. Olha also said she was from the Ukraine." I paused and thought a moment. "You said you read about Petiura in the newspapers." I gave Hannibal a quizzical look.

Hannibal nodded and replied: "Sholom Schwartzbard, a Ukrainian national, shot Symon Petiura on a Paris street in the spring of 1926. A sensational trial followed. Even though Schwartzbard freely admitted killing Petiura, he was acquitted by a French jury."

"Why?" I asked. "Who is Schwartzbard and what was his motive?"

"Schwartzbard is a Jew. His entire family was murdered during the anti-Jewish pogroms in the Ukraine during 1918 and through 1921. Petiura was the head of the Ukrainian People's Republican Army. Many Jews, including Schwartzbard, blamed Petiura for the killings."

"I remember reading about civil war in Eastern Europe," I responded. "The newspapers said that the Bolsheviks were involved, and they won the war."

"Yes," said Hannibal. "Over 35,000 Jews were killed. All political factions were involved in the murders. However, most Ukrainians believed that Petiura tried to stop the killings. They consider him a national hero for opposing the Bolsheviks. Obviously, others disagreed."

"What about Schwartzbard?" I asked.

Hannibal leaned back, though a moment and replied: "The newspapers told many stories during his trial in Paris. Some said he was a Soviet agent. Other said he acted alone." He paused and then added: "Who knows?"

"Hummm," I responded. "Olha and Lesya may know something that the Soviets do not want revealed."

"Probably," replied Hannibal. "I hope the pair find a safe haven. Whether or not Olha's husband was a murderer of Jews doesn't justify killing his wife and daughter."

I was silent for several minutes. "Agree," I finally said. "Anyway, it's done." I gave another sigh and put the episode away in my memories. "Time to think about something else," I muttered.

Hannibal heard and smiled. "We have permission to visit Monet's gardens. Shall we have breakfast and walk over? According to our map, the gardens are just down the street."

I love it when Hannibal says just the right thing.

## Wednesday evening, July 17

Hannibal and I walked from the hotel to the garden after breakfast; the day was bright and sunny, with a slight breeze. We passed a few shops and houses along the main road and arrived at Monet's house and gardens after a few blocks.

Blanche saw us coming and met us at the door. She had a basket of cut flowers. "Bonjour, Caroline and Hannibal." She waved. "As you can see, I have already been to the garden. Several artists are there, painting in the morning light." She paused and shielded her eyes from the sun with her free hand. "The gate is right over there." She pointed.

After many thank yous, Hannibal and I walked over to the gate by the house. On the gatepost, I saw a small bright yellow box. A little card was fixed on the side. The words read: 'Bienvenue dans notre jardin. Marchez prudemment et profitez. Veuillez placer vos commentaires dans cette case. Je vous remercie!!'

Hannibal looked over my shoulder and interpreted for me: "Welcome to our garden. Walk carefully and enjoy. Please place your comments in this box. Thank you!"

"That's nice," I responded. "I have pencils and paper in my purse."

We walked through the garden in front of the house first. It had many vistas, perspectives, symmetries and colors. It was divided into beds that had flower clumps of different heights and volumes. Fruit and ornamental trees were accented by long-stemmed hollyhocks and banks of annuals in a riot of color and variety. A central alley was covered over by iron arches laced with climbing roses. It was beautiful.

Hannibal and I found a couple of white wooden lounging chairs under the arches at the far end. We sat down in the shade and watched a couple of nearby artists in the process of their creations.

I took a pencil and some paper out of my purse. Soon I was engrossed in my scribbles. Hannibal got up and walked over to one of the artists and engaged in quiet conversation. I was by myself, surrounded by the loveliest gardens that I had ever seen.

After a while, I walked over to Hannibal and the artist. We exchanged pleasantries, and then Hannibal and I walked away and left the man to his work.

"Shall we go to the garden across the road?" Hannibal asked.

"Yes please," I replied. We walked back through the gate, crossed the road and passed through another gate into an even more beautiful place.

"I believe Claude Monet called this his water garden," said Hannibal.

I didn't answer, the beauty was overwhelming. We found a bridge over a pond and stream, and the water flowed slowly. The bridge rails were wound with blooming wisterias.

As we walked, we saw stands of bamboo, blooming nymphaea, weeping willows, tall maple trees and water lilies floating in the pond. Beds of roses and annuals lined a path that wound through a lawn of untrimmed grass. We couldn't see outside the garden; the surrounding vegetation formed an enclosure. We were in a private little world.

I found a couple of yellow wooden lounging chairs in the shade of a weeping willow near the bridge. We sat down, and I continued to refine my comments for the box at the gate by the other garden. Finally, I was satisfied. I made a copy for my diary and one for the box. When I finished, I showed my work to Hannibal.

## Impressions

Monet's garden, answers come, cloudless sky, blue and bold.

So many flowers, seek the sun, dark and white, red and gold.

Insects buzz and lilacs grow, tall maples soar and willows weep.

Bridge in mist, o'er troubled flow, somber stream, dark and deep.

Our time passes, like morning dew, hold my hand, walk with me.

Search for secrets, find what's true, ephemeral garden, observe and be.

To the bridge and touch the flowers, find the gate, beyond the glade.

Mood uplifted, gift of hours, must hasten steps, plans are made.

He read, smiled and said: "You are an artist with words. It's beautiful."

I reached over and kissed him. Our wonderful excursion ended by mid-afternoon, and we strolled back to the hotel. Tomorrow we leave for Paris. Our investigations that began in Le Havre will continue in the City of Light.

# 19

## CITY OF LIGHT

*Thursday, Evening, July 18, 1929*

Well! That was exciting! I drove our Duesenberg into Paris this afternoon, and we are still alive. Our road from Giverny connected to Avenue Victor Hugo as we entered the suburbs of Paris. I had taken the time to study the map carefully before we left Giverny, so I knew the route to the Hôtel Ritz.

Traffic increased as we approached the Arc de Triomphe. Parisians drive at one speed; it's always as fast as the car will go. I squinted my eyes, worked the clutch, the gearshift, the gas pedal and joined the crowd. I'm sure my fingerprints are permanently engrained on the steering wheel.

Finally, we reached the Arc de Triomphe, which is surrounded by the biggest roundabout I have ever experienced. Around and around we went, full speed, jockeying for position, trying to find our exit on the Champs Elysées. Finally, after three circles, I gritted my teeth, downshifted, floored the gas pedal, swerved in front of a lorry and turned. Fortunately, the street was the Champs Elysées.

I glanced over at Hannibal. He had both hands firmly braced on the dash. I'm sure his life had just flashed before his eyes, and he was privately preparing to meet his maker.

Champs Elysées was the right street. After a few kilometers at breakneck speed, we reached the Place de la Concorde, which is another roundabout. Our experience was a little calmer this time, and I made the correct exit on Rue Royale. After a few blocks of dodging traffic, we turned right on Rue Saint Honoré and then left on Rue Castiglione. Finally, we entered the Place Vendôme. The Ritz was on the left.

I made a turn around the traffic circle and drove up to the main entrance. I then shut down the car's engine, turned to Hannibal and smiled. I wasn't about to let him know I had been frightened out of my wits.

Hannibal looked at me, gave a big sigh and said: "Nice driving."

"Humph!" I responded.

Hannibal got out of the car slowly, walked around to my side and opened my door for me. I stepped out and looked up at the façade of the Hôtel Ritz. Wow!

Hannibal arranged for our baggage, valet parking of our car and check-in. Fortunately, our trunks had arrived from Le Havre the day before. He also retrieved a letter that was waiting for us at the front desk.

Hannibal read it, walked over to me and said: "The letter is from Capitaine Inspecteur Soucet. It's what we expected. We can discuss it tomorrow."

While I waited for Hannibal to finish the check-in process, I walked around the sumptuous lobby and gawked like a small-town American girl. Of course, this description of me is precisely true; the veneer of sophistication is not very deep.

After about twenty minutes, we made it to our grand suite. I have never experienced such opulence. After the bellman left, I gave Hannibal a big kiss, and he responded warmly. I think he finally relaxed a little.

Later, I decided to take a bubble bath. What a soothing experience! I spent an hour in the tub and almost fell asleep. Finally, I got out, combed out my hair and added a little perfume. I then opened one of my trunks and retrieved my Chanel white silk lounging pajamas, matching robe and soft white slippers.

After appropriate dressing and primping, I felt so relaxed. I looked in the bathroom mirror, smiled at myself and said: "Not bad, not bad at all." I twirled around a couple of times, giggled and sauntered into the parlor.

Hannibal watched my grand entrance from his seat on the sofa, chuckled and said: "You are lovely, Mrs. Jones." He stood up, put his arms around me and we kissed. We then relaxed for a while on the sofa, snuggled and looked out of our big bay window at the view of Paris.

Hannibal had thoughtfully ordered room service with champagne while I was taking my bubble bath. It arrived just as the sun slipped toward the horizon and behind some clouds. It gave off a golden glow. How beautiful!

After a delightful light dinner and several toasts to our good fortune, I sat down at this writing desk and finished my diary entries. What a day!

## Friday evening, July 19

After breakfast in our room this morning, Hannibal and I sat down in the parlor with cups of coffee. I read Inspecteur Soucet's letter. It gave us the name of our Gendarmerie contact in Paris, Lieutenant Inspecteur Henri Renault. It also provided a phone number and an address near the Paris Palais de Justice on the Île de la Cité.

"I will give Inspecteur Renault a call this morning," said Hannibal. "I'll try to set an appointment at his office on Monday." He smiled and added: "You will have the rest of today and all-day Saturday to shop."

"I'm so excited!" I replied. I thought a moment and added: "Sunday the shops will be closed, so perhaps you can show me some sights in Paris."

"Good idea," responded Hannibal with a smile. "However, I think we need to discuss the possibility of a long-term stay in Paris.

Our investigation may take some time. Also, I have done some homework on our finances, and I want to share some ideas with you concerning investments."

I thought a moment before replying. Finally, I asked: "How long do you think we should stay in Paris?"

"At least a year," responded Hannibal. "Maybe longer." He smiled again and added: "I know some people, and perhaps we can lease a Paris townhouse."

"You mean live in Paris? Sounds wonderful!" I thought a moment as I recalled Hannibal's comment about finances. I then blurted out: "Can we afford it?"

Hannibal chuckled a little. I could tell that he knew what I was thinking. He replied: "Oh, I think so; our net worth is a little over one-hundred ninety million dollars." He looked at me and added: "We have done very well in the stock market. However, that brings me to my second point. I think we need to make some changes in our finances for the future."

Intellectually, I knew we were extremely wealthy. Emotionally, however, I couldn't get my head around the fact. I still think in terms of being poor and counting every penny. I took a deep breath, let out a sigh and concentrated. "OK," I said. "What do you have in mind?"

"Have you watched the U.S. stock market lately?" responded Hannibal.

I thought a moment and replied: "Yes, I try to keep up to date." I paused as I recalled some recent newspaper articles in the New York Times that I read while we were in Le Havre. "We had a sharp dip in stock market averages in March, but the averages have since recovered. We are at an all-time high." I looked at Hannibal's face closely. "Are you concerned about the future?"

"Yes, I am," responded Hannibal. "As you said yourself some time ago, this crazy stock market can't last forever." He paused and added: "My banker contacts in New York have some serious concerns, and so do I."

I waited; I knew Hannibal had done his homework; he always does.

Hannibal slipped into his military briefing mode. I smiled; I couldn't help it. It was so typical of him. However, I also paid close attention.

Hannibal stood up and looked out the window for a moment. He then turned to me and said: "We have accounts at Chase National Bank, Bank of the Manhattan Company, Hanover Bank of the City of New York and Manufacturer's Trust of Manhattan. We also have accounts at Bank of America in Los Angeles and Credit Suisse in Geneva. Each account has a mix of cash, bonds and stocks."

"OK," I responded. "We are diversified with regard to banks, and that's a good thing."

"Yes," replied Hannibal with a smile. I know he was pleased with my instinctive approach to reducing risk. "However, I suggest we change our portfolios held by these banks to be even more defensive."

"How so?" I asked.

"We have been overweight in common stocks, which have done very well since the war," he responded. "For the future, I think we should shift to about fifty percent bonds, forty percent stocks and ten percent cash, primarily in U.S. dollars, Swiss francs and gold."

He paused and added: "Our bond portfolio should be heavy with U.S. treasury bonds, which we can have our bankers buy at subscription directly from the U.S. Treasury, some corporate bonds in well-managed companies and some bonds issued by the Credit Suisse Bank. If we just clip coupons on the bonds at an average of over four percent per year, our income will be just over four million per year." He smiled and added: "Do you think you can live on that?"

I grinned and replied: "I'll do my best. A girl has to shop, you know."

Hannibal laughed and then thought a few moments. I could tell he was recalling a well-thought out plan. Finally, he said: "The stocks in our portfolios should be a mix of common and preferred stocks in well-managed companies that can weather hard times. We will get some dividends, but I think we should hold these stocks primarily for capital gains."

Hannibal gave me time to absorb this information, and then continued. "Our bankers have sent us prospectuses on common stocks for a number of companies. I picked eight."

Hannibal walked over to the table, retrieved a piece of paper and handed it to me. I read the list of eight companies, each with a paragraph showing returns over time and a risk assessment. The companies were: U.S Gypsum, Ford Motor Company, Standard Oil of New Jersey, Coca Cola, U.S. Steel, Ingersoll-Rand, John Deere and Homestake Mining. I recognized all eight from my readings of newspapers.

Hannibal handed me another list and continued: "Our bankers also sent information on preferred stocks for Curtis Publishing, Electric Power and Light and the New York, Chicago and Saint Louis Railroad. I like all three."

I read the second list, thought a moment and then said: "Are you suggesting we sell our holdings in our current stocks, including my stocks in several car dealerships, and buy the bonds and stocks that you just identified?"

"Yes," replied Hannibal. "I also think we should do it soon, as in this month."

I got up from the sofa and joined Hannibal at the window. Finally, I said: "You know these companies far better than I do." I put my arm through his and added: "I trust your judgement." I then said: "Go ahead, as you propose."

"OK," responded Hannibal. "I'll send telegrams this afternoon."

I then looked up at Hannibal's face, grinned mischievously and said: "Can we talk about shopping now?"

Hannibal laughed and kissed me on the cheek. "Of course," he responded: "I suggest that you check at the concierge desk downstairs. They can set you up with private showings at all of the best fashion houses."

"What a marvelous idea!" I exclaimed. "Can I make appointments?"

Hannibal laughed and said: "Yes, I think so. You are the shopping expert." He paused and then added: "While you are waiting for your appointments, there are several classy department stores on the Champs Elysées and nearby streets. These include Printemps, Galeries Lafayette and Le Bon Marche." I can show them to you if you want."

"Do I want?" I responded. "You've got to be kidding!" I giggled. "I'll be dressed and ready to go in an hour." I thought a moment. "What should I wear? Oh, my heaven!"

Hannibal laughed as I ran for the walk-in closet near the bathroom. The closet had my trunks full of clothes.

I heard Hannibal say as I rounded the corner: "I also know a place for lunch that you might like." There was a pause and then: "How does the restaurant on the observation deck of the Eiffel Tower sound?"

"How does he know these things?" I thought to myself as I rummaged through my trunks. "Someday I will figure it out, but not now. Where is my Chanel outfit?" I then realized what Hannibal said about lunch. "The Eiffel Tower? Wonderful!" I said loud enough for Hannibal to hear. I heard more laughter in response.

## Sunday morning, July 21

Saturday was a very successful shopping day. Hannibal and I visited Printemps and Galeries Lafayette. I found a beautiful Lanvin-designed full-length wool coat with fox fur trim at Printemps. It had long dolman sleeves with single button details at the cuffs. The front of the coat was asymmetrical, with seven button closures. The top button closed high on the simple neckline. The coat was fully lined with rayon and had interior pockets.

I accented the coat with a lovely matching Poiret fox fur pillbox style hat and fur-lined navy-blue leather gloves. At Galeries Lafayette, I found tall black leather boots with medium heels. In just one day, I made a very nice start on my new winter wardrobe!

Hannibal was very patient with me. At Printemps, he even bought a dark grey Burberry cashmere scarf that had dark brown stripes through it. Very fashionable. Of course, I helped him pick it out.

As promised, we had a sumptuous lunch on the observation deck of the Eiffel Tower. What a view!

We returned to the Ritz late afternoon. As Hannibal suggested, I made appointments for private showings of winter dresses and accessories through the concierge. My appointments are spaced out over the next three weeks, so I will have nice breaks in our investigation activities.

My first appointment is at Coco Chanel's salon, which is located at 31 Rue Cambon. The following week, I will visit Jeanne Lanvin's fashion house, which is at 15 Rue du Faubourge - Saint Honoré. I want to look at more fur-trimmed coats. Three weeks from now, I will visit Elsa Schiaparelli's salon, which on Rue de la Paix. Rumor has it that Schiaparelli plans to move to 21 Place Vendôme in the near future; I will have to keep track.

Today is Sunday, and Hannibal promised to take me to the Louvre. Based on Hannibal's description, the place is huge. We will just see some highlights, and return for more exploring on future dates. Ah, Paris, the city of light!

# 20

## THREADS OF CRIME

*Tuesday morning, July 23, 1929*

Hannibal had scheduled our appointment with Lieutenant Inspector Henri Renault on Monday morning at ten o'clock. The Inspecteur's office was located in Gendarmerie Centrale, 36 Quai des Orféures, next to the Palais de Justice. We decided to take a taxi from the Ritz; neither of us wanted to drive in Paris traffic.

After a room service breakfast, I dressed in my conservative summer Lanvin-blue dress with white trim. It was made of chiffon and lace fabrics and had three-quarter sleeves. The hem was just below my knees. The waist had matching little bows on each side. The dress accented my slim figure. I wore creamy-white silk hose, dark blue low-heeled shoes and my yellow silk scarf for accent. I had diamond stud earrings to match my engagement and wedding rings.

"Elegant, yet conservative," I concluded, as I preened in front of our bathroom mirror. "I'm in summer colors, just right for warm weather in Paris."

I sensed Hannibal watching me as I applied finishing touches to my hair. I turned around. He was standing in the doorway, and he smiled with a twinkle in his eyes. "Very nice," he said. "You'll make a great first impression."

I sniffed, tossed my head back in my best snooty manner and replied: "Oh, I'm so glad you think so." We both laughed.

Hannibal wore a light grey single-breasted business suit. His tie had Lanvin-blue and white stripes to match my dress. I sauntered over to him, fingered his tie and said: "Nice touch." He just chuckled.

We were ready. Hannibal called down to the front desk for a taxi. We took the elevator down, and the taxi was waiting at the door.

The ride over to the Îsle de la Cité took us down the Rue Castiglione to the Rue de Rivoli. The weather was beautiful. We passed the Jardin des Tuileries and the Louvre.

"What a wonderful place," I thought to myself as I watched out the window. On Sunday, Hannibal and I had visited the Louvre, and I was still overwhelmed by its vast size and immense collections.

"I could spend a month in that place," I mused, as we passed the buildings of the old Tuileries palace that was now the Louvre. After a few minutes, we turned right and crossed the bridge to the Îsle de la Cité.

We arrived at Gendarmerie Centrale just in time for our appointment. Inspecteur Renault's  office was not difficult to find; his name was on the directory in the building lobby.

After a short walk down the hall, we entered a small, oak-paneled anteroom. A very nice-looking young lady rose from her desk and said: "Puis-je vous aider, Monsieur? Madame?"

"Oui, Mademoiselle," responded Hannibal. "Je m'appelle Hannibal Jones et voici ma femme Caroline. Nous avons rendez-vous avec l'Inspecteur Renault."

"Ah, yes," replied the young lady in perfect English. "I am Yvette, Inspecteur Renault's assistant." She smiled warmly and added: "The Inspecteur will be happy to see you."

"Whew!" I thought to myself. "She speaks English, thank goodness."

Yvette led the way to the inner office and opened the door. I saw a well-dressed, relatively young man sitting at a plain oak desk. Files were stacked everywhere: on the desk, on the floor and on a credenza behind the desk.

I glanced around. A plain oak table and a half-dozen chairs rested under large windows on the right side of the room. The left side was lined with bookcases. I saw a mix of books, papers and files in the bookcases; all nooks and crannies were filled. "Busy man," I thought to myself.

I turned my attention to Yvette, who was completing the introductions. Inspecteur Renault had risen from behind his stacks of files and had walked around his desk. He greeted and shook hands with Hannibal. He then turned to me.

"Ah, Madame Jones," he said in a soft and melodious voice. "Capitaine Inspecteur Soucet told me so much about you." He smiled with a twinkle in his eyes.

I returned his smile in a courteous manner and offered my hand. Renault formally took my hand, bowed slightly and kissed it.

"Careful, Caroline," I thought to myself. "He's French." To Renault, I continued my slight smile and replied: "So nice to meet you, Monsieur Inspecteur." I glanced over at Hannibal, who was suppressing a chuckle.

Inspecteur Renault smiled graciously, in spite of the gentle rebuff. He looked over at Hannibal and said: "Please, Monsieur Jones, would you and Madame Jones join me at my table by the windows?" He motioned with his hand toward some seats that allowed us to have the light over our shoulders.

Hannibal and I took our seats, and Renault joined us. Soon the social niceties were over, and we got down to business.

Renault looked at Hannibal and said: "Inspecteur Soucet's letter asked me to brief you on the connection of the Le Havre robbery ring to the Emporium owned by Simon Goldhirsch here in Paris."

"Yes, replied Hannibal. "Based on Inspecteur Soucet's findings, Grégorie Durant, the mastermind of the robberies and murders in Le Havre, made regular trips to Paris and to the Emporium. He also said that Simon Goldhirsch, the owner, has connections to Paul Carbone, a known leader of the Unione Corse, a Le Milieu crime family in Paris."

"Yes," responded Renault. "We have not been able to prove it, but it is likely that Goldhirsch, who is a licensed jeweler, remade the stolen jewelry from Le Havre and sold it in his Emporium, or through other shops or on the black-market."

I asked: "Do you have investigative files that we may read?"

Renault turned to me and said: "Yes. Inspecteur Paul Clemenceau, my best undercover agent, has put together a very large file." Renault retrieved a folder from his desk, turned to Hannibal and me and showed us a photo. "This is Inspecteur Clemenceau. You may read everything we have."

He then turned back to his desk and picked up a larger folder that overflowed with notes and photographs. He handed the file to me and said: "You may use my table to review Clemenceau's file and make as many notes as you wish."

He looked at Hannibal, then back to me and said: "Yvette will help you build a file of your own."

"Thank you," I responded. I leafed briefly through the files. All of the notes were written in French. I looked at Hannibal, and he nodded.

"I will review the files in detail and make notes," Hannibal said. I knew that Hannibal's notes would be very thorough and in English. I nodded to Hannibal and smiled. We both returned our attention to Renault.

Renault's expression grew very serious. He said: "Please be very careful with the files and your notes." He paused and then added in a low voice, almost a whisper: "Trust no one other than Yvette, Inspecteur Soucet, Inspecteur Clemenceau and me. We are all of the Gendarmerie."

Hannibal and I looked at each other with surprised expressions. Hannibal turned to Renault and asked: "What is our assignment on this case? It seems that we might get involved in larger issues than just the sale of stolen property."

Renault nodded and replied: "Your work in Le Havre was the first proof that a highly organized ring, connected to the Le Milieu in Paris, was and is involved in robbery and murder."

Renault's smile disappeared. He then said: "We suspect that members of the Sûreté, the French National Police Force, and especially elements of the Sûreté Paris department, or Préfet de Paris, provides protection to certain Le Milieu gang members. Your assignment, if you choose to assist, may involve investigating possible bribery and corruption within the Sûreté."

Hannibal asked: "Do rivalries exist between the Sûreté and the Gendarmerie? I know that both organizations have nation-wide police powers."

Renault smiled grimly and responded: "Sadly, rivalries exist. The criminal element knows this all too well. Gang leaders, who we call the parrain, often play one police force against the other. Parrain such as Paul Carbone and François Spirito have formed friendships within the Sûreté."

"Oh my," I thought to myself. "Who knows what these gangsters and their corrupt police conspirators might do?" To Renault, I said: "Such an investigation might be dangerous."

Renault sighed again and responded: "Yes, your work will be quite dangerous. Again, be very careful who you trust."

I looked at Hannibal. He returned my look with a steady gaze. I could tell he was waiting for a sign from me. I leaned back in my chair, turned and looked out the window. I was quiet for quite a while.

Finally, I returned my attention to Hannibal and said: "We've had dangerous assignments before." I nodded my assent.

Hannibal turned to Renault and said: "We will take the case, wherever it leads."

Renault gave a big sigh. I could tell he had been holding his breath. He then replied: "Thank you. Please be assured you will be well paid."

I grinned and said: "Well! That's good. I have appointments for shopping at the Coco Chanel, Jeanne Lanvin and Elsa Schiaparelli salons." I then added: "My tastes are quite expensive."

Hannibal and Renault laughed; both understood my real meaning.

Our discussions continued. Soon, we had notes, photos and an annotated map spread out on the table.

As we looked at the map, Renault said: "The Unione Corse has rivals in Paris, and there are many unsolved gangland killings. Rival gangs include the Gang de la Brise, which is headed by parrain Ange Salicetti. These two gangs originated in Corsica, but most of the suspected members operate in Paris and Marseille."

Renault paused and then added: "We are certain that both gangs engage in a variety of criminal activities, yet the Sûreté had made few arrests."

"Do you know where these gangs operate in Paris?" I asked.

Renault nodded and responded: "All three have a strong presence in the Quartier Pigalle, which overlaps portions of the Ninth and Eighteenth Arrondissements, or districts." He paused and then added: "In addition to robbery and murder, the gangs engage in prostitution, illegal gambling, extortion, kidnapping and drugs, including opium and heroin."

I noted Renault's expression as he spoke. Apparently, he viewed the Quartier Pigalle with distaste. He said: "Inspector Clemenceau spends much of his time in Montmartre, which is in the Eighteenth Arrondissement, and in the Quartier Pigalle, working under cover, with little cooperation from the Sûreté."

He paused and added: "In the Quartier Pigalle, the gangs rule the streets. We know some of their key members. However, we do not have evidence on their organizational structure, how they operate and proof of who committed various crimes. Your evidence from Le Havre was our first proof of criminal activity."

He shook his head sadly. "We of the Gendarmerie have made a few arrests, but most often, our suspects are released by the Sûreté due to lack of evidence or persons willing to testify against them."

I looked at the annotated map on the table. The Emporium, our suspect jewelry store, was marked on the map. Its location was near the corner of the Rue Jean Babtiste Pigalle and Rue Pierre Fontaine, right in the middle the Quartier Pigalle. "How convenient," I thought to myself.

We continued to leaf through the files. However, they were much too large to review at one sitting. Besides, everything was written in French.

After half an hour or so, Hannibal looked at Renault and said: "I'm sure you have many cases and your workload is heavy. I would like to return to your office, perhaps tomorrow, and review these files in detail on my own."

"Yes, of course," replied Renault. "I will leave all of the pertinent files on this table. If I'm not here, Yvette will assist you, if you have inquiries."

Hannibal looked at me. I knew Hannibal planned to make notes in English for my benefit. I rose from my seat. After goodbyes and handshakes with Renault, we departed. So much work ahead!

## Tuesday noon, July 23

Hannibal has left for the day, and I am ready for my afternoon appointments. A taxi will be downstairs in a few minutes, but I have time for these few scribbles in my diary.

Hannibal and I got up early this morning, dressed in business attire and had breakfast downstairs. As planned, Hannibal will visit Inspecteur Renault's office, review his files and make notes in English. There was no point in my going with Hannibal; he had to do the translations.

We discussed a walk through the Quartier Pigalle over coffee and breakfast. We both wanted to get a sense of the businesses, people and activities. Of course, we also wanted to spy on Simon Goldhirsch in his Emporium.

"I could go alone to Pigalle while you are at Renault's place," I ventured. "It would save time."

Hannibal frowned, thought a moment and replied: "A lone female might be too conspicuous, even in plain, ordinary clothes." He looked at my fashionable, expensive business outfit and smiled. His smile then disappeared, and he added: "If Pigalle is a center for gangland activity, going alone might be too dangerous."

I thought a moment and replied: "You are right. We should go together." I grinned and added: "I'll take my revolver."

Hannibal smiled grimly, and his eyes had a steady gaze. "Good idea," he said. "I'll take my forty-five."

We agreed that we would go together on Thursday or Friday, and we would dress in non-descript clothes to blend in with the local folks.

"So, what should I do while you are at Renault's office?" I asked.

Hannibal leaned back in his chair, took a sip of coffee, smiled and replied: "Could you move your appointment at Coco Chanel's salon to this afternoon?"

"What a wonderful idea!" I exclaimed. Images of elegant outfits danced in my mind. "I'll phone the concierge right away!" I paused, thinking. "I will have to change clothes!"

Hannibal just laughed, settled in with his coffee and watched.

I rushed to the phone, called the concierge and explained the situation. The nice concierge lady promised to call me back in a few minutes. I paced back and forth as I waited. I thought about what I should wear. I occasionally glanced at Hannibal, who wisely, didn't say a word. I could see he was doing his best to suppress chuckles. It was infuriating.  Finally, the phone rang.

"Yes?" I answered the phone with as much dignity as I could muster.

The smooth voice of the concierge came over the phone. "Chanel had a cancellation from two until four this afternoon," she said. "The models will be showing the latest in fall fashions. Only one other guest will be in the showroom." She then asked: "Would I be interested?"

"Yes," I replied, again in my dignified voice. "I will be there. Please confirm my appointment with Chanel." I hung up the phone and rushed to the walk-in closet next to the bathroom. Oh, what should I wear?!

# 21

## FIGHTING FASHIONS

### Wednesday morning, July 24, 1929

Coco Chanel's salon was more exciting than I ever imagined. I visited her opulent parlor, met an attentive hostess, viewed stunning displays of exquisite fashions, experienced an attempted kidnapping and survived utter mayhem.

The afternoon had a very pleasant beginning. The Ritz concierge had a taxi waiting for me at one o'clock. I was totally prepared. I wore my newest Chanel white summer dress with navy trim, a short, matching white and navy jacket and appropriate accessories. "I am the epitome of the latest fashion," I thought to myself, as I sauntered out the door of the Ritz and to the opened door of the taxi.

The taxi dropped me off at 31 Rue Cambon at precisely one-fifty-five, according to the ornate clock set in the window of the Chanel salon. Perfect!

A very attractive young lady met me just inside the door. "Bonjour, Madame, puis-je vous aider?" She asked.

I replied in my best French: "Oui, Mademoiselle, merci. Je m'appelle Caroline Case Jones, et j'ai rendez-vous à 14 heures."

"Ah, yes, Madame Jones," the young lady replied in perfect English. "We are so glad you could come. Welcome to Chanel's Salon. I am Suzanne, and I will be your hostess."

Whew! I was concerned about my ability to communicate. "Problem solved," I thought to myself.

"Please follow me into the parlor," said Suzanne. "We expect our other guest very soon."

I followed Suzanne. We exited the lobby and entered a parlor through a central interior doorway. The parlor was overwhelming. Light streamed through two tall windows on the right side wall. The furniture was eclectic, and included Queen Anne style chairs as well as Louis XIV bureaus and other pieces. Crystal objects d'art, brass candle holders with decorative candles, vases with cut fresh flowers and marble accent pieces were everywhere.

A large bureau rested between the windows on the right wall. I could see hallways leading from the parlor at both ends of the back wall, and each hallway was accented with a folding room divider in the corner that had an oriental motif. The back wall had a bureau and a couple of small tables, but no windows.

The left wall had tall, decoratively filled bookcases on both ends and a huge mirror with a gold baroque frame in the center. A sofa rested under the mirror, and end tables with lamps sat on both sides of the sofa.

A large, wooden, rectangular coffee table had been placed in front of the sofa, and a smaller, round, glass-topped table rested in the center of the room, directly under an exquisite crystal chandelier.

The round table held a silver tray with a teapot, china cups and saucers, little sugar cookies, condiments and linen napkins.

Somehow, the eclectic décor worked. It was beautiful. Suzanne took my coat, offered me tea and cookies, and asked me to please be seated on the sofa.

As I sipped my tea, Susanne saw my glances toward the hallways. She said: "Models will come in from the hallway across the room, on the right of the back wall. Dressing rooms, a three-way mirror, a table with fitting tools and a small dais are down the other hallway." I continued to look around, taking in every detail.

After a few minutes, we heard the outside door open. Suzanne excused herself and walked back across the room and through the parlor door.

I couldn't help myself, I got up from my seat and peeked down the hallway to the left. I could see a pair of curtained dressing rooms on the left, and a three-way mirror was on the right. A small dais rested in front of the mirror, along with a table that held scissors, a pin cushion full of pins and measuring tapes.

I tip-toed back to my seat on the sofa. After a few minutes, Suzanne appeared in the parlor doorway. She was accompanied by a dark-haired, stylishly dressed young lady who was obviously another client.

Suzanne made the introductions in English. "Madame Caroline Case Jones, this is Mademoiselle Annette Salicetti," she said.

I put down my tea, smiled and responded: "So nice to meet you; please call me Caroline."

"Please call me Annette," replied the young lady in accented English. "I'm so excited to be here." She looked at me closely and said: "You are American, Yes?"

I laughed. To myself, I thought: "We Americans must be so obvious." To Annette, I replied: "Yes, and this is my first visit to the Chanel salon." How about you?"

"Oh, yes," responded Annette. "I was born in Corsica, but now I live in Paris and sometimes Rome." She grinned mischievously and added in a whisper: "My grandfather is paying for this!"

I laughed. I could see that Annette and I would get along just fine. I now recognized the accent; Annette's native language was Italian. Something in the back of my mind hinted that I had heard the name Salicetti before, but I couldn't place it. "Oh, well," I thought to myself. "I'll figure it out eventually."

Suzanne offered Annette tea, and soon the three of us were seated on the sofa. Suzanne explained the clothes that would be modeled and how fittings would be done for our selections.

"We will begin with Autumn day dresses, progress to more formal attire, and then to outer garments, including jackets, coats, gloves and furs," Suzanne said. "Based on your inputs during the appointment process, we hope we have narrowed down our showings to fashions that match your tastes."

Suzanne rose from her seat, walked to the center of the room near the tea table and signaled toward the hallway across the room from the sofa. After a moment, a model walked out from behind the folding room divider. She walked slowly around the room, posed, turned and then stopped near Suzanne, who then explained the outfit. After an appropriate time for our viewing, the model returned down the hallway.

This process was repeated over and over, with a new outfit each time. Annette and I asked questions and indicated which outfits we especially liked. I picked out a couple of day dresses, an outfit with daring slim-cut black pants, a black cashmere pullover top and a matching jacket. I also selected a business suit, an evening gown and a full-length black wool coat with sable trim. Annette made her selections, and we both oohed and ahhed over the choices.

After an hour, we were ready for fittings to prepare for tailoring. Annette and I changed into our selected outfits in adjacent dressing rooms and took turns on the dais in front of the mirror. As I walked back and forth between the dressing room and the mirror, I noticed a door at the end of the hallway with a 'sortie' sign, but I didn't pay much attention. "Must mean exit," I mused to myself.

I was in my dressing room and had just changed into the black pants and black pullover cashmere top. I was still barefoot. My little dressing room had a full-length mirror, and I turned around a couple of times. "Not much tailoring needed," I thought to myself. "It fits nearly perfectly."

As I finished this thought, I heard scuffling sounds and screams from Annette's dressing room. "Aheeeh! Aheeeh!" This was accompanied by both female and male curses. The female voice was Annette's. "Oh, mon Dieu!" was next. That voice was Susanne's.

I flipped back the curtain of my dressing room. A quick glance revealed four large men, all in dark clothing, struggling with a fighting Annette. Her screams of "Aheeeh!" were followed by her exclamations in Italian. I understood them, and none were very polite.

I saw scissors on the little table by the three-way mirror. I darted past the melee, grabbed the scissors, pivoted and stabbed with all my strength into the face of the man holding Annette from behind. The point penetrated deep into the man's face by the side of his nose and stuck. I lost my grip on the scissors as the man screamed in agony, released Annette, staggered back against the wall and fell to the floor.

Annette broke free, avoided the grasp of a second man and hit a third man in the face with her fist. Her blow was not heavy, but it startled him enough so that I could aim my left foot to the side of his knee. I ran a couple of steps, delivered the blow with my foot, and he went down.

Annette saw me. I said: "Run!" She did, down the hallway into the parlor. I was right behind her. The remaining two men were right behind me.

I saw a brass candle holder on the bureau as I entered the parlor. I grabbed it and dropped to my knees. The candle fell out of the holder.

The man right behind me couldn't stop, and he fell over the top of me.

The second stopped, which was his undoing. I swung the heavy brass candle holder at his left knee. I heard and felt bone break. He screamed and fell, holding his knee. The screams continued.

The man who had fallen over me was getting to his feet, but I had to deal with the one I had knocked down in the hallway. He had made it into the parlor. His eyes were blazing.

As I started to rise to meet this threat, a resounding crash and the tinkle of broken ceramic echoed in the room. Suzanne had come up behind the man from the hallway and smashed a vase full of flowers over the back of his head. He dropped like a stone. Water and red roses scattered all over the floor.

Still on my knees, I pivoted. I had my brass candle holder. The man who had fallen over me was halfway to his feet. I swung my candle holder with all my strength. The blow hit him full in the face. He fell sideways, but he struggled to get to his feet.

He didn't make it. Annette followed Suzanne's example and smashed another vase of flowers over the back of his head. He dropped. "Down for the count," the thought flashed through my mind. White chrysanthemums joined the red roses on the floor.

I stood and surveyed our opponents. Two in the parlor were out cold. The one with the smashed knee was struggling to get to his feet. I walked over, swung my candle holder deliberately and with all my strength. The man dropped to the floor and didn't move. I wasn't sure if he was dead, but I really didn't care.

I then padded carefully through the water and flowers on the floor into the hallway. The man with the scissors stuck in his face was still screaming. I walked over and swung my candle holder. The screams stopped.

I turned around. Susanne and Annette stood in the doorway to the parlor. Both had their mouths wide open and had looks of amazement in their eyes.

I'm sure my eyes were still blazing. After a couple of moments, I calmed down, took a deep breath and asked: "Are you both OK?"

They nodded and didn't say a word. Dead silence reigned for a full minute.

Finally, Annette turned to Suzanne and asked: "May I use your phone? I want to call my grandfather."

Suzanne pointed to a phone on the bureau on the far side of the parlor. Annette walked over and made her phone call.

In the meantime, the women who had modeled the clothes walked into the room, along with the seamstress who had been fitting our clothes. These ladies were followed by a lady I had not yet seen.

She was a little older than the rest, but still very beautiful. She looked around the room and fixed her eyes on me. She said in accented English: "I am Gabriele Chanel. Apparently, I missed all of the excitement."

I smiled wryly and replied: "Sorry for the mess. I really do like your fashions."

Annette walked over and said: "My grandfather will be here shortly; he will take care of the mess and pay for the damage."

Gabriele 'Coco' Chanel nodded and replied: "I understand. We will wait."

My mind clicked; I made the connection on Annette's last name. I looked at Annette and asked: "Is your grandfather Ange Salicetti?"

Annette smiled, nodded and replied: "He knows how to take care of such things." She then looked at me with steady eyes and added: "Thank you. You saved me."

I smiled and nodded. No words were needed.

Coco began giving orders. The front door was locked and Suzanne was stationed by the window to await Ange Salicetti. A couple of the women brought mops and buckets and cleaned up the broken ceramics, the flowers and the water. The four men were left where they fell.

After a few moments of watching the activity, I realized that I still had the brass candle holder in my hand. I walked over, placed it on the coffee table, turned and asked Coco: "May I have some tea?"

Coco smiled and said: "Of course." She looked at Annette and then back to me and said: "Please, you are both my customers. Have a seat on the sofa and I will pour."

Soon the three of us were sitting on the sofa drinking tea. At first, we talked about recent unfortunate events and how the clean-up process was going.

Coco glanced around the room a few times and seemed satisfied. She gave no indication that she wanted to involve the police.

"Interesting," I thought to myself as I sipped my tea. "Reminds me of Chicago." I smiled politely to Coco, and her eyes twinkled. I think we understood each other.

Annette was delightful. She was clearly supported in a very affluent life style. She had a free spirit attitude, smiled a lot, and I instantly liked her.

After a few minutes of girl talk about the clothes we had selected, she looked directly in my eyes and said: "This is not the first time my grandfather's enemies have tried to kidnap me."

"Oh?" I thought a moment and then replied. "Are members of the Unione Corse among his enemies?"

Annette's expression changed to surprise, and she responded: "You know about them?"

I looked at her for a long moment. "The enemy of my enemy is my friend," I thought to myself. I decided to take a chance. To Annette, I said: "Yes. My husband and I are private investigators, and we are very interested in the Unione Corse."

Both Coco and Annette stared at me for a long minute. I returned their looks with a steady gaze.

Finally, Annette said: "I live on the Rive Gauche, in Montparnasse." She smiled and then looked around. She found her purse, took out a notepad and a pencil and scribbled a note.

She handed the note to me. "My phone number and address," she said. Her smile broadened, and she added: "I think we can be friends."

"Well!" said Coco. She sipped her tea and then added: "You two may have adventures together. Please keep me informed. I like adventurers."

Annette laughed and responded: "I will. I'm so looking forward to it!"

We were talking quietly when we heard the front door open.

A small, impeccably dressed grey-haired man walked into the parlor, followed by four very large men also dressed in business suits.

Annette said: "My grandfather." She got up, walked over to the elderly gentleman and began talking in a low voice in Italian. I picked up much of the conversation; I had learned Italian during my Wabash Valley days from immigrant coal miners. Monsieur Salicetti listened carefully, glanced my way several times and asked a few questions.

After a couple of minutes, he turned to Coco and asked: "Pouvons-nous utiliser votre porte arrière pour retirer ces hommes?" I understood. He wanted to use the back door to remove the 'evidence.' I heard a few groans from the evidence, at least some of the men were waking up.

"Oui, Monsieur Salicetti. Je l'apprécierais beaucoup," replied Coco.

Between Salicetti's men and Coco's employees, the parlor and the hallway soon looked much as it had before the most unfortunate incident.

As the clean-up was in its final stages, Monsieur Salicetti walked over to me and said, in heavily accented English: "My granddaughter told me about you."

He smiled and added: "I know how to return a favor, Madame Jones. If you ever need help, call me." He then handed me a gold-engraved business card, nodded politely to Annette, Coco and me, and left with his men.

The mess was gone. I looked at the clock on the bureau. "Five o'clock," I said with a smile. I turned to Coco and said: "I apologize for running overtime. Suzanne has my order. Would you please ask her to phone and get me a taxi? In the meantime, I will change into my regular clothes."

Coco laughed and said: "Of course!"

I was on my way back to the Ritz before five-thirty. When I arrived about six, I went straight to the room. Hannibal was sitting on the sofa, reading, when I walked into the door.

He looked up, smiled and asked: "Good evening. How was your day?"

I smiled in return and replied: "Oh, just an average day at the salon. If you order some champagne and room service dinner, I will tell you all about it."

# 22

## MEAN STREETS OF PARIS

*Thursday noon, July 25, 1929*

Hannibal was appropriately impressed with my adventures at Coco Chanel's salon. We continued our discussion over our in-room breakfast and coffee.

"Your experiences on Tuesday take shopping to a whole new level," he said with a grin. "You also made a very interesting friend. Inspecteur Renault's files show that Ange Salicetti is the head of the Gang de la Brise, one of several major crime families with operations in Paris, Marseille and Corsica."

I thought a moment and then replied: "We also know that Paul Carbone, who was connected to the robbery and murder ring in Le Havre, has operations in Paris. Carbone and Salicetti are competitors."

"Yes," responded Hannibal. "Renault's files say as much. His undercover agent, Inspecteur Clemenceau, put together files on Carbone and Salicetti. Both men are parrain, and lead Corsica-based crime families." Hannibal paused and then added: "As far as we know, only Carbone had a connection in Le Havre."

After a moment. I said: "So, we know that the assault on Annette Salicetti was directed by one of her grandfather's competitors."

Hannibal picked up his coffee cup, took a sip and leaned back on the sofa. He looked at me with his steady gaze and asked: "Did you see this morning's newspaper?" He reached over to the end table by the sofa, picked up a newspaper and handed it to me.

"No," I replied. "It's written in French."

"Take a look at the photos on the second page," Hannibal responded.

I opened to page two. Photos of the faces of four dead men looked back at me. Another photo showed that the bodies lay on a quai along a waterfront. Several uniformed policemen stood near the bodies. The headline read: 'Corps de quatre membres de la pègre Parisienne retrouvés en Seine.'

I looked closely at the faces of the dead men. "Oh, my goodness!" I exclaimed. "These are the men who assaulted Annette Salicetti at Chanel's salon on Tuesday!'

"I thought as much," replied Hannibal. The headline says that the four were found in the Seine."

"Oh," I replied. I was silent for a while as I recalled my actions during the fight at Chanel's salon. I remembered the groans as the four men lay on the floor just before they were removed by Salicetti's men.

"What happened to them afterwards is not my doing," I thought to myself. Still, I felt a little uneasy. "Oh, well," my thoughts continued. "I can't change the past."

Hannibal watched me for a few moments and then said: "The article goes on to say that the four were known members of the Unione Corse."

I nodded and responded: "Based on Renault's comments, his files and events at Chanel's salon, it's pretty clear that Carbone and Salicetti are at war." I thought a moment and then added: "My Salicetti connection might be useful."

I looked at the stack of notes that Hannibal had made from Renault's files. They were spread out on our coffee table, along with several photos from the files. I picked up one of the photos, which showed a man in a Gendarmerie uniform. I looked at Hannibal.

"That's Inspecteur Paul Clemenceau, Renault's undercover agent," responded Hannibal. "Based on his employment record, he normally dresses in non-descript clothes and works undercover in the Quartier Pigalle."

"Hummm," I responded. "We should coordinate our efforts with Clemenceau."

Hannibal nodded. We were both quiet for a while. Finally, Hannibal said: "Are you ready to prowl the streets of Pigalle?"

I asked: "We need common street clothes. Any ideas?"

Hannibal smiled and replied: "I stopped at a second-hand clothing store in Montparnasse after I finished at Renault's office on Tuesday." He got up, walked to the closet and returned with a package. "These are for you," he continued. "I hope I got your size right."

I opened the package. Inside, I found a couple of dowdy-looking dresses, a plain hat, and walking shoes. I stood up, held one of the dresses up against my body and walked over to the mirror in the bathroom. I then returned to the parlor, grinned mischievously and said: "Just my size, I'm sure. How gauche!"

Hannibal laughed.

## Thursday midnight, July 25

Hannibal and I spent Thursday evening in the Quartier Pigalle. Hannibal had his service forty-five in a shoulder holster under his jacket, and I carried my Smith and Wesson revolver in my purse.

Our taxi dropped us off at the Moulin Rouge, located at 82 Boulevard de Clichy. The red windmill on the roof glittered with lights.

We watched people come and go. The crowd included a few dressed in elegant evening outfits, but most were dressed in ordinary Parisian street clothes. We blended with the latter. Bawdy music drifted out from the Moulin Rouge.

I looked up at Hannibal and said: "Must be quite a show."

Hannibal grinned and replied: "So I'm told."

I gave him a dig in the ribs.

We crossed the street and walked about two blocks along the Rue Pierre Fontaine toward the corner with Rue Jean-Babtiste Pigalle. I looked all around and memorized details.

Scantily dressed females walked the streets and stood in doorways, propositioning potential customers. There were dozens of them, all within a couple of blocks. We saw several men and girls walk away toward doors in alleys and other out-of-the-way locations.

Sinister-looking men, better dressed than most, occasionally spoke with the street girls. Invariably, the girls deferred to these men; I could see fear in their eyes.

"Gangsters," I concluded to myself. "They control the street trade." My thoughts continued: "Reminds me of the old days," I mused wryly. "However, in the U.S., the activities were usually indoors and not so obvious."

We turned left at the corner of Fontaine and Pigalle. The Emporium was tucked into a small niche along an alley not far from the corner, on the left side of the street. The window near the door was lighted and held a number of displays of jewelry. We stopped and looked.

I spotted a silver cigarette case and a matching lighter. "Look," I said to Hannibal.

He looked and nodded. "Matches the description of the case and lighter taken in Le Havre," he replied. "Let's go inside."

A little bell over the door tinkled as we entered. A portly, bald, middle-aged man flipped back a curtain from a doorway to a back room and stepped into the main room. He had a green eyeshade and wore glasses with an attached jeweler's magnifying lens. He stood behind a glass display case filled with a variety of jewelry.

I looked down into the display case. Broaches, combs, necklaces, bracelets, earrings and finger rings, some encrusted with precious and semi-precious stones, were arranged in an eclectic fashion.

The man smiled slyly and said: "Bonsoir, Monsieur et Madame. Je m'appelle Simon Goldhirsch. Bienvenue dans mon Emporium. Puis-je vous aider, s'il vous plaît?"

Hannibal replied: "Bonsoir, Monsieur Goldhirsch. Nous avons remarqué un briquet argenté et un étui à cigarettes dans la fenêtre. Ils sont très beaux. Pouvons-nous les voir s'il vous plaît?"

I understood enough to know that we had just met Simon Goldhirsch, and Hannibal had asked about the cigarette lighter and case in the window. I prudently kept silent.

Soon Goldhirsch had the lighter and case on the top of the display case. Hannibal picked up each, in turn, and inspected both sides. The back side of both items were newly burnished. He also opened the case. The inside was lined in red velvet. The case and lighter were clearly expensive items.

I watched closely. "Both had engravings that were burnished out," I concluded. I looked at Hannibal, and he nodded.

Hannibal discussed price with Goldhirsch. Soon negotiations were finished. Actually, the price was a bargain. "Stolen goods sell at a discount," I thought to myself.

Hannibal pulled French francs from his pocket and counted out the agreed upon amount, carefully, as if every franc was precious.

"Nice touch," I thought. Soon Hannibal had his new purchase in a plain paper sack, along with a receipt. Hannibal said his goodbyes, and we walked out the door.

"Bonsoir, monsieur et madame," said Goldhirsch as the door closed behind us.

Hannibal and I strolled down the street. "I will send these, along with the receipt, to Soucet in Le Havre," said Hannibal quietly. "I'm fairly certain he will be able to match the case and lighter to his photos of those items that belonged to Sir Albert Brunswick, who was murdered on June 22 in Le Havre."

"Well done," I responded as we walked. I looked around. Streetlights were coming on up and down Rue Jean-Babtiste Pigalle. The crowd had thinned, except for a few single men and girls of the evening.

After a half-block of walking, we crossed the street and started back toward the corner of Pigalle and Fontaine. As we reached the other side, Hannibal leaned over and said, in a low voice: "Did you notice the man watching us as we crossed the street?"

I glanced back briefly and saw a plainly dressed man under a streetlight. I responded: "It's Inspecteur Clemenceau. I recognize him from his photo."

"I thought so," replied Hannibal. "Keep walking. We don't want to blow his cover."

We turned left at the corner and continued on Rue Pierre Fontaine. What's down this street?" I asked as we strolled.

The Folies Bergére is near the corner of Fontaine and Rue Richer," replied Hannibal. "It's about a kilometer away. I want to get a taxi from a different location rather than here or near the Moulin Rouge."

I understood; we would be less conspicuous. "Good idea," I responded.

I thought a moment and then said: "Tell me about the Folies Bergére." I looked up at Hannibal's face with a mischievous grin. "And don't tell me you don't know."

Hannibal chuckled. After a few moments of walking, he responded: "The Folies Bergére has been around for a long time. Many of its entertainers are American." He looked at me with a twinkle in his eyes and added: "I have been told that the entertainment is quite revealing."

"Hummf," I responded. I also gave Hannibal another dig in the ribs.

After about twenty minutes of walking, we reached Rue Richer and turned left. At 32 Rue Richer, the building that housed the Folies glittered. The façade was new, in the latest Art Deco style. A marque advertised 'Josephine Baker en Revue.' Like the Moulin Rouge, the crowd included some well-dressed couples in addition to ordinary Parisians.

The area around the Folies was a beehive of criminal activity. Street girls worked the crowd, even right in front of the Folies Bergére. We saw several pickpocket men and girls, also working the crowd. They were very efficient, not one victim even noticed they had just been robbed. In addition, we saw more men in expensive suits, and they were not tourists, patrons of the Folies or customers of the street girls. What a place!

Taxis were all around. I thought about going inside the Folies, but Hannibal had already hailed a taxi. "Some other time," I thought, with a rueful smile.

Soon we were back at the Ritz. After we had a quick bite to eat from the coffee shop, we returned to our room. Soon we settled on the sofa, comparing notes and planning our activities for Friday.

I began by saying: "We had quite an evening. I learned a lot."

Hannibal nodded and responded: "We need to contact Inspecteur Clemenceau before we do anything else."

"I agree," I replied. "He was aware of us tonight in the Quartier Pigalle. Do you know how to contact him?"

"I got a phone number when I was at Renault's office on Tuesday. According to Yvette, Clemenceau lives in Montparnasse, on the left bank of the Seine."

"That's wise," I replied. "He has a safer residence than his usual haunts in the Quartier Pigalle."

"I'll give him a call first thing tomorrow morning," responded Hannibal. "After a night of undercover prowling, I'm sure he will sleep in."

"Good idea," I said with a smile. I leaned over and kissed Hannibal on the cheek. He smiled and returned the favor.

## Friday midnight, July 26

Today began and ended well. Hannibal called Clemenceau at about nine o'clock. After a brief conversation, Hannibal returned to the sofa and sat next to me. I was dressed in my white Chanel lounging pajamas. As always, Hannibal was already fully dressed.

"Clemenceau will meet us at the new La Coupole Brasserie on Boulevard du Montparnasse for lunch at noon," said Hannibal. "The La Coupole is near his apartment."

"Did he mention seeing us in Quartier Pigalle last night?" I asked.

"Yes," replied Hannibal with a smile. "Clemenceau said we blended into the crowd nicely, but he had our description from Renault." He paused and then added: "He had been briefed by Renault concerning our investigative activities."

"Very observant of him," I responded.

Hannibal nodded and said: "He seemed genuinely glad to have our help."

"Hummm," I mused. "I think we can dress normally for our meeting at La Coupole, as long as we are not too flashy," I ventured. I definitely did not want to wear my dowdy Pigalle sleuthing dress.

Hannibal grinned, nodded and replied: "I think so. I saw an advertisement in the newspaper, and the place is upscale, but the food is very reasonably priced. It opened just two years ago." With a twinkle in his eyes, Hannibal added: "I also read in the newspaper where La Coupole is a hangout for the Avant Guard artistic crowd."

"Sounds like fun," I responded. "It's a long way from the Quartier Pigalle, and we can spend time with Clemenceau, at an inconspicuous table. I want to get his input on potential Sûreté corruption as well as what we should look for in Pigalle."

Hannibal and I arrived at La Coupole just before noon. The place was new, fresh and filled with patrons. "Perfect," I thought to myself. Hannibal arranged for a table inside, next to a window.

I spotted Inspecteur Clemenceau a few minutes after twelve noon. He saw us and walked over to our table. He was dressed in a business suit, very unlike the clothes that he wore in the Quartier Pigalle on Thursday evening.

Clemenceau smiled as he approached. "Monsieur and Madame Jones, I presume," he said in perfect English.

Hannibal rose from his seat and offered his hand. "Yes," he responded. "We've heard many good things about you, Inspecteur." The two men shook hands. Hannibal turned to me and said: "Caroline, please meet Inspecteur Clemenceau."

I smiled and nodded. "Inspecteur Renault told us about your work," I said. "He speaks very highly of you."

"Thank you," replied Clemenceau. "And you are known to the Gendarmerie as 'the cat in the window." His smile broadened. "Your exploits are extraordinary and of great service."

"Thank you," I responded. "Would you please join us? We were about to order lunch."

Soon the social pleasantries were completed and lunch was ordered. We got down to business.

Clemenceau began with: "The Emporium owned by Simon Goldhirsch is an outlet for stolen jewelry. Thanks to your evidence, charges will eventually be filed and as a minimum, Goldhirsch will likely get a lengthy prison sentence."

"Eventually?" asked Hannibal.

Clemenceau replied: "The Gendarmerie hopes to gather enough evidence to also arrest members of the Unione Corse, Goldhirsch's sponsors and source of supply." He paused and his voice lowered to a whisper: "We are after Paul Carbone and François Spirito."

Hannibal and I both nodded. I then said: "We noticed that prostitution and pickpocketing are rampant in the Quartier Pigalle." I added: "Do the police have plans regarding these activities?"

Clemenceau's face had a sad look. "We of the Gendarmerie have made some arrests of the gangster sponsors of these activities. All of our arrests were suspected members of the Unione Corse."

He sighed and then continued: "However, the Sûreté, specifically the Préfet de Police of Paris, quietly released those arrested due to lack of evidence and witnesses who were not willing to testify in court."

Clemenceau looked first at me, then Hannibal and said: "We do not have much public support with regard to prosecuting prostitution. Many of our citizens view it as a victimless crime."

I squirmed a little in my seat, as I recalled my previous line of work in the Wabash Valley. After a moment, I replied: "It is much the same in America." Both Hannibal and Clemenceau nodded, and nothing else was said.

After a couple of moments, Hannibal said: "Inspecteur Renault hinted that known gang leaders, the parrain, may have influence within the Préfet de Police of Paris. Do you have evidence?"

"None that would stand up in court," replied Clemenceau. "However," and his voice lowered to a whisper: "The Directeur Generale of the Sûreté, Jean Chiappe, has been seen in the company of both Paul Carbone and François Spirito."

Hannibal and I looked at each other. "We now have a name," I thought to myself. To Clemenceau, I said: "I understand your frustration."

Clemenceau nodded and replied: "Any evidence of corruption that you can uncover would be most appreciated."

The waiter brought our lunch. The three of us ate in silence.

As we finished, Clemenceau stated: "While you are in Quartier Pigalle, pay close attention to the building across the street and two doors down from Goldhirsch's Emporium." He smiled and added: "I think you will find the people who come and go of interest."

Hannibal and I looked at each other. Nothing more was said about business, and the luncheon passed with social pleasantries. The waiter came, and Hannibal and the Inspecteur split the bill. Clemenceau said his goodbyes and left.

"We have a place that requires long-term surveillance," Hannibal said, as we watched Clemenceau walk out the door.

"Agreed," I replied. "When we get back to the Ritz, let's get out a street map and select a spot for inconspicuous snooping."

# 23

## PREPARATIONS FOR SNOOPING

*Sunday evening, July 28, 1929*

Hannibal and I spent the weekend planning our next moves. Saturday mid-morning, we relaxed on the sofa in the parlor.

After a few sips of our third cups of coffee, Hannibal began the conversation. "We should follow up on Clemenceau's suggestion about surveillance," he said.

"Hummm," I mused. I thought a moment about the area surrounding the building across the street from the Emporium that Clemenceau had mentioned. Finally, I said: "I recall that the intersection of Rue Fontaine and Rue Pigalle had another street between them at the intersection, just northwest of the building that Clemenceau mentioned."

Hannibal leaned back on the sofa and closed his eyes. After a moment, he responded: "Yes, the street is Rue Chaptal, and it bisects the angle between Fontaine and Pigalle from the northwest." He looked at me, and his eyes showed the obvious question.

I smiled at Hannibal's puzzled look and replied: "There is a large, three-story building at the intersection between Chaptal and Pigalle. The top floor has a window that gives a view straight down Pigalle, which runs to the northeast."

"Ah," responded Hannibal. "Great place for a surveillance post. We could see the fronts of both the building of interest and the Emporium." He grinned and added: "Very good!"

I smiled; the compliment was appreciated. I took another sip of coffee and said: "Perhaps if we agree to share information on the Unione Corse, Annette's grandfather can help us get permission to use the room behind that window."

I waited as Hannibal digested my comment and then continued: "I could visit my new friend Annette and discuss it." I grinned and added: "She was clearly ready for an adventure."

Hannibal frowned a little and said: "A little risky, but you should be OK." He leaned forward and scribbled a few notes on a notepad that lay on the coffee table. He then looked up and said: "I have contacts in Germany that used to supply our Chicago lab with cameras and other optical equipment."

I'm sure my face had a blank look.

Hannibal smiled and said: "Remember my Leica thirty-five-millimeter camera that we used for surveillance back in the Wabash Valley? It came from my German contact."

"And?" I asked.

Hannibal grinned more openly and replied: "The firm makes cameras and lenses for the new motion picture industry. Maybe they have some equipment we can use for long distance surveillance."

"Wonderful!" I exclaimed, as the implications crystalized in my mind. I added: "We each have our homework for Monday." I paused and then asked: "What about Sunday?"

## Monday evening, July 29

Sunday was a day of relaxation. Hannibal and I visited Montparnasse on the left bank of the Seine, stopped in a couple of shops, and had lunch at La Coupole. I felt refreshed as we wandered the streets. Hannibal pointed out places of interest; he had obviously visited Rive Gauche before. "A man of the world," I thought to myself, as I put my arm through his.

One of the shops that Hannibal wanted to show me was a bookstore and publishing house with the name 'Shakespeare and

Company.' We took a taxi from the Boulevard du Montparnasse to just north of the Palais du Luxembourg. The store was located at 12 Rue de l'Odéon. We browsed through the books. A very nice American lady, apparently the owner, helped us. I think her name was Silvia.

We bought a couple of books, including one by a new American author named Earnest Hemingway. Sylvia said Hemingway now lives in France, and he was a frequent visitor to the bookstore. His new book is titled: 'The Sun Also Rises.' It was written in English, and I'm looking forward to reading it when I have time.

Today, Hannibal and I made lots of phone calls. We both have meetings on Tuesday.

Annette was all bubbly about getting together for lunch. She suggested the Le Dôme Café at noon. I accepted. She gave me the address, which is 108 Boulevard du Montparnasse. Hannibal said it has been a hangout for artists and writers since the war. Sounds like fun!

Hannibal made arrangements to meet a Paris representative of Arnold and Richter Cine Teknik, his German camera supplier. We would go on our separate errands and meet back at the Ritz for dinner.

## Tuesday Evening, July 30

I arrived at Le Dôme by taxi from the Ritz just before noon. I saw Annette, who waved gayly from just inside the main door. I also saw two very large men standing near Annette.

Both had no nonsense expressions on their faces. They tipped their hats as I approached, moved to a table just outside the main door and sat down. Their eyes constantly searched all around, both inside the café and along the sidewalk.

"My bodyguards," whispered Annette as I drew near. "My grandfather insisted." She grinned mischievously.

"Good idea," I replied. I looked around. I saw a scattering of local folks and a couple of scruffy looking characters seated just inside.

The scruffy pair were lamenting in English about the old days. One said: "Joyce and Hemingway never stop by now. The old days are gone forever." His companion seemed to agree. Both men sipped wine. I saw a couple of empty bottles on the table.

The maître d' escorted Annette and me to a nice table in a corner by a window. After the usual pleasantries about dresses and the arrival of our recent purchases at the Chanel salon, we got down to the hot topic of the day.

"I need your help for an adventure," I began. "My husband and I plan to spy on members of the Unione Corse."

"Oh, my!" Annette replied. "How can I help?"

I described our intended target buildings on Rue Pigalle. "We want to watch and take photos of the people that enter and leave the Emporium, owned by Simon Goldhirsch, and the building across the street. We suspect that the Unione Corse has operations in that building."

I paused as I watched Annette's reaction. She fidgeted a little and grinned.

I then said: "There is another three-story building at the intersection between Chaptal and Pigalle that would make a perfect surveillance post. My husband and I are particularly interested in the third story room with a window that provides a view of our target buildings."

Annette leaned forward and whispered: "I bet you want my grandfather to get you set up in that room."

"Hummm," I thought to myself. "This girl is quick and smart." To Annette, I replied: "Yes. Hannibal and I could set up a hidden camera with a telephoto lens in the room. We would have a perfect view of our targets."

Annette leaned back in her chair as the waiter approached. We looked at the menu. "I suggest a salad and fillet of sole," said Annette. "I have been here many times, and it's the best in Paris."

"Done," I replied. "Shall we add wine or Perrier?"

"Ah, you Americans," said Annette with a laugh. "Perrier sounds fine."

I laughed in response. The waiter took our order and left.

Annette leaned forward, looked directly in my eyes and asked: "Are you working for the police?"

I was taken a little by surprise. "This girl is no one's fool," I concluded. I decided to be truthful. I replied: "Yes. We are working for the Gendarmerie, not the Sûreté and their subordinate unit, the Préfet de Police of Paris."

"Ah," mused Annette. "They are rivals, just like my grandfather and the Unione Corse."

It was my turn to lean back in my chair and watch Annette's face. Her eyes held steady.

After a moment, I said: "I think so. Our Gendarmerie employers suspect that the Unione Corse has made arrangements with members of the Préfet de Police of Paris for protection of their activities." I paused and then added: "My husband and I are after Paul Carbone, François Spirito and their contacts in the Préfet de Police."

Annette chuckled and acquired a mischievous grin. "My grandfather will love this one," she replied. "However, I think he would want to share in the information that you obtain by your surveillance."

I thought a long moment before replying. "Ange Salicetti will use our information to go after the Unione Corse with vengeance," I thought to myself. "However, I have skirted the fringes of gang warfare most of my adult life," my thoughts continued. "Sometimes justice is served outside the law," I finally rationalized. I could see no downside to such an outcome.

I set twinges of conscience aside, and to Annette, I said: "Agree. My husband and I will not tell the Gendarmerie about our arrangement with your grandfather, although I think they will eventually figure it out."

Annette looked long into my eyes. Finally, she said: "Fair enough. I will talk to my grandfather." Her eyes regained their twinkle, and she added: "I think he will agree to help you."

"Thank you," I replied, and I meant it.

Annette giggled and said: "You're welcome. However, there is one more thing. You must promise to keep me informed every step of the way. I'm so excited!"

I laughed and said: "I promise."

Our conversation turned to the outfits that we purchased at Coco Chanel's salon. The lunch soon arrived, and we had a great time. We finished at about two o'clock. Annette said she would call me at the Ritz in a day or so. What a lunch!

Back at the Ritz, I took a bubble bath, fixed my hair and changed into my black Schiaparelli lounging outfit before Hannibal returned from his errand. I also ordered room service dinner, with champagne, for six o'clock.

"My treat," I said to myself as I completed the final touches to my hair. "I hope Hannibal likes what I ordered." I was beginning to understand French food, fine dining and Hannibal's preferences.

Hannibal showed up just after five o'clock. I heard the door open as I stood by the window, looking out over Paris. I turned just as Hannibal entered the parlor.

"You look lovely this evening," Hannibal said with a smile. "You are the cat in the window again."

I smiled demurely and replied: "Why merci beaucoup, Monsieur." I then gave Hannibal my best imitation of a purring kitten. "Welcome home," I said, as I sauntered over to him and gave him a big kiss. He returned the favor, several times.

Soon he had shed his coat, tie and shoes, and we snuggled cozily on the sofa. After a few minutes, I said: "I have been slaving over dinner ever since I got home from work. I hope you like it."

Oh?" replied Hannibal with a grin. "What time will room service arrive?"

I gave him a dig in the ribs and responded: "OK, smarty, they will be here at six o'clock."

I paused and then added: "I ordered chicken liver pâté and crackers, baguettes and sweet cream butter, a selection of cheeses, coquilles Saint Jacques, a garden salad with buttermilk dressing and blanquette de Veau. For dessert, we are having chocolate mousse. Of course, we will have champagne."

"Sounds wonderful," replied Hannibal. "I'm hungry, so I guess I will snack on you while we wait." He gave me a kiss on the neck.

I giggled. "Later, dear, after dinner." I kissed him again. I'll be dessert after dessert."

Hannibal chuckled and said: "I look forward to it." He scooted around, looked into my eyes and added: "So how was your day?"

"Very productive," I replied. I then told him about my meeting with Annette.

"Very good," responded Hannibal when I finished. "You did the right thing. Hopefully, Salicetti can make arrangements for our surveillance post."

He paused and then continued: "While you were doing the fun stuff, I made arrangements for some state-of-the-art camera equipment."

"Tell, me all about it," I replied. I was genuinely interested; I loved photography, especially with regard to sleuthing.

"Well," said Hannibal, "Arnold and Richter will provide us with a thirty-five-millimeter camera with an Astro-Berlin telephoto lens. The combination of camera and lens is quite heavy, so it will be mounted on a tripod for stability and to reduce jitter. The telephoto lens has a side-mounted, wide-angle spotting telescope to locate targets. The camera and lens can take close-up photos of targets that are hundreds of meters distant."

"What about developing the film?" I asked.

"Good point," replied Hannibal. "Arnold and Richter will also provide all the dark room equipment that we will need. We can set everything up at our surveillance post, if Salicetti can make arrangements."

I thought a moment and then said: "We will have to find a back entrance to the building. We can't let the bad guys see us."

"I agree," replied Hannibal. "I'll do a little reconnaissance tomorrow."

There was a knock at the door. Hannibal looked at his watch and said: "Six o'clock. Right on time." He stood up and got ready to answer the door. Before he turned to go, he said: "I'm already looking forward to dessert."

I giggled.

## Friday evening, August 2

Annette called this morning. We have our room for a surveillance post, and Hannibal found a back entrance to the building on Wednesday.

On Thursday, Hannibal found a couple of U.S. Army surplus cots, blankets and mess kits at a second-hand store in Montparnasse. "Lots of old U.S. equipment was left in France after the war," he explained.

Early this morning, Hannibal and I took a taxi from the Ritz to our new surveillance post. We wore fashionable clothes as we left the Ritz, but I carried a hanging bag with our dowdy outfits. I also had a paper sack with drinks and sandwiches for our first evening of surveillance and a briefcase with notepads and pencils.

We got out of the taxi on Rue Chaptal, right by the alley that led to the building with our new third-story hideout.

A man in a business suit met us in the alley. He gave Hannibal a set of keys. Nothing was said, and the man silently departed. "Creepy," I thought to myself, and I shivered a little. Hannibal opened the back door behind a small loading dock, and we entered the dimly lit building. Stairs led up to the second and third floors. No one was around.

We soon found our third-floor room. It was a vacant loft at the far end. The second-floor underneath was used for storage by a couple of shops on the ground level. The loft room had a simple water tap and a sink, that was all. Otherwise, it was completely empty. A very rudimentary bathroom was located by a second stairwell just outside the room. Simple, but we could manage. The view from the window was perfect.

Hannibal and I changed clothes and returned to the alley. Within ten minutes, the Arnold and Richter truck entered the alley and stopped by the little loading dock.

Hannibal and the driver unloaded two non-descript crates. The building had no elevator, so they had to carry the two boxes up the three flights of narrow stairs. The process took about thirty minutes. I kept watch outside in the alley, but I didn't see anyone.

Hannibal had also arranged for the delivery of the army surplus equipment just after the Arnold and Richter truck left the alley. I marveled at Hannibal's attention to detail with regard to equipment and timing of deliveries.

Soon everything we needed was in our room. Hannibal assembled the camera, telephoto lens and the tripod. He set everything up back from the window so it would not be noticed by people on the street. I set up the dark room equipment. By noon we were ready.

# 24

## DEATH OF A GOOD MAN

*Saturday afternoon, August 10, 1929*

Surveillance is hard work! Hannibal and I set up shop last week on Friday in our surveillance post, and we collected a wealth of photos and notes over seven days. As best we could tell, no one, especially the persons coming and going from our target building, ever noticed us.

Each morning, we took a taxi from the Ritz to a different location on either Rue Fontaine or Rue Chaptal, several blocks northwest of our surveillance post. We wore different nondescript clothing each day, so we blended with ordinary Parisians on their way to work.

We walked along the crowded sidewalk with the morning work traffic and slipped into the alley behind our building. Using our key, we entered through the service door behind the loading dock and walked up the stairs to our loft.

After a couple of days of surveillance, we named our target building 'the Headquarters.' We spent about fifteen hours each day watching, taking photos through our window and making notes.

About eleven o'clock at night, we closed up shop and left through the service door. Our walk along Rue Fontaine to the Moulin Rouge was just in time for the evening show to let out and the midnight show to begin; Parisians are night people. Again, we blended with the crowd. There were always plenty of taxis around the Moulin Rouge, and we made it back to the Ritz about midnight.

The effort was worth it. We have most of the evidence needed to complete our file. We have just one more task with regard to the Headquarters; we plan to burglarize the place. On Friday night, we locked up our surveillance post, but we left our equipment. We may need to snoop again at a later date, during and after our burglary.

I took a bubble bath this morning, fixed my hair and put on one of my new Chanel summer outfits. I slipped quietly out of the bathroom and joined Hannibal in the parlor. He was already dressed, groomed and busy at our work table, arranging photos and making notes. How does he do it?

Hannibal looked up as I entered the parlor. "Good morning sunshine," he said with a smile. "Let's go downstairs for breakfast this morning. Think you can make it?"

"Hummf," I muttered. My brain was still fuzzy. Actually, a nice breakfast down in the sumptuous morning room sounded pretty good. "OK," I articulated. This time my voice was at least intelligible.

I felt better after a leisurely breakfast. Hannibal and I returned to our room about ten o'clock, ready for work. We laid out dozens of photos in organized stacks. Each stack had photos of a single person, along with notes.

"Let's review," Hannibal began. "As expected, we have photos of Simon Goldhirsch, as he walked across the street to the Headquarters every other evening. He carried a small sack in, and left with a box."

"Yes," I responded. "He probably carried money in to the Headquarters and took stolen goods out." I paused, smiled wryly and added: "Busy man."

"We also photographed the regular Headquarters crew," Hannibal said. "Four men, dressed in normal business attire, who arrive separately around eight o'clock in the morning and leave after five in the evening."

"Accountants and bookkeepers," I mused. "I would love to see their ledgers."

"You're probably right," replied Hannibal. "The evidence of their work will be one of the objectives of our planned burglary."

I pointed to three stacks of photos and notes, all in a little group on the table. "These three guys look like the men we saw in the crowds around the Moulin Rouge and the Folies Bergére, I stated. "I remember two of them for sure; they were talking with several of the street girls."

"They probably control the girls," Hannibal agreed. "It would be nice to have an organizational chart."

I grinned and replied: "Another objective for our burglary."

"Yes," said Hannibal. "We have lots of objectives; what we need is a plan."

I thought for quite a while. Hannibal waited patiently. Finally, I said: "It's too risky for the two of us to do it. If we're spotted, we will lose the whole game." I grinned wryly and continued: "If we're not shot on sight, the bad guys will, as a minimum, move elsewhere. We would have to start from scratch."

"Agree," responded Hannibal. "We need a good second-story person."

I nodded and said: "I expect that Annette's grandfather can supply us with a first-class burglar."

Hannibal laughed and then replied: "You have such interesting friends."

I smiled and continued my train of thought: "We could show our burglar how to use a camera and flashlight to photograph any ledgers and other records, page by page, that he might find."

Hannibal nodded and responded: "The burglar could also take photos of anything else of interest. If he does it right, the occupants of the Headquarters will never know he was there."

"I will call Annette on Monday," I replied. "I'll even promise to buy lunch." I thought a moment and then added: "She's resourceful and full of surprises."

Hannibal laughed again.

I looked around the table. Another stack had several photos of Inspecteur Clemenceau. "Our Inspecteur friend is a regular on the street," I stated. I thought a moment and added: "He is playing a dangerous game."

"Agree," responded Hannibal. "He has good intentions, but he's a little obvious."

I turned to a final stack. This guy interests me the most," I said, as I picked up the top photo. "He was well-dressed, and he came in and out several times." I paused a moment and then continued: "Each time, he carried a briefcase."

"He also came by automobile," said Hannibal, as he picked up a photo of the man next to a car. "We have a photo of his license plate." Hannibal smiled slightly and added: "I was on the phone with Inspecteur Renault this morning. He gave me a name."

My face expressed the obvious question, but I replied: "You were a busy guy before I got up this morning."

Hannibal responded: "Yes, well, our person of interest is Inspecteur Jean-Paul Symone, and he is a member of the Préfet de Police in Paris, which is under the Sûreté."

"The Sûreté! I exclaimed. "We have our connection."

"I think so," responded Hannibal. "It's interesting that his visits are so blatant." His expression changed to a frown, and he added: "Look carefully at this photo." He picked up a photo from the stack and handed it to me. "I snapped this photo yesterday and developed it last evening."

"I took the photo from Hannibal and looked carefully. I saw the man of interest, who now had the name Jean-Paul Symone. He was getting into a car. I could read the license plate.

I then looked around the image of the car and man. Finally, I spotted what Hannibal was driving at. Inspecteur Clemenceau was standing about fifty meters away, across the street, by the corner near the Emporium. "Oh, my goodness," I exclaimed. "Clemenceau is in plain sight."

"I would be very surprised if Clemenceau has not been spotted," said Hannibal. "He is in danger." He paused and added: "I told Renault this morning when I was on the phone."

"Good," I replied. "I hope Renault warns Clemenceau."

"He will," said Hannibal.

Hannibal and I spent the rest of the afternoon reviewing and organizing our notes. We also started a draft report.

## Saturday evening, August 10

As we were about to call it a day, the phone rang. Hannibal walked over to the phone by the entryway and answered. After a full minute, Hannibal returned. His expression was very grave. I looked into his eyes and waited.

"It was Renault," said Hannibal. "Inspecteur Clemenceau was shot in front of his apartment building less than an hour ago. He's dead. Renault wants us to meet him at the scene." Hannibal paused and then added: "I have the address. His apartment building is on Rue Stanislas, not far from La Coupole. I told Renault that we are on the way."

"Right," I responded. I went to the closet and took out our leather crime scene case that we had created in Le Havre. We both grabbed light jackets from the closet. Within two minutes, we were out the door.

Hannibal and I got out of our taxi at the corner of Boulevard du Montparnasse and Rue Stanislas about twenty minutes later. We walked up Rue Stanislas and passed the Église Notre Dame-des-Champs on the left.

We saw Inspecteur Renault on the right side of the street in front of an apartment building. Several police cars were parked nearby, along with an ambulance.

Inspecteur Renault saw us as we approached and waved us over. We saw a body on the sidewalk, covered with a dark blanket. Blood oozed out from under the blanket. "Inspecteur Clemenceau," I said to myself.

Renault's expression was a combination of sadness and fierce temper, both under control. "Your warning was correct," he said in a soft voice as we drew near. "I need your help." His expression changed to one of grim determination. "Would you inspect the crime scene?"

"Yes," replied Hannibal. He set our leather case on the sidewalk and took out his Leica thirty-five-millimeter camera. He then walked over to the body, pulled back the blanket and studied the victim.

While Hannibal was busy, I asked: "Any witnesses?"

"None that would say much," replied Renault. "A couple said they saw a car drive by, heard two shots and saw the man fall." He pointed to the body. "I have their names."

"Drive-by shooting," I mused. "Sounds professional."

"Yes," replied Renault. "No one has come forward with a license plate number. The couple that saw the shooting said the car was a black sedan, probably a late model Citroën B10."

He paused and pointed. "The car came up the street on this side and continued in that direction." He pointed up the street away from the intersection of Boulevard du Montparnasse and Rue Stanislas.

"That's something to go on," I responded. "If it's OK with you, I will follow along the path of the car as it drove along the street."

"Please do," replied Renault. He turned and spoke a few words to several uniformed gendarme, who stood nearby. They nodded and went about their tasks of keeping gawkers away.

I turned, walked back down the street and back up, next to the curb. I looked carefully in the gutter as I approached the body. I spotted what I was looking for.

Two bullet casings lay in the gutter, about ten meters from the body. I took a small paper sack and a pencil from my jacket pocket and used the pencil to pick up the casings. These I dropped in my sack.

I then walked over to Hannibal. He was taking photos. "Two bullet casings," I said, as I held up the sack.

Hannibal replied: "Good. Two wounds on the victim, both through the chest. The autopsy will tell us more." He pointed to our leather case and added: "We have the fingerprint stuff in the case."

Between us, we soon had two fingerprints from the bullet casings. Hannibal took photos of the casings and close-ups of the fingerprints. I returned the casings to the sack.

I saw Renault watching. "You two are very efficient," he said. "We can compare these fingerprints to those of known criminals in our files." He looked into the sack at the casings. "Nine-millimeter," he said.

I handed him the sack with the casings and the sheets of paper with the fingerprints. "We have photos, and that will be sufficient."

I turned to Hannibal and asked: "Did you find exit wounds?"

"Yes," replied Hannibal. "Both bullets passed all the way through and out the back. "He thought a moment and added: "They were probably jacketed, perhaps military rounds."

We both turned and scanned the front of the apartment building. Hannibal spotted a hole in a door frame, just behind the body. "One bullet for sure," he said.

He took out his pocket knife and dug out the bullet, being careful not to damage it. Soon he had it in a sack. "Nine-millimeter," he confirmed. "It's jacketed, with nice grooves from the gun barrel. If we find a gun, we can match the bullet."

I looked around for the second bullet. I saw a new chip in the stone façade next to the wooden door frame. I look around.

"Nothing, I mused. "That bullet could have ricocheted anywhere. However, one bullet is good."

Renault walked over from his conversations with the uniformed gendarme. Hannibal explained what we had found and handed him the sack with the bullet.

"We will follow up with what we have," I said. "Can you let us review the autopsy report and tell about any matches with the fingerprints?"

"Of course," replied Renault. "You both are marvels. Thank you." His voice was sincere.

Hannibal and I looked around the crime scene for another thirty minutes or so, but there was nothing else, except a man watching us from across the street near an alley.

I looked closely. The man was thin, almost haggard. He was dressed in a dark business suit and had a fedora hat that obscured his face. He saw me watching and raised his head.

The sun illuminated his features for a moment. His complexion was dark, as if he had a Mediterranean ancestry. I saw a long scar on his left cheek. He turned and quickly disappeared in the alley.

I turned toward Hannibal, who was facing away, talking to Renault. "OK, Caroline, a suspicious character, but he's gone." I had other things to think about.

A crew from the ambulance took away the body and cleaned up the blood. I watched for a moment. "Sad," I mused. "He was a good man."

I walked over to Renault and asked: "Did Inspecteur Clemenceau have a family?"

"He was a bachelor," replied Renault. "However, his family is quite prominent." He paused and smiled. "Perhaps you are familiar with the name Georges Clemenceau."

I drew a blank. "I will ask Hannibal," I thought to myself. To Renault, I said: "I'm sure you will follow up with his family."

"Yes," replied Renault, "One of my saddest duties."

Hannibal and I buttoned up our leather case and prepared to leave. Renault watched us and said: "I can have someone drive you back to the Ritz."

"No, thank you," replied Hannibal with a smile. "We want to avoid being conspicuous when we arrive at the Ritz, so we will catch a taxi." He paused and added: "We will keep you informed."

"As you wish," replied Renault. "Good hunting."

# 25

## A DANGEROUS GAME

*Sunday noon, August 11, 1929*

After our murder scene investigation last evening, Hannibal and I returned to the Ritz. We were not very hungry, so we picked up a couple of sandwiches and coffee at the little café near the lobby. We sat in silence on the sofa in our room, eating our sandwiches and sipping coffee.

As we finished, I broke the silence. "Clemenceau was the victim of a professional hit." I paused and then added: "I would bet that the hit was ordered by the parrain, the leaders, of the Unione Corse."

"Agree," replied Hannibal. "We need to connect the evidence we found at the scene to the hit man and the hit man to the Unione Corse." He leaned back on the sofa and then added: "We have fingerprints, a bullet, two nine-millimeter bullet casings and two witnesses that saw a black car, probably a late model Citroën B10."

I thought for a moment and then responded: "Renault may not find a match to the fingerprints in his criminal data base. Professional hit men often do not have criminal records."

"Yes," replied Hannibal. "Also, the autopsy report will probably just verify what we already know about the cause of death."

We were silent for a couple of minutes. I finished my coffee. Finally, I said: "Renault said that Inspecteur Clemenceau was a bachelor, but had a prominent family. He also mentioned the name Georges Clemenceau." I looked at Hannibal closely. "Do you know what he meant?"

Hannibal finished his coffee, returned my gaze and responded: "Inspecteur Clemenceau may be related to the former French Prime Minister, Georges Clemenceau. As far as I can recall from my time during the war, Georges Clemenceau had only one son Michel, who is also quite prominent. Perhaps our Inspecteur was a distant cousin or great-nephew."

I took a deep breath and let it out slowly. I then said: "If our Inspecteur was a relative, I'm sure there will be high-level interest in solving his murder and bringing the murderer to justice."

"I think so," responded Hannibal. "According to French newspapers, Jean Baptiste Chiappe, the former Director of the Sûreté, is now the Préfet de Police of Paris. "Also, recent leftist French newspapers confirmed that Chiappe is a friend of Paul Carbone and François Spirito, the parrain of Unione Corse."

"Hummm," I replied. "Then Soucet's insight is now public knowledge. The rivalry between the Gendarmerie and the Sûreté has a strong political element." I paused and then added: "Who are the bad guys, really?"

Hannibal shook his head and smiled.

Silence reigned for several minutes. Finally, I said: "More than ever, we need to get inside the Unione Corse Headquarters on Rue Pigalle. In addition to records of stolen goods, we need to look for records of bribes to members of the Sûreté and payments to a professional hit man."

Monday evening, August 12th

I called Annette late this morning. As usual, she was all bubbly and upbeat.

After the usual pleasantries, I said: "I have another favor to ask. Can we meet for lunch?"

"Of course," replied Annette. "I'm so excited to hear about your adventures." There was a pause; I could hear Annette speaking to someone else. After a moment, she came back on line. "My bodyguard said we can meet at La Coupole without a problem. I am free today. How about one o'clock?"

"Perfect," I responded. "Please tell your grandfather that I will have a file for him soon."

"I will make sure he knows," said Annette. "See you at one o'clock."

After I hung up the phone, I checked my calendar for the remainder of the week. I had an appointment on Wednesday afternoon at Jean Lanvin's Fashion house at 15 Rue du Faubourg-Saint Honoré, that was all.

"I can ask Annette if she wants to join me at Lanvin's on Wednesday," I mused. I smiled a little ruefully and continued my thoughts: "It will be fun, but perhaps less exciting than our last outing at a fashion salon."

I walked into the parlor. Hannibal was writing at our work table. He looked up and said: "I heard your conversation with Annette. I will have a file ready for you later today."

"How very thoughtful!" I replied. "I suppose you will include the results of our surveillance."

"Yes," responded Hannibal. "I will include extra prints of all of the photos, with annotations of time, place, and so on. I will even include the photo of Inspecteur Jean-Paul Symone, his car and Inspecteur Clemenceau in the background. Since Clemenceau is dead, we will not give anything away that would compromise his undercover activities."

"I'm sure Salicetti will appreciate knowing that the Unione Corse is involved with the Sûreté, I replied. "Maybe he can nose around and add information, including names, to our files."

"That's the idea," Hannibal replied. "What are your plans for your meeting with Annette?"

"Well, in addition to getting her grandfather's help in finding a suitable burglar, I'm going to invite her to join me at lunch again tomorrow. I can give her your file at lunch. I will also invite her to join me at Lanvin's on Wednesday."

Hannibal laughed. "Shopping again. I suppose I should check our bank account to make sure we can cover your purchases."

"OK, smarty, you do that," I replied with a grin. "I understood Hannibal's jest. He wanted me to have a good time; the past week had been pretty stressful. I walked over and kissed him on the cheek. He kissed me back and gave me a hug.

The meeting with Annette today went as planned. As before, her bodyguards sat at a table just outside the main door of La Coupole, and Annette and I sat at a corner table inside, by a window.

Annette ordered a delicious soup, salad and baguette combination, along with gelato for dessert for both of us. We had a great time together, in addition to business.

With a mischievous grin, she promised to talk to her grandfather about a burglar. We made another luncheon date at La Coupole Café for tomorrow at one o'clock, and she agreed to join me at Lanvin's on Wednesday. Annette said she would have news concerning a suitable burglar at our next lunch.

The only sad note was her recognition of the death of Inspecteur Clemenceau. "I heard about your Gendarmerie colleague," she said. "I'm so sorry." She put her hand on my arm and added: "I will see if my grandfather can help find those responsible."

I returned to the Ritz at about three o'clock. Hannibal was waiting. As we sat on the sofa, I gave him all of the details.

"When I finished, he said: "I have a file ready for her grandfather. Later, we can work out how we want to supervise a burglary. However, that can wait. I have other news." He smiled and watched my face.

After waiting for a full minute, I fidgeted and said: "Well?"

"Remember our discussion about an apartment in Paris a couple of weeks ago? I made some phone calls, and we have an appointment with a real estate broker on Wednesday next week. After I described our preferences, he promised to show us several rather nice apartments."

"Sounds wonderful!" I responded. "I'll wear my latest dress from Chanel's salon!"

Hannibal laughed. "However, I have to take a train to Geneva this evening to arrange a transfer of funds to our Paris account. I also have to finish the asset re-allocation for cash, stocks and bonds that we discussed in mi-July. I'll be back on Tuesday, in time for our apartment hunting expedition."

"And I will continue shopping," I replied with a giggle. "Bring back lots of money."

"Good heavens," responded Hannibal. "Paris will never be the same."

"Hummf," I responded with my best snooty look. "I'll look very nice, you'll see." I joined Hannibal in laughter.

## Tuesday evening, August 13

Hannibal is away on his business trip, and I have our Ritz suite all to myself. It's very quiet without Hannibal.

I arrived at La Coupole Café just before one o'clock today. Annette was already there, along with her two bodyguards. The maître 'd escorted us to a corner table inside, and the bodyguards sat at an outside table, like our last luncheon. After the usual pleasantries, I slipped Annette the file for her grandfather.

Annette leafed through the file and looked very carefully at the photos. I was a little surprised; her review seemed almost professional. "There is more to this young lady than just a wealthy dilettante," I thought to myself.

After a couple of minutes, Annette looked up, smiled and said: "Very well done; my grandfather will be pleased."

"Thank you," I replied.

The waiter came over and took our order. At Annette's suggestion, we ordered a salad, ratatouille, baguettes and in deference to my American tastes, Perrier.

Annette smiled as we explained our order to the very patient waiter. "The ratatouille is a French peasant stew," she said. "It's delicious." I could tell she was waiting to tell me something besides lunch order suggestions. "Patience, Caroline," I thought to myself.

As we sipped Perrier and waited for our food, I finally asked: "Did your grandfather have anyone in mind for our burglar?"

Annette smiled coyly and replied: "Yes. We decided to provide the very best burglar in Paris." She leaned close to me and whispered: "Me."

My mouth dropped open and I sat back in my chair. My mind raced, and I thought: "Of course!  Annette's sense of adventure, fighting spirit and family connections all point to such an admission." Finally, I said: "I should have guessed." Annette giggled.

"When should we do it?" Annette asked as she sipped her Perrier. Her demeanor shifted from humor to a business-like, professional expression.

I liked her implicit assumption that I would join in the adventure. "A girl after my own heart," I thought to myself.

I thought for a full minute. Finally, I replied: "My husband will be out of town until next Tuesday. If we work together, I think we can plan on Thursday or Friday."

"I looked at your photos carefully," responded Annette. "There is a skylight in the building that you have labeled 'the Headquarters.' We can approach over the rooftops, enter the skylight and drop down inside." She paused and then added: "I have the proper equipment."

"I have a camera that works well in low light," I said. "I also have a good flashlight." I paused as Annette digested the implications of working together and taking photos.

I then added: "We need to photograph records and ledgers page by page, and anything else that can help us prove the connection of Unione Corse to receipt of stolen goods, bribery of Sûreté officials, and murder." I then added: "For our safety, it's important that the building occupants never know that we were there."

"We will need several hours," Annette mused. "I have found that after midnight and before four o'clock in the morning works best." She smiled and her eyes twinkled.

"What a partner!" I thought to myself. To Annette, I said: "We can use our surveillance post to stage our operations. I also have film development equipment there, and I can develop our photos afterwards."

"I have a tight black pullover sweater, slim-cut tailored black pants and soft-soled, lace-up shoes," said Annette. "I also have a black backpack for my equipment and black leather gloves. How about you?"

"A tight black outfit makes perfect sense," I thought to myself. I smiled and then replied: "I have a suitable black outfit straight from Chanel's salon and black gloves, but I will have to get shoes and a backpack." I giggled a little and added: "We must be stylish about this."

Annette joined me in a giggle. "I remember the outfit. It's perfect. I can help you buy the shoes and backpack this afternoon," she responded.

We spent the rest of our lunch date memorizing our route from the surveillance post to the skylight on the roof of the building that housed the Unione Corse headquarters. Adventure awaits!

## Wednesday Evening, August 14

Annette and I had a wonderful time at Lanvin's on Wednesday. The experience was much the same as our experience at Chanel's, except for the attempted kidnapping. We each bought several outfits, all for the fall season. I'll model my outfits for Hannibal when he returns.

## Friday morning, August 16

The burglary went as planned. Last night just after midnight, Annette and I arrived separately. I came by taxi to a corner on Rue Fontaine, a couple of blocks away. I walked to the building that housed the surveillance post. We met in the alley behind the building.

We were both in ordinary street clothes, and we each had a backpack. I carried mine in a large shopping bag labeled 'Chanel Salon.' "No point in advertising that I'm a burglar," I had concluded. Annette had a similar disguise for her backpack, except that hers was a bag labeled 'Schiaparelli.'

Annette and I went inside and changed from our street clothes to our burglar outfits. Soon we were ready.

We followed our memorized route through alleys to our destination. It led through dark, deserted, narrow passages behind buildings that faced Rue Pigalle. We crossed Rue Fontaine and entered another alley that passed behind the large building next to the headquarters.

The large building had a fire escape ladder that ascended to the roof. We went up, crossed the roof over to the headquarters building and found the skylight that we had observed in the photos.

I watched in fascination as Annette opened her backpack, took out some tools and expertly removed the wood frame and a large pane of glass from the skylight. She then looked down inside the open hole. "About five meters to the floor," she whispered.

I looked in the hole. Enough light filtered through the windows into the room below to allow us to see shadowy details.

Annette rummaged in her backpack again and took out a neatly rolled up rope ladder. She used a short rope to attach one end of the ladder to the base of a nearby vent pipe, made sure the fastening and pipe were secure, and dropped the rolled ladder in the hole in the skylight.

I looked in the hole. The rope ladder reached the floor with about a meter of ladder to spare. I looked over to Annette and said: "I'll go first. If something goes wrong, you can fish me back up."

"Understand," whispered Annette. She verified the security of the fastened end of the ladder.

I kept my backpack on. It held my camera, a flashlight, a notepad, pencils and a fingerprint kit. I put on my gloves and slipped through the hole in the skylight. I swayed a little as I descended, but I made it to the floor without a problem. Whew!

A couple of minutes later, Annette joined me. She also wore gloves. She grinned at me in the dim light and whispered: "Let's get to work!"

We looked around. The place was a regular business office, with desks, chairs and filing cabinets. I made a sketch of the room layout. We found plenty of files. Annette read the French entries, and we soon figured out, given our objectives, the important files.

We worked with the flashlight and camera and took dozens of photos. I had extra rolls of film, and we changed rolls four times. I also laid out a cloth, dusted a number of items with black powder and lifted fingerprints. I had a little whisk brush to clean up the black powder. It was Annette's turn to watch in fascination.

Annette had a wristwatch, and she kept track of the time. We finished at about three in the morning. We made sure everything was back in its proper place. Finally, we were satisfied that no evidence of our snooping remained.

I shouldered my backpack and ascended the rope ladder. After I reached the roof, Annette followed me up.

I watched as Annette pulled up the rope ladder, replaced the glass pane and its frame and cleaned up the evidence of our entry.

We packed up our stuff and checked all around to make sure no evidence remained of our work on the roof. We then returned to the building that housed our surveillance post and changed into our street clothes.

After we finished, I said: "I'll come back to my darkroom equipment tomorrow and develop the film. I'll call you when I'm done."

"Sounds good," replied Annette. "My bodyguard knows where to pick me up. Do you need a ride?"

"No," I replied. I'll leave my stuff here, walk down Rue Fontaine and catch a taxi as people start arriving for the normal workday."

"Good idea," Annette replied. "Give me a call when you are ready for another lunch." She grinned mischievously. "I've had such fun!"

"Me too," I replied. I meant it; the whole night had been exhilarating. I couldn't wait to tell Hannibal.

We changed clothes and Annette departed. I just had to wait until daylight and the beginning of the workday.

# 26

## PREPARING FOR CLOSURE

*Tuesday night, August 20, 1929.*

At noon today, I took a taxi from the Ritz to the Gare de l'Est, the station that serves trains between Paris and Geneva. Hannibal's train arrived at noon. I was so glad to see him!

After kisses and hugs, I said: "I have so much to tell you!" My face, I'm sure, beamed like a mischievous school girl.

Hannibal looked at me with a smile and replied: "Oh? I can guess that you have had adventures other than shopping." His smile broadened a little.

"How does he always know?" I thought to myself. To Hannibal, I responded in my best mysterious manner: "I think we should brief Inspecteur Renault." I sniffed, paused for effect and added: "I'll tell you all about it when we get back to the Ritz."

I could see that Hannibal was intrigued. However, he just smiled and said: "OK."

"Humph," I thought to myself. "I'll make him wait." I replied: "So how was your trip?"

"It went well," he responded. "Our finances are finally in order, and we can weather the coming storm." He looked at me, and his smile faded.

He then said: "A storm is coming, and it will be severe. My banker friends have grave concerns about world economic activity. It's just a matter of time before stock markets, worldwide, react."

I'm sure my expression sobered as my mind turned to finances. To Hannibal, I responded: "Should we stay in Europe?"

Hannibal was quiet for several minutes as he collected his bag from the porter and we headed to the taxi stand. We got in a taxi and headed back toward the Ritz.

As we were speeding along, he said: "I think we are much better off in France than we would be back in the United States." He looked at me, smiled again and added: "Our life style will not change. We can shop for a long-term place to live in Paris, at least for a year or so."

I thought about Hannibal's sobering comments about the economy and his assessment for our future. Based on our previous conversations on the subject, I felt secure. I smiled and we held hands.

As we drove up to the Ritz, I said: "What time are we going shopping for an apartment tomorrow?"

"We have an appointment with an agent at ten in the morning," Hannibal replied. He looked at me with that steady, twinkly-eyed gaze of his and added: "In the meantime, I am looking forward to hearing about your adventures."

Soon we were in our room at the Ritz. We ordered a light lunch through room service. Hannibal unpacked, showered and changed clothes. I freshened up and changed into my white silk lounging outfit.

By two in the afternoon, we had finished our late lunch and had made ourselves comfortable on the sofa in the parlor. I spread out files, notes, photos and fingerprint pages on the coffee table.

I then began my tale of adventure. "Annette and I are burglars," I said with a grin. "According to her, she's the best in Paris."

Hannibal raised his eyebrows and looked at me for a full minute. Finally, he replied: "I'm sure you were successful."

"Yes," I responded. "We left no evidence of our break-in, and we took these photos, which I developed last Friday." I pointed to the neatly arranged stacks on the coffee table. "We have photos of ledger pages, files with names and phone numbers and even some fingerprints. We also have photos of two very interesting, hand-written notes that we found under a glass cover on the top of one of the desks."

Hannibal spent the next hour going over the photos, files and notes. He compared them to the notes that we had already made. I watched, puttered around the room, looked out the window and sipped a cup of coffee left over from lunch.

Finally, Hannibal leaned back on the sofa, smiled and said: "Thanks to you and Annette, we have enough evidence to complete our case. I will call Inspecteur Renault immediately." He then looked long into my eyes and added: "Good job." His look and voice were sincere.

I tingled a little and then kissed Hannibal lightly on the cheek. He gave me a hug. His words and reactions meant a lot.

After a moment, Hannibal got up and walked to the phone in the entryway.

I overheard snippets of conversation. Finally, Hannibal said: "Friday at ten o'clock. We'll be there."

Hannibal walked back into the parlor and sat down beside me on the sofa. He said: "I spoke with Yvette. Inspecteur Renault is out of town. He will be back Friday, and we have an appointment at ten o'clock."

"Good," I replied. "We need to write a report, prepare a briefing for Renault and write a shorter report for Salicetti."

"Agree," responded Hannibal. I will translate the notes and captions that are in French, and then we can compose our reports in English together. The briefing notes can follow."

I thought a moment, then said: "We also have to remove our rented camera, darkroom and other equipment from our surveillance post."

"Right," responded Hannibal. "I will call Arnold and Richter and arrange to meet them on Saturday at the surveillance post. They can also have the cots and other stuff we bought for our time there." He paused and then added: "You can deliver the keys to Annette along with the report for her grandfather."

"Yes," I replied. "I'll call her and try to arrange lunch."

We spent the rest of the afternoon translating and writing. We finished at about six in the evening. We had two finished reports and notes for a briefing. We put down our pens and pencils and relaxed a few minutes.

As we relaxed, I said: "I will give Annette the report for her grandfather and the keys to our surveillance post at lunch on Saturday, if that works for Annette." I lifted the Salicetti report from the coffee table for emphasis, and then put it down. "You'll be cleaning out the surveillance post."

"Good," replied Hannibal. His face had a thoughtful expression. He then said: "Ange Salicetti may be able to perform certain acts of justice that are not possible for the Gendarmerie."

We were both silent for a while, as we thought about the implications.

Finally, I smiled and said: "Don't we have an appointment tomorrow?"

Hannibal had a blank look for a brief moment. His eyes widened a little, and he replied: "Ah, yes. Tomorrow is Wednesday. I had completely forgotten." He grinned and added: "Ten o'clock, real estate agent and apartment hunting."

"Let's dress up and go downstairs for dinner," I replied. "You can tell me all about it over a couple of glasses of champagne."

## Wednesday evening, August 21

I got up early this morning, which was very unusual. I was fully dressed in my best snooty Chanel summer outfit by nine o'clock. Hannibal had dressed in a light gray business suit. He laughed as I paraded out of the bathroom into the parlor.

"Humph!" I uttered in response to his chuckle and smile. "I look very nice."

"Of course, you do," Hannibal replied, with a slight smile. "I am also impressed by how quickly you put everything together this morning."

I looked closely. His smile appeared sincere. "You are just very lucky to escort me," I continued. "I am the epitome of Paris fashion."

"Lovely indeed," replied Hannibal.

I looked at his face again. Other than a little twinkle in his eyes, I could detect no sarcasm. I gave him a condescending smile and said: "You are forgiven, but only if you buy me breakfast."

"Happy to," replied Hannibal. He offered me his arm. I took it and we sauntered out the door.

After a nice breakfast in the morning room downstairs, we were ready for pick-up by the agent at just before ten.

As we waited near the front door of the Ritz, Hannibal said: "The agent's name is David Feldstein, and like us, he is an American-born expatriate. He specializes in finding upscale homes for Americans."

At precisely ten o'clock, a neatly dressed, middle-aged man walked in the front door. He looked around, spotted Hannibal and me and walked over.

"Major and Mrs. Jones, I presume?" He said as he approached.

"Yes," replied Hannibal. "You must be David. We talked on the phone." The two men shook hands.

Hannibal turned to me and said: "Caroline, this is David Feldstein. He promised to help us find an apartment."

"I'm pleased to meet a fellow American in Paris," I responded with a smile. "I'm so glad you will help us. Call me Caroline." I offered my hand.

"A pleasure to meet you, Caroline," replied David, as he looked at me with a steady gaze. "Please call me David." He took my hand gently and formally.

"Different than Frenchmen," I thought to myself. "More reserved, without the suggestive twinkle in the eyes." I was beginning to understand why Americans were so easily spotted in Europe. "We are different," I concluded.

David was speaking, and I focused my attention. "I have narrowed our search to three apartments, all beautifully furnished and all in the Seventh Arrondissement. All three have views of the Eiffel Tower."

David paused and let the information sink in. He then continued: "If you purchase, they range between one and a half and two and a half million American dollars. The owners are also willing to lease with an option to buy. Leases run for one year, pre-paid, at between one-hundred and one-hundred eighty thousand per year."

I did a quick mental calculation on the lease option. "Cheaper than staying at the Ritz," I concluded. "The Ritz would cost us about two-hundred forty thousand."

"What about maid service and a cook?" I asked.

David looked at me, smiled and responded: "Both together would run about eight thousand per year." He paused and added: "Miscellaneous fees to include valet parking and maintenance will add another two thousand."

"So, our total annual expenses for the lease option would be between one-hundred ten and one-hundred ninety thousand," I responded. "Still cheaper than the Ritz," I thought to myself.

David smiled and answered "Yes." He turned to Hannibal and said: "Caroline asks very good questions."

Hannibal gave me an approving look and said: "Yes, she does." He turned to David and added: "Be careful. Caroline understands very well the value of a dollar."

David laughed, and I joined in. "Let's discuss value and other details on our way to the first apartment. My car and driver are right outside."

We had a wonderful day. I completely forgot, for the moment, about our crime investigation.

We went to the apartment on Rue du Champ de Mars first. It was luxuriously furnished and occupied the first two stories of a four-story limestone building. It had a completely unobstructed view of the Eiffel Tower. Parking for our Duesenberg was in a garage under the building. A staircase led from the main floor directly to our garage underneath.

The apartment had over six-hundred square meters of floor space. It featured hand-painted ceilings with crown moldings, elaborate marble work, elegant Versailles parquet floors, exquisite crystal chandeliers, grand windows and a dramatic staircase leading off a stunning double height entrance hall.

The front entrance door opened onto a balcony facing the Eiffel Tower. A flight of steps led from the balcony down to the sidewalk. A turn-off lane paralleled the street in front of our building; a couple of cars could pull up in front without extending out into the street.

We walked through the large living room, a library, an elegant dining room, a very large kitchen, a master bedroom with two dressing rooms, two walk-in closets and a luxurious bathroom. The living room and master bedroom both had stunning views of the Eiffel Tower. Beautiful!

Two extra bedrooms, each with an adjacent bathroom, provided options. One could be converted into a workroom, the other would be available for guests.

After I oohed and ahhed over the apartment, David bought us lunch at the restaurant on the viewing deck of the Eiffel Tower. We could see the apartment building from the restaurant window. David said the lease cost was one-hundred fifty thousand dollars per year.

After lunch, we visited the other two apartments. Both were beautiful, but I had fallen in love with the first one. I looked at Hannibal as we departed the last apartment.

Hannibal looked at me, smiled and said: "I'm glad you are pleased."

We got into the car and David's driver headed back towards the Ritz. David, the perfect host, said: "Think it over and call me when you are ready."

"We will," I replied. What a day!

## Thursday evening, August 22

After much discussion, Hannibal and I agreed to lease the first apartment. It will serve as a base of operations for further detective work, should it arise, while we live in France.

We decided to re-model the smaller of the two extra bedrooms into a workroom. It will have bookcases, a work table, a writing desk, and chairs. The adjacent bathroom will be converted into a photo development darkroom.

We also decided to add a Frigidaire to the kitchen and a very new appliance: a temperature-controlled cooler for wine.

The very large oak-paneled library will serve as a study. In addition to the existing bookcases and books, we will add a conference table with a half-dozen chairs, a desk and chair, two easy chairs and a coffee table. Existing lamps and side tables gave a warm and cozy look. A large window looked out toward the Champs de Mars.

Over the next week, we will shop for a few decorative pieces and perhaps some artwork. Our extra expenses will total less than twenty thousand dollars.

Hannibal called David late this morning. David brought the paperwork to the Ritz, and we met downstairs for lunch.

Soon the paperwork was done. David agreed to arrange for a cook and maid. In addition to another luxury apartment, our building has four small apartments for servants; two are for our luxury apartment.

David also recommended a decorator. We agreed. The decorator will manage our upgrades, buy linens, new window treatments, and so on. He will also manage the move of our belongings from the Ritz. We will walk in our finished new Paris home on Rue du Champs de Mars on September 15. How exciting!

As I write these words, I marvel at my change in status. Less than ten years ago, I worried over meeting monthly expenses, including groceries. Now Hannibal and I have a fixed income over four million dollars per year, not including our lucrative fees for detective work.

"I'm a very lucky girl," I mused. "Still," my thoughts continued: "I worked very hard to get here."

In a few minutes, Hannibal and I will turn out the lights and go to bed. As I close this diary for tonight, my thoughts turn to our presentation to Inspecteur Renault in the morning. We have a busy day tomorrow.

# 27

## ENDINGS AND BEGINNINGS

*Saturday Evening, August 24, 1929*

The last couple of days passed in a swirl. Hannibal and I had our meeting at Gendarmerie headquarters on Friday. On Saturday, Hannibal cleaned out our surveillance post, and I had lunch with Annette at Le Dôme Café. As I arrived for lunch, I saw the sinister man with a scar again; I'm being watched.

Hannibal and I arrived at Inspecteur Renault's office at Gendarmerie Centrale just before ten o'clock on Friday. We were both conservatively dressed. I wore my latest Chanel summer outfit, and Hannibal wore his light grey business suit. I carried a leather notebook, and Hannibal had a very full briefcase. We were ready.

Yvette escorted Hannibal and me into Renault's office. We were pleasantly surprised; both Renault and Capitaine Inspecteur Soucet were standing at the conference table, looking at notes and a map of Paris. Both raised up and smiled as we walked in.

"Ah, so glad to see you again," said Soucet. "We are looking forward to completing our crime puzzle today."

After the usual pleasantries, we all sat down around the conference table. Yvette had a notepad; this was a formal presentation. Hannibal fished in his briefcase, took out a neat bound report, and laid it on the table.

Hannibal then rose from his seat. He set up his table-top easel with flip charts and began the briefing in his usual, clipped, military manner. I always marveled at his ability to put so much information in just a few short sentences. I sat in a chair next to Hannibal, ready to do my part.

"Thanks to Caroline, our report includes photos of ledger pages, files and other records that were taken inside the Paris headquarters of the Unione Corse crime organization," Hannibal began. "She also obtained fingerprints from common office items inside the building."

He paused for effect and then added: "The report also includes many photos taken during a week of surveillance from a hidden vantage point outside the Unione Corse headquarters building. These photos provide clear images of persons who work in or who visited the headquarters during the period August 2 through August 9."

I looked at the faces of Soucet and Renault. Both were paying rapt attention to Hannibal, with occasional glances at me. Hannibal flipped his overview chart to a diagram that showed the Unione Corse organization. He then turned to me.

I remained in my seat and said: "To our knowledge, the Unione Corse is totally unaware that we had them under surveillance or that I gained entry to their headquarters on Rue de Pigalle."

Soucet and Renault both smiled and nodded.

Hannibal picked up the narrative. "As a result of the analysis of our photos and fingerprints, our report contains the names of the Unione Corse parrain leaders, their immediate beau voyous subordinates and a number spécialistes, including murderers for hire, burglars, and fences who operate in Paris. In addition, our report has an organizational chart that ties the Paris organization to units in Le Havre, Lyon, Grenoble, Corsica and the main headquarters in Marseille. We also know that the Marseille headquarters is in a building at the corner of Rue Beauvau and Rue Pavillon."

Hannibal flipped his overview chart to the next page and continued: "The photos of ledger pages show payment amounts and dates next to coded entries. This was an attempt to keep the names of the individuals secret, in case the ledgers were compromised."

Hannibal paused, smiled and continued: "However, one of the desks had a hand-written page under a glass top on the desk. The 'cheat sheet' as we call it, was clearly for the personal use of one of the clerks who made the payments. The sheet lists the codes with names. After correlating the cheat sheet to the ledgers, we know names, dates and payment amounts."

Hannibal looked to me, and I said: "Among many others, payments were made to Simon Goldhirsch, Rikard Gagnon and Jean-Paul Symone." I watched the faces of Renault and Soucet as I mentioned the names.

Both men acquired expressions of surprise. They looked at each other and then back to me. Soucet said: "Jean-Paul Symone is a high-ranking official in the Sûreté, second only to Jean Babtiste Chiappe, the Préfet de Police of Paris."

Silence reigned for a full minute. Finally, Hannibal said: "We already know about the Goldhirsch connection. However, the name Gagnon is of interest because of the large amounts paid and the dates."

Hannibal paused and then continued: "Gagnon received two payments of equal amounts, one on August 5 and the other on August 11. Inspecteur Clemenceau was murdered on August 10."

I picked up the narrative. "Gagnon was also listed in a file of phone numbers and names. He is clearly someone who was contacted often enough to be listed in the file." I paused and then added: "I think it is worthwhile to match Gagnon's phone number to an address."

"Yes," responded Renault. "We can do that." He turned to Yvette and said: "Contact our operatives and follow up immediately." Yvette nodded, rose from her seat and left the room.

Renault turned to me, smiled grimly and said: "Our operatives will find the address and go there today."

Soucet looked at Hannibal and then back to me. He then said: "The payment to Symone is an entirely different matter. As you can imagine, it has political implications."

Everyone was silent for a while. Finally, Renault looked at Soucet and said: "I will leave Symone to you. However, I can follow up on all of the other names on the list, including Gagnon."

Soucet nodded, sighed and replied: "Yes."

Soucet looked at Hannibal. He smiled and said: "You both have earned your fee." He then looked at me and his eyes twinkled. "I expect that you had an interesting experience in gaining entry to the Paris Unione Corse headquarters, but I will not press you for details."

I gave a slight sigh of relief. My contacts with Annette and her grandfather would remain confidential. To Soucet, I smiled sweetly and replied: "Thank you."

Soucet's smile faded and he said: "Please be careful. Your work may not have gone unnoticed."

Both Renault and Soucet looked at Hannibal, who nodded. Nothing else was said about the dangers of our work.

After a moment, Hannibal said: "That concludes our briefing. Details are in the report."

Hannibal sat down in his chair and patted my hand under the table. He looked at Soucet and Renault in turn then said: "Caroline and I have arranged a lease on an apartment in Paris." He smiled and continued: "We plan on staying in the city for at least a year."

"Wonderful!" replied both Soucet and Renault, almost in unison. Everyone laughed.

Soucet then said: "We will have as much work for you as you are willing to do." Renault nodded vigorously.

Our meeting soon ended. Hannibal and I departed, had a nice lunch and returned to the Ritz. After our briefing at Gendarmerie headquarters, we needed to unwind a little.

We spent the afternoon looking at photos of furniture and artwork that had been provided by our decorator. Dinner downstairs began at six and lasted until eight. I had several glasses of champagne.

Saturday morning came too soon. I rolled out of bed at about eight o'clock. Of course, Hannibal was already up. Coffee and breakfast arrived at about the time I toddled out of the bathroom, still in my black silk pajamas. I had forgotten my robe.

"Good morning," said Hannibal with a smile. "Breakfast is light, you have a lunch with Annette at noon."

I mumbled something; I needed coffee. After a full cup, my mind slowly slipped into gear. "Yes," I replied to Hannibal's statement of five minutes earlier. "I will be ready and dressed by eleven." Hannibal laughed.

I arrived at Le Dôme Café at five minutes until noon. As before, Annette waved to me from inside, and two bodyguards sat at a table outside.

I gave Annette the report for her grandfather after we were seated. We ordered from the menu, and then Annette leafed through the report. Finally, she looked up, smiled and said: "Very thorough. My grandfather will be pleased."

I nodded in response. As I did so, my eye caught a movement at an outside table at the far end of the patio from Annette's bodyguards. I saw the face of the man with a scar. He saw my glance in his direction, got up and departed quickly.

Annette saw my look and expression of surprise. She then looked out the window. The scar-faced man was already off the patio and headed down the street.

Without a word, Annette rose from her seat and went outside to her bodyguards. I watched as she whispered something. One of the bodyguards got up and headed after the departing scar-faced man. Annette returned inside to our table.

After she sat down, she said: "I think we were too late; I'm sure our person of interest will disappear down some alley before my man can catch up."

I gave Annette a full description of the scar-faced man. We were both silent for quite a while.

The waiter brought our lunch. We had both ordered soup, salad, baguettes and chocolate mousse for dessert. The food was delicious, but the sight of the scar-faced man had unsettled both of us.

The second bodyguard returned to the table with his companion as Annette and I were finishing the chocolate mousse. He looked at Annette through the window and gave a negative expression.

Annette sighed and said: "I should let you know that my grandfather insists that I return to Rome. Paris has become too dangerous for me."

I sighed. After a couple of minutes, I responded. "I understand. I will miss you."

Annette smiled and replied: "And I will miss you." She placed her hand on my arm and added: "I will contact you by letter when I get settled in Rome."

I nodded and tried to smile. Lunch, and much more, was over.

I soon departed. As I got into a taxi, I looked back to our table inside Le Dôme. Annette saw me and waved. I cried a little as the taxi headed back toward the Ritz.

## Sunday morning, September 1

Hannibal and I had a busy week. We reviewed the decorator's plans for our new apartment and shopped for art and a few pieces of furniture. I also had an appointment at Schiaparelli's salon on Rue de la Paix. All of the activity helped take my mind off the fact that Annette had departed Paris.

Hannibal understood, and he did his best to keep me occupied. By the end of the week, I was almost back to my usual self. We move into our new place in two weeks!

On Friday morning, we got a phone call. I remained in the parlor on the sofa as Hannibal answered. I was reviewing photos of new drapes for the windows in our apartment.

After several minutes, Hannibal returned to the parlor and sat down beside me. "That was Renault," he said. "The Gendarmerie arrested Gagnon yesterday."

"Good news!" I exclaimed.

"It gets even better," replied Hannibal. "The gendarmes found a 1910 Browning nine-millimeter semi-automatic pistol in Gagnon's apartment. The rifling in the barrel matched the grooves in the bullet we found at the scene of Clemenceau's murder."

"I'm sure Renault has a sense of closure," I replied. "I think he and Clemenceau were friends as well as colleagues."

"Agree," responded Hannibal. "Renault seemed quite certain that they have an ironclad case. He said that Gagnon will probably get the guillotine."

I shuddered a little. After a few moments, I asked: "What about the others?"

"Well," replied Hannibal, "Goldhirsch was also arrested. Renault thinks he will get a long prison sentence." Hannibal paused and then added: "The jewelry store and the headquarters of the Unione Corse across the street were raided and shut down. Many others connected with the Paris operation were arrested."

"What about other cities?" I asked.

"Don't know," replied Hannibal. "When I asked, Renault just said that the Marseille headquarters is under surveillance."

I thought a moment and then asked: "What about Symone and the Sûreté connection?"

Hannibal smiled wryly and said: "Symone was arrested on Monday. However, by law, he was turned over to the Paris Préfet de Police, along with all of the evidence."

"Let me guess," I responded. "The evidence disappeared, and Symone was released."

"The very next day," replied Hannibal. "However, according to Renault, Symone has since disappeared. No one seems to know what happened to him."

I thought for a few moments and then said: "Symone knew too much. The Sûreté, the Unione Corse and even the Salicetti people had reason to make him disappear."

"Yes," replied Hannibal. But we will probably never know."

I thought a long time. Finally, I said: "Salicetti will probably hunt for the scar-faced man."

"Yes," replied Hannibal. He looked at me with a steady gaze and said: "Be careful, even in public places. Remember what happened to Clemenceau."

"I will," I responded. I reached over and gave Hannibal a reassuring kiss on the cheek.

# 28

## NIGHT TRAIN

### Tuesday Evening, September 10, 1929

September began well. I had an appointment at Chanel's Salon at ten o'clock on Monday, September 2. I said goodbye to Hannibal in our room. Hannibal's last words to me as I went out the door were: "Be careful!"

"I will!" I replied as I closed the door and hurried down the hallway. I didn't want to be late.

A taxi took me from the Ritz to Chanel's. I arrived at precisely ten o'clock. Suzanne, my favorite hostess, met me just inside the front door.

I was so excited to view the latest in fall and winter fashions! The models paraded around; I made my selections, and Suzanne supervised the fittings. At noon, Coco stopped by and we three girls had high tea, with scrumptious finger food, scones, and chocolate-covered strawberries. I had a wonderful time.

Among my many purchases, I bought a lovely pair of black, worsted wool pants and a light gray, pull-over cashmere sweater. The pants had four gold buttons on each side panel, fit snugly at the top, and the legs flared in the latest style. I also bought a very chic black suede jacket with sable trim and low-cut black boots.

All four items fit perfectly. I decided to wear my new outfit. "I'm at the top of Paris fashion," I said to Suzanne as I twirled around. We both giggled.

At just before one, Suzanne phoned for a taxi; I had to get back to the Ritz. Suzanne promised to send all my purchases to the Ritz when the alterations were finished. All I had to carry was my purse.

I waited with Suzanne by the door. At one o'clock, two taxis arrived in front of the salon. "Odd," I thought to myself, "Someone else must have called for a taxi." I looked around but didn't see anyone. "Oh, well," my thoughts continued. "I'll take the first one."

I said my goodbyes to Suzanne and got in the first taxi. "Emmenez-moi au Ritz, s'il vous plaît," I said to the driver. I was very proud of my growing vocabulary in French.

"Oui, Madame," responded the driver. I noticed that the driver of the second taxi had a puzzled expression on his face as we drove away.

The driver stopped less than a block away. Before I could react, two burly men got in the taxi, one on each side. I screamed and tried to fight my way out.

I hit the man on my left with a left-handed uppercut to the chin and jammed my right elbow in the ribs of the man on my right. Both men grunted and uttered words in French, probably curses.

I scrambled over the top of the man on my left, pushed down on the door handle and got the door open. I was half-way out when rough hands grabbed my waist and legs and pulled me back in. I hit my head on the door frame as I continued to fight. The blow stunned me.

The last thing I remember was my jacket being ripped open and my sweater being pulled down from my shoulder. I saw a hypodermic syringe. A sharp prick tingled in my upper left arm. My struggles grew feeble, and I passed out.

I woke up in the dark. I felt utterly wretched. I was lying on my right side in a moving conveyance. I tried to squirm, but my hands were bound behind my back. My ankles were also tied together. My stomach heaved and I threw up. The taste was awful. I shivered uncontrollably and passed out again.

My next conscious thought was the recognition of dim light. I looked around. I was in a small, oak paneled room. Light came in a window. I noticed a loud, rhythmic clackety-clack sound. The room swayed back and forth. I forced myself to full consciousness. I looked around again. "OK, Caroline, you are on the floor in a passenger compartment on a train," I concluded.

I saw the vomit on the floor next to my face. I squirmed and was able to move away. I squirmed a little more and finally sat up. The compartment swirled around. I closed my eyes. After a couple of minutes, my nausea passed.

I turned from facing the window. I saw a man sitting in the corner next to the door. He was on the bench seat that spanned the width of the compartment.

He was watching me. I focused and muttered: "The scar-faced man!" He heard my mumbling. His lips curled into a mirthless smile, and his eyes glittered in the pale light.

"Good morning," he said, in perfect English.

Before I could scream, he added: "If you scream, I will put a gag in your mouth. I will not be gentle." His smile went away.

I chose not to scream. I tried to speak. I couldn't get words out. Finally, in a hoarse voice, I asked: "Where are we going?"

"To Marseille," said the man. Monsieur Carbone wants to meet you."

"Why?" I responded.

"Information," the man stated. The mirthless smile returned and then faded. "Afterwards, who knows?" His eyes glittered.

I thought for several minutes. "Not good, Caroline," my thoughts surmised. "Escape is my only option." To the man, I said: "Water."

The man stood, reached into the overhead baggage rack and retrieved a thermos. "I have coffee." He looked at me closely and added: "Monsieur Carbone wants you in good condition to talk, so

I have been instructed to keep you alive." He then bent over and said: "I will tie your hands in front so you can drink. Lean forward."

I leaned forward. He untied my hands, but for just a moment. I rubbed my wrists gingerly, and the circulation returned. I saw that my binding was thin hemp cord.

Soon the man had my hands bound in front. I looked closely. The cord was tied in simple square knots. I looked down at my ankles. The cord and knots were similar.

The man stood, unscrewed the lid on the thermos, and poured a cup of coffee. He handed me the cup. I took a sip. "Not up to Ritz standards," I thought to myself. "But it's hot." After several sips, my head cleared and my throat felt better.

The man sniffed as he stood over me. "It stinks in here," he said. "I will clean up your mess, but I have to get towels and water from the lavatory."

He looked at me closely and added: "My three companions are in the next compartment." He sneered and added: "You met them in the taxi. Drink your coffee, and don't do anything foolish."

With that, the man turned, opened the door and stepped out into the passageway. The door closed. I heard him speak to someone in the next compartment but couldn't make out the words; the train noise was too loud.

A few seconds later, the door opened and a man's face appeared. He looked at me and then the vomit. He sniffed, grimaced and closed the door.

I looked around the compartment. I saw a couple of suitcases and an umbrella in the luggage rack. I also saw my suede jacket. Bench seats stretched across the compartment, from door to window, on both sides. A small, built-in table rested under the window. There was nothing else.

The train continued its loud clackety-clack progress in the growing morning light.

The scar-faced man soon returned. He had a double handful of paper towels. Several were soaking wet. He laid everything on one of the bench seats, reached down and picked me up roughly. I held tightly to my coffee cup. He seated me on one of the bench seats. I silently put my coffee cup on the seat beside me.

The man bent over and started cleaning up the vomit on the floor. For just a moment, his back was toward me. I braced against the seat back, raised my legs and feet, and slammed my booted feet as hard as I could into the man's back. He lurched forward and hit his forehead on the edge of the table. His head snapped back. He sprawled to the floor, face down, across the vomit.

I rolled forward and landed with my knees on his back and then slipped my tied wrists and arms over his head, under his face and down to his neck. I pulled back very hard and held the cords tightly across his throat. There was a little struggle, but soon the man was completely limp.

For a full minute, I knelt on the man's back. Slowly, I caught my breath. My internal fury subsided. I listened carefully. No sounds came from the compartment next door. Luck was with me; the train noise was too loud.

After I settled down, I rolled off the man's back to a sitting position on the floor. I used my teeth to work loose the knots in the cord around my wrists. In less than a minute, my hands were free. I untied my feet and stood up. My wrists and ankles hurt, but I put the pain out of my mind.

"OK, Caroline, what's next?" I muttered. I pulled one of the suitcases from the luggage rack and set it on the seat. The train whistle blew, long and loud, and it began to slow. "We're coming into a station," I concluded. "I have to hurry."

I opened the suitcase. In addition to clothing, I found a Browning semi-automatic pistol, two magazine clips with ammunition and my purse.

"What luck!" my thoughts continued. I took out the pistol, pulled back the slide and checked the chamber. It was empty. I shoved one of the magazines into the butt of the pistol, pulled back the slide again and let it slip forward. A round was in the chamber. I set the safety.

Next, I opened my purse. Everything was there, including my driver's license and cash. A quick look in the suitcase showed nothing else of use.

I put on my jacket, placed the Browning and the extra magazine into my jacket pockets, threw my purse strap over my shoulder and waited.

The train slowed to a crawl. The whistle blew again. I looked around. The scar-faced man on the floor moved slightly, but he was still out cold. "Alive," I concluded, with mixed feelings.

My coffee cup had not spilled; it still rested on the seat where I placed it a few minutes earlier. I finished drinking my coffee, picked up a couple of the wet paper towels on the seat, and wiped my face, neck and the front of my sweater that had flecks of vomit. I felt cleaner and better.

The train was nearly at a stop. I opened the door, stepped out into the passageway and headed for the door at the end. Several other passengers were in the passageway, and I moved in between several.

As I reached the door, I heard a yell. I glanced over my shoulder. Three men came out from the compartment next to mine. They were in the passageway, trying to weave in and around other passengers. They headed straight for me.

I slipped out the door, gauged the speed of the train and jumped. I landed on my feet, but I fell and rolled. In a few seconds, I was up and running down the tracks, away from the station.

Two pistol shots rang out, followed by a whizzing sound. Both shots missed. I glanced back. My three pursuers were over fifty meters behind. I made a sharp left turn and headed across the train yard.

Another train was just starting to pull out from the station. It was headed back in the direction from which my train had come.

It was a freight train with several boxcars. The engine was now only about a hundred meters away. I ran, crossed the tracks in front of the engine and after another left turn, ran parallel with the train as it passed. My pursuers couldn't see me.

I stopped, turned, gauged the slowly increasing speed of the train and then ran alongside in the direction that it was headed. After matching the train's speed, I grabbed a steel ladder near the end of one of the boxcars and hauled myself aboard.

I climbed to the roof, lay flat and looked around. My pursuers had crossed the tracks behind the freight train. However, they were running across the rail yard away from the train.

"Stroke of luck," I thought. "Stay down, Caroline. Those thugs will take a while to figure out that I've caught this freight." My new train continued to pick up speed.

After about five minutes, we were moving very fast, perhaps thirty kilometers per hour. I sat up and looked around my perch. I spotted a hatch, crawled over and opened it. Very carefully, I lowered myself into the hole. I held on the edge of the hatch and dropped. The fall was less than three meters.

Light from the open hatch provided dim illumination. The boxcar was nearly empty, except for a few crates and machinery at one end. I looked around. Packing pads lay in a corner. I walked over, spread out a couple of pads, and lay down. I was totally exhausted.

The train whistle woke me up. I stretched, rubbed my eyes and sat up. My mouth was very dry, and I was sore all over. Dim light filtered through the open hatch on the roof. I had no idea how long I had slept, but it was still daylight. I felt the train slowing. The whistle blew again.

"We are coming into a station," I muttered. "Where?" I thought for moment. "I don't think we stopped while I slept. The scar-faced man on the other train said we were going to Marseille. This train is going in the opposite direction. If we started in Paris, then we are somewhere between Marseille and Paris, and headed back toward Paris."

I tried to remember maps of France that I had looked at in the past. Finally, I gave up. "I need to see outside of this boxcar," I concluded.

I then remembered the chase after I had jumped from the other train. "Those thugs will have figured out that I am on this train," I concluded. "They will have checked to determine its next stop."

I let my thoughts continue. "If they obtained a car, they could have arrived at this station before this train." The conclusion was obvious. "I may have a reception committee waiting for me."

"I have to get out before we reach the station," I muttered. "How?" I looked up to the hatch and then over at the crates at the far end of the boxcar. I got up. I was dizzy for a moment, but I steadied myself on the side of the boxcar.

I found the door on the side of the boxcar and tried to slide it open. It didn't move. "Locked from the outside," I muttered. Again, I looked over at the crates at the far end. I staggered and swayed over to them.

There were over a dozen, all the same size. I lifted the corner of one. It wasn't too heavy, maybe fifty pounds. "I can do this," I muttered. Within a few minutes, I had built a pyramid under the open hatch in the roof.

I adjusted my purse over my shoulder and made sure my Browning and extra magazine were secure in my jacket pockets. I climbed up. The whole pyramid swayed, but I moved carefully so I wouldn't fall. I was able to reach the open hatch and pull myself out on the roof.

I could see a station just ahead. The train continued to slow; we would stop soon. I moved over to the steel ladder near the end of the boxcar, climbed down, and jumped.

I landed on my feet but immediately fell. I tried to roll, but I ended up sprawled on my face. "Nice landing, Caroline," I muttered.

I stood up, brushed myself off and looked around. The first thing I noticed was a sign next to the tracks. I peered closely. It read: 'Mâcon.'

The sun was setting into a mist in the distance. I looked toward the station just ahead. Four men stood on the platform. "This is a freight train," I surmised. "They are not waiting for passengers to get off, and they are not going to board a freight train as passengers."

I quickly walked away from the tracks and into a nearby field. "Maybe they saw me, and maybe not," I thought. "OK, Caroline, get into the countryside."

After a few hundred yards, I crossed a dirt road. There was a vineyard on the other side. A few bunches of shriveled grapes grew on nearby vines. "Harvest is finished, and these are the leftovers," I mused.

"Oh, well, it's not time to be fussy about the menu," I muttered. I picked and ate hungrily. Never did grapes taste so sweet.

# 29

## HUNTED

*Wednesday morning, September 11, 1929*

I didn't sleep well last night. Memories are still raw from my adventure near Mâcon. Men died; others were crippled, and I was involved. Continuing to write my story seems to help; I need to clear my mind.

After jumping from the freight train near the Mâcon station on September 4th, I spotted my four pursuers on the station platform. "Those gangsters had to have come to this station in a car ahead of me. They will soon figure out that I jumped from the train, and they will begin a search," I concluded.

Since I couldn't go toward the station and the town on the other side, my only option was to disappear into the countryside. Light was fading, but I could see well enough. I half-ran from the railroad yard into a field, across a road and into a nearby vineyard. After my quick meal of grapes still on the vines after the harvest, I felt better. I continued through the vineyard to the other side.

"Take stock and make a plan, Caroline," I muttered, as I slipped through the rows of vines. "Let's see, I have a Browning semi-automatic, two magazines with twelve rounds of ammunition and my purse, money and identification."

I stopped and looked over my outfit. I smiled; I was wearing my newly purchased Chanel black wool pants, grey cashmere pullover sweater, black suede jacket with sable trim and black boots. "A little dirty from rolling around on the ground after jumping from the train, but that can be remedied."

I looked around and listened. Water tinkled nearby. I peered through the bushes and fence at the edge of the vineyard. A piped water source and cattle trough rested in the closely cropped grass just a few meters away.

I walked over to the cattle trough, lifted my purse strap from my shoulder, took off my jacket, pulled up my sleeves and splashed water on my face and hair. A linen handkerchief from my purse became a washcloth; my fingers served as a comb, and my hands brushed the dirt off my pants and sweater. I shook out my jacket and consumed a long drink from the pipe that poured water into the trough. I felt much better, and my mind cleared.

I turned around 360 degrees and scanned the countryside. A second gravel road, on the far side of the pasture, ran parallel to the one I had crossed. Lights gleamed from a farmhouse to my left along the road, about two hundred meters away. Except for a few cows in the pasture between me and the farmhouse, nothing moved in that direction.

A sound drifted out of the gloom. An engine chattered in the distance. I looked right, down the road. Lights from a car appeared; it was about half a kilometer away. I watched for a few moments. It moved very slowly, as if its passengers were looking for something. "Not local folks on their way someplace," I surmised. "It's probably the bad guys." I thought a moment. "I can't take a chance. Best get to the farmhouse as quickly as possible."

I put on my jacket, shouldered my purse, checked my pockets for the loaded gun and the extra magazine, fluffed my hair and headed toward the farmhouse. I could hear the car in the distance, as I walked up the lane to the house and approached the front door.

"OK, Caroline, take a deep breath and get ready to speak French." I knocked on the door. Voices and sounds of movement came from inside. After a moment, the door opened.

Light streamed out into darkness. A few seconds passed as my eyes adjusted to the light. A middle-aged lady stood in the doorway, and she said: "Puis-je vous aider, madame?"

"Oui, s'il vous plaît; Je suis pourchassé par de mauvais hommes. Aidez-moi à contacter le gendarme," I replied. My French was probably fractured, but the lady seemed to understand.

Her eyes widened. She turned and exclaimed: "Pierre! Pierre! Venez ici!

A tall, gray haired man in work clothes appeared out of the lighted room. I also heard a younger male voice from deep inside the house. The lady stepped back and Pierre stood before me.

Pierre eyed me carefully. In retrospect, I'm sure he had never seen anyone quite like me, a slightly disheveled young woman, dressed in high fashion, standing at his door, with a pleading look in my eyes.

"Do you speak English?" I asked.

Moments passed in silence. Finally, Pierre said: "Yes, a little. I learned during the war."

I breathe a sigh of relief and said: "Please, may I come in? I'm being hunted."

"Yes, yes," replied Pierre. He opened the door wide; I stepped inside, and he closed the door.

I looked at the lady of the house. She stared back. A teen-aged boy entered from another room and stared. After a few moments of mutual appraisal by everyone, Pierre said: "Why?"

"I work with the Gendarmerie, and very dangerous criminals are after me. Please, can you contact a gendarme? The criminals are very close; they have a car."

"Nous n'avons pas de telephone," responded Pierre. He paused, looked at me closely and then translated slowly: "We do not have a telephone."

He turned to the boy and said: "Robert, va en ville et retrouve Jacque, le gendarme! N'utilisez pas la route; passer par le pâturage!"

I understood. Robert would go through the pasture to town and find Jacque, the local gendarme. "Quick thinking on the part of Pierre," I thought to myself. "He told Robert to stay off the road."

Robert ran to the other room. I heard him scurrying around for a moment, and then the back door slammed.

Pierre looked at me for a long moment. I just stood there; I didn't know what else to do or say.

Finally, Pierre looked over at the lady of the house, then back at me and said: "Veuillez rencontrer Marie, ma femme." He thought a moment and repeated slowly: "This is Marie, my ah, wife." Marie nodded graciously.

"My name is Caroline, and I am American," I responded.

"Oui," replied Pierre with a smile. "I understand." He looked at me with a steady gaze and added: "We will do what we can for you. Please have a seat and tell me why you are being hunted." After I sat on a comfortable easy chair, Pierre and Marie sat down on a nearby sofa and waited for me to speak.

I gave him the short version: "My husband Hannibal Jones and I are private detectives. We work with Capitaine Inspecteur Soucet of the Gendarmerie Nationale. Recently, we helped identify members of the Unione Corse crime family, and they were arrested, some for murder. Other members of the crime family kidnapped me to extract information. I escaped, and four gangsters from the Unione Corse are after me. They will kill me if I'm re-captured."

I then pointed to the door and said: "The gangsters are in a car on the road a short distance away. They will probably stop here."

Pierre looked at Marie and spoke quietly in French. I could tell he was translating my English narrative.

As Pierre talked, Marie looked back and forth between Pierre and me. Her expression gradually changed to one of grim determination. When Pierre finished, she was quiet for a full minute. She then said: "Les criminels ne doivent pas entrer dans ma maison! Nous protégerons Caroline. Pierre, prends ton fusil!"

Pierre smiled and said: "I have a shotgun. Jacque, the Mâcon gendarme, will not get here for some time. Marie and I will help you."

As he finished, we heard a car approaching the house. Pierre walked to a nearby closet and rummaged around. Within a minute, he came back and stood by the door. He had a double-barreled shotgun and a handful of shells. Marie hurried to the kitchen and returned with a heavy meat cleaver.

Not to be outdone, I slipped my pistol from my jacket pocket and thumbed off the safety.

Both Pierre and Marie were startled at first when they saw my pistol, but then smiled. Marie went to the side of a window near the door, peered out cautiously and whispered: "Quatre hommes, tous armés de pistolets!"

Pierre looked at me. I nodded. "Ready," I said.

Pierre swung open the front door and stepped outside and to the left. I followed and stepped to the right. Lights from the car and the open door illuminated the scene in front of us.

Four men, led by the scar-faced man, had gotten out of their car and stopped twenty meters away in the lane. Pierre and I moved into the shadows; our four opponents remained in the light. "Bad tactics," I thought to myself. "They are vulnerable."

Pierre's shotgun boomed. I took aim and fired two shots. Screams echoed in the night.

Two men fell, and the other two returned fire. Bullets struck the house. One of the fallen men scrambled to his feet, screaming in pain. I could see him looking wildly around. His choices were a nearby barn in the gloom of the night or the car.

"If he heads towards the car, he will still be in the light," I thought grimly. The man saw me raise my pistol and aim carefully. He wisely ran and stumbled across the yard toward the barn in the dark. I didn't have a clear shot, so I didn't fire.

As this was going on, the other wounded man was helped up by a companion, and the three also ran across the yard toward the barn. The two unwounded men continued to fire as they ran. More bullets struck the house.

The gunfire stopped. The silence was eerie. I looked over at Pierre, and he looked at me. Neither of us was hit. "Watch the barn, I will disable the car!" I exclaimed. Pierre understood, re-loaded his empty barrel and moved off toward a fence near the barn.

I ran to the car, carefully avoiding the beams of the headlights. I remembered enough about cars from my days in the Valley to know about sparkplug wires and distributor caps. I lifted the latches and threw open the side panel to the engine. Wires to four sparkplugs were clearly visible in the light.

I started pulling. With a heave, four wires sailed off into the night. I quickly opened the driver's door, found the light switch and turned off the headlights. Done! I ran toward Pierre at the fence.

"Four men, two wounded, in the barn," I whispered to Pierre as I approached. "It's dark. How many exits?" I paused, thinking. "Sortie," I said and pointed to the barn.

Pierre nodded and replied slowly: "Three: a large door on this end, one on the right side and another in back."

"How long before Jacque arrives?" I responded.

Pierre thought a moment, then said: "Half an hour or more."

"Humm," I muttered. I looked at the barn in the gloom. "You stay here and watch the front. I'll go around back. We can both also see the side door. They will be trapped until Jacque arrives."

Pierre nodded. "A loft door," and he pointed.

I looked at the barn. Above the front door, I could see an opening in the loft. "Good vantage point for the enemy," I muttered.

Pierre nodded and said: "Ready."

I slipped quietly around the fence that formed an enclosure on the right. A door led from the enclosure into the side of the barn. In less than a minute, I arrived at a point where I could see the back and side doors. "Good," I thought. "All exits covered."

I heard Pierre shouting to Marie, who remained in the house. I didn't get all of the conversation, but it was clear that he told Marie to watch for Robert and Jacque from the back side of the house. Marie answered, and then silence. The lights went out that were visible in the house.

We didn't have to wait long before the men in the barn tried to slip out the back and side doors. The back door slowly opened. One man out, then two. I fired two rounds. One man gave out a groan and both hastily retreated back into the barn. Pierre's shotgun boomed and splinters flew from the side door as it slammed shut. "Good eye, Pierre," I muttered with satisfaction.

Silence descended upon the battleground. Time seemed to drag. Finally, a car engine chattered in the distance. I watched as Marie slipped out from behind the house and ran toward the road. After a couple of minutes, the car engine stopped.

At least five more minutes passed. Finally, I saw Marie moving around the side of the house to the back. She was followed by Robert and a uniformed man carrying a rifle. "Jacque," I concluded. "Reinforcements have arrived."

I watched both the barn and the house. "Marie is explaining the situation to Jacque," I surmised. Finally, Jacque slipped around the side of the house and stealthily approached Pierre by the fence. After a brief conversation, Pierre moved along the fence toward me.

"I explained the situation," whispered Pierre as he stood by the fence next to me. "Jacque will watch the front and loft doors. I will watch the back. Can you watch the side door?"

"Yes," I replied. "Will others come?"

Pierre smiled and said: "Jacque called Paris before he left Mâcon." His smile broadened. "You are well-known to the Gendarmerie." His smile changed to a frown. "Men are coming from Paris, but their trip will take several hours."

I replied: "I think two and possibly three of the enemy are wounded. However, they still may attempt to escape." I looked at Pierre closely. "We have to keep watch."

Pierre nodded and said: "It is good to fight along-side of an American again." His eyes twinkled. "Like 1918."

"Thank you," I replied. "You saved me." I looked into Pierre's eyes with a steady gaze.

Pierre shrugged his shoulders a little and said: "It is nothing." His eyes twinkled again.

Hours slowly passed. Dawn lighted the eastern sky. Jacque had moved to a tree about twenty meters from the front of the barn, where he had a good view of the front and loft doors. I could see his rifle as it pointed in the direction of the barn. Pierre had moved along the fence to a position about twenty meters from the back door, and his shotgun rested on a fence rail. I stood by a small gate in the enclosure and watched the side door.

"The enemy is in bad shape," I thought to myself. "They may get desperate." I shifted my position a little and watched the side door intently. The dawn light increased.

Jacque moved slightly, and he sighted along his rifle. I watched his face and sensed that he saw something at the barn. A pistol shot rang out, followed by the crack of Jacque's rifle. A cry of 'Oh!' came from the barn, followed by a sodden thump. I could hear the snick-snick of Jacque's rifle as he jacked another round into its chamber.

Pierre's shotgun boomed at the back of the barn. At the same time, the side door opened and a man slipped out. He saw me by the fence. It was the scar-faced man. He raised his pistol and fired wildly in my direction. Pop! Pop! The shots echoed, and then four more. A couple of bullets hit nearby fence rails. I watched carefully.

The scar-faced man's pistol slide was back and open. Empty! He fumbled in his pocket and pulled out another magazine.

Before he could re-load, I stepped through the gate, moved forward and said: "You've had your six, and it's my turn." Pop! Pop! I calmly shot him through both knees. He dropped his pistol and fell to the ground, screaming.

The aftermath passed in a swirl. I heard shouts from Jacque and Pierre. They rushed the front and back doors of the barn. There were no more shots. Two men were dead. One had fallen from the loft door as a result of Jacque's shot. Pierre's shotgun blast had finished a second man at the back. Pierre and Jacque found a third inside, severely wounded. I watched as the scar-faced man groaned in pain on the ground in front of me. I didn't try to help him.

Marie and Robert came out of the house. I walked slowly over to the front of the house and sat in a chair. Marie came over and sat next to me. I unloaded my Browning; I had six bullets left.

Hannibal, Soucet and a host of gendarmes arrived mid-morning. The men took care of the vanquished enemy.

# 30

## PARIS INTERLUDE

*Thursday, September 12, 1929*

Writing about the aftermath of the Battle of Mâcon helps me put bad dreams to rest. The fight was disturbing, but afterwards, my experiences were good. Pierre, Marie and Robert had saved me, and Hannibal and I spent a couple of pleasant hours with them before we returned to Paris.

After the battle, Capitaine Inspecteur Soucet, assisted by Jacque and a hoard of other gendarmes, hauled the two surviving gangsters, both severely wounded, off to the hospital. The two dead men were also quietly removed. I chose not to watch. All was done by noon.

Soucet told us that Lieutenant Inspecteur Renault led a raid on the Unione Corse headquarters on Rue Beauvau in Marseille. A number of beaux voyous gangsters were arrested. However, Paul Carbone and François Spirito were not there.

"Our information indicates that they have left France," said Soucet. "However, we have decimated their organization, and I think the Unione Corse will not be a major factor in the French underworld for quite some time."

"Good news," I replied. "Maybe we won't have to look over our shoulders for bad guys for a while."

Hannibal slowly nodded in agreement, but he only said: "I hope so."

After business was finished, Marie fixed a wonderful farm lunch, or déjeuner in French. She invited Hannibal and me to join them. During our meal, Pierre and Hannibal helped me in English when I didn't understand the French conversation.

I asked many questions. I learned that Pierre's family name was Beaune, which was also the name of a nearby village. Pierre was grooming his son Robert to take over the thriving vineyards and farm. Each year, Pierre sends his chardonnay grapes to a local community winery, which produces wine under the Appellation Mâcon Villages. Pierre let us sample the wine at lunch, and it was wonderful.

Robert beamed when he explained his plans to study viticulture at the university. Marie and Pierre shook their heads in wonder at the modern winery methods Robert described.

Hannibal and I listened, and we agreed to quietly fund Robert's education. It was the least we could do. Hannibal explained our plans to the Beaune family and promised to make arrangements. Marie and I shed a few tears when Hannibal and I departed after lunch.

Hannibal had driven the Duesenberg from Paris. Our drive back to the Ritz took about six hours, and we didn't hurry. On the way, Hannibal talked about our impending move from the Ritz to our new apartment. The memories of the battle faded for the moment; Hannibal is such a kind man.

### Saturday morning, September 14

I slept in this morning, our last day at the Ritz. I'm all packed. Tomorrow we move into our new apartment on the Rue du Champs de Mars. Our decorator provided photos and floor plan diagrams.

Hannibal and I examined the photos and floor plans over breakfast coffee. We have 600 square meters of floor space on the first and second floors of the building. The apartment has a living room and master bedroom, both with views of the Eiffel Tower, a lovely master bath with walk-in closets, a library, a workroom, a darkroom for photography, a spare bedroom with an adjoining bathroom and underground parking for the Duesenberg. The photos show crystal chandeliers, wood parquet and marble floors, hand-painted frescos on ceilings and exquisite window treatments and furnishings. Dazzling!

Our decorator took care of the details. Everything that we can think of is done. Madame Lynette Laval, our cook, and Mademoiselle Susanne Fayette, our maid, have already moved into their separate quarters in our building. We even have a stock of groceries and wine. I will miss the Ritz, but the apartment will be so much better. I'm so excited!

After all of the good news concerning the apartment, Hannibal and I discussed events back in the United States. The New York newspapers are full of articles about the stock market. The Dow Jones industrial average peaked on September 3rd, but it has been declining steadily since then. Hannibal's predictions of hard times may be coming true. Fortunately, Hannibal saved our fortune, and we are financially secure, no matter what happens.

## Monday morning, September 16

Hannibal carried me over the threshold of our new apartment yesterday afternoon. Lynette and Susanne watched from inside the living room, standing at attention in their best formal manner. At first, they had expressions that combined surprise, puzzlement and slight shock.

However, Hannibal and I laughed merrily during the whole process, especially when he dumped me on the sofa and gave me a big kiss. Lynette and Susanne joined in the laughter. I'm sure they have decided that working for us will be different compared to any previous employment. Such crazy Americans!

Capitaine Inspecteur Soucet called early this morning. He asked for an appointment. Hannibal and I will meet with him in our library at ten o'clock on Friday morning.

Soucet was very mysterious about why he wanted to meet with us. All he said over the phone was that he had concerns about the political situation in Europe, and he needed our help. He suggested that we read the Paris newspapers. What on earth? I guess we will find out Friday.

## Wednesday evening, September 18

Our new apartment is just wonderful. Lynette is a fabulous cook, and Susanne chases every speck of dust with a diligence that tops anything I have ever experienced. Susanne should have seen my home on a Wabash River houseboat, just six years ago. So many things have changed.

## Friday evening, September 20

I received a letter from Annette Salicetti this morning. She has settled in Rome, and according to her bubbly writing, her affairs are going well. She even has a new boyfriend. She hinted that her grandfather's operatives raided the remaining Unione Corse operations in the Pigalle District of Paris. She said: "I think, Caroline, you will be safe in Paris; my grandfather watches over you."

I wrote a reply, with many thanks. I told Annette about my experience in Mâcon and about our new apartment in Paris. I also suggested that she go shopping. After all, Rome has fashion houses too. I gave her my love and best wishes. I miss my friend; perhaps we will meet again.

## Saturday morning, September 21

I don't know quite what to think about our meeting with Soucet yesterday. It lasted from ten o'clock in the morning until four in the afternoon.

Soucet arrived at ten o'clock on Friday. I proudly gave him a complete tour of our apartment; I couldn't help myself. Hannibal smiled in his typical enigmatic way and followed as I escorted Soucet all around, even to the parking garage. Soucet was gracious as usual, and he provided compliments at appropriate moments.

Finally, I ran out of steam. Hannibal politely suggested that we adjourn to the library. Soon we were seated around our lovely new conference table. Lynette served tea and other refreshments.

After a couple of minutes of silence while we sipped, Soucet began. "My colleagues and I are very concerned about events in Germany."

Hannibal leaned back in his chair, folded his arms and waited. I had read a few things about political turmoil in Berlin and Munich, but that was all. I'm sure my expression combined puzzlement and expectation. What did Soucet have in mind?

Soucet continued: "After the war, the Treaty of Versailles imposed severe restrictions on Germany. As a result, the German people have demonstrated much resentment. Riots against the German government, which adheres to the treaty, are common."

Hannibal nodded and said: "The Germans resent the loss of territory, restrictions on their military and most of all, the payment of massive war reparations to the victors. The reparations are a huge drag on the economy."

Soucet responded: "So far, the reparations have been mitigated by generous loans from the United States, but I fear that this flow of funds may soon end."

I listened carefully. Hannibal and Soucet were much better informed than me. However, I asked: "Why would American loans end?"

Soucet said: "Good question. I fear that the New York stock market is on the brink of collapse. Have you watched it lately?"

"Yes," I replied. "Hannibal warned me, and we have prepared our finances." I paused and then added: "Hannibal and our bankers say that if the market collapses, so will the economy."

"The effects will be world-wide," responded Soucet. "As with other countries, the United States will seek its own interests. Loans to Germany will most likely end."

"I agree," responded Hannibal. "My banker friends say the same." He paused and then asked: "Do you expect more unrest in Germany as a result?"

"Yes," replied Soucet. "In addition to my role in the judicial police, I have duties in other agencies. We are especially concerned about the rise of the National Socialists under the leadership of a fanatical new leader named Adolf Hitler." He added: "Hitler has vowed to abrogate the Treaty of Versailles, stop all war reparations, re-build the German military, regain territory lost as a result of the treaty and eliminate non-Aryans from German life."

Soucet paused a moment, and then added: "Our sources tell us that Hitler routinely uses his Sturmabteilung, his SA Brownshirts, for intimidation, beatings and even murder. His targets include political opponents, including Marxists and Social Democrats, and people he considers undesirables, especially the Jews."

"I read about Hitler and the Nazi Party in the French newspapers," replied Hannibal. "Apparently, Hitler has gift for public speaking."

"He is also a capable organizer," responded Soucet. "The Nazi's now have 153 seats in the German Reichstag, the most of any political party."

"I see," responded Hannibal. "And you are concerned that Hitler may gain more power if the German economy declines?"

"Precisely," replied Soucet. "Hitler thrives when the people resent the current German government. Our intelligence services need to learn more about Hitler, the Nazi Party and the details concerning his plans to return Germany to a position of power in Europe."

"And how do Hannibal and I fit in?" I asked.

Soucet smiled and responded: "How do you feel about doing intelligence work?"

"You mean becoming spies?" I blurted. I'm sure my face expressed surprise.

Hannibal and Soucet laughed. Finally, Soucet replied: "Yes, that's exactly what I mean. Your demonstrated investigative and clandestine operations skills would be most valuable."

"Oh!" I responded. I didn't know what else to say. However, my pulse quickened, and I fidgeted a little.

Soucet looked at me, smiled and sipped his tea for a moment. His expression then changed to a slight frown, and he said: "Hitler is not our only intelligence concern."

Even Hannibal had puzzled look. We both waited.

"Italy was an ally during the war," Soucet finally said. "However, they have a new dictator named Benito Mussolini."

I looked at Hannibal. After a moment, we both looked at Soucet. I'm sure our faces expressed the obvious questions.

"From my reading of British and American newspapers, Mussolini seems popular in Italy, in Britain and even among Italian-Americans," I ventured.

"Yes," replied Soucet. "However, Mussolini has also banned any opposition in Italy. His fascist government is ruthless, even murderous, and opportunistic. His Camicie Nere, or Blackshirts, operate in Italy much like the SA in Germany. In these ways, Mussolini is similar to Hitler, the rising power in Germany."

Hannibal nodded and said: "From what I have read in the newspapers, both Hitler and Mussolini have ambitions for expansion beyond their current borders."

Soucet nodded sadly and continued. "Hitler and Mussolini have similar domestic fascist programs. Although Mussolini currently aligns Italian foreign policy with the United Kingdom and France, particularly over the issues concerning Austria, the Balkans and influence in North Africa, we are concerned about a possible change to an alliance between Mussolini and Hitler in the future."

Silence reigned for quite a while. Finally, Hannibal said: "As I understand it from my war experience, French intelligence activities were under the Deuxiéme Bureau, and the Bureau is under the Sûreté. Has that changed?"

Soucet lowered his gaze, frowned and was silent for a while. He finally said: "Perhaps. The lines of authority are very murky."

He then looked up and added: "For now, you would continue to report to me, should you agree to do our work."

"I would hope so," I replied. "I do not wish to become another Mata Hari."

Both Hannibal and Soucet looked at me in surprise. After a moment, Hannibal smiled and said: "I understand. Mata Hari was executed by the French for being a double agent for the Germans during the war."

"Many think that she was a scapegoat for the French intelligence services; they had many failures during the war," I replied. I gazed intently at Soucet and added: "Like then, the French intelligence services have, as you said, murky lines of authority."

Soucet squirmed a little. After a full minute, he said: "I understand your concern." He then added: "Rest assured, if you decide to help us, you will be protected."

Hannibal looked at me with an expression of appreciation, coupled with a little surprise. He turned to Soucet and said: "Caroline and I have much to discuss. Can we give you an answer on Monday?"

Soucet rose from his seat and said: "Of course. I can assure you that we desperately need your help; we will give you protection on assignments, and we will pay you well."

"Thank you," replied Hannibal. He looked intently at Soucet, and added: "There is one more thing: Caroline and I will not accept any assignment that goes against the interests of the United States."

Soucet smiled with a confident expression and replied: "Rest assured that the old alliance between our countries will always be respected."

"Good enough," responded Hannibal. He then offered his hand to Soucet. The two men shook hands.

Soucet turned to me, and I offered my hand. Soucet smiled, took it, kissed it lightly in a formal manner and said: "Ah, le Chat dans la Fenêtre, I look forward to working with you."

"OK," I thought to myself, "How does he know?"

# 31

## EPILOGUE

*Monday evening, September 23, 1929*

This morning, at the request of Capitaine Inspecteur Soucet, Hannibal and I agreed to assist the French intelligence services. We will investigate the activities and intentions of Adolf Hitler and Benito Mussolini. Where will our spy work lead? I don't know.

Soucet emphasized that the work will be dangerous; both men have already used murderers and street brawlers as instruments to gain political ends.

After appropriate training, including languages, Soucet envisions trips to Berlin, Munich, Vienna, Rome and the Mediterranean. We will enter a world of murder, political turmoil and deceit. Friends may become enemies, and enemies may become friends.

Our cover as 'rich, expatriate Americans' will serve nicely. Hannibal has many business contacts, including camera manufacturers in Berlin and bankers in several cities. In addition to designer clothes, I have an interest in impressionist and other modern art; our visit to Giverny was a catalyst. In Italy, we have Ruth, our friend from Chicago, who has a villa in Tuscany, and Annette, my Paris burglar partner, who now lives in Rome.

For the time being, our Paris home will be our 'safe house.' During our travels, we will stay in the finest hotels and resorts.

According to Soucet, our research and clandestine activities in Germany, Austria, Italy and the Mediterranean may take several years. How exciting!

# THE CAT'S PAW
# MURDERS

Scheduled for publication in late 2022, *The Cat's Paw Murders* will be the fourth novel in the Caroline Case mystery series. In 1930, Caroline and Hannibal Jones become paid espionage operatives for the French government. As wealthy expatriate Americans, they have the perfect cover. They are tasked with gathering intelligence about the intentions, methods and organizations of Adolf Hitler and Benito Mussolini. As part of their espionage duties, they bring murderous criminals and spies to justice, legally and otherwise. However, competing French politicians and bureaucrats fight for funds and influence. Caroline and Hannibal face extreme danger from certain French authorities as well as sinister Nazi secret police and their criminal associates. As Caroline and Hannibal pursue and dodge the bad guys, they take sleuthing to a sophisticated, intricate and exciting new level.

# ABOUT THE AUTHOR

Frank L. Gertcher is a retired scientist and a current writer of murder-mysteries. He was born in Clinton, a small town in Indiana. During his childhood, Frank and his father fished and trapped on the Wabash River for a major portion of their family income. Frank's teenage years were spent on a farm in Sullivan County. As an adult, he served 23 years in the U.S. Air Force and had another 22-year career building weapon systems for the Department of Defense. Frank's publications include eight books and a number of papers in scientific journals. He has traveled to and lived in many places around the world, but he is still a Hoosier at heart. When not traveling, Frank and his wife Linda now live in the lovely Shell Point Retirement Community near Fort Myers, Florida.